GALLOWS WAY

DAOMA WINSTON

SIMON AND SCHUSTER • NEW YORK

Published by Simon and Schuster
A Gulf+Western Company
Rockefeller Center, 630 Fifth Avenue
New York, New York 10020

Manufactured in the United States of America
1 2 3 4 5 6 7 8 9 10

Library of Congress Cataloging in Publication Data

Winston, Daoma, date.
  Gallows way

  I. Title
PZ4.W784Gal [PS3545.I7612] 813'.5'4 76-23114

ISBN 0-671-22345-3

For Ray Winston, my mother

BOOK ONE

1

Six roads led to Darnal. Of these only one deserved the name. It was smooth and flat, worn by the heavily laden wagons that rolled to Durham's Station and its railroad depot or to the newly established tobacco processing plant, or else passed through, heading southeast to the state capital at Raleigh. The other roads were no more than trails that ran past tiny subsistence farms and the vast acreages held by single landowners to small plantation hamlets. In the heat of summer a fine haze of golden dust hovered over them. When rains came, they turned red, thick, and mired.

Darnal, as befitted the county seat, was two streets larger than the other villages, but both of these were unpaved with stone. It had a small square, in which the major point of interest was a long horse trough that dated from colonial times. Nearby were hitching rails, one broken and hanging to the ground. A few feet beyond were three stone benches surrounding a stone tablet that commemorated the date on which North Carolina became the twelfth state to ratify the Constitution of the United States. In the sixty-nine years since, the white stone had been weathered dark, decorated by birds, and defaced by known miscreants who, sometime after midnight in this same month of May 1858, had decided that the original decision had been an error and should be obliterated.

On the square stood a single-story building of paint-blistered wood. It was called Hell's Tavern, after David Heller, who had built it ten years before and still ran it. It was frequented by the small farmers, artisans, and mechanics of the neighborhood, and had a particularly appropriate location, with its back adjacent to the county calaboose around the corner.

Jordan House, a three-floor establishment fronted with white columns, encircled by railed galleries hung with fragrant honeysuckle, dominated the other side of the square. It was to Jordan House that the politicians came when they had business in the county courthouse only a few steps away. It was to Jordan House that the men who owned the surrounding plantations came for occasional recreation away from their own acres. They gathered in the gaming rooms for cards, drink, and conversation, confident that Eamus Jordan would give them due respect and forget their indiscretions.

It was here that Lafe Flynn sat. He leaned back in a large armed chair that wasn't large enough to accommodate his big body. He eyed the other men there and understood their feelings completely. For a good part of his thirty years he had been such a man and he understood the need to ride away from the prinking and primping of the women who surrounded him. He had also known the need to ride back at full gallop.

His amused thought was interrupted by a sudden change in the hum of the voices. He had been tired of the walls of his suite in Jordan House and had already found the smoky gaming room not much to his liking either. He was ready to be diverted.

Eamus Jordan, standing at the bar nearby, was much less anxious for sport. At the first loud word, his nearly bald head jerked up. The spectacles perched on his pudgy nose seemed to mist with anxiety.

"Oh, no," he murmured pleadingly to no one. "Oh, damn it! No, I say!"

Across the room, the cards suddenly flew in the air. A chair scraped the floor with a raw and ugly sound. The hum of voices stilled, so that when the next words came they were audible. Indeed, though they weren't spoken at a shout, they might as well have been.

"You're a fool to deny it," Gentry Beckwith said. "You know the truth of it the same as I do."

"Be quiet," Oren Henderson answered. "Be quiet, and pick up your cards."

Lafe knew the two men by reputation and name. He had made it his business to learn quickly about the people of the county when he had first come to Darnal a month before.

Oren Henderson was from the plantation called Galloway, where tobacco was raised. He was tall and slender, with a narrow thoughtful face and long dark eyes.

Gentry Beckwith was from the Beckwith plantation, owned by his father, Alexander. Gentry was of middle height, but bulky and thick in the arm and thigh. He was fair, and through the thinness of his skin his hot blood burned a fiery red.

Soon, Lafe knew, his various errands would take him both to Galloway and to the Beckwith plantation. Soon the task for which he had been preparing would begin.

"I asked her," Gentry was saying. "I did, Oren. Again today, the more fool me, I guess."

Oren nodded sympathetically. His collar felt tight, and he ran a finger around it. The cards in his left hand were sticky with sweat. He frowned down at the table, refusing to meet Gentry's bloodshot blue eyes.

Gentry demanded, "How many times is it, do you suppose?"

Oren shrugged, more in despair than in indifference. "Pick up your cards, Gentry. Let's get on with the game."

"And she smiled so sweetly. She looked at me and smiled, and I swear my ears deceived me. I swear, just from the look of her, I heard her say, Yes, Gentry. Yes, I will. So I reached out to take her into my arms, Oren, and she said, tapping my cheek with her fan, 'Gentry, what ails you? I'm sorry. I truly am. But did you mishear me? I can't marry you. I can't and I won't and I never will.' That's what she told me, Oren."

Listening, Lafe thought, Lovesick calf. What a fool! Why want a woman who doesn't want you? His contempt was

11

thinned by a bitter remembrance, and he admitted to it, but allowed no dwelling on it.

He was tired, bored. His shoulders and back were heavy with the pressure of loneliness. In this past month in Darnal he knew no man as friend. He knew no woman even as acquaintance. He was there because he believed he must be. What had begun as adventure, as quixotic enterprise for a drifting man, for a man escaping from his past and memories, had become a reality and responsibility. It surprised him, for he'd known no such feelings before. To learn his own possibilities had turned into the greatest adventure. In these past few years he'd been tempered. He was not the boy, as he called it now, that he'd been before. He was different. He knew it. Duveen knew it, too. Between them, they had forged from the young dandy called Lafayette Flynn a new man. For good or for ill, it was done.

"Oh, no," Eamus Jordan groaned. "Oh, damn it! No, I say."

"Your sister, the beautiful Marietta Garvey," Gentry was shouting, "is no more than a cold-blooded man-hating spinster, and that's what she's going to remain all her life."

Lafe slowly raised his head, slowly pushed himself from the uncomfortable chair, moving without thought or calculation.

He was a man built on a very big pattern. He stood six feet three inches on his bare feet, with massive shoulders, a broad deep chest, and a heavy neck, yet he was lean, granite hard, and moved with an easy grace that could be disarming to the unwary.

"A twenty-four-year-old man-hating spinster," Gentry whined. "And you can't tell me different."

"That'll do," Oren cried. His chair fell away as he lunged across the table.

Gentry fell back staggering and came up with a glass in his hand. He drew a deep noisy breath as he smashed it deliberately. "More than that, she's a heartless flirt who enjoys conquest but gives nothing in return."

12

"You'd have her if you could," Oren shouted. "And that's the only reason you insult her."

Gentry launched himself forward brandishing the smashed glass in his clenched fist. Its jagged edges glittered evilly, inches from Oren Henderson's throat.

The other men shifted back, watching and silent, and allowed the two ample room. Eamus Jordan moaned softly as the two men closed, and Oren sank to his knees. Gentry, standing over him, bleeding from the nose, raised his fist for a second strike with the bloodied glass as Lafe Flynn cut through the silent circle of onlookers, caught Gentry by the scruff of the neck, and pitched him with ease into the far corner of the room. While Gentry lay there cursing, Lafe pulled Oren Henderson to his feet.

A babble of voices rose behind them as he led Oren outside.

"Can you ride?"

Oren nodded, unable to speak. He clasped his left arm just below the shoulder with his right hand. Between the fingers dark blood seeped slowly.

"Galloway, isn't it?" Lafe asked. For all that it showed, he might have made no exertion at all. His longish russet hair still lay in waves to his collar, which was neatly in place. His cuffs remained impeccable, his jacket, too.

Oren stared at him. "Yes, Galloway."

"I'll ride with you."

"No need, sir," Oren gasped. "I can make it myself."

"Of course," Lafe agreed dryly. "But we'll be certain, shall we?"

He helped Oren into the saddle, placed the reins in his hands, and folded them tightly around the pommel. He gave the dark spreading stain on Oren's coat sleeve a brief glance, but made no comment on it.

They rode silently, side by side, Lafe thinking that this would be his first visit to Galloway, Oren thinking of Marietta.

It was her fault that he and Gentry, friends from youth,

had made such fools of themselves in the gaming room at Jordan House. It was Marietta's fault, and her fault alone, that he, Oren Henderson, who should have been master of Galloway, was no one and nothing. And he was going home to her, because there was no place else to go.

At last a high flicker of light shone momentarily through the trees.

"Galloway," Oren said, hunching over the pommel. And in a whisper, "Marietta will be waiting."

She stood very still, her small feet as if rooted to the hardwood floor, her slender body tensed for the struggle to free herself.

The hounds barked in a long sustained chorus. Listening, straining to hear beyond their noise, beyond the song of the crickets and the rustle of the settling mockingbirds, she made out the sound of horses' hooves.

Immediately, she caught up a candle and swooped through a long window to the second-floor gallery. The air was sweet with wisteria and honeysuckle. She drew a deep gasping breath without noticing the luscious perfumes. The candlelight was blinding. She held it away from her and leaned against the scrolled railing, her full-skirted gown billowing like pink foam around her.

The drum of hooves came closer. Her practiced ear picked out two different gaits. There were two horsemen. Two. Not the one for whom she had been so anxiously waiting.

Where was Oren? Why was he so late in town? she asked herself silently; and she prayed silently at the same time, Let this be Oren now. Let him be riding in with a friend.

She peered along the curved drive that ended at the two tall white pillars which marked the main approach to Galloway. Holding her breath, she waited. If this was a two-man night patrol, and not Oren, then these horsemen would sweep by, riding on through the dark to search for slaves who were abroad without walking papers.

Instantly there formed in her mind's eye an image she had

never forgotten. Four dark bodies swaying in the night wind, limp and dangling at the ends of ropes that disappeared into the thick foliage of the live oak trees. Instantly she heard in her ears again her father's angry curse, and her mother's shrill scream. Her vision blurred now with the tears of an old memory. The candle trembled in her hand.

Finally she saw the shadows of men. They didn't sweep past the pillars but swung in between them. They came toward her, silver-speckled with moonlight, riding beneath the gray of the creeper vines that veiled the gnarled limbs of the trees. Even before she saw their faces, she knew something was wrong.

The one sat straight and very tall, enormous in the saddle. She saw him to be a stranger.

The other leaned over the pommel. She didn't need to see his face to know him. She had always been aware of his shape and form. She had always had the sense of his presence. Alarm chilled her heart in mid-beat. The breath went thin in her throat. The man sagging against the pommel was Oren.

For a single instant longer she stared into the silvery moonlight. Then she whirled, skimming through the tall windows. A tendril of wisteria adrip with blossoms caught in the hem of her gown, as if to hold her back willfully. She jerked free. Soft scented petals fell in a silent cloud and were crushed beneath her feet as she hurried on, her slippers tapping out staccato signals as she raced down the stairs. From somewhere in the dimness below, Aunt Tatie appeared, crying, "Miss Marietta! Wait, wait! The night air's poison, child!" At the same time she felt the old woman place a gossamer scarf of white woven French lace around her shoulders.

Tall Elisha appeared, holding a light before him, his dark face hollowed at cheek and temple. "Miss Marietta?"

With no answer, and no pause, she thrust her candle at him and was at the doors and had flung them wide before he could move.

15

"What's out there, child? What ails you?" Aunt Tatie was shouting.

"It's Oren," Marietta gasped as she skimmed the gallery, the steps, and stumbled to an awkward and breathless stop at the hitching post. She ignored Lafe, who turned while still securing the reins to stare at her.

"Oren," she cried. "What is it? What's happened to you?" She flung herself at him, and his horse danced and shied and snorted; and Oren himself wavered dangerously in the saddle, clinging to the pommel with his right hand and holding his torn left arm rigid against his body. "Oren, tell me! What have they done to you?"

Oren tried to speak but couldn't. Dear Christ, he asked himself, when will she learn? When will she stop wearing her heart on her sleeve? When will she stop embarrassing me, and shaming herself?

Her wide slanted eyes glowed like precious stones. Her heart-shaped face was pale with fright. "Oren, please . . ."

She felt strong fingers curl tightly at both her shoulders. She was lifted bodily, spun away, and set on her feet with a jar that seemed to rattle her bones.

Lafe said, "My dear girl, if you'll stop clawing at your brother, I'll help him down. He's cut, but he's hardly at death's door."

"He's not my brother," she retorted hotly. She didn't notice that it might be an odd time to make such a denial. It was one that was second nature to her. She had made it over and over again through the years. Oren Henderson was not her brother. He was the son of her father's second wife. He was not related to Marietta by blood. He wasn't, and she didn't want him to be.

Lafe knew nothing of that. But he allowed his straight black brows to rise, and even as he eased Oren from the saddle, he gave Marietta a long and pensive look, thinking her comment and the intensity with which it had been made strange. At the same instant he decided that she was surely one of the most beautiful women he had ever seen.

16

She was tall, even though he himself stood nearly a full head higher. Her form was slender, and from the billows of her gown her waist rose narrow and graceful as a flower stem. Her bosom was high and round and full, the pale skin gleaming through the lace of her shawl. Her features were perfectly made, a firm chin and jaw, high cheekbones. In that light he couldn't tell the color of her eyes, but they were pale, he knew, glowing with heady brightness, and set deep and slanted beneath full curving brows.

Oren leaned heavily on him, groaning softly now.

She cried, "Oh, come in. Come in quickly. I'll send one of the boys for Dr. Pinchot right away." Her arm went swiftly about Oren's waist in what was partly support and partly a reassuring hug.

"There's no need for a physician," Lafe told her. "This is something we can attend to ourselves, I think. If you'll permit me to help, that is."

She didn't answer. She was hardly aware of his presence then. All her attention was directed at Oren as the three moved up the steps together and into the house.

Aunt Tatie stood waiting under the many-globed chandelier, now alight. Its pale rays showed hard disapproving lines on her broad dark face. "Spoiling yourself with that stuff, Mr. Oren. That's what you're doing. And your legs like yeast dough from it. Mr. Oren, honey, you're hurting yourself."

"He's had one or two, but he's not in his cups," Lafe told her. And then, "We'll need some hot water. And some cloths, if you have them handy."

She gave him a straight steady look, and he knew that he had been weighed, measured, sized heart and soul. Then she said, with a bob, "I'll get them, sir."

Elisha followed her to the back of the house.

Marietta was making soft sympathetic murmurings. "Oh, Oren! Does it hurt greatly? There's so much blood. What on earth were you doing?"

He was rigid, resisting her touch, the concern in her voice.

17

Now there was this to explain. And what a bad time. Just when he had to ask her about the note. Not that he wanted to. It was only that he saw no other way.

"I was fighting," he said at last, the words edged with warning chill. "What else could it have been?"

There was a sharp hoot of laughter from the top of the stairs. "Fighting again, my dear brother Oren. Can't you do anything else? Why, I swear, every time you go to town it's the same thing. You'd suppose a man could find more use for his energies. Were I a man, I would."

Lafe gazed upward. A girl stood in the shadows at the top of the steps. She leaned over the rail, her face tilted down. He judged her to be sixteen. She was small but plump.

Marietta spoke to her absently. "Hush, Coraleen. Can't you see your brother's hurt?"

"I see he's on his feet. And if the two of you turned him loose, I wager he'd stand well enough alone."

Lafe concealed his amusement, though it lit a gleam in his dark blue eyes. "If you'll lead the way, ma'am," he told Marietta, "then we'll be able to follow."

"Can you go up, Oren? Or shall we do a bed for you on the settle in the morning room?" she asked, ignoring Lafe.

"Of course I'll go up. You needn't make such a fuss," Oren told her.

She nodded and ran ahead. The room to which she hurried was dark, only a silvery bar of moonlight striping the floor. She snatched up a taper, lit the lamp quickly. She pulled back the bed curtains and turned down the dark green spread.

"Here now," she said when Oren was beside her. "Lie down at once, and let me see what it is."

Aunt Tatie bustled in, a basin of steaming water in one hand, a jar of unguent in the other, and white cloths trailing over her arm. "Miss Marietta, you let me do the doctoring. It won't be the first time I've tended Mr. Oren. And I expect it won't be the last either."

Marietta made a soft sound of impatience and continued

to bend over Oren, drawing away his bloodstained jacket and shirt. Her eyes widened even more and her face grew paler when she saw the still-bleeding wound, crescent-shaped and jagged, in the flesh of his upper arm. "How did you come by this?" she demanded. "Oren, you must tell me what happened."

"I had words with Gentry Beckwith," Oren answered wearily. He turned his head away. "I don't want to talk about it now, Marietta."

Coraleen stood at the foot of the bed, running a length of curtain through her small white hands. "Oh, I'll wager you don't want to talk of it," she chortled.

"You must tell me," Marietta insisted. "I demand to know why you had words with Gentry. Do you hear me, Oren? Do you?"

"I hear you," he said tiredly. "We'll speak of it later, if you please." He looked meaningfully at Lafe.

"I say we'll speak of it now," she cried, though she had seen Oren glance at the stranger and understood he had made a silent plea for her to respect his privacy, and her own. She was too upset, too angry, to care. "Now," she said. "Tell me, Oren."

Aunt Tatie had nursed Marietta with mother's milk, and cuddled her out of midnight dreams. She had bound Oren's wounds before and purged him in illness and bathed him in fever. She had earned certain rights, and knew her due. Now, she interposed her ample bulk between Marietta and Oren. "Miss Marietta," she said, "will you give Mr. Oren a minute to catch his breath? He's hurt, and lost blood. And had a long ride out from town. Whatever words said are said, ain't they? What's the use you badgering him?"

Marietta flashed an angry look at the older woman, but didn't argue.

Coraleen said brightly, "Perhaps my brother would rest better if he were alone." And then, to Lafe, "Sir, it appears there's no one here to remember the good manners we were raised to. And no one to introduce us either. So I'll do the honors myself, if you'll forgive me for being so forward. I'm Coraleen Henderson. And this is my sister, Marietta Garvey."

Lafe bowed first to Marietta, then to Coraleen, who responded with a deep and careful curtsey. "My name is Lafayette Flynn," he said.

"Now that's done with," Coraleen trilled, "may I suggest that we—"

Marietta's warm husky voice overrode Coraleen's words. Turning from Oren to look at Lafe, she said, "I thank you, Mr. Flynn, for your help. Will you stop in the parlor below with me for a few minutes and take some refreshment before you leave?"

Having inspected Oren's wound and seen him relax under Aunt Tatie's silent ministrations, Marietta was able to observe Lafe Flynn clearly for the first time. She saw his height and breadth, and the crisp russet hair worn long. She realized that his blue eyes had a twinkle in them.

He, aware of her earlier abstraction, her closer attention now, said with a teasing note in his voice, "I think this is a good time to introduce myself again, ma'am. I'm Lafayette Flynn. And I'm usually called Lafe." With that he bowed once more.

She ignored his levity, saying, "It's a pleasure, sir." She made him a small prim curtsey, then rose. "You'll accept our hospitality in return for your kindness to Oren?"

Lafe had an appointment in town, and knew very well that time was passing. But he was intrigued by Marietta. He wondered what she would be like when she wasn't fussing over her brother. He nodded. He watched as she cast a long look at Oren, then turned to lead the way down.

Coraleen trailed after, pouting. With that expression her pink-and-white face took on the look of childhood, so that she appeared even less than sixteen. She would have liked to flounce off to her room, but she feared that neither Marietta nor Lafe Flynn would notice her absence.

He said as he reached the lower hallway, "Miss Garvey, I wouldn't want to deceive you by accident. I'm hardly an acquaintance of your brother's. In fact, I'm certain he doesn't know my name."

"And what of it? You brought him home. Which was more than Gentry Beckwith troubled himself to do. I'm very grateful to you, sir."

"We both are," Coraleen said sweetly. She fluttered her lashes over her brown eyes and smiled. "Please do sit down, Mr. Flynn. And I'll have coffee brought in. Or would you prefer a brandy? Surely, Marietta, there's a brandy in the cellarette, if Mr. Flynn prefers it."

Lafe stood before the fireplace. "Coffee will be fine."

"As you like, of course." Coraleen tugged at the bell rope. When a small young Negress appeared, she gave the order.

Lafe noted that the girl looked at Marietta, who said, "Yes, Dora. Ask Essie for fresh coffee, please."

Dora nodded, hurried out.

Lafe considered that small exchange, decided that Marietta Garvey was mistress here, and Coraleen by the look on her youthful face didn't like it.

Now she said coldly, with a sudden sharp gleam in her eyes, "That Dora should be sold off, Marietta. She's an insolent chit who's never learned her place."

Marietta turned her head so quickly that her long black hair slid like a drape along her shoulder. "We don't sell our people. And you know that as well as I do, Coraleen. My father never did it. Nor my grandfather before him. We've not bred slaves for sale. Nor bought them either. Not for generations. I don't propose to do it now."

"Papa's been dead for over a year," Coraleen said sadly. "Things change, Marietta."

"That won't," Marietta retorted. She seated herself on a red velvet love seat and folded her hands against the billow of her gown. "And now, Mr. Flynn . . ."

Coraleen smiled sweetly and then said, "Mr. Flynn, you must prepare yourself at this point. My sister's about to demand answers to her questions. Sometimes she has a bitter and overweening curiosity about men's affairs."

"Coraleen, do hush." Marietta gave the girl a sharp glance. "Mr. Flynn doesn't know you well enough to recognize your attempts at humor for what they are."

"I shall remedy his ignorance if I can." Coraleen laughed.

Again Marietta eyed her. But she said, turning to Lafe, "It's very important to me that I understand. Can you tell me what happened? Were you there when Oren fought with Gentry?"

"I was indeed," Lafe said dryly. "Though I wasn't a part of it until I made myself so."

"And you saw it, heard it all?"

He nodded.

"Then what happened?"

"It's downright unwomanly," Coraleen cried. "When will you learn, Marietta?"

"Hush," Marietta said. "I must know. Why did Oren fight with Gentry Beckwith, Mr. Flynn?"

"You embarrass our guest," Coraleen murmured.

"Not at all," Lafe protested. And it was true, too. He hardly listened to Marietta's questions. He was completely taken up with her husky voice, the brightness of her eyes. Still, he was glad of the small delay when Dora came in to serve small cups of coffee. When she had gone, he delayed longer, savoring the strong black brew.

Marietta endured his silence as long as she could, but finally she said, "Well then?"

"There were words," he answered.

"About what?"

He looked away from her intent face. He noted that the white globes of the lamps were painted with small golden roses wreathed in pale green leaves. He saw that the draperies were of a heavy golden damask. A silver candelabrum stood on the mantel.

Marietta was staring at him. "You hesitate, Mr. Flynn. About what were the words?"

"I think you must ask your brother," Lafe answered at last.

22

"Gentry spoke slightingly of me," she said in a soft voice.

"I'll say only this. Now that I've seen you, I know for certain that I'd have done the same as Oren did."

"He struck Gentry first," she said, and now there was acid in her tone. "I don't want him to fight for me. I've told him so. There's no need."

"But Oren thinks there is. It's what a man does, ma'am. As you surely know yourself."

Coraleen had been silent, she considered, long enough, and too long for bearing. She turned on Marietta. "You see! It's all your fault, as you knew all along, and as I knew, too. If you'd any sense in your head, you'd accept Gentry's attentions and say yes to him and marry him and be done with it."

"*You* may do that if you like, for I never will," Marietta replied. "And I'd be glad if you kept your advice to yourself in the future." She turned, smiling now, to Lafe. "We continue to inflict our family problems on you. I apologize." Her glance strayed toward the door. She was uneasy about Oren. She wondered how he fared now. She wanted to sit beside him and look down into his face.

She had always loved him. In the moment when he descended from the carriage to set his feet on the earth of Galloway for the first time, she had recognized him as the answer to her heart's hopes. She had been fourteen then, and Oren sixteen. The ten years that had passed had changed nothing, except to increase the intensity of her feelings. He was a part of those good times when her father had ruled the plantation, the best days of her life.

Lafe sensed the withdrawal of her attention and understood. Now that she had subjected him to her inquisition, she was done with him. He smiled to himself, thinking that she wasted such intensity on a brother. But he rose. "I must be getting back to town. Thank you for the coffee."

Coraleen cried, "You'll come again, of course. Surely, now that you know the way, you'll visit us. And Oren will certainly want to thank you for your help."

Lafe already knew that the fires of hell wouldn't keep him from Galloway, but it wasn't the right time to say so. He looked politely at Marietta and waited for her to repeat the invitation.

"I hope you'll accept our hospitality in the future, Mr. Flynn," she told him with equal politeness.

"I'll be delighted, of course." He stared deep into her eyes. They were a strange color. Light, as he had thought, but with a deeper glow within that recalled the dark flash of amethysts in firelight. He smiled to himself. Yes, she had eyes like amethysts. Her lips were lovely. Sculptured. A clear fresh red untouched by artifice. They would be sweet to kiss. He remembered Gentry Beckwith's words. Of one thing Lafe was certain now that he'd seen her: Marietta remained unmarried by her own choice. He knew too, beyond any doubt, that such a woman could never accept Gentry Beckwith. But he, Lafayette Flynn, was another man entirely. Though she didn't know that yet. She will, he thought, his eyes scanning the voluptuous curve of her breasts, his smile deepening.

Her expression sharpened in response to his appraising look, and a faint frown appeared between her brows. A quick current seemed to sting the air between them. Aware of it, Marietta looked away as a loud "miaow" filled the silence and a huge white cat stalked from the shadows beyond the stairs.

"Snowball," Coraleen cried prettily, and she bent down. "There you are, my baby. Snowball, come to me."

The cat raised emerald eyes, skimmed daintly past the flounces on Coraleen's skirt, and leaped into Marietta's arms, snuggling its head into the white curve of Marietta's throat and making deep, contented purring sounds.

Lafe made his farewells then and started for the door, aware, as he did, that Marietta hurried to the steps. She was going up to Oren.

Coraleen accompanied him outside. In the shadows of the gallery she caught his arm while she smiled up into his face. "Mr. Flynn, you will come again?"

"Of course."

"You've not been in the town long, have you?"

"A month, just about." He went on slowly: "I've opened a tobacco-buying company. Golden Leaf, I call it."

"Why then, you're not just passing through. You're here to stay, aren't you, Mr. Flynn?"

"As long as the county grows tobacco, I'm here to stay," he said lightly. It was at least a partial truth.

"It's a wonder I've not seen you before this."

"I wonder at it, too."

"But I'll make sure to remedy that situation, believe me."

She was a child to him. And a forward one at that. Pretty, but with sharp, foxlike eyes that were unfathomable when he looked into them. It must be a trial to her to have as an older sister Marietta Garvey. But, yes, as Marietta herself had been so insistent to make plain, Oren Henderson wasn't her brother. Then Coraleen was not her sister either. Lafe recalled that he'd known their real relationship before. Part of what he must do in Darnal was to listen to gossip, and gossip aplenty there'd been about Marietta Garvey and Oren and Coraleen Henderson, and how Galloway had come by its name. Yet none of it had been truly meaningful to him until he'd seen Oren go down under the jagged edge of Gentry Beckwith's glass. Even then, he might not have truly understood had he not looked up as he rode between the white stone pillars and seen the candlelight and the billow of a pink gown and the tall slender form of Marietta leaning forward from amid the wisteria blossoms to search the darkness.

He stepped to the hitching post, although Coraleen still held him. He undraped the reins and reached up to pat the horse's head.

She caught his hand, took the reins, and looped them quickly around his wrist. "You're fairly caught, Mr. Flynn, and my prisoner now." She dimpled at him, her smile sweet but somehow strangely empty, he thought. It was as though the muscles obeyed, but the feeling that should have given warmth to the impulse wasn't there.

He extricated himself, made a small mocking bow. "What's been caught, fairly or not, can be freed, ma'am. If a man wishes it."

"Oh, but you don't know, Mr. Flynn," Coraleen said. "You've been given warning. And now you must beware."

"I shall," he said, smiling coolly. Beware he would. Coraleen Henderson would make a nice younger sister to him perhaps. But no more than that.

"And if it's my sister you're thinking of," she went on, intercepting the slanted glance he sent toward the house and interpreting it with annoyance, "then I must warn you of that, too. She's not interested in men, nor in marriage." Here Coraleen leaned forward and rose on her tiptoes so that her lips were bare inches from Lafe's and he need only incline his head to kiss them. "Poor Marietta's like her mother, you know. The woman died by her own hand, after three years of being locked up in her room. And Marietta's like her father, too. Who also died strangely. There are streams of bad blood in both her parents, you see, and they've formed a river in Marietta."

Lafe turned his head from Coraleen's offered lips. He smiled narrowly. "Now that you've told me all about Marietta, you must, someday soon, tell me all about the Hendersons, about you and Oren."

"It will be my pleasure, I promise you," she answered.

He mounted, leaned down, tipping his hat back so that the moonlight made shadows on his face. "And I promise to give you the opportunity, Miss Coraleen. As soon as it can be arranged. Until then, I'll bid you good night."

"Good night," she whispered. She watched until he disappeared down the driveway, then went slowly inside.

There was a murmur of voices from above. Oren and Marietta. The two of them together. They had secrets between them. At least they believed so. And she, Coraleen, was always the outsider.

A small smile twisted her lips. She had a secret, too. She allowed herself a moment of deep satisfaction, and her smile broadened. Oh, yes. She had a secret, too. She climbed the steps on silent tiptoe, holding her gown close to her sides, concentrating on the murmur from above. Outside the door of Oren's room she stopped. She held her breath and listened.

Oren was saying, "It was nothing, Marietta. When men drink and play cards, as you know very well yourself, anything can happen, and often does."

"But Gentry? Gentry Beckwith? I can hardly believe it of him. Or of you. He's been our friend since childhood, Oren."

It was, Oren thought, only that which had kept him from calling Gentry out to face him in a duel. That and the fear of a full-blown scandal. Otherwise he would already have told Gentry to be at Death Meadows to settle the matter honorably by pistol. Aloud Oren said, "Sometimes friends fall out, Marietta."

"Surely not over some trivial disagreement."

"Sometimes even that happens."

"Yes," she agreed, suddenly giving way. "Perhaps you're right that friends do fall out. But when they do, it's not over small things, I believe." She was silent for a moment, thinking of her father. Lawrence Garvey had ridden to every plantation in the county venting his rage at what had happened at Galloway. After that he had had precious few friends. Marcus Swinton, the banker, had had been one. Dr. Pinchot had been another. Then she said, choosing her words carefully, "Oren, was it because of me? Did Gentry insult me, is that it?"

Oren didn't answer.

Listening still, Coraleen nodded. A thin smile curled her lips. It would have been something that Gentry said about Marietta. Why else would Oren fight?

"If you won't tell me," Marietta was saying, "I shall go to him myself. I shall demand an explanation from him."

"You can't do that," Oren answered quickly and with heat. "You mustn't do that. It would be a humiliation to me. It would shame me. What sort of a man would I seem if my sister should swing her skirts about me?"

"I'm not your sister, Oren," Marietta said softly.

27

"Very well," he agreed. "If you insist, you're not my sister. Then what shall we be to each other?"

She wanted to tell him. The words rose up, sweet and loving on her tongue: Oh, Oren, you've always known what we are to each other. Why pretend any longer? But something held her back. Some thin ribbon of pride bound her.

Snowball, curled at her feet, suddenly mewed and uncoiled, his eyes open and glowing green.

Marietta swiftly crossed the room, jerked open the door.

Coraleen said coolly, "I thought Oren must rest, but you're disturbing him, Marietta. Since all this is your fault, the least you could do would be to allow him to mend."

"You've been sneaking about again, haven't you?" Marietta demanded. "Standing at the door and listening like a common spy."

Coraleen looked at Oren. "Am I invited to see you for a moment, brother Oren? Or shall I apologize for my intrusion and creep away?"

He put an arm over his face, murmured, "Enough of this, the both of you. Just leave me alone."

From the doorway Aunt Tatie cried, "Out, out. Mr. Oren says it, and so do I. I've brought a potion for him. And I want him to take it."

On the steps Coraleen said in an angry whisper, "It's your fault, Marietta. You're the cause of the talk. No wonder Oren must defend you. Why don't you marry Gentry and be done with it? How long will you hold out, waiting and hoping. You know that Oren'll never, never—"

"Mind your tongue, Coraleen," Marietta said icily.

"I won't! It's time someone told you the truth. You can make great cow eyes at him for the rest of your life, but Oren won't ever have you as you want."

With a will of its own, Marietta's hand lifted and lashed out in a hard stinging blow that left the print of five fingers on Coraleen's cheek.

As Coraleen fell back against the wall, her eyes blazing, Marietta turned and went into her room.

"You'll be sorry for that," Coraleen said in a soft whisper. "You just wait and see."

Marietta, leaning her forehead against the closed door, heard those words and tasted a rueful bitterness. She should never have lost her temper. Coraleen's childishness was better ignored than fed by angry outbursts.

You'll be sorry for that. Words Coraleen had said many times over the years.

Marietta heard the echo of them and shuddered, suddenly cold.

2

Lafe took his watch from his vest pocket. He stroked the smooth gold case before he snapped open its lid to study the time. He was late indeed. But Duveen would still be waiting.

He spurred his horse to the gallop, the last few miles spinning away beneath the flashing hooves. Fireflies sparked among the dark foliage of the trees like precious jewels mysteriously propelled aloft. Watching them as he rode, he thought of Marietta's eyes. He'd stayed longer than he intended at Galloway. Coraleen Henderson had hung on his arm, delaying his departure. But it was Marietta Garvey who had held him there, though she neither knew it now nor cared.

A grin of amusement flickered across his face. He had believed himself well cured of such nonsense. He was a man of thirty, and too old surely to be enchanted by a perfect oval face. And not only age but experience, too, should have taught him a caution he apparently hadn't learned. "Jeanne," he said softly to himself. "Jeanne. Remember, Lafayette Flynn. Jeanne of the melting look and sweet smile and the soft promising curves."

It was five years since he'd seen her, since he'd seen his home. Five years of wandering for love of Jeanne. And now nothing was left of that love. It was ashes in his mouth. It had been, he realized, ashes even on the misty lavender morning when he had left the Vieux Carré and New Orleans.

It was all behind him, he reminded himself as he stabled

his horse at the back of the hotel and then started across the yard to the lantern-lit entrance.

There was nothing left in him of that young hothead who had killed his rival for Jeanne's affections, only to find that there were others she favored. He was a different man in 1858 and saw the world through different eyes. He was able now to view even his own emotions with the same sardonic wonder that he applied to those of others.

Yet the image of Marietta Garvey remained with him. The look of her as he had first seen her, leaning above the wisteria vines on the gallery, her face perfect and pale in the light of the candle she held, the dark hair ashine, her willowy slimness a breathtaking silhouette. Even in her distraction she exuded a strength and purpose, and a glowing heat that stirred him. He knew that to court her would be to court danger. Marietta was a risk he could not afford. But he was determined that he would see her again. He would have her. And nothing would stand in his way.

Ahead there came a sudden loud shout. A lurid curse in a voice Lafe recognized. A door opened and slammed, and Gentry Beckwith reeled into the lantern light, shoving big Duveen before him and at the same time yelling drunkenly, "Speak up, boy! What's your name, and what're you doing here? What're you hanging about for? Answer me, or you'll end up in the calaboose tonight answering the deputies, and in the stocks in the morning answering to the whip."

Lafe moved fast, with the grace of a challenged jungle animal, a smooth and sudden flow of taut muscle and tendon, his big hard body at the ready. But his voice was silky, asking, "What's this, Mr. Beckwith? What's going on here, sir?"

"No business of yours, Mr. Flynn, if that's truly your name as Eamus Jordan told me. I've already noticed once tonight that for a stranger you've a long nose indeed."

Though his fists were clenched at his sides, Lafe managed a gentle, conciliatory laugh. "I'm by nature a man opposed to violence of any sort," he told Gentry. "So I try to be reasonable when I can, as will most reasonable men. Which is why I interfered with you earlier."

Gentry swayed on his feet, suddenly grinning. "I'm a reasonable man, too, Mr. Flynn. But surely you'll agree that it's beyond reason for you to intervene with me whenever I raise my head." He turned his back on Lafe, nudged Duveen's large and immovable bulk. "Damn it, boy! Speak up, I say. What're you hanging around here for? Who do you belong to?"

Lafe moved swiftly and neatly, slipping his own bulk between Gentry and Duveen. His broad shoulders were rigid, a light burned deep in his eyes. "This is my man, Mr. Beckwith. He's here because I told him to be."

Gentry stared Lafe up and down, fell back a step, and stared again. "Your man, is he? Then order him to learn better manners. Teach him to speak up when he's asked a civil question. Explain to him that it's not safe for his kind to be on the streets of this town, nor the roads of this county, without walking papers in hand."

"He's a mute," Lafe said shortly. "Which is why he didn't respond to your questions." And to Duveen: "Go inside and have Mr. Jordan make up a tray for me. A big pot of coffee, some bread and cheese, and tomatoes—fresh, mind you— or whatever else cold, to go with, instead."

Duveen nodded, dark eyes hidden under drooping lids, and disappeared through the door with the soundless tread of a cat.

"I was hasty," Gentry said. "But when I see one like him, and what a worker he'd be. Surely worth fifteen hundred on the block. And dressed up in a fine suit . . . hell, it makes me wonder."

"We wonder at all things, don't we?" Lafe asked pleasantly.

"*You* surely do." Then, "Did you get Oren home safely?" Lafe nodded.

"He's not badly hurt, is he?" Gentry's bloodshot eyes were anxious, but there was a truculent set to his jaw.

32

Lafe shook his head, and waited.

"I didn't try to really hurt him. We're friends," Gentry went on. "And the whole thing shouldn't have happened." His voice thickened with sudden heat. He went on accusingly: "If you'd not taken it upon yourself to interfere, I'd have brought him home myself, and we'd have talked it out on the way."

"If you hadn't thoroughly maimed each other first."

"We wouldn't have. We both know when to stop," Gentry retorted.

"My apologies then. But it didn't appear that such a brawl could end well. And as Mr. Jordan was dancing nervously at his bar and praying for help from the Lord, I thought to do the man a favor and save for him what furnishings I could."

Gentry seemed to forget his sudden heat. He grinned. "I suppose it would have been a brawl, Mr. Flynn. Oren's hotheaded and doesn't take it kindly when he hears the truth about his sister."

"Nor would any gentleman," Lafe said in a deep quiet voice. "Particularly when he knew the words uttered to be otherwise than the truth."

Gentry gave vent to a bitter laugh. "He knows. He knows." Without another word the blond man went reeling away toward the stable.

Lafe shrugged and went inside. He had no intention of seeing another citizen safely home that night. As he crossed the wide lounge, he heard his name called. He turned in response.

"Mr. Flynn, sir. Mr. Flynn, if you have a moment for me . . ." It was Eamus Jordan. He hurried toward Lafe. "A moment only."

"Yes, Mr. Jordan. And what can I do for you?" Controlling his impatience to get to his suite, Lafe took out two small black cigars, offered one to the older man.

Mr. Jordan accepted his with a quick smile, gave it a careful and suspicious sniff. "Ah, Mr. Flynn, you deal in a de-

33

lightful weed. This isn't made from one of our tobaccos, I warrant."

Lafe grinned but didn't answer.

Mr. Jordan offered a light, and after Lafe had bent his head over the chimney lamp, he used it himself. He slowly blew out a thick cloud of smoke. "Prime," he said appreciatively. "Wherever it comes from, you plainly know good stuff."

"I should, sir. Since that's my business."

"So I've heard. And I've even seen the warehouse you've just begun to build. Which is part of what I wanted to say to you. We're glad to have you here with us, Mr. Flynn. If there's any way we can make you more comfortable, anything you need, then you must be sure to make your wishes known to us."

"I thank you, Mr. Jordan." Lafe narrowed his eyes against the glee that he knew must be beginning to glow in them. Though he hadn't thought of it at the time, and had used it only as an excuse when he spoke to Gentry, his earlier gesture in the gaming room had already begun to pay dividends.

"And I thank *you*." A fleeting grimace touched the hotel-keeper's lips. "Your help was most welcome this evening. I feared for a serious round, sir. I assure you, every chair and table in the gaming room has been broken at least once before. Every mirror and every last decoration, as well. When the young bloods begin to rowdy, there's hardly a thing left unscathed. Including the gentlemen themselves."

"I saw it might be so."

"And I suspect you saw more than that. Heard more, too, Mr. Flynn. I feared for a duel. Oren Henderson sometimes speaks before he thinks. And Gentry Beckwith usually does. Certainly Oren has good cause. But Gentry is the best shot in the county. I fear that there's already been enough blood spilled."

"Fortunately we were able to stop it," Lafe said evenly. Yet he was remembering the Dueling Oaks where he himself

34

had killed, and had turned away as victor to know he had won no triumph.

"*You* were able to stop it," Mr. Jordan was saying. "No one else could have. The element of surprise, sir. I only hope that by tomorrow Oren's head will have cleared. He'll not pursue this further. They're such old friends."

"I believe it'll be forgotten."

"We can't be sure. The Hendersons and Garveys are an odd lot. Oren dotes on his sisters, both of them. Though only Miss Coraleen is actually related to him by blood. Still, he feels the same for Miss Marietta. Even though," he added, "when her father died a year ago the plantation was left to her."

"Was it?" Lafe asked, his interest quickened. "Now that's a strange thing, isn't it?"

"Of course she allows him the running of the place, as any woman would. Yet it's not the same as when a man builds his own property. Still, Lawrence Garvey was an odd man in some ways," Mr. Jordan said.

"And how was that?"

Mr. Jordan shook his head. "I don't speak ill of the dead. As for how he disposed of his plantation, that makes a sort of sense, I suppose. For it really was the Garvey plantation all the way back. Lawrence came down from Virginia, and brought Virginia tobacco with him, and married his second cousin, Beatrice Garvey. Garvey's Acres came to him through her. When he married Kathleen Henderson, he took on her two children, Oren and Coraleen, but he never adopted them. And I suppose when he made his will he considered that what had belonged to the Garveys must remain with them."

Lafe made a sound of grave agreement. A burst of raucous laughter came from the gaming room, and a grandfather clock chimed softly. He was well aware of the passing of time, but he kept his eyes on Mr. Jordan's face. To talk to Duveen was important, but the history of Galloway and its beautiful mistress held him.

"And, perhaps," Eamus Jordan continued, "considering what happened there, at Galloway, I mean, and what came after, Lawrence Garvey can be understood, even sympathized with."

Now here, Lafe thought, was a man who pretended to balanced judgments, and who could, perhaps, be useful. Lafe made a mental apology to Duveen and said aloud, smiling, "Mr. Jordan, may this guest buy for the hotelkeeper a small libation?"

"I'll accept with pleasure." Mr. Jordan led the way to the gaming room, chose a small corner table from which he could observe the room, and waved Lafe to a chair. "Your pleasure, sir?"

"An ale, thank you."

"Ale it is, and for the two of us." Within moments the hotelkeeper returned. He seated himself. "Your health, Mr. Flynn."

"And yours, Mr. Jordan." Lafe sipped, weighed the heavy mug in his hand, and said softly, "I noticed that you spoke once of Garvey's Acres, then another time of Galloway. How is it that the place has two names?"

"Galloway," Mr. Jordan answered, "that's what the plantation is called now, and has been for the past nineteen years. For that's when Lawrence Garvey himself went into the county courthouse across the square and changed it on the grants and deeds. It was considered, then, a peculiar thing to do. Now I see it as his reminder and reproach for what happened there." Mr. Jordan drew a deep breath. "Galloway . . . it became that from Gallows Way. My own father was present at its baptism, and what I know, I know from him. Though I doubt that anyone still living knows the whole of it."

Lafe sipped his ale, waited.

"You're a stranger hereabouts, so I must tell you that the Quakers had been active in this area in those days. They were quiet in every instance, except in their abolitionist talk. And soon after the Nat Turner rebellion in Virginia

36

we had a small uprising here at Beckwith plantation. It was dealt with firmly, as it had to be, of course. But there was a lingering nervousness in the county over the next ten years. Our night patrols were increased. We paid five instead of two dollars per head for reports to owners of curfew violators, and any slave found wandering about without a pass was dealt with most severely."

Lafe thought of Gentry's handling of Duveen. Plainly not much had changed in the past nineteen years.

Mr. Jordan was saying, "My father was on such a patrol the night it happened. Now, remember that Lawrence and Beatrice Garvey, along with little Marietta and Aunt Tatie, were away in one of the eastern counties, visiting relations. Their overseer, a man named Jennings, was of good repute and well trusted by them.

"The group, and my father with them, came upon Jennings' body on a path between Garvey's Acres, as it was called then, and the Beckwith plantation. A Garvey slave was bending over the dead Jennings, rock in hand. A Beckwith wench, her neck broken, was at his feet. The patrol took him. He broke away, fled. They found him hiding in the Garvey slave quarters. He said he and Beckwith's girl had been in the habit of meeting after curfew, that Jennings had come upon them, broken the wench's neck, and that he himself was only trying to protect the girl when he killed Jennings. None of which mattered, of course. When they tried to take him away, there was some interference from three other slaves. So they took the four of them. They hanged them in the live oaks on the road to the plantation and left them there."

"Hanged them," Lafe repeated softly. "And Lawrence Garvey away from home."

Mr. Jordan nodded solemnly. "A grave error, Mr. Flynn. That's how I see it now. But it appeared differently to those involved at the time. The killing of a white man, the fear of insurrection . . . And then there was Garvey himself, reputed to be too easygoing a man, one who permitted religious services for the slaves, for instance. It was thought that these four must be made an example."

"And then?" Lafe asked.

"The Garveys returned the following evening. It was late, it's said. Dark. Though the moon had risen."

Mr. Jordan went on softly, and Lafe imagined how it must have been: Lawrence Garvey, his wife, his five-year-old daughter, his middle-aged slave, Aunt Tatie. They were tired, glad to be approaching home at last. Lawrence urging the horses on as they approached the gates, and then, looming out of the dark, the dangling black shadows of the hanged men.

The woman screaming. The man grabbing the child, turning her head to his breast so that she would not see.

"Beatrice Garvey never recovered from the sight," the hotelkeeper went on. "She is said to have risen in her seat, screaming wildly, to have continued to scream all that night through and the next day. She took to her bed and rarely left it after. She died, by her own hand, by hanging, sir, just three years later."

"And Mr. Garvey?" Lafe asked. "What of him?"

"He was distraught, as you might imagine. In those first days after, he went about the county saying he had been robbed of his property. He finally went to court, in suit, trying to recover one thousand dollars apiece for those four men, one of whom it turned out was Aunt Tatie's son. It came to nothing, of course. Except that he increased his reputation for being an odd one. And no doubt he was, having, perhaps, as I said in the beginning, good reason to be."

"And Miss Marietta?"

"A fine girl, and smart as a whip. Of course she has Oren to run the plantation for her, and Blandish, their overseer, too."

"But there's been no slave trouble in the area since?" Lafe asked.

"Why, no, certainly not," Mr. Jordan said quickly. "You understand that there are occasional ripples of worry. Each time something happens elsewhere, we have our rumors flying. Two years ago, when that madman John Brown went on his Kansas rampage, there was some anxiety. But it was for nothing. Though we do continue our patrols, as we must. A precaution only. You've no reason to fear for trouble, Mr. Flynn. This is a safe county, and we make sure to keep it so. Your investment will be protected, believe me. Which calls to my mind . . . Since you've begun the warehouse, I see that you plan to remain in our town. Will you be building a house also? Or will we have the continued pleasure of keeping you here at the hotel with us?"

"I'll just stay where I am, Mr. Jordan." Lafe paused, then, in deference to a newly conceived idea, said, "At least for the time being. A man without a family hardly needs an entire house. There's just me and Duveen, my man, of course. We do fine in the suite you've given me. I do believe, however, that I shall have need of a temporary office to be used until the warehouse is completed. Perhaps you have another room adjacent? We could remove the bed, install a desk and some chairs perhaps."

"Delighted, Mr. Flynn. I know just the place, and I have a desk for you right now. A fine rosewood, only a bit scratched, but nothing that a good polish won't deal with."

"Then you'll see to it for me?"

"I will, Mr. Flynn. I will indeed. Rest easy, and by morning you'll have only but to walk some eight feet to your new office."

Lafe nodded, rose. "Then I'll bid you good night."

Mr. Jordan accompanied him to the end of the hall, then went dancing happily away, already calculating the additional profit he would have from such a well-paying and steady guest.

The lamps were lit when Lafe entered his rooms. A tray was set on the big round table before the gallery doors, and Duveen stood in the middle of the room, his head down, his massive hands once again clenched into hamlike fists.

Lafe regarded him for a long moment, then said quietly,

"I know it's hard. But consider it now. The thing is, is it too hard for you?"

Duveen shook his head from side to side, the muscles in his thick neck standing out like heavy ropes.

"No, Duveen. I'm serious. Think about what I'm asking. Is it too hard? You know as well as I do that what happened in the yard downstairs will happen over and over again. Is it too hard for you? Which might make it dangerous. Dangerous for you and for me as well. Remember, if you lose your temper once, then it's all finished. What we've come to do is wrecked for good. We'd have to start over somewhere else, and it mightn't even be possible to do that the way things are. You don't have to do it, you know. You can go North and out to Canada. There are plenty who will help you. You don't have to stay here. Not unless you want to."

Duveen looked at Lafe, his long silent stare answer enough.

Lafe understood and accepted it. Gentry Beckwith, and others, too, might provoke Duveen, but not beyond endurance. Lafe nodded, sat down at the table, waving Duveen into the chair across from him. "We'll have some coffee while we go over it."

Duveen, seated, poured the mugs full, buttered bread and covered it with thick hunks of cheese, which he daintily trimmed first. He served Lafe, then helped himself.

He was an enormous man, his skin smooth and dark as black velvet. His head was completely bald. His black eyes were deepset under thick overhanging brows. A long pale scar zigzagged across his cheek, and his broad lips had a downward twist, accentuated by another long pale scar.

He couldn't speak because he was maimed. Years before, he had been rented out by his owner in a slack cotton season and had ended up as a dock worker, hauling bales aboard the ships that would take them from New Orleans to English markets and mills. He'd been a tractable twenty-year-old, accustomed to the casual treatment provided by a slaveholder who didn't believe in damaging her property, and completely unprepared for a gang driver who considered him no more than an animal. He'd suffered abuse he'd never known, until one day he exploded in fury, cursing his tormentor. The gang driver had had Duveen bound to the whipping posts, had torn out his tongue, and left him hanging, choking slowly on his own blood.

Lafe had come upon him there. He'd cut Duveen down, while holding at pistol point the man who had maimed him. With his fists Lafe had beaten from the man the name of Duveen's owner. Within the hour, he'd bought Duveen, brought him to the shadowed house in the Vieux Carré, and set about nursing him back to health.

Lafe's parents encouraged him. They were slaveowners, but not people who countenanced brutality. His sisters, Elizabet and Andrea, were involved in their complicated social affairs. His older brother, Claude, who had dealings as an attorney with Duveen's owner, and considered the woman a simpering fool, evinced no interest in the affair.

The same week that Lafe bought Duveen the gang driver fell ill. Within days he and each of his three small sons were bloated and blue with plague. They died of strangulation. Duveen showed no surprise on hearing this. It was, Lafe thought, as if he had already known it would happen.

When, five years after, Lafe stood under the Dueling Oaks and raised his pistol, and at the word *Fire* killed Anton Devereaux with a single shot, Duveen was standing only a few feet away.

Duveen was there, too, when Lafe learned that the man he had called out to duel and killed for naming him a liar had been telling God's truth and no lie at all.

Jeanne, his beloved of bitter remembrance, had promised herself not only to Lafayette Flynn but to Anton Devereaux as well, then sat back prettily, waiting to see what would happen, and on that to make her decision. By the time her horrified parents had discovered Jeanne's deceit and whisked her away to England on one of the Flynn ships, it was too late for Anton Devereaux. Hearing Lafe announce his be-

trothal to Jeanne, Anton had called him a dreamer.
"Jeanne," he said, "has promised herself to me." "I'm not
dreaming," Lafe had answered. "You lie, then," Anton retorted. And at dawn the next day, for telling the truth as he
thought it, he had died.

It was then that New Orleans had lost its savor for Lafe.
When he left, fleeing his memories, Duveen, by his own
choice, went with him. By that time Lafe had taught him to
read and write, using as text the papers of manumission
which Claude, though silently disapproving, had drawn up.

Duveen learned the skills of a free man through the words
that had made him free.

Now, to attract Lafe's attention, Duveen tapped his right
wrist hard. It was one signal they used between them. The
other was one Duveen had taught himself. Using his teeth
and lip, he had learned to whistle. And that whistle, like the
Pied Piper's flute, was known to draw up certain followers.

Lafe looked at Duveen inquisitively. The man shoved the
coffee mug closer, pointed to the bread and cheese. Lafe
grinned. "I'll eat, I promise you. I could eat near anything,
I'm that hungry. Though why I should be, I don't know. My
supper still lies on my gut."

Duveen nodded his understanding. There was none of
the familiar food here, no sweet shrimp or gumbo, nothing
to truly fill a man's stomach or satisfy his palate.

It seemed to Lafe that the last thing a man forgot of his
past was the food of his childhood. It was as if his insides had
a memory all their own and sent out signals, tantalizing and
ephemeral, that stirred the appetite without possibility of
relief, and at the same time stirred longings that could never
be appeased by food, but only by turning the hands of the
clock and sliding backwards into a past misty with the debris
of long years in between.

Lafe knew that his time of longing for home was done.
He had shed it as a snake sheds its skin, without thought or
concern or effort. He had, not realizing it then, been a misfit
in that society to which he had been born of a Creole mother
and an Irish father. He had belonged fully neither to his

mother's multitudinous family nor to his father's distant one. He had been too tall from the day he stood on his feet. His hair had been too red even after it darkened to a deeper shade. His eyes had always remained a too piercing dark blue. He had been too boisterous in his manner—with a loud booming laugh and a temper that flashed—to blend easily with the Creole gentlemen of his acquaintance. As a younger man he had remained a craggy outsider in spite of ruffled shirts and embroidered vests and silver buttons. He had given up the ruffles and buttons, though he still preferred silk next to his skin and finely tanned leather in his boots. No one would call him a dandy these days, but he looked prosperous, and was, and made no effort to conceal it. The years of wandering had taught him, more than he'd ever known before, the benefits of wealth; and since he had them, at the insistence of his father and Claude, he allowed himself to enjoy them. A man not driven to earn his own living could indulge himself. And if such indulgence led to dangerous pursuits, the freedom to take the risk was even sweeter.

He had made his first gamble by accident one evening as he and Duveen rode out of Natchez. He had no destination in mind, and no particular reason for traveling except the restlessness which had driven him since he'd left New Orleans.

It was dusk, the blue and heavy dusk of midsummer. Across the river there were flickers of lightning and ominous growls of thunder.

He had rounded a tree-lined curve, Duveen just behind him, and come upon a carriage. Pulling out to pass around, he saw a young black girl trotting close by its wheel, and the taut-drawn rope that bound her two wrists and kept her running. She was well formed, might even have been beautiful had she not been so starved, with the bones showing through her golden flesh. Her clothing was tattered and soaked through with her sweat. She breathed in quick harsh gasps, and her bare feet left small bloody spots on the dirt road.

43

Lafe saw the long look Duveen gave her, and moving his hand close to the saddle, he pointed ahead. He glanced into the carriage as they went around it. Two plump women sat within, their hats bedecked with pink feathers, their faces sleek and satisfied.

When they had overtaken and ridden well past them, he said, having already made up his mind, "Duveen, ride on into the next town. Go to the inn and take a room for me. Make sure that you're seen. Do you understand?"

Duveen raised sad dark eyes. He shook his head.

"I'm going back."

A grin spread against Duveen's harsh features and softened them. He wasted no more time. He raced away into the newly fallen dark.

Lafe pulled over into a stand of thick brush. While thunder growled overhead, he pulled a long dark greatcoat from his pack and threw it cloakwise over his shoulders. He tied a handkerchief over his face and drew the broad brim of his hat down so nothing showed but a gleam of eyes. He laid his pistol across his thigh.

Soon the carriage jolted into view. He allowed it to pass, then followed, trailing it until the sky was India-ink black, and its two small lamps were brilliant by contrast. By then the girl was hardly able to keep her feet, and when he hailed the carriage to a sudden stop, she collapsed into the dark shadows near the wheel.

Lafe rode close, leaned down and cut the ropes that bound her. "Hide nearby," he whispered. "Wait for me to come."

He thrust his pistol from beneath the makeshift cloak and looked in the carriage window. "Your jewels, my good ladies," he growled. "Hand over what you have!"

Amid twitters of fright, the ladies obeyed.

The Negro driver on the front seat sat mute, his hands carefully clasping the reins in full view.

Within moments Lafe was off across country. He stopped in the shelter of the trees to remove his meager disguise, then hurried on toward town.

44

He found Duveen waiting and explained what he had done. Two hours later they set off again. They had a carriage now, a woven hamper stocked with food, and a full outfit of clothes.

The young slave girl stood up fearfully when they stopped at the edge of the dark road. She heeded Lafe's "Girl? Where are you, girl? I've come to take you to safety," but she was plainly poised to run until she saw Duveen.

She allowed him to hand her into the seat. She snuggled under the wrap he put around her shoulders. She ate hungrily of the food he put in her lap.

Lafe had the carriage rolling a moment after he picked her up. When the two women reached town, an alarm would be raised. They'd lost their property and would offer rewards for its return, jewels and slave alike. Lafe drove north along the river. By the time they stopped again, the girl was dressed in suitable clothing. She wore a plain gold wedding ring. She sat on the driver's seat beside Duveen while Lafe lounged within.

He took lodgings in a hamlet for himself and for the couple he owned. He was lavish with his money in the tavern, and drank a boisterous toast to Chief Justice Roger Taney, who handed down the Dred Scott decision, which kept men slaves whether they were on free soil or not.

At dawn the next morning he, Duveen, and the girl set out on the long journey to Ohio. By the time they arrived, the girl had told them her story. She was seventeen. Her name was Amélia. Her master had wanted her, and made the mistake of being honest in his desires. Her mistress, with the support of her mother, had sold the girl and was delivering her to a Natchez brothel when Lafe stopped them.

They saw Amélia last in late September in Cincinnati. Duveen had somewhere obtained a list of addresses. She was to stop at each one and she would be passed onward until she arrived at the Canadian border and a new life.

Afterward, time seemed to hang on Lafe's hands. He was not pleased with himself. He found that he spent hours reliving his encounter on the Natchez road, and the memory was pleasurable to him. At length he and Duveen went South again and continued their travels.

Now, reflecting on their adventures as he chewed the bread and tasteless cheese, he studied Duveen. Then he asked, "Tell me, why do you stay with me?"

The big black man reached for paper and plumed pen. He scratched slowly, blotted with care, then passed over what he had printed in his childlike block letters. I NEED TO. As Lafe read the words, Duveen drew from his pockets the papers of manumission.

Lafe nodded his understanding. Duveen needed to do this work because he was a free man. There were many like him, without whom the task would not have been possible. Nor would it have been possible without men like himself. These two kinds were required, with their special knowledge and their special skills, to fill the hidey holes provided by those along the way.

"The Golden Leaf Tobacco Company will prosper here," he told Duveen.

Duveen grinned.

"You've made the arrangements?"

Duveen nodded again.

"You're pretty sure of your people, are you?"

Duveen winked.

"They'll have enough for clothes and food for several days?"

Duveen reached for paper and pen again. The note he passed to Lafe said, JUST ENOUGH, BUT NOT TOO MUCH.

"Friday after dark? At the wooden bridge we decided on?"

Duveen's answer was a wide and enthusiastic smile.

"You'll be glad to get started, and I don't blame you. I feel the same," Lafe said. "The inactivity isn't to my taste any more than to yours. But still, it's taken this month to do what was needed to be done. We've made our beginnings."

Duveen finished his coffee, gave Lafe's empty mug a questioning look.

46

"I guess I've had enough. What I'd like would be some decent liqueur, like my father's Benedictine. But I suppose it's best not to think on that. Though I'm not much in the mood for brandy, at least not the sort made from Georgia peaches, which is the best we could get from Mr. Jordan. And I'm certainly not in the mood for the stuff the men around here drink—damn stuff burns their tongues at night and their tails at morning." Self-conscious at having mentioned the word that might remind Duveen of his disability, Lafe hurried on. "On second thought, maybe I'll have the peach brandy after all."

Duveen made a sound that was as close to a chuckle as he could come. His deepset eyes gleamed with humor. He printed, I ORDERED SOME. IT'LL BE READY WHEN I GO FOR IT.

Lafe grinned. "You know me better than I know myself, it seems. But what man really knows himself?"

Later, alone, with the brandy glass that should have been a goblet warming in his hands, and the lamps turned low, he watched the shadow of the window curtain move along the round braided cotton rug in the middle of the room. What man really knows himself? he wondered again, but this time silently.

Did Oren Henderson? Did Gentry Beckwith? Did Duveen?

Lafe took a sip of brandy, rolled it on his tongue, and then swallowed it. He felt the trail of burning heat it carved as it went down his throat. He sighed. No, this stuff would surely never take the place of his father's brandies or liqueurs, luxuries men like his father took for granted, though they had been straw wrapped and packed in baskets and packed again and crated and shipped from the teeming wharves of Marseilles.

It was possible to learn to take anything for granted. From the worst horror to the greatest joy.

On the drift of breeze, there came the scent of honeysuckle, and with it the thought of Marietta Garvey.

Lafe leaned back his head, closed his eyes.

He wouldn't leave it to chance. He'd make certain that he saw her soon again.

3

Oren raised his head to listen as the dogs bayed.

"It's nothing," Marietta said quickly. "Don't disturb yourself."

"I'm not disturbed." He got to his feet. His face was still too pale, she thought. His left arm showed bulky under his sleeve where Aunt Tatie had bound his wound. He went on: "It seems to me that the hounds are too close by."

"Do you think so? Then I'll send Dora to look."

"I'll go myself, Marietta, but thank you."

"But should you be up and about? I expected that you would stay in bed today. I told Elisha—"

"Yes," Oren cut in impatiently. "I know. Elisha told me. I preferred to come down. There's nothing wrong with me. It's hardly more than a scratch. I'm a big boy, Marietta, and I don't like you to fuss so."

She leaned back, smiling. She folded her hands neatly together. "I'm sorry, Oren. Perhaps I've been overconcerned. But that Gentry Beckwith should—"

"It was my fault more than his." Now Oren's voice was sharp. A flush came up on his cheekbones. As the dogs bayed again, he caught up his crop, muttered, "Excuse me, Marietta," and stalked outside.

She hesitated at the table, knowing that he didn't want her to follow him.

Her uncertainty vanished when she heard his voice raised in an angry bellow. "Damn your empty heads and lazy bones! Which one of you did it this time?"

She hurried out. In the front gardens, where the oleanders and rhododendrons were set out in formal rows, Oren stood towering over two small boys. His whole body seemed swollen with rage, and the twins, Beedle and Needle, named so by their mother, Essie, the cook, for no reason Marietta knew, cowered before him.

"Answer up! I want to know." Oren raised his crop threateningly. "Somebody's going to get whipped for this. I don't want those hounds in here where they eat the oleander leaves. If they do, they'll get sick. They'll die. I've explained it more times than I've patience for. Now you tell me . . ."

Marietta was dimly aware of a gig rolling briskly up the track, of sunlight on a pale blue parasol, but she continued her headlong rush to where Oren stood.

The ten-year-olds nodded together, whispered together. "Yes, Mr. Oren. Yes, you told us. And it won't happen no more."

"Which one of you did it?" he demanded.

The boys looked up at him, then at each other, identical faces drawn with identical fear.

"Oren," Marietta cried. "Oren, wait a minute."

She had watched Beedle and Needle grow from infancy and deemed them clever and decided she would never send them into the fields. Now they did half-hand chores, directed by Aunt Tatie and Elisha. When they were full grown, they would be house servants. She couldn't bear to have Oren abuse them.

But he didn't seem to hear her call. He raised the crop, lashed out with it in a long swinging blow that caught both Needle and Beedle in its descent. The boys yelled. The dogs barked and leaped around them.

Marietta, watching Oren's arm draw back and lift, cried out, "Oren, I tell you, no! We never use the whip at Galloway." Even as she spoke, she hurled herself at him. She pulled the crop from his hand and threw it away. "We didn't when Papa was master! We shan't while I'm mistress here."

49

"Ah, yes," he answered, his mouth thinned with bitterness, and angry embers burning in his dark eyes. "Not while *you're* mistress here. As you so often remind me." And today, he thought, today was the day he must speak to her about the note. It could wait no longer.

"But I don't . . . I didn't mean . . ." She stopped herself, suddenly realizing that she had an interested audience.

The twins were listening, wide-eyed.

The gig had rolled up. Gentry Beckwith and his younger sister Sara had stepped down and were listening, too.

Marietta saw the swift color rise in Oren's face. She turned to the twins. "The two of you, scat. Get the hounds out of here this instant, and yourselves, too. And if that gate's ever left open again, then you'll find out! Now, go on. Move it, I say."

"Oren! You're all right then!" Sara's breathless cry preceded her. She came up in a swift gliding run that made her appear to float on the surface of the velvet green grass. "Oh, I was just devastated by what happened. And my father was, too. Oh, Oren, I can't tell you what a night I spent. But you're all right, aren't you!"

"Of course," Oren said. He looked past the shimmering golden curls, the blue silk parasol, to Gentry, who was approaching slowly. Oren wondered what he had heard, what he had seen.

Sara said, smiling now, her hand pressed to the curve of her breast, "Oh, I'm so happy." And then, turning to Marietta, "How are you, honey? And where's Coraleen?"

"I'm fine," Marietta answered. "And Coraleen's inside." Her tone was cool. Her eyes, fixed on Gentry, were bright with anger.

He moved his bulky shoulders uncomfortably. The guilt he felt was written on his face, and worse than that, it twisted like a viper in his chest. "Marietta . . . Oren . . . I don't know what got into me," he said softly. "I just . . . well . . . I'm sorry."

"He came home drunk as a lord," Sara announced cheerily. "Drunk as a lord, I tell you." She dimpled at Oren.

"And I'll bet you were just the same. The two of you, what a pair. Aren't they a pair, Marietta?"

Marietta agreed coolly, her eyes still fixed on Gentry.

"And of course when he told Papa and me what had happened, why, we were just furious with him. He'd had a fight with Oren, he said. And Papa just jumped all over him. And—"

"Hush," Gentry cut in. "Neither Marietta nor Oren is interested."

"Oh, but I am," Marietta told him. "I'm truly interested in what happened last night. In all of what happened, in fact. I'd like to know how you came to wound Oren, and why. And—"

Oren said, flushing once more, "Marietta, please."

"It was my fault," Gentry told her. "He had every right to strike the first blow. I'd had one too many, and said what I shouldn't. I freely own it. I'm sorry, and I've said so. What more can I do?"

He could stop his proposals, she thought. He could ride away and never come back. He could disappear forever into thin air. Any of these would please her. She didn't want his attentions. But the Beckwiths were Galloway's closest neighbors. Some propriety must be observed, so she said nothing of her feelings. She turned away, saying, "Come inside. Why do we stand out here?"

Behind her back, Oren and Sara exchanged glances, hers hopeful, his a warning.

Gentry observed this, and decided that he might have been wrong. Sara had provoked him the night before, shouting angrily even as she wept, "You *think* you cut Oren! Oh, you're all just like animals, every last one of you. Brawling, fighting, dueling if you can tease some fool innocent into it. I'm sick of hearing your tales. Why, even you, Gentry, you, my own brother, and Oren, two of the best . . . Why should you fight Oren?"

"And why not?" Gentry had demanded. "Is it because you want him? Is that why he's got to be kept whole and perfect? So he'll be a husband to you? Then think again, little sister.

Because you'll not get him. And the sooner you face up to it the better for you."

"You know nothing of it," she cried.

Now, having seen the looks that passed between the two of them, Gentry saw that there was something here he hadn't counted on. Oren wanted Sara as much as she wanted him. If only he could think of some way to get those two off together, leaving him alone with Marietta. If only he had a chance to talk to her for a little while. Maybe she'd listen to him. Maybe this morning would be different from yesterday noon, when she'd smiled so sweetly and said, *No, Gentry. I'm sorry.*

But he wasn't able to think quickly enough, and before he could make a move they were all indoors, and Coraleen was rushing down the stairs crying, "Oh, Sara, how glad I am to see you."

"And I'm glad to see you, too." Sara answered, with another sideways look at Oren.

"Then come along to my room. I've so much to tell you." There was Lafe Flynn to talk about, and the promise of future adventures, Coraleen thought, as she seized Sara's hand. But she felt resistance and let go at once. "Don't you want to?" Now her smiling lips had begun to pout. She had always considered Sara her ally against Marietta. Sara understood her grievances better than anyone. But now . . .

Sarah answered quickly, "Of course I want to go up with you. But in a little while."

"We'll have iced tea," Marietta said. "And Aunt Tatie's rhubarb pie that should be ready just about now."

"I'd like some," Gentry said in haste. He was very nearly giddy with relief. If Marietta hadn't forgiven him, she'd not be offering him the hospitality of the house.

The five settled in the sunlit parlor. Dora and Elisha served the tea and pie.

Oren raised his head toward the window. "Listen. Is that the hounds again?"

"I don't hear anything," Coraleen told him.

He ignored her, got to his feet quickly. "I'd better just see. The boys keep leaving the gate open. I don't want to lose my dogs to oleander poisoning if I can help it."

Sara leaped up. "I'll go with you. If they're back in the gardens, the two of us can run them into the yard faster."

"Thank you," he answered gravely.

They hurried out, and Marietta, listening to their quick footsteps in the hallway, frowned thoughtfully. Seizing his opportunity, Gentry said, "Coraleen, it occurs to me that we've clear run out of chives and chervil at home. Do you suppose you could ask Aunt Tatie to give us some starters?"

"Of course I can, and be glad to." She smiled teasingly at him and reached for the small silver bell at Marietta's elbow. "But since when do you concern yourself with kitchen affairs?"

He turned beet red, muttered wordlessly.

"Ah, never mind." She laughed. "I'll go and attend to it myself, so you can talk to Marietta alone." With that, and a triumphant look at Marietta, she left the room.

Gentry's color slowly became normal. He sighed aloud. "I don't know what gets into Coraleen sometimes. She can be sweet as sugar and then tart as a lemon. And you never know—"

"She still has some growing up to do," Marietta answered.

"But she's old enough to understand I wanted to talk to you." Gentry sighed again. "Marietta, I don't want to talk about her. I just want to tell you . . . I'm sorry for what happened."

She nodded. "Very well. Let's not speak of it further."

"I'm glad I didn't hurt Oren badly."

"So you should be."

"Marietta, listen . . . if that Flynn fellow hadn't interfered, I'd have come to my senses and brought Oren home, and you'd never even have known."

She said softly, "It's just as well I do know, however. And you can stop worrying, Gentry. Oren's refused to tell me just

53

what it was that you fought about. I realize that means you said something about me that he felt he couldn't let pass."

Gentry's face was scarlet, his pale eyes glistening as if with fever. He burned truly, but it was with the heat of embarrassment. "I'd never . . . if I hadn't been drunk—"

"I don't care," she cut in. "You don't seem to understand, so let me say it plainly. I don't care what you say about me, and I shall make that quite clear to Oren, if I haven't already. You're nothing to me, Gentry Beckwith. Nor shall you ever be." Her voice was level, her look, too. This time there was nothing soft, or smiling, or kind. "I'd have no interest in a boy, Gentry. And that's what you are."

Gentry, silenced by a sudden cold anger, didn't reply. He couldn't imagine now why he'd ever wanted her. She wasn't womanly. He saw it finally. She was a harridan, and a spinster harridan she would remain. He heaved himself up from the chair. "I'll not trouble you any longer," he said.

"But of course, Gentry, we shall always be friends," she told him, her voice light.

He left without replying.

She turned to look out the window. Oren and Sara were walking side by side, Oren towering over the small blond girl. A frown grew between Marietta's dark arching brows. She wished she could hear what they were saying.

It was as if Oren were conscious of her gaze. He glanced at the window, then looked quickly away. He said, "Sara, please, try to understand."

"All I know is that she refused Gentry yesterday. Again, Oren."

"He told me," Oren said bitterly.

"Well, then . . ."

"But maybe she'll change her mind, Sara."

"She won't. I know Marietta. She's not made of flesh and blood like you and me. She doesn't bend. She doesn't change her mind. She'll never marry Gentry."

"If only I had something of my own," Oren said. "If only her father hadn't cut me out so completely . . ."

"Yes, my darling. Yes, I know. It's so unfair to you and

54

Coraleen. And you work hard running the plantation, taking the responsibility on your shoulders. It's terribly unfair. But what can we do?"

"I don't know," he told her. The words were so unhappy that she caught his hand in hers and tugged him off the path, deeper into the shadow of the oleander bushes where the house was hidden from them, and they were hidden from the house.

She raised her face to his. "I don't care, Oren. But the thing is, no matter how I feel, my father would never allow it, never, not if you don't have something."

"I can't blame him for that. But what am I supposed to do? I hear there's still a fortune to be made if you get a bit of cash together and pull up a few coffles of slaves and get well around the law safely."

"Oren!" she gasped. "You couldn't go blackbirding!"

"Well, then what?"

"You'll think of something. I know you will. That's why I'm waiting, Oren."

He bent and gathered her into his arms, buried his face in the softness of her breasts. "Oh, I want you so, Sara. Sweet God, how I want you."

They leaped guiltily apart at the stamping sound of Gentry's approach.

Sara brushed the blond curls from her cheeks, ran small quick hands over the bosom of her pink gown, gently touched her lips, as if pressing into permanence the warmth of Oren's kiss. Then she stepped out of the shade of the concealing bushes, with Oren following her.

"Let's go," Gentry said shortly.

She saw the anger in his eyes. "What's the matter, Gentry?"

"We're leaving now." Gentry went to the gig.

Beedle darted to him, thrust up a basket of herbs. "For you to take home, Mr. Gentry," he said grinning. When Gentry didn't move to take it, Sara did. Within moments the two had driven down the road.

Oren waited until they were gone from sight. Then he

went indoors. He found Marietta where he had left her earlier. "What happened between you and Gentry?" he demanded.

"I made plain my feelings for him. This time I know he understood."

"You'd no reason to make an enemy of him, Marietta," Oren protested.

She deliberately widened her eyes. "Did I do that? Why, then, I'm sorry, Oren."

Now was the time, he thought. There would be no better. The longer he waited, the worse it would be. He seated himself beside her. "Never mind, Marietta. Gentry will get over it. I've something more important to discuss with you."

Her heart gave a small quick flutter of hope. He looked serious, his handsome face showing new lines of anxiety. Could he think she would ever speak to him as she did to Gentry Beckwith? She said, "Oren, what's of such moment that makes you look so?"

"We need money to pay our bills, Marietta. I've been to see Marcus Swinton. He's perfectly willing to make a loan to Galloway. He knows that our crop is planted. We'll get a good price when we harvest. I don't want you to worry your pretty head with the details, but I shall need your signature, Banker Swinton says. *Your* signature, Marietta, since you're the owner of Galloway."

"We need the money?" she asked gently.

"To pay the bills that have fallen due."

"Won't our creditors wait?"

"They will, but they won't continue to supply us."

"I don't understand."

His dark eyes narrowed, but he said quietly, "You want me to run the plantation for you, Marietta. Then you must allow me to do what I think best." It hurt him to have to admit to this failure before her. The less said of it the better.

"Naturally you must do what you think best," she answered, but she was doubtful, and it came through in her voice. She went on quickly: "Let me have the paper, Oren. I'll sign it right now."

"Thank you, Marietta." He rose, left her for a few moments. When he returned, he put a parchment into her hand and a pen. "Quickly," he said. "Before the ink dries."

She put pen to paper and looked up. "You think it's necessary, Oren? We couldn't do without?"

"I'd not ask if there was any other way."

She caught a word or two, *security, in the event, the month of May.* But she had no time to read with him standing so impatiently over her. And what did it matter? Oren said it was necessary to sign. She signed.

He took the document from her, waved it to dry her inked signature. "All right," he said. "Now I'll go in to see Marcus Swinton."

"You must give him my regards, Oren. And you might ask him to stop by for a visit. It's been a while since I've seen him."

"I certainly will," Oren promised. But he knew he wouldn't pass the message along. The less Marcus Swinton saw of Marietta just now the better it would be. Later, Oren told himself, it would be all right. With this loan he would straighten out the plantation affairs, and show Marietta that her trust in him was well placed. But for the moment he wanted her to go on in happy ignorance.

At the sound of horse hooves Oren looked from the window. He saw Needle come darting through the gate to catch the reins Lafe Flynn tossed to him. Beedle swung the gate shut quickly and gave Oren a quick proud grin as he went to greet Lafe.

"So you've remembered this time," Oren said, smiling. "You've earned you and Needle a sweet for that. Go tell Aunt Tatie that I said so."

The boys scampered off as Lafe swung down from the saddle. "I see just what I came to see, Mr. Henderson. That you fare as well as I thought you would."

"I do, and thank you," Oren answered. "And thank you for your help last night."

"A small thing," Lafe murmured, glancing toward the house.

57

From an upstairs window, Coraleen watched for a moment. Then she hurried to her mirror. She smoothed her brown waves and pinched her cheeks. She rearranged the lace at her throat. Breathlessly, she hurried downstairs.

Lafe had just greeted Marietta and been invited to sit down when Coraleen came bursting in. "Mr. Flynn, it's good to see you again so soon."

He grinned at her. "I promised I'd come back, I believe. And I always keep my promises."

"How nice to know." She smiled sweetly at Marietta. "Oh, I almost forgot to tell you. Elisha says that Mr. Blandish is tying up out back, and asks to see you, Marietta."

"To see me, you mean," Oren put in.

"Elisha spoke of Marietta, Oren." Coraleen tossed her head. "I do think I can manage to carry a message correctly for such a short distance."

Oren said, "If you'll excuse me for a moment . . . I'll speak to Mr. Blandish and return."

When he had gone, Lafe said, "I'm glad the wound proved to be nothing."

"So are we."

"I fear I've come at an inopportune moment, however."

"Not at all," Coraleen cried.

But Lafe was looking at Marietta. She was plainly abstracted. This was not as he'd planned. He got to his feet. "I hope I may call again, Miss Marietta."

Now he had her full attention, but it was Coraleen who cried, "And why not? Surely you don't expect to be turned away from our door."

She sounded like an overenthusiastic child, he thought, and waited for Marietta's reply.

"We'll be glad to have you whenever you're in the neighborhood, Mr. Flynn. And you mustn't hurry away now. Oren will be back soon."

He sat down again, stayed for a short time to make small talk with Coraleen, while he studied Marietta openly.

She was uncomfortably aware of his gaze. Once again she

58

felt the air between them grow heavy with quick sharp currents. She sensed a quickening within that startled her. It was only natural, she reminded herself, that she should notice that he was a man of exceptionally good looks and bearing. But she was concerned only with Oren. It was a relief to her when Lafe departed, seen off by a smiling Coraleen.

But Lafe forgot Coraleen as soon as he reached the road. Marietta filled his thoughts. He wasn't downhearted that she seemed hardly to attend to him beyond superficial courtesies. He could be patient, when patience was needed. And there was time.

Eamus Jordan gave him a message from the telegraph room, which was conveniently located in a first-floor cubbyhole in the hotel, a matter of some pride to Mr. Jordan.

Lafe exchanged comments about the fine weather with the proprietor, then went to his suite.

There he read that his sister Elizabet was to be married. His family expected him to appear at the wedding. He grinned broadly. It was nice that they wanted him at home, but he had no intention of going. He planned his reply, went down to send it off, and spent an hour listening to the varied conversations in the gaming room.

Much later that night, when Darnal was dark and still, he and Duveen worked quickly and quietly.

The one room in the warehouse that was to be his office was nearly completed. The wooden floor was laid. Now, while the town slept, they cut out a square trap door and covered it over with lengths of paper.

"Tomorrow night will be harder," Lafe said when they were done.

Duveen nodded.

"And moving the dirt out will be risky."

Duveen shrugged his massive shoulders, spread his big hands.

"Yes," Lafe agreed. "It *is* the only way. We'll just have to be as fast as we can."

59

When they returned to the hotel, Lafe sat before the gallery window, going over papers sent to him by Claude from New Orleans. The Golden Leaf Tobacco Company was a part of the Flynn shipping empire, and the papers his brother had prepared, silently disapproving, Lafe knew, were evidence of that fact. He was immersed in his study of them when he heard a faint sound on the gallery.

He reached immediately for the pistol on the small table beside him. Holding it against his thigh, he rose and stepped silently to the open doors.

There was a ripple of movement in the vines along the railing, although there was no breeze. He waited, allowing his eyes to adjust to the darkness. He saw the tall high-backed chair tilt slightly, and he glided to it, his pistol aimed. Then he grasped the back of the chair and gave it a single hard rock that shook it and spun it around.

"What do you want?" he demanded, and found himself looking into Coraleen Henderson's laughing face.

"My goodness, Lafe, do you mean to kill me for visiting you?" she asked.

"You take a grave risk when you creep about a man's window in that fashion, Miss Coraleen."

She smoothed her hair. Her voice was still full of laughter. "I see that I do. But what do you fear so, Lafe? Have you dangerous enemies about?"

It was, he knew, his mistake. And there was no way to retrieve it. He forced a grin. "Perhaps I fear visits from young ladies."

"You've no doubt had many. You should have become well accustomed to them."

"I've had some."

"Then you'll forgive me for being forward. But you took your leave too quickly this morning. I'd barely time to be civil to you, and then suddenly you were gone."

"Next time I'll stay longer." Now the banter was gone from his voice. "But I think you should return home at once, Miss Coraleen. You shouldn't be here, you know."

"I don't care," she told him. "I do as I like."

"I do care."

She gave an angry sigh. "Oh, very well. But nobody will know I was here. I slipped away when Oren and Marietta thought I was in bed. The stable boys would never dare tell on me, and why should they?"

"You know, as I do, that the roads hereabouts are not safe after dark."

"They're safe enough for me." She pouted.

"And if the patrol saw you . . ."

"But they wouldn't see me. I know how to avoid them, believe me."

"Oh, I do believe you." He paused, grinned. "I also believe that if you were my sister or daughter, I'd give you several powerful smacks on the bottom. Somewhere along the way, you've not learned all that you should."

"It wasn't because no one tried," she said airily.

"I begin to believe that, too."

She eyed him. "Never mind me, Lafe. Just tell me, do you have dangerous enemies?"

"I hope not. And I hardly think I have."

"Yet you're rather quick with that pistol of yours," she said, smiling. "I wonder who you expected to find in the rocking chair beside your window."

"If I'd expected an enemy, I'd have fired first, wouldn't I?"

"I doubt that," she said dryly.

"Do you? Why?"

"Because I think you're a man who prizes his honor. And men who do rarely shoot before they know their target."

"I take that as a pleasant compliment." He looked down at her and heard the chime of the grandfather clock. "If you wait while I get my hat and my horse, I'll see you home."

"You'll what?"

"I'll see you back to Galloway, Miss Coraleen. I'd not sleep if I knew you were on the road alone."

"How gallant you are," she purred. "I do confess, in spite of what I said before, that I was a bit nervous."

"But you came on anyway."

61

"Oh, yes. I always do. Were I to allow my fears to stop me I would never have what I want."

"Come along," he told her, drawing her with him across the gallery and then down the steps and around the hotel into the stable yard. They met no one, and Lafe was relieved. How would he explain a midnight visit from Miss Coraleen Henderson? He untethered her horse and tossed the reins up to her. When he had mounted, they rode out together.

"We Hendersons do keep you busy, don't we?" she asked, satisfaction in her voice.

He turned his head, regarded her silently. She considered this no more than an adventure, he supposed. The prank of a girl still not quite grown up. And yet, when he looked into her eyes it seemed to him that he saw no child staring out at him. She could be a menace to him and all he wanted. He said soberly, "Miss Coraleen, I want you to know that I'm flattered by your visit. But if you should take such a foolish risk again, I would feel, as an acquaintance of your brother and sister, and as a grown person responsible for the young around him, that I must speak honestly with your family."

"You wouldn't," she gasped. "It's nothing to do with Oren and Marietta."

"But it has. Since you're a minor, and under their care."

"But Lafe," she wailed, "you'll spoil everything."

"I shouldn't like to do that. But if I'm not to, then you must promise not to come alone to the hotel again," he answered.

"Very well. I promise." She agreed quickly, but was seething inside. She thought of the way he had crept out to the gallery, his pistol at the ready, when he heard her moving there, and she wondered whom he had expected to find.

4

The June sun was warm, and a blue haze hung on the ridges to the west. Above, soft fleecy white clouds drifted slowly closer. Marietta hugged to her the bouquet of newly cut roses. They were a brilliant scarlet, touched with the glitter and sheen of dew, and gave off a heady fragrance. It was a fine day, and later she and Oren would ride out together. Aunt Tatie was already supervising Essie at the preparation of the picnic lunch. Marietta turned toward the house, reminding herself that she must be sure to stop by Mr. Blandish's cabin to arrange for his wife, Letty, to come to do some mending.

When the hounds yelped, she swung back toward the yard to see Jed Blandish come through the gate and close it carefully behind him.

"Why, Mr. Blandish," she said, smiling. "I was just thinking of you. Would you ask Letty to come up for half a day sometime this week?"

He pulled off his hat, regarded her dourly. "I'll tell her." Then, "Do you have a minute for me, Miss Garvey?"

"You know I do. Come inside. I'll just give these flowers to Elisha, and we can talk as long as you like."

He didn't reply, but followed after her. She was aware of his set jaw and hangdog look as she spoke to Elisha, and by the time she had led him into the morning room, she knew there was some problem.

He waited until she was seated, and then standing before her, his hat in his hand, he said, "Miss Garvey, I was hired by your father. He taught me Galloway, and how it ought to be."

She saw his glance go to the big gold-framed portrait hanging between the two windows draped in blue rep. Lawrence Garvey. A good man, who had died too soon and left her alone to maintain the plantation he had loved. She allowed Oren to do the managing because it was what he wanted. Until she learned about the loan she had been confident in her decision. Now she had begun to wonder. Jed Blandish's long pause, his obvious unwillingness to continue, made her uneasy.

She murmured encouragingly, "You've done a fine job of it, Mr. Blandish."

"But I can not. Not any more."

Startled, she cried, "What? What do you mean?"

"It's Mr. Henderson, I'm sorry to say. His way isn't mine. And it's not your father's either. You'll have to decide how Galloway's to be run. *You'll* have to, Miss Garvey."

With those words out, Jed Blandish gave a sigh of relief. He sat down, put his hat on his knees. He was a man of fifty-five, bone-thin and leather-hard, with a shock of sun-streaked blond hair and a long full blond mustache. He had come down from the mountains to the west when he was a boy, and worked on two plantations before Lawrence Garvey hired him as overseer after the catastrophe at Galloway. He was a strict man, but fair and soft-speaking, and he dealt well with the slaves. He had married a Darnal girl, Letty Jones, and had three growing sons. He had been content for his first eighteen years at Galloway. But these past twelve months had wiped all that away. Oren Henderson was no Lawrence Garvey. It was Jed's opinion that Oren was spoiled by all that the older man had done for him, and mulishly determined to prove himself the older man's equal, without advice or help from anyone else. Now Jed saw by the expression on her face that Marietta didn't like what she had heard. But he couldn't help that. He'd had to speak.

She said softly, "I think you'd better explain, Mr. Blandish."

64

"No plantation can be run by two masters, Miss Garvey."

"But you know that Mr. Henderson—"

Jed cut in. "Mr. Henderson does wrong. And won't listen when I point it out. And when I've tried to speak to you, he shunts me aside."

"Shunts you aside?" she echoed. "But I'm always available to you. You've only to—"

"Only to come up to the house." Jed's face had a stubborn look. "As I did . . . and when was it . . . weeks ago? And Mr. Henderson came out and sent me away with a bug in my ear. And he meant it, too. He said you didn't want to be bothered. That he would deal with me, with whatever came up."

"I see," she said softly. Then she smiled at Jed. "All right. Now that you're here, what was it that you wanted to discuss with me?"

He took a long folded sheet of paper from his pocket. "These are the supplies I needed. Needed, mind you. Nothing there that could be called foolish extravagance. At least your father wouldn't have thought so. You'll see what's been crossed out. He narrowed the list down to a bare nothing. We can't make do with what's left. I'll ask you to read it and decide. You, Miss Garvey."

Slowly she ran her finger down the list. Nails, lumber, paint. These were for the slave quarters a mile beyond the house and separated from it by a grove of pines. The old buildings needed continual repairs to keep them habitable. Now with the planting completed, and before the first harvests were begun, was the time to do them. Oren had crossed off all the essential materials. He was wrong to have done that, of course. It was work that had to be done. Sick men, weary men, could not be relied upon to do a day's labor, her father had always said. She looked up at the portrait again and imagined she saw her father's bearded face nod at her. Jed Blandish was right.

She said, sighing, "You must do this work, and buy these things, of course."

"Thank you. And what of the rest?"

65

She read on. Salt, sugar, molasses, meat. Crossed out again. Whatever had Oren been thinking of? Hungry men couldn't do a day's labor either. If you owned slaves, you fed them. Otherwise they were a worthless investment. She could hear her father saying that, could remember the look in his eyes when he saw starving people, and he had seen them, she knew.

"You can't do away with the foodstuffs here, Mr. Blandish," she said finally.

"Very well." Relief made the overseer's eyes glitter. "And now, Miss Garvey, what of the future? Mr. Henderson won't be pleased that I've come to you. It'll surely make for trouble. What are we to do?"

"We?" She gave him a cool smile, reminding him that they were not conspirators against Oren. She went on: "*I* shall explain it to Mr. Henderson."

"And if he says I'm not to trouble you?"

"He won't." She rose, smiling. "Don't worry about it any more. And do remember to tell Letty that I'd like to see her."

He got up quickly. "Thanks, Miss Garvey. I hope I did the right thing."

"Of course you did. We'll work it out."

But she found that evening that it was not as easy a problem to solve as she had hoped it would be.

When she told Oren of Jed Blandish's visit, he went white-faced with anger.

"He'd no call to do that," he said hoarsely. "I know exactly what's needed. He's accustomed to having too free a hand. There's waste. I must put a stop to it."

"Mr. Blandish must have those supplies, Oren," she said softly. "He's been ordering for Galloway for eighteen years."

"And become lax at it." Oren's long dark eyes burned. "And to have the gall to come up here, behind my back . . ."

"He only did what he thought was right."

"You think so, too." Oren's hands became fists. "See here, Marietta, if I'm to take responsibility for Galloway, then I

66

must have the authority. You know nothing of running a plantation. You mustn't interfere."

More than anything she wanted to cry, Yes, yes, Oren, you're right. I don't want to hear about the plantation. You see to it for me. But her father's will had left the property, and all on it, to her care. She must accept the maintenance of it, even though, as now, it seemed a struggle beyond her capacities.

She said only, "I shan't interfere in the future, Oren, but you must allow me to take part in your decisions. We must work much more closely together than we have in the past. I see that I've been remiss. I should have been helping you, and I haven't."

He saw that he wouldn't move her, so accepted what she offered as a graceful compromise. He would, he told himself, deal with it later. "Very well, Marietta," he answered. "We'll work together from now on."

"Then suppose the two of us go for a ride tomorrow morning," she suggested. "We could stop by and see Mr. Blandish."

"If you like," he answered indifferently.

But the next morning when she came down in a green riding dress, with a small green feathered hat perched on her curls, she found that he had already left the house.

Neither Elisha nor Aunt Tatie knew where he had gone.

She tried to contain her disappointment, pacing from room to room. There was a fleck of dust on the staircase. She called Dora to polish the treads. She spied a set of handprints on the window and rang for Elisha. When Snowball curled herself against her, she shooed the cat away.

It was soon after that that Aunt Tatie told her that Lafe Flynn had come to call.

"To call on me?" Marietta demanded.

"It's what he said," Aunt Tatie answered. "Did you know you got on your hat?"

Marietta reached up, touched it, and laughed. "I must have forgotten it."

"He's still waiting."

"Show him in," Marietta said.

Just as she did, Lafe appeared in the doorway. "Good morning, Miss Garvey."

"Good morning. I'm rather surprised to see you, Mr. Flynn."

"Surprised? Now why is that, I wonder? You said I might call if I were ever in the neighborhood. And I was."

"Of course. But what I meant was . . ." She stopped in sudden confusion. She couldn't explain to herself the strange effect Lafe Flynn had on her each time she saw him. She was sharply aware of the blue of his eye, the width of his shoulders.

"What did you mean?" he asked softly.

"If it's Oren you've come to see, and I suppose it is, then I fear you've missed him. He set out for town several hours ago."

"I know." Lafe smiled. He took a seat, stretched out his long legs. "I saw him in Darnal before I left for Galloway." Lafe didn't consider it necessary to mention that Oren had already had several drinks by the time he had seen him.

"Then what can I do for you?" Marietta asked.

"For a beginning, you can stop calling me Mr. Flynn. My name is Lafayette. My friends call me Lafe. And I much prefer it."

She leaned back in her chair, not smiling. She gave him a level look. "Isn't that rather familiar on such short acquaintance?"

"I intend it to be, Marietta. I don't believe in wasting my time—"

"Now see here—"

His booming laugh silenced her. He leaned closer. "I'm a very straightforward man, Marietta."

"Forward certainly," she answered in a dry voice.

He laughed again, enjoying himself. He took out a small cigar and lit it.

As he waved out the light, she said severely, "I don't recall that you asked my permission to smoke in my presence."

68

"I don't recall that I did either. Nor did I ask you your permission to call you by your Christian name. I doubt, ma'am, that I'll ever ask your permission. Except for one thing." His mouth turned in a teasing smile. "And perhaps I won't even then."

She felt heat burn in her cheeks. "Mr. Flynn, would you like to state your business before you leave?"

"I'll be glad to. If you call me Lafe."

"Then what is your business?"

"On second thought, perhaps I'd better not divulge it now."

She stared at him, trying not to smile. "I find it difficult to understand you."

"Perhaps you do now. But if you'll allow me a little time, then I'm sure you'll have no problem, Marietta."

"If you won't tell me why you're here—"

"Didn't Coraleen explain to you what I'm doing in Darnal?" he asked.

Marietta shook her head.

"And you've heard no gossip about me?"

"I don't listen to gossip," she said.

"Ah, now I begin to see." Lafe pressed out his cigar. "You considered that this might be a personal call, is that it?"

Again she felt heat burn her cheeks. "Why on earth should I?"

"Why on earth not?" When she didn't reply, he went on: "After all, you're a most attractive woman, and I'm an unmarried man."

"But you're not making a personal call," she said finally, trying to control her impatience. What did he want of her? Why did his smile, his laugh, so disturb her?

"I'm afraid you have the wrong of it, Marietta. I *am* making a personal call. Not on Oren. But on you."

"As you said yourself . . ." she began coldly, but ended by laughing. "You're straightforward indeed."

"And as you said, I'm simply forward." He remembered saying the same thing to Coraleen. It had been true then, and the observation remained true of him as well. But he was

69

a man, and thirty years to Coraleen's sixteen. And regardless, he saw no reason to delay the courtship he intended. "I'll agree with you, Marietta," he said, "but I don't apologize for it."

She rose to her feet. "As you can see, I'm dressed to go out. If this is merely a personal call, then I hope you'll forgive me, and excuse me."

"It's that. But, beyond that is something else. I asked if Coraleen had told you why I'm in Darnal. You say she hasn't. My reason may well interest you."

"And that is?"

"I'm here to do business."

She waited, seeing the gleam in his eye, the square stubborn lines of his face.

"The Golden Leaf Tobacco Company is mine," he went on. "And when you harvest, I hope you'll remember that. I pay good prices, as good as any you'll get. And cash on delivery, of course. One day, when you've the time to spare me, perhaps we can have a drive around the plantation together. We might be able to approximate your harvest."

It would be Oren who would ride with Lafe. But she said nothing of that. She observed only, "The harvest is a long way off. We begin in mid-July, and it takes five to six weeks."

"So I had supposed. But it doesn't hurt to talk now. And possibly to come to some terms. What leaf do you grow?"

"We grow Bright."

"And you use charcoal for curing?"

"We do now."

"That's very advanced. I approve."

"My father was a farsighted man," she said, glancing at the portrait of Lawrence Garvey.

"He must have been."

"He came originally from Virginia, where tobacco has been grown for years." She went on thoughtfully: "You must be farsighted yourself. Else why would you open a tobacco warehouse in Darnal? There are not that many acres of tobacco under cultivation in the county yet. Galloway. Beckwiths'. Perhaps three others. The rest are all still in cotton, though it no longer does that well here."

"Three or four plantations will do me," he said cheerfully. "As long as I am the buyer. And I mean to be certain that I am."

"We believe that soon the whole county will go for tobacco. It's a good cash-yielding crop, and does well in this soil. However, there are some who still refuse to believe it."

"You can see that I do." He paused. "You surprise me, Marietta. You know more of the business than I would have thought."

"I learned some from listening to my father," she answered. But she thought that in this past year Oren had shielded her more than he should have from such affairs. She went on: "If you like, my overseer, Mr. Blandish, and Oren will show you the fields."

"I prefer to deal only with the owner, Marietta."

"Do you?"

"Indeed I do. It always simplifies business affairs."

"In this case, Oren acts for me," she answered. "However, I'm sure we'll discuss it together."

"I shall discuss it with you," he told her firmly.

It seemed to her that the conversation and the visit were quite finished. But she wanted to prolong it. It was pleasant to speak with Lafe Flynn. She seated herself, said, "You've come to Darnal to buy tobacco, and I gather you plan to remain."

"As I told Coraleen, I'll be here as long as I find crop to move out." He thought of the small earthen room carved out beneath the warehouse floor. He and Duveen had completed it, furnished it with mats for sleeping, with jugs and toweling cloth, with dried fruits. Slowly, cautiously, working always in silence by shaded lamps, they had readied the place. Soon he would receive his first telegraph message; soon he would move out the first of his "crops."

Marietta asked, "And from where are you originally?"

"I hail from New Orleans, Marietta. I have a mother and

a father, both quite pleasant people. I have two sisters, one of whom has just married. I also have an older brother. Nice, but a bit stuffy for my taste. We are fairly respectable people. I think you'd agree, if you allowed yourself to know us."

"Mr. Flynn," she protested, "I've not asked for your pedigree."

"Lafe, if you don't mind. And as for the pedigree . . . I thought I might as well say it all and have done with it forever. Now you know everything about me."

"And you're from New Orleans," she said, at once intrigued and intimidated. "So far away from here. So different. It's hard to imagine how you would find Darnal. I could understand your locating in Durham's Station, small though it is, since it's a train stop. But somehow . . ."

He laughed. "Ah, it's not necessarily size that counts, you know. But I did have to search to find Darnal, believe me. And I did think to settle in Durham's Station, but somehow it didn't please me. I decided to be closer to the crop. I can wagon the hogsheads out for shipment. It doesn't matter too much to me. They go by rail anyway, you know, to the wharves of Norfolk, or else cross to the Mississippi by cart and go off the docks at St. Louis. Either way they get to New Orleans. And on my father's ships they sail across the ocean."

"Ah," she said, " the manufacture is abroad then."

"Largely. Except for some chewing stuff done up in Durham's Station."

"It should all be handled in this country. Then we'd see more of the profit."

"Oh, yes, I agree. But, of course, one would have to pay more of the taxes, too."

She nodded. Then, "And yours is a New Orleans family?"

"On my mother's side. My father came there as a young boy."

"Do you speak French?"

"Of course. It's my mother's native language." He grinned. "It troubled her that I spoke both languages when I first used words."

72

"Say a few words for me, Lafe."

"Would you understand them?"

"No. I have learned no French, nor had the opportunity to."

"Then I won't say a few words for you."

"But why not?"

"If you won't understand me, why should I?" he asked.

"To amuse me perhaps."

"Would you have me do parlor tricks to satisfy your whim?"

She blinked once, then again. She leaned back her head and laughed heartily. "Oh, you're right, of course. I sound like a chittering fool, don't I? 'Oh, speak French to me,' " she mocked herself.

He looked at the long clean line of her throat and suddenly his mouth was dry, his lips burning. He wanted to press them against the warmth of her flesh. Patience, he told himself, and said easily, "Someday I'll show you New Orleans and you to New Orleans. You'll hear French spoken as it should be."

"I wouldn't want to go. Not anywhere. My life is here. I don't care about any other place."

"Do you mean that you're not curious even to see it?"

"Why should I be?"

"You might learn something. You might find something you don't have here."

"All I want, all I'll ever want is here," she answered, thinking of Oren and Galloway.

Lafe said dryly, "I'm sure you must believe so now. But suppose everything were different."

"It won't be."

"You can't know that, Marietta." He watched her intently. "Suppose, for instance, that slavery were to be outlawed, and every state became free soil."

"It couldn't happen, Lafe." She didn't even notice that she had used his first name. She went on: "President Buchanan would never allow it. And the Supreme Court . . . Chief Justice Taney—"

73

"No man, not even a president, lives forever, Marietta. Nor even a chief justice of the Supreme Court."

"Then there would be others to take their places, to enforce the laws of the land, and protect private property."

"And others to take the places of those who feel human beings can't be private property."

"It can't happen," she repeated. "A change would destroy us all. How would we harvest our crops? How would we live? What would become of us? The South would be destroyed."

"Do you think so?" Lafe asked carefully. "I, for myself, sometimes wonder. I begin to think we rely too much on slave labor, Marietta. I fear we don't exploit our natural resources as well as we should. Slave labor isn't necessarily the most efficient, I've been seeing."

"But it's all we have, or are likely to have." She was suddenly put in mind of her father by the quiet conviction in Lafe's words. She looked up at the portrait. A farsighted man, Lafe had called him. It was as if she were speaking to Lawrence Garvey when she said, "I loathe the idea of change. All I want is to keep everything as it has always been. For his sake, my father's, I mean. It's what he would want."

"A noble sentiment," Lafe said softly. "But might it be no more than a reflection of your cowardice?"

She jerked her head around to look at him. A silken black curl slipped along her cheek. "You have a cutting tongue, Lafe."

"You've no idea how cutting my tongue can be," he retorted. "I accused you of no cowardice. I asked only that you consider your motives."

"I know them," she answered shortly. Oh, yes, she knew them well. Keep all as it was. Yes, yes, that was the necessity. For then Oren would remain here. Time musn't go forward. The hours musn't pass, nor the days nor weeks. All must remain as it had been when they were younger, when her father was still alive.

A bell rang in the distance. "Noon," she said. "The hands

74

will be stopping to eat. Will you join me at the dinner table here?"

She heard her own words with surprise. She knew she had no reason to encourage this man. But he was personable in his looks, and interesting to talk to. She found herself somehow loath to see him go. Real conversation was impossible with Oren lately, for no matter how begun, it always ended in disagreement.

Lafe had gotten to his feet. He smiled down at her. "I've overstayed my welcome, I think. But you must ask me again another time."

"You've not overstayed your welcome," Coraleen cried from the doorway. "And I shall ask you again. Right now. Do stay for dinner with us, Lafe. If you go away now, then I shall not have had a visit with you." She cast a narrow-eyed look at Marietta. "I didn't even know you were in the house. My dear sister never thought to tell me we had a guest."

"A business visit," Lafe said.

"But stay and explain," she insisted.

He looked at Marietta, saw her nod, and said, "Why, thank you. I'd like to. Mr. Jordan is a pleasant man and a good host, but his kitchen . . ."

"Our kitchen and our cook, Essie, have a fine reputation in the county," Coraleen trilled. "You won't be sorry, Lafe, to learn that bit of truth for yourself." She caught him by the arm. "Come along now, and I'll show you our gardens. And when it's time I'll bring you in."

He glanced at Marietta again.

"Yes, please do go with Coraleen, Mr. Flynn—"

"Lafe," he interjected.

"Lafe, then," she said impatiently. "I'll have a word with Dora. We'll sit down in half an hour."

As he followed Coraleen down the hallway, Snowball darted by, skirting the fringes of her gown, and shot in a furry white arc into the morning room and into Marietta's arms.

He looked back to watch her hold him, and Coraleen, star-

75

ing adoringly into his face, suddenly thought, He's mine. Mine. She shan't have him. She has Gentry, anyone else she wants. She can pick and choose as she pleases, but Lafe Flynn is mine, and Marietta will never have him.

But she saw how Lafe's glances went to Marietta over the white-covered dinner table.

Dora served the crisp fried chicken, the yam pie, the giblet gravy and corn bread, the beans and rice, and kept the tall glasses filled with lemony tea, while Lafe admiringly engaged Marietta in conversation, occasionally tossing a kindly smile at Coraleen. She seethed in silence until she noticed him look at the portrait of Beatrice Garvey that still hung on the wall over the sideboard.

The portrait had been there when Coraleen first came into this dining room, a frightened six-year-old. She had hated it on sight, just as she had despised Beatrice's daughter, Marietta, at first glance. No one had taken the portrait down, even after Coraleen's own mother, Kathleen Henderson, became the mistress of Galloway and sat at this very table. For the last ten years, Beatrice Garvey had continued her reign from the wall, when Kathleen was alive, and after, when Kathleen succumbed to a fever two years after her arrival at Galloway.

"That's Marietta's mother," Coraleen said. "You can see the likeness, no doubt."

Marietta stiffened at Coraleen's tone.

"A beautiful woman," Lafe said, and with a nod of his head at Marietta, continued: "And indeed there's a very strong likeness."

"Yes," Coraleen said. "Beatrice was very beautiful. At least on the outside."

Marietta attempted diversion by offering a dish of preserves to Lafe. He shook his head "Thank you. I don't know how long it's been since I've eaten so well, but I can hold no more."

Coraleen pressed on. "It was a pity that she died so young."

Marietta's mouth tightened, but she said softly, "I'm sure that Lafe isn't interested in our family affairs."

"Oh, but he must be. See how he admires your mother's beauty."

"I do, indeed," Lafe said. "You do greatly resemble her, Marietta."

"You'd not have admired Beatrice so greatly if you'd seen her after," Coraleen said sweetly. "Why, then, in those years just before she died, she must have changed."

"She was ill," Marietta said, remembering all that she didn't want to remember: the dark shadows leaping from the blackness of the live oak trees, her mother's shrill screams that went on and on for days. And after, the terrible silence in the house. The whispers with Dr. Pinchot, the closed doors, and Aunt Tatie's warm arms holding her. And then . . . three years later . . .

"Ill?" Coraleen's laughter was soft and edged with malice. "Ill indeed. Why, I suppose some call what troubled her an illness. Though I wouldn't. For I've heard that she was plainly, simply mad."

The blood drained from Marietta's face, leaving her white to the lips. Her hands, clenched at the table's edge, were as white at the knuckle as the cloth on which they rested. But her voice was steady. "Coraleen, be quiet. I don't like to reprimand you before Lafe, but I will not hear you talk so."

Lafe looked at her, then at Coraleen, marveling at Marietta's ability to control herself, and at Coraleen's daring. He had no intention of injecting himself into the quarrel between these two. It would do his suit no good to turn either of them against him, or perhaps, he thought wryly, to turn both of them against him, united in the face of a stranger's partisanship.

Coraleen, seeing the whiteness of Marietta's face, her clenched hands atremble, knew she had found the weapon for which she had searched for so long. Marietta feared her mother's madness. She feared what she remembered. Coraleen

77

jumped to her feet, ran, and pressed a kiss on Marietta's cheek. "I'm sorry, Marietta. Please do forgive me. I don't know what devil makes me say these awful things."

Marietta suffered the embrace, the smiling apology. At last she said, "Do try to be good, Coraleen. You're embarrassing our guest." And then, as Oren came into the room, "Oh, Oren, I'm glad you've returned. Lafe has been visiting us."

Lafe rose. "I hope your arm's not troubling you?"

"Not at all," Oren answered. He took a chair, waved Lafe back to his seat. "I removed the bandages last week. There's scarcely a mark left to see."

"I'm glad to hear it. Your quarrel with Gentry had good consequences for me, you know. I've had the pleasure of the company of your two charming sisters. And the first decent meal I've had since I came to Darnal."

Oren laughed. "Eamus Jordan will save on his food bills when he can. You must make certain to come to Galloway often."

"I shall," Lafe said, his eyes on Marietta.

Marietta, watching the two men, and listening to them speak, forgot Coraleen's behavior. She allowed herself the joy of studying Oren's face, his narrow dark eyes, the way he moved his hands. Then she looked at Lafe. He was plainly a gentleman, and handsome. He was witty as well as intelligent. He was a person of substance. In short, he was surely all that a woman could hope for in a husband, and the first man she had ever met who might rival Oren. If only Oren could be made to see Lafe's interest in her . . . If only he could be made to imagine her interest in Lafe . . .

In that instant she made up her mind.

She leaned forward, smiling. "Lafe, we're having a small dinner party at Galloway a week from Saturday night. I do hope you can come."

"We are?" Coraleen cried. "Oh, what a wonderful idea! When did you decide?"

"Just this very moment." Marietta's cheeks were flushed

now. "We've been much too sober lately, I think. No wonder you're restive, Coraleen. And you, too, Oren. I think it's my fault. This past year . . ." She stopped herself briefly, then hurried on. "But it will be different now." She looked back at Lafe. "Do say you'll be with us."

"Of course I will," he promised genially, and thought, By that Saturday evening I'll be back from Durham's Station, and Duveen will surely be well on his way to Norfolk City.

5

It was a fair Saturday. The sky spread a cloudless blue over-head, and the hills to the west were wreathed in a faint lavender haze, but the peaceful stillness that usually enveloped Galloway was gone. The dinner Marietta first planned had grown into a full-fledged party. Ten hands had been brought up from the fields to hang colored lanterns and to set up the long banquet table from which the buffet, in preparation for three days now, would be served. There were shouts and laughter. There was the clatter of hammers, the rasp of saws as the stand for the fiddlers was put together.

Jed Blandish gave orders, moving quickly from one group to another, as brisk as a lieutenant preparing an attack, while Marietta watched from the gallery, planning and imagining how it would be, the general on whose slender shoulders the responsibility for the campaign must fall.

It would be the finest party the county had seen in years, and would be remembered forever, she told herself.

Moreover it was to be only the first step in her strategy. She had further plans to implement. And all of it to one end only: that Oren be brought to see her as she was—not as his sister, but as the woman who loved him.

She wanted him to see her dancing in Lafe's arms, leaning back to smile into his face. That would be different from watching her with Gentry, whom Oren took as much for granted as he did Marietta herself. If she was successful, then Oren would feel what she had felt watching him with Sara.

He would realize at last that he loved her. Together, they would run Galloway with a single hand and single mind.

Now, as she watched, Gentry came riding between the gateposts. There was an urgency in the clatter of the horse's hooves. She wondered what was wrong. It was hours early for the party, and he was plainly disturbed. He dismounted, plunged into the group that surrounded Jed Blandish, and was lost for a moment to Marietta's sight. When he reappeared, he was pulling Mr. Blandish with him to the gallery steps. He swept off his hat, bowed. "Good day, Marietta. Can you tell me, is Oren inside?"

"Yes, he is, Gentry," she answered. "But what is it? You seem very upset. Is something amiss?"

"I must talk to Oren at once."

"Come in, then." Marietta's eyes rested briefly on Gentry's red face. Then she looked at Mr. Blandish. "What is it?" she asked again as they followed her to the door.

Gentry said, "Mr. Blandish tells me that your head count was all right this morning."

"But of course," she said, frowning. "It always is."

"You take a good deal for granted, Marietta. I think you'd better have the count done again, and right now. We've had a loss at our place."

"A loss?"

"I'd like to speak with Oren about it, Marietta. It isn't a matter for you to deal with."

She smiled at him and didn't argue. "Come inside, both of you. I'll send for Oren at once."

But when he joined the three in the morning room, she didn't leave as they obviously expected. Instead, she seated herself opposite Gentry and said, "Gentry, perhaps you'll explain all this."

Oren leaned at the mantel, his dark eyes narrowed, and waited.

"We had one missing at head count last night," Gentry began. "But my overseer found an empty bottle of rum, and we thought the poor fool had gotten himself drunk and was

81

in the fields sleeping it off. Though I'd like to know where he got that rum, I can tell you. By this morning, when he hadn't turned up, we conducted a search. The man's gone from the plantation."

"But gone where?" Marietta asked.

Gentry shrugged. "Perhaps west to the hills. Perhaps east to the coast. Who knows?"

"I should think he's wandering about in the woods, and will soon be hungry and come back," she told Gentry.

"Perhaps he will, and perhaps he won't, but I'm concerned about it, and I think you should be, too." The last of Gentry's words were directed only to Oren. "You had better do another head count, and I'd consider it a favor if you had your housing searched, too, just in case. My man could be concealing himself among your people, you know."

Oren turned to Jed Blandish. "You heard?"

The overseer nodded. "I heard. But I don't think you'll find any runaway of yours at Galloway, Mr. Beckwith."

Gentry frowned at him, and Oren said, "Do as Mr. Beckwith asks, Mr. Blandish."

The overseer glanced at Marietta, and she answered his look hurriedly. "Yes, yes, perhaps you should make a search. And, Mr. Blandish, in the meanwhile I'd appreciate it if you'd see that word is passed among our people. None of them are to go out tonight after dark, not to set their rabbit snares, nor for any other reason. I presume the patrols will be very active, and we don't want anyone hurt."

"You're right, Marietta," Gentry said. "There'll be a lot of activity. My father's in town right now setting up some extra bounties. We're going to offer rewards. Alive or dead."

"Is that wise, Gentry?" Marietta asked. "You may make more trouble than it's worth."

Oren cut in. "What else can he do? This has to be stopped right now. Suppose this boy gets away. Then there'll be more and more."

"Oh, I think you make too much of it. What's happened? A single boy has taken off into the fields." She shook her head, turned away. "But do as you like. I've the party to think of." Then she swung back. "Gentry, I won't have my guests troubled, do you hear me? You'd better tell your father to see to that, too."

"Now, Marietta, nobody's going to stop your guests. We'll be here in our fine feathers, and so will everyone else. Nobody's going to spoil you party."

"I take that as a promise," she said lightly.

Later she was to remember those words. But now she said, "Mr. Blandish, will you get back here to see that all's taken care of, and as soon as you possibly can?"

"I will, Miss Garvey."

"And you'll make certain that the musicians are given special rations for their dinner this noon?"

"I'll see to it, Miss Garvey."

"And have the gardeners start to bring up the flowers for the house?"

"They're attending to it right now."

Oren grinned at her. "Marietta, you're as nervous as if this were a wedding, and you the mother of the bride."

"As nervous as the bride herself," Gentry said.

"I want it to be nice," she answered.

She hurried upstairs, thinking that Oren had come closer to the truth than he imagined.

All this trouble taken was for Oren, although he didn't know it. But it was for Galloway, too. The Garveys would no longer be withdrawn from the society of the county.

She had sent runners out with the invitations, and they had come back with acceptances. Idle curiosity would bring some, old friendship would bring others. Either way she was satisfied. There would be light and music and laughter in Galloway once more.

"Marietta," Coraleen cried. "Do come and look at my hair. Please, please, you must help me."

Marietta smiled to herself, shook her head. Coraleen was behaving as if this were the most important party of her young life. And perhaps, Marietta thought as she went into

83

Coraleen's room, there was good reason for her feeling. After all, she was only sixteen, and she had been allowed just a few adult entertainments away from home. And at Galloway there had been none to amuse her and accustom her to the idea.

"You see?" Coraleen wailed. "It won't curl properly."

"Oh, but it will." Marietta set to work, her fingers nimble. She drew back a lock of hair here, turned it under, fixed it with a pin. She drew a second strand through her fingers. "You have nice hair. Soft as silk, Coraleen."

"But it won't stay in place."

Marietta laughed. "Look in the mirror now. You'll see that it does."

Coraleen looked, preened, holding her head stiffly as she turned to survey her coiffure. "It's just as I hoped. Now that you've done it, Marietta." She smiled. "Thank you for helping." And in a rush, "And for having this party."

"I've been too long about it, I think," Marietta answered soberly. "But it will be different from now on."

"Do you think Lafe will come?"

"Certainly. He said he would."

"Still, we've not seen him since that day he was here, Marietta."

"I expect that he's a busy man, Coraleen. Surely he has more to do each afternoon than to ride out here and converse with us."

"He rides out. Even if not here. That I can tell you, for I've seen him myself."

"Oh, have you?"

"Indeed. He has a wagon, and he and a very large black man sit together on the seat. In the back there's a huge packing case. It's red with large yellow black-eyed daisies painted on it."

"You've observed them very closely, I gather." Marietta laughed.

"I was on the bluff yesterday when he went by on the Durham's Station Road. We couldn't speak of course. I'm not certain that he saw me. But I did wonder if he would come tonight."

"We'd have heard if he planned not to," Marietta said firmly. "And now I have things to do." She bent to scoop up Snowball, who had followed her into the room.

"I'll be ready in good time," Coraleen said. "We should be on the gallery together when the first guests arrive."

"Meanwhile, I advise you to rest."

"Oh, I will. I want to be just perfect, Marietta."

Before Marietta went downstairs, she stopped in her room to look at the gown she had chosen to wear. It was cherry red silk, flounced and ruffled at the hem. White insets of lace trimmed the bodice and tiny sleeves that would barely cap her shoulders. She smoothed the fullness of the skirt, then put it away. Her slippers were on the table. They were red, too, with satin ribbons.

In the kitchen all seemed well. Essie was busy at the fire. Dora sliced cabbage for a slaw. Elisha and Aunt Tatie watched over the preparations.

"If you need me, I shall be up in my room," she told Aunt Tatie.

"We're doing fine, Miss Marietta," the older woman said. "Have yourself a little lie-down."

"I'll want Dora for a while, I think," Marietta said.

"Send down for her when you're ready," Aunt Tatie told her.

It was unnecessary, after all, to send down for Dora. Aunt Tatie herself appeared in Marietta's room at exactly the right time. "They can get along without having my nose stuck in every pot for a little while," she said firmly. "I want to see you turned out."

She helped Marietta into the stays that cinched her narrow waist, drew the strings tight, and tied small snug bows to hold them. She adjusted the crinoline, then lifted the frilled and frothy red silk over Marietta's head so carefully that not a single curl was disturbed.

She stood back and surveyed Marietta with solemn satisfaction. "You look good. Just right," she pronounced. At that moment the distant mournful baying of the dogs broke the still evening. Aunt Tatie said nothing, but she raised her head, listening.

Marietta frowned. "They're using dogs to search the Beckwiths' woods."

Aunt Tatie nodded, her eyes hooded, her mouth tight. She took up the strand of pearls from the table, and Marietta went to stand before the cheval glass while the older woman placed them carefully around her throat and hooked them.

Marietta stroked the small gleaming beads. These pearls had belonged to her mother. These, and every jewel Marietta owned, had come to her on her mother's death.

Her gay mood was dampened as memory overtook her. The day before her father was so suddenly killed by the gun he had just cleaned, the same pearls had disappeared. Marietta had searched the house, every nook and corner of it, before telling her father. Then, together, they'd looked again. The next morning the pearls were on her dressing table, in full sight, where they couldn't possibly have been missed before. And two hours later the house echoed with the hideous gunshot that had taken her father's life, and Coraleen had emerged from the morning room screaming, "Papa's dead. He's shot himself. Marietta, my God, he's shot himself!"

Only later, after she had calmed down under Dr. Pinchot's ministrations, could Oren and Marietta understand why she had said that. She'd been on the gallery outside. She'd heard the terrible sound, crossed into the room as Lawrence fell over his desk, the rags and cleaner still beside him, the smoking gun under his hand. She hadn't stopped to see and think before, assuming him a suicide, she rushed out to scream of Lawrence's death.

And so the sudden strange reappearance of the pearls had been forgotten. Grief had obliterated the memory of it; and only now, wearing them again for the first time since, Marietta remembered, and asked herself what could have happened. How had the pearls been lost, then found?

She looked into the mirror again, saw that Aunt Tatie's eyes were fixed on her reflection. She was about to ask if Aunt Tatie remembered, knew about the pearls, but the dogs bayed loudly, close now. "They're near to Galloway," she said softly.

"Yes."

An image flickered through Marietta's mind. A single hanging figure. Slowly, within black shadows, it became four. She swallowed hard. She said, "Aunt Tatie, you recall it, don't you? What happened at Galloway when I was a child."

Aunt Tatie didn't answer. She moved away. She lit a lamp, adjusted the bed coverlet and curtains. She gathered the gown Marietta had discarded and hung it away in the wardrobe.

"You do," Marietta insisted. "Just as I remember it myself."

Aunt Tatie finally nodded her head.

"It's all still in my mind. What happened that night, Aunt Tatie. And what happened after. But do you know, I never understood the why of it. I always wondered. But I didn't dare ask my father. I couldn't hurt him by making him remember." She drew a deep breath. "Tell me about it, Aunt Tatie. Why did they come to Galloway and kill four of our people?"

"Why they did it? I don't know."

"But what happened?"

"There was a dead man laying there, and the Beckwith girl was dead, too," Aunt Tatie said finally. "I know about it because there was some who saw enough of it to understand. The overseer was good when Mr. Lawrence could see him. But he had an eye on the Beckwith girl. She had a boy she was sweet on here. They'd slip out and meet, and nobody' was worse for it. The overseer wanted her. He met her one night and tried to take her. She fought him. Our boy found them struggling and killed the overseer, but she'd already got her neck broken." Aunt Tatie turned now, looked into the dusk beyond the window where the colored lanterns swung in the twilight breeze. "Our boy came home to Galloway after he broke from the patrol, and hid. He just wanted to wait for Mr. Lawrence, knowing he'd have justice from him, and not from anybody else. So . . . so they came and got him, and there was a fight. They took him, and they took the three others."

Marietta fumbled to hold the older woman's hand. "And one of them was your own son," she whispered. "How you must hate us, Aunt Tatie!"

"Hate you?" the older woman asked. "Maybe, for just a minute, when I saw him hanging, maybe then I did. But no. You didn't do it. Nor your papa either. Nor your poor mama, though they paid heavy for it. No, I never hated any of you. I couldn't live with that, could I, Miss Marietta? I had to have something else to go on." She smiled suddenly. "And I better get to the kitchen. You know Essie gets scared without me to nag at her."

There was no time to say more. Coraleen rapped at the door, crying, "Marietta, I think we must go down at once."

"I'm ready." Marietta snatched up a crimson and white lace fan, and hurried out to Coraleen.

They descended together and found Oren in the lower hall already waiting.

"You both look lovely," he said.

And he, Marietta thought, he was even more handsome than usual. His dark curly hair lay brushed across his high brow. His eyes seemed to burn with excitement as he looked first at them and then along the road toward the gates, where the first of the guests were arriving now.

Needle and Beedle, dressed up for the occasion, dashed out to take the horses' reins, and having allowed the first couple, the Filenes, to alight, to lead the carriage away.

Henley and Eustacia Filene approached the steps smiling. He was minister of the Darnal church, a man of sixty. His eyes were a muddy gray, his complexion pale, with a gray-ish cast. He had thick iron-gray hair, and heavy gray side whiskers that framed a protruding, pointed chin. His wife, whose white-streaked hair was drawn into a severe topknot, long out of fashion, was a stout woman tightly laced into whalebone stays that did little to narrow her waist and a great deal to inhibit her breathing. Gasping, she rushed to greet her hostess.

"Marietta, my dear girl, how good to see you." Eustacia Filene kissed the air near both Marietta's cheeks. She did the same with Coraleen, and then allowed Oren to bow over her hand.

"Children," the Reverend Filene said, "we were delighted to have your invitation." He cleared his throat, as if preparing to offer a sermon, but before he could launch his speech, other guests drew up, much to Marietta's relief.

Swiftly the gardens of Galloway filled. The fiddlers played. There was laughter and quick conversation, some bantering and some sober. As Marietta watched the servants carry trays of punch and stronger stuff, she listened to the talk.

"The broadsides will go out tomorrow," Alexander Beckwith was saying to the small group that surrounded him. "We'll get him if he's still in the neighborhood."

"If . . ." one of the listening men murmured.

"You waste your time. You waste your money," the Reverend Filene said. "He's well away from here, I'll warrant."

"And doing only the good Lord knows what," Mrs. Filene agreed with a shudder. "One runaway slave is a source of infection. It spreads. It spreads into rebellion."

"Marietta, child. How are you?" The voice was deep, familiar, and Marietta swung about, smiling with delight. "Oh, Mr. Swinton, I'm so glad that you could come."

He bowed over her hand, then held her lightly by both shoulders and looked down into her face. "You're lovely. My only regret is that I don't see you more often. I suggested to Oren that he tell you I'd like you to drop in any time you're in town. I've waited, expecting to see you, but you've never come, have you?"

She wondered only briefly that Oren had mentioned no such request by Marcus Swinton. One which she would have been pleased to honor the moment she heard it. She said, smiling, "I'll do as you ask very soon. But tell me, how are you?"

He was a tall man, thin and long-boned, his flesh eaten away by time. But he had young eyes, hazel in color. A lock of his thinning brown hair lay across his forehead, and each time he brushed it away it slipped back. He was her father's age, and had been Lawrence Garvey's good friend. "I'm well enough, I suppose," he answered, "though my gorge rises at the talk I hear around me."

"Talk?"

"Ah, Marietta, Alexander Beckwith has lost a slave and he's fiery-eyed about it. What does he expect? I ask. What did he and all the others think would happen? They chortled at the compromise made back in 1850 that divided our nation into slave soil and free soil. And what hosannas went up when the Fugitive Slave laws were passed! As if they could protect us."

"But don't they?" Marietta asked. "A man can be fined, jailed, for helping a runaway and not returning him to his proper owner."

"Can be, perhaps, and sometimes is, but only when these laws are enforced, and where they are enforced. Which is only on slave soil. So we now have a fine crew of slave hunters. And they are wicked men, I think."

It was true, Marietta thought. The business of hunting down slaves was ugly. Remembering the day-long baying of the dogs near Galloway, she shuddered.

Marcus saw and shook his head at her. "Forgive an old man his maunderings. Why do I despoil your mood with such talk? What'll be will be. And nothing I say or do will change that." He took her arm. "Come, let me get you some refreshment while I think of gayer conversation. I see Elisha with the tray."

But as they approached the place where Elisha stood, Coraleen seized Marietta's arm. "I must talk to you," she said urgently.

Marietta excused herself, promised to rejoin Marcus in a moment, and allowed Coraleen to lead her away. When they were alone, Coraleen breathed, "He's not here yet, Marietta."

"I see that."

"Perhaps he won't come." A pout began to form on Coraleen's lips.

"Perhaps not," Marietta agreed. But she still hoped that Lafe Flynn would arrive, even though her disappointment had deepened with every moment that passed. It was, she told herself, chiefly because of him that she had so suddenly decided to have the party.

Now a small frown creased her brow as she saw Oren bending to talk to Sara. who smiled prettily up at him and playfully tapped his arm with her fan.

"It'll spoil everything for me," Coraleen said. "If Lafe doesn't come, I'll die."

"You won't," Marietta told her. "You'll help me begin to plan another entertainment."

But Coraleen only sighed and wandered off.

Soon after, Marietta saw Lafe arrive. He came through the crowd toward her, his russet head towering over the others. He wore narrow fawn trousers and a slim fawn coat. His silk shirt was white, his flowing silk cravat a sharp contrasting black. As he moved by the ladies, covert glances followed him.

Unaware of the looks he drew, Lafe made his way quickly to Marietta.

She drew a deep breath, startled to find that her heart was beating so quickly. Now, she thought. Now I must play my part well. It was easy to give him a warm welcoming smile, to look at him with pleasure, to say, "Lafe, I'm glad you've come. I'd about given up the hope that you would. And Coraleen, too."

"Thank you, Marietta." He stood looking down at her, a faint smile on his lips. He was pleased by the warmth in her voice, her eyes. They marked a greater cordiality than she'd shown to him before. He wondered at it, but only briefly. At last, unable to restain himself, he said, "You're beautiful, Marietta."

91

She covered her sudden confusion with a smile. "You must meet everyone, Lafe. Since you're fairly new to the neighborhood, there must be many you don't know as yet."

"A great many, I believe. But I didn't come here this evening to repair that lack. I came solely to see you again."

"And see me you do, and shall. But remember that I'm the hostess, and I have a hostess's duties to perform. Come, let me present you to the Reverend and Mrs. Filene. He is the Episcopal minister. I think you'll find them congenial, but if you want to make a great impression on the lady, contrive to ask Mrs. Filene about the city of London. She was there in 1851 at what they call the Great Exhibition. She'll be delighted to tell you all she saw, and I warn you, it was much."

"Very well," he said with a laugh. "Take me to Mrs. Filene, if you must." He looked at the dancers waltzing now. "But I'll tell you, I'd sooner stay at your side, Marietta. And I'll be separated only if I have the promise of a dance when you feel that you're free to honor me so."

"Done then." She presented him to the Filenes, and as she murmured an excuse heard Lafe say something about England. He was launched into the society of the county, and would swim there without any trouble, she knew.

When she looked back at him later, she saw that Coraleen was hanging on his arm, drawing him away from the Filenes.

She made her way to Oren's side. "I don't know why we've not done this before," she said.

"Such gay affairs cost a pretty penny, Marietta. You mustn't think you can afford it often."

"And why not? We've all we need and more. And there'll be a good harvest. Mr. Blandish thinks so, and so do I."

"You know nothing of it, Marietta." He grinned, softening the words. "And I don't want you to. You're too lovely to waste your time on mundane things."

She was saved from having to comment by Lafe, who came to claim her for the promised dance.

She stepped into his arms, knowing that Oren's gaze followed her, and glad of it. The gladness brought a shine to her amethyst eyes, a glow of color to her cheeks, a joy to her laughter as she tilted her head to look into Lafe's face. His hand tightened on her shoulder, and as he moved forward in a long step, his thigh pressed through the voluminous folds of her gown and brushed hers. The touch was like an ember under draft. Heat flared from that point, blazed up, scorching her body, and lingered warmly.

"You're enjoying yourself," he said lightly.

"Indeed I am. It's the first party we've had in a very long time."

"You've been in mourning this past year, I understand."

She nodded. "Yes. For my father. But it's been far longer than that since we've had an entertainment."

He thought he understood. Eamus Jordan had told him that her father had fallen out with his neighbors after the hangings at Galloway. He had been a man out of his time then, and would be the same even now.

Lafe said, "Then you're wise to remedy the situation. No life can be pleasant without socializing, I think." It was Lawrence Garvey that Lafe had in mind. It must have been hard for him to be surrounded by those with whom he disagreed, by those who held his views in no respect. Had his death truly been an accident? Lafe wondered.

"I quite agree," she was saying. "And already Oren has reproved me. He feels I am too extravagant and says I mustn't believe I can do this often."

"He must be a careful manager. Which surely won't hurt Galloway."

She suddenly thought of the note Oren had presented for her signature. If requiring a loan was a sign, then Oren was not the manager she had thought. It would explain his warning, albeit a smiling one, against extravagance. She decided she must ask him about it in more detail. But it would be difficult to do so without upsetting him. And that she didn't want to do.

"I wonder, Marietta, how did you come by your musicians?" Lafe was asking.

She brought her wandering attention back to him. "My

father found a few fiddles someplace. And the boys made their own drums. And those jugs are something they've always made music on. My father felt his people must be happy, and music is good for that. He was much criticized in some quarters for that and other benefits he allowed. I carry on, so I'm criticized for it, too, I suppose." She thought of Oren again. He opposed her determination to carry out her father's policies. She must find some way to persuade him.

Lafe grinned at her. "Marietta, there's none so blind as those who will not see. Your father was right, of course. And you are, too. But so many close their eyes to the obvious." It was a quality of the human character that could, at times, anger Lafe almost beyond endurance, though at others it was one for which he was intensely grateful. This evening was one of those times.

He had ridden hard since the night before, his project successful only because those who will not, do not see.

The young man who had met Duveen near the small wooden bridge had slipped away from Beckwith's plantation, following the directions given him. Those hours before the search was begun had allowed Duveen and Lafe a good head start. They'd had time to dress the boy, drive him to Durham's Station and see him safely aboard the train, clothed as a young woman, and with an escort for safety's sake. All this because when the empty rum bottle was found it was assumed that the young man had gotten drunk on its contents and hidden himself away to sleep.

Beyond Lafe's broad shoulder, Marietta saw Coraleen, who lingered nearby, her face in the shadow. Then she saw Oren and Sara swing by, intent on each other. She called out a greeting but neither of them responded.

Lafe's fingers tightened at her waist, reclaiming her attention. She found it a pleasure to dance with him, more so than she had anticipated. He held her so lightly, yet moved her so firmly. Again she turned her shining dark head to look at Oren.

Soon after, the music paused. She excused herself, saying

that she must see to her other guests, and Lafe acquiesced with smiling disapproval, and a promise not to allow her too long away from him.

She agreed, but silently reminded herself that she mustn't encourage him too much. She had no intention of misleading him. She offered only a small flirtation, which would do no harm. He mustn't be led to think otherwise.

She spoke to Oren and Sara, to the Filenes again. She had a few words with Marcus Swinton, then paused beside Gentry for a moment, but didn't stay. He was too bright of eye and too flushed for her liking. She danced a full set with Alexander Beckwith, another with Dr. Pinchot. Then, wanting to catch her breath, to smooth back her disheveled curls, she went into the house.

She had just started up the steps when she heard a faint sound. She stopped, looked about her.

The lamps flickered. Shadows danced on the walls. The air was scented with flowers. Outside the music began again; there was clapping now and singing.

Inside all was still, except for the small rustle of the window curtains. But now she heard a peculiar sound again. A piteous murmur that sent a ripple of cold up her back and prickled the flesh on her arms. She looked quickly around the hallway, but saw nothing.

The thin groan was repeated, and this time she realized that it was Snowball calling to her. But something was wrong. Something had to be wrong for Snowball to make a sound so different from its usual triumphant miaow.

"Snowball," she whispered. "Is that you, Snowball? Where are you hiding? What's the matter?"

As if in answer to her question, there was another long anguished murmur.

She walked up and down the hall, looked into the shadows under the refectory table, searched all the corners. Finally she lifted her gown and bent and crept under the back of the stairs.

In the dim light of the hidden nook she found Snowball.

95

The big cat lay stretched out, stiff and straining, its back almost bowed, its legs splayed at an unnatural angle from the tensed body. Its lips were drawn back over clenched teeth, and its small whiskered chin was wet with foam. Its green eyes were wide and dull.

Even as Marietta choked back a scream, the cat gave one more pitiful sound. Then it went silent, its body shaken with one last heave as it died.

"Snowball," Marietta whispered in horrified disbelief. She knelt, staring, unable to look away from the four broken legs. How could it have happened? There was no animal trap about which could have inflicted such wounds. There was no beast that could have done such a thing to Snowball.

Marietta pushed herself to her feet, stood wavering, her hands over her eyes. She must do something. She must call Elisha.

And at that moment Coraleen was there, crying, "Marietta, you must come with me. You must stop them. Oren and and Gentry are quarreling again. You must do something at once. Because it's all your fault! It's up to you to make them stop it, I tell you. Make them stop it before something awful happens."

She didn't seem to notice the body of the cat at Marietta's feet. She didn't seem to notice the pale hurt look on Marietta's face. She stamped her foot. "Marietta! Come on!"

Marietta gave the dead cat a last anguished stare from tear-filled eyes, then caught up her gown, driven by the new fear Coraleen had brought her, and hurried outside.

Oren and Sara had been kissing in the shadows of the corner of the garden. The girl, arms around Oren's neck, clung to him in hungry passion, and he held her.

Gentry, wavering with more to drink than he could safely carry, had been in search of Marietta, but had come upon the two instead and torn Sara from Oren's arms, snarling, "Keep your distance from my sister!"

Sara cried, "Oren loves me, I told you. He loves me, and I love him, and one day we'll be married."

Gentry's laugh was low, ugly. "Oh, do you think so? My

dear sister, you dream. And you'll dream your youth away waiting. Oren will never marry you. And he knows it, if you don't. I shan't allow you to shame me and besmirch the Beckwith name. Save yourself and your reputation for a man who has something to offer you."

Oren, white-lipped, his eyes narrow, said quietly, "Gentry, have a care. You say too much for your own good. Even though you're Sara's brother, and an old friend . . ."

Again Gentry laughed. "Even though . . . My dear Oren, you know as well as I do that Marietta has conceived an incestuous passion for you. She wants you for herself. She'll never make it possible for you to be anything but what you are. A cadger on Galloway's wealth, pretending to earn your keep. And now, even worse to my mind, a betrayer of a young girl. But Sara's my sister, I won't allow . . ."

"Sara, forgive me," Oren was saying as Marietta came upon the scene. "I can't let this pass."

"Can't let what pass?" she demanded furiously. "How dare the two of you carry on so? How dare you behave thus?"

She remembered with hot bitterness that Gentry had promised her no one would spoil her party. And here he stood berating Oren, insulting him for all to listen to.

Neither of the men spoke.

A crowd had begun to gather now. There were whisperings all around as those closest repeated Gentry's words to Oren.

Marietta cried, "Nothing that Gentry Beckwith says can hurt me, Oren." Then, appealing to Gentry, "You don't mean these idiocies. Tell Oren so."

Both men ignored her.

Then Oren said, "Gentry, you've gone too far. I won't fight you now, as you're a guest at Galloway. But there's another day, and another place. You know well what I mean. We'll make the arrangements."

"No," Marietta screamed. "No, no, no! You'll do no such thing. I won't have it, I tell you."

Coraleen wept noisily in Sara's arms.

97

Oren bowed to Gentry and said again, "We'll make the arrangements." Then he turned to Marietta. "Come, compose yourself." He offered her his arm. "It's time we rejoined our guests."

6

Oren paused outside to look at the warehouse. It was a low two-story building made of rough-cut lumber that still smelled fresh. At one end there was a wide opening that would permit the entry of wagons for loading. Three workmen were hanging a gate there. The front door was double width, flanked by two small bronze lanterns. A neatly painted sign, with the words GOLDEN LEAF TOBACCO COMPANY in black, hung from two brass-headed screws.

He looked at it twice before climbing the four steps to the door. He mopped his face before he want inside.

It was much cooler within than on the street. He heard the sounds of a hammer, the murmur of voices, and went across the rough floor to a window, where a workman directed him to an open door at the end of the building.

It was there that he found Lafe Flynn, seated behind a desk, legs asprawl. He straightened when Oren entered saying, "Good morning, Lafe. Do you have a few moments for me?"

"Of course. Sit down." Lafe waved him to a straight chair. "What brings you to town on this hot Monday morning?"

Oren settled himself, crossed his long legs. "I think you must know. You heard what I said to Gentry Beckwith."

"I did hear. I had hoped that you'd taken the time to sleep on it."

"I've slept and awakened feeling exactly the same. Did you imagine that I could possibly change my mind?"

"Sometimes men do, and often that's the better part of wisdom," Lafe returned.

"Cowardice has never been a weakness of mine," Oren answered. "I don't propose to be accused of it now."

"No one would think it," Lafe returned. "You've two sisters to think of, man. The risk is very great."

Oren grinned. "Which makes it all the better, Lafe. I hope you'll consent to make the arrangements for me."

Lafe hesitated for a long moment. It was no real business of his, and he had other things to think about. But a refusal seemed impossible. He asked, "Don't you think it would be best to allow more time to pass? When your temper is cooled, you may well find you don't want it after all. I'm sure that Gentry doesn't, and already rues his behavior."

"My temper is quite cooled, thank you," Oren answered. "I must have satisfaction, regardless of what Gentry feels."

"And what of Coraleen and Marietta?"

"I must do what I think best."

"Very well, Oren," Lafe said finally. "I'll go to Beckwith's this afternoon. I take it you go by the standard code?"

Oren nodded. "And I'll ask you to say nothing of this to Marietta when you see her. The less she knows the better. I'm sure you understand."

"I do understand, though I don't see how she can be kept out of it. However, she'll hear nothing from me."

When Oren left him, Lafe went to the Beckwith plantation immediately. He delivered Oren's message. Gentry agreed grimly to meet him at the time specified two days later, and he sent no message of conciliation back. From there Lafe went to see Dr. Pinchot and then the Reverend Filene. To each he spoke the standard words of caution, knowing that they wouldn't be heeded.

By late that afternoon word had spread through Darnal. Oren and Gentry would meet at Death Meadows on Wednesday.

By the next afternoon it had reached Galloway, as well as the other county plantations.

Coraleen had heard it from Needle and Beedle, who excitedly relayed to her what they had overheard Elisha telling Aunt Tatie.

Red-faced, eyes glittering with tears, Coraleen burst into the morning room, where Marietta sat alone.

"Do you know?" Coraleen shouted. "Have you heard what Oren's going to do?"

Marietta rose quickly, alarmed. "What is it, Coraleen? What's amiss?"

"Everything, everything. Oren and Gentry will duel. They meet tomorrow. And you know what Gentry is, how he handles a pistol. He's killed two men already. You must stop them, Marietta."

The room seemed to spin. Darkness gathered in the corners and moved out to assail her. Marietta closed her eyes briefly. She breathed slowly, fighting for control. She had planned the entertainment with such joy and hope. And what had come of it? What had come of all her foolish plotting? She had only wanted Oren to see her with fresh eyes, perhaps be a bit jealous that Lafe lavished so much attention upon her. It had seemed so simple. Yet it had all gone awry. Oren had eyes only for Sara. Gentry was drunk and determined to spew his insults. Now they would fight.

And there was Snowball, too. She could still see too clearly that painfully maimed body, still hear the piteous moan the animal made as it died.

The quarrel between the men had put it out of her mind. But once all the guests had finally gone, she had returned to the nook under the stairs. Elisha had found her there weeping.

He had lifted Snowball's body and carried it away for burial. They did not discuss it, but Marietta knew that someone at Galloway had killed Snowball. Some hand had seized the cat, twisted its legs, and left it under the stairs to die in agony.

Hands pulled at her now. "Marietta, do something!" Coraleen screamed.

She forced away the memory of Snowball, the cat she had loved, that was gone. She said thickly, "Where's Oren, Coraleen? Do you know?"

"In town, I think."

"I'll stop it," Marietta said grimly. She hurried out, ordered Elisha to ready the carriage.

Coraleen went with her, weeping still and wringing her hands. But by the time they reached town, she was dry-eyed, her cheeks flushed.

Marietta was pale, clutching her reticule to her side. With Coraleen trotting beside her, she stopped on the threshold of Eamus Jordan's gaming room. It wasn't a place that women of her sort entered, but she'd have gone in were Oren there.

He wasn't, so she turned away, ignoring Mr. Jordan's effusive greeting.

Outside again, she hesitated. Oren wasn't among the three men standing together in the square. He wasn't walking along the road. She decided quickly, and went hurrying past Hell's Tavern and around the corner to the calaboose.

Elisha caught up with her. "Miss Marietta," he protested. "You and Miss Coraleen can't go in there. What would people think? What would they say?"

She didn't speak, but only glared at him.

Sighing, shaking his head, he dropped back. He wished Mr. Oren would appear, or Mr. Marcus. Or anybody who could stop her.

But no one appeared. Marietta opened the door, sailed inside, with Coraleen following.

The small room was dim, its two windows barred, as if to prevent the bright sun outdoors from entering. A man sat with his chair tipped back against the dingy wall, staring at her from under the brim of his hat.

He didn't rise when she stood before him and announced, "I wish to see the sheriff."

"He's out of town."

"And when will he be coming back?"

The man grinned. "Don't know. He didn't say. Maybe late tomorrow, though. Maybe even the day after."

"Then who's in charge?" she asked impatiently. "Surely someone does the sheriff's business when he's away."

The man grinned again. "It's hard to say. I guess I'm in charge."

"You and no one else?" she asked despairingly.

"Me and no one else," he repeated.

She saw his enjoyment, and understood. She didn't know his name, but he knew hers. He knew that the sheriff had already heard of the coming duel and had left town to avoid having to do anything about it. This man, too, would certainly do nothing about it.

Marietta persisted anyway. "Is there any lawman in town who will help me prevent a shooting?"

"I'm the only lawman in town," the man answered. "And I can't leave here. Not until the sheriff comes back. Whenever that is. I've got three out back, and only one in shackles. It wouldn't do to leave them alone. So I can't go anywhere to stop anything."

Her tense shoulders sagged. She turned away without another word. It was useless. She was facing the usual conspiracy of silence. There wasn't a man in town who would help her keep Oren and Gentry from going through with the duel.

"Lafe Flynn," Coraleen said softly, grabbing her elbow. "Marietta, perhaps he'll listen to you. Or to me."

They hurried back to Jordan House. Mr. Jordan once again greeted them effusively, and effusively apologized when Marietta asked for Mr. Flynn. "Mr. Flynn rode away several hours ago, taking Duveen with him. I've no idea when they'll return."

"He didn't say where he was going?"

Mr. Jordan shook his head regretfully.

"Nor when he'd be back?" Marietta pressed him.

"I fear not, Miss Marietta."

Marietta nodded her thanks and turned away.

"What will you do now?" Coraleen demanded.

"I'll stop it somehow" was Marietta's answer.

"Gentry?"

"He won't back down."

103

"Nor will Oren. So it's no use to talk to him."

"No," Marietta agreed. "I realize it's no use, Coraleen." But Marietta's determination was only strengthened now. She would not be stopped, and there was nothing she would not do to prevent the meeting at Death Meadows.

At sunup she stood at the window. The gardens of Galloway were bathed in pale pink light. A few stars still glimmered in the sky. She wore a riding habit of dark brown, with a white stock at her throat. A brown hat was tilted over her curls.

Soon she heard quiet footsteps in the hallway.

Moments later Oren appeared below her. He went toward the stables. In a little while she heard the clip-clop of a horse's hooves, and he went cantering down the road.

She drew a deep breath, touched the pistol she had earlier thrust into her belt. Yes, she would go to any length to stop this, to protect Oren.

She heard, in the distance now, the baying of the hounds, the receding hoofbeats. She hurried out to the stables.

Needle and Beedle reared up from their pallets, rubbing their eyes sleepily, just as the clamor of the morning wake-up bell began.

"Get the gig ready for me, boys. And hurry it up. I've not got much time."

"Now, Miss Marietta? Where can you go now?"

"Right now," she said sharply. "And I said hurry."

They exchanged frightened looks. Then, as Needle led the black stallion out, Beedle ran to get Elisha.

He came running. His careful expostulations didn't stop Marietta. She hardly listened to his anxious words. She climbed to the seat, waited impatiently to be handed the reins.

Instead, when the horse was harnessed, the gig ready, Elisha climbed up beside her. "I'm going, too, Miss Marietta."

She nodded. They set out without another word.

They couldn't be long behind Oren, she knew, though it

would take them longer to traverse the four miles on the track in the gig than it would take Oren riding across country. Still, she could count on some extra time. It would be a while before the men gathered, and they would wait until the morning mists had lifted. They would wait, surely, until the sun was strong and bright.

Elisha knew their destination. Scowling but silent now, he followed the trail worn smooth by generations of hot-headed men.

Huddling within her light cloak, Marietta shivered and set her teeth and touched the pistol at her belt. When they climbed the last ridge and were overlooking the meadow, she gasped aloud.

"They're about ready," Elisha said softly. "We'd better stop here."

"Whip up the horse, I tell you," she cried. "Hurry, Elisha! Hurry!"

Below, on the flats, she saw that Oren had already dismounted and stood facing Gentry.

She saw Lafe standing at one side and Alexander Beckwith at the other.

She saw Dr. Pinchot and the Reverend Filene.

If she hadn't been so angry, and so frightened at the same time, she would have laughed to see them raise their set and outraged faces as she climbed down from the gig.

They might be ready to kill each other, but they were united in their horror that she had ignored the conventions, broken through the conspiracy of silence.

Oren, tight-lipped and gray, stared long at her, then turned away without a word. Gentry in no way acknowledged her presence.

She walked into the midst of the men, then stood stiff and straight, braced rigid, with her cloak tight around her. "You fools!" she cried. "How dare you! I don't care what anyone has said, or will say, about me. Nothing matters to me except that no one die."

"Go home, Marietta." It was Oren's voice, cold, hard. "You don't belong here."

Dr. Pinchot grumbled a disapproving "Ladies shouldn't be on the field of honor, b'gad. I never saw the like in all my days."

"Field of honor," Marietta said bitterly. "Field of fools, I say. Field of murder, that's what I say. Oren, please, please, come to your senses. Withdraw your challenge while there's still time."

He remained silent.

"Gentry . . . Mr. Beckwith, will you help me?" she cried.

Neither Gentry nor Alexander looked at her, nor answered.

"Very well." She drew the pistol from under her cloak. "You see this? It's my father's gun. That's right. This gun belonged to Lawrence Garvey. You all know well what he was like. Recall how often you all have told me I resemble him." She cocked the pistol, moved it slowly from one man to the next. "We shall remain here, as we are, until the two of you, Oren and Gentry, think again. And be sure, if you make a move toward each other, I'll be the one who fires first."

There was a moment's hush, broken only by the distant trill of a nightingale. Then Oren spoke, his face suddenly red. "In the name of God, Marietta . . ."

She stared hard at him.

"Child, no," the Reverend Filene rumbled.

Marietta pivoted, her arm outstretched before her, and looked along the pistol's barrel. The minister went silent.

Then Lafe strolled toward her, smiling faintly, his dark blue eyes alight with laughter. "Marietta, I believe you don't fully understand what you do here."

"Stay back," she warned. "You're not exempt."

He spread his hands, still smiling. "But suppose you do stop this now, Marietta, and send us home to sleep on it. What then? What of tomorrow, and the day after, and the week that follows? Do you intend to keep your brother always with you, under the threat of your father's pistol?"

"I'll worry about tomorrow when it comes," she retorted. "Stay back, I say." Her fingers tightened around the pistol grip. She felt the chill of cold steel in her flesh. This was the gun that had destroyed her father. In that same instant she realized that she could not pull the trigger. She could not shoot Lafe Flynn. A force stronger than her own will prevented it.

Then Lafe had reached her, and his hands had closed around hers, enfolding both pistol and fingers in a grip of iron. "Forgive me, my darling. But I'll have the gun before you harm someone with it, if only yourself."

She struggled. She clawed him and kicked him, but he took the pistol from her grasp. He tucked it into his belt.

"Now go to the gig," he drawled. "Go and leave us to finish up this sorry business as quickly as we can."

When she fought him, crying, "No, no, you can't send me away!" he whipped her cloak around her, binding both her arms to her body in its voluminous folds. He lifted her off the ground, struggling still, and thrust her into the gig. "Whip up the horse," he told Elisha harshly. "Take Miss Marietta home at once, and see that she stays there. I'll be along presently, and we'll discuss this affair then."

The gig rolled off with a jolt. It sped up the ridge and over it, leaving a rising cloud of pink dust in its wake.

Lafe turned back to the men, the gleam of amusement gone from his eyes, his face a mask of anger. "She's right, as you all know. There's no need for this. Take a moment or two to consider."

Dr. Pinchot stamped his feet impatiently. "Consider, consider. This is a field of honor, sir. What are you about?"

"Let us allow these two to decide," Lafe retorted. "What of it? You two alone must face each other." He looked at Gentry. "Well? You know your words were poorly chosen. Do you withdraw them?"

Gentry hesitated, swallowed. Finally he said, "I can't withdraw what I—what everyone—believe to be the truth."

"Oren? You know better than anyone that Gentry's insult is a lie. Will you demand your satisfaction when in truth you already have it and need no other?"

"What's this?" Dr. Pinchot exploded. "Is the second become an advocate? Do you require, young man, that Oren Henderson go to court to uphold his honor in this affair?"

"You're bloodthirsty for a physician," Lafe drawled. "But no matter." He turned back to Oren. "What do you decide?"

"The challenge stands," Oren said coldly.

"Very well." Lafe backed away. "Then I suppose we must begin."

It was only for Marietta's sake that he was concerned, and he had done his best to stop it just for her. For his own part, these two men might kill each other, if they liked, and if they could find no better reason for dying.

Oren and Gentry looked at each other for a long moment. Then both turned away. With their backs to each other, they each counted off twenty paces.

"Yes," Lafe said quietly.

The two men turned. Now they were face to face and confronting each other, their pistols hanging at their sides.

"Ready," Lafe said. He looked first at Oren, received a nod. He looked at Gentry, received his nod.

"Aim." At his command, the two arms came up, both steady, the pistols gleaming in the sun.

"Fire!" Lafe's voice was only a whisper on the word.

The pistol cracks were sharp in the still air.

Marietta heard the exchange. She stiffened for an instant, cried out wordlessly, straining to look behind her from the moving gig.

Elisha frantically whipped the horse, and they jounced wildly downhill. Freeing herself from her cloak, she tore the reins from Elisha's fingers. "Obey me, Elisha. Turn back. I order you to turn back at once. I must see what's happened."

The horse had already begun to circle. Elisha took the reins unwillingly. Unwillingly he tugged them hard, giving the uneasy animal direction. Now the gig jounced wildly back uphill.

Marietta sat straight, tears streaming down her cheeks.

The gig tipped precariously on its wheels as it gained the ridge for the second time.

Elisha cried out and fought the horse to a stop.

At that moment there was the sound of a single third shot.

Oren was on his feet. He lowered his pistol, turned away as Gentry stumbled back and fell.

Marietta sagged back, suddenly boneless, worn with relief. "Very well," she said dryly. "We'll go now."

"Mr. Gentry's down," Elisha muttered.

"His father's there. And Dr. Pinchot. They'll not need us."

Elisha nodded, turned the gig on the track for Galloway as Oren and Lafe knelt with the doctor beside Gentry's still body.

He lay with his head turned to the side, his mouth open, his blue eyes wide and bright. A red stain spread slowly over his right shoulder, seeping onto the white shirt beneath his waistcoat. He looked up at Oren and said in a pain-filled whisper, "Oren, my friend, your aim is still not as good as it should be."

"I didn't shoot to kill," Oren retorted dryly.

"I know. Neither did I."

Alexander Beckwith didn't speak. His hands were clenched at his hips, his face was stony and gray as granite. "Dr. Pinchot," he said at last, "do what you can here. Then I want to take my son home from this place."

7

Lafe rode between the white pillars and up to the road to
Galloway. This was the fourth time in the past four weeks
that he had come here. Each time before, he had seen
either Oren or Coraleen in pleasant but brief visits. But
Marietta had firmly refused to receive him. Now he was
determined that he wouldn't leave until he had spoken to
her.

He made his first request of Elisha, who welcomed him
at the door.

Then Coraleen appeared. "Oh, Lafe," she said delightedly,
"how nice that you've called."

The second request was made to her. "I'd like to see your
sister, Miss Coraleen. Will you tell her I'm here?"

"Oh, I doubt that she's changed her mind."

"Miss Coraleen . . ." Elisha began. "I'll just go up and
say—"

"Be quiet, Elisha, and leave us. I want to speak privately to
Mr. Flynn."

The voice was imperious and somehow threatening. Lafe
decided, not for the first time, that the child needed a good
paddling to teach her better manners.

Elisha went down the hallway, his long dark face full of
disapproval.

Coraleen laughed, put her arm through Lafe's. "You come
with me," she ordered.

He went with her, curious to know what she would say
now, aware that in a little while he would send her upstairs,

or to whatever place Marietta was hiding herself, with a message. He knew, too, that he would remain here at Galloway until Marietta made her appearance.

Coraleen led him outdoors again, to a wicker love seat in the corner of the side gallery. She pressed him down into the cushions, then snuggled beside him as if there were not quite enough room for the two of them.

He shifted away from her, crossed his long legs, and said, "All right, Miss Coraleen. What do you want to say to me?"

"You should understand, Lafe. My sister's still very angry at you. And it's so unjust of her. She should have been glad that you kept her from making such an enormous fool of herself. But no! She blames you for the duel, for sending her off, probably even for saving Oren's life and Gentry's, too."

"I saved no one, as you remember," he answered dryly.

"But Oren wasn't injured, and Gentry's wound is very nearly healed now."

"So I've heard."

"And he and Gentry go about together as always. It's as if there had been no challenge between them."

"Yes. I know that. And it's just as well. What's done is done. They're wise to realize it."

"Then Marietta's quite wrong to be angry with you."

"I'll discuss that with Marietta, Miss Coraleen."

"Miss Coraleen! Miss Coraleen!" She tossed her brown head. "Why do you say that?"

He grinned at her. "It's a mark of respect, isn't it?"

"It makes me feel a stranger to you."

His grin broadened. "Then I'll call you Coraleen as if you were a child. And perhaps that's fitting."

"It's not!" she blazed.

"Then prove it by telling Marietta I'm here and want to see her."

"So you can persuade her not to be angry with you?"

"Yes," he said simply. "For that reason, and others, too."

"You'll not be able to. Not if she refuses to see you," Coraleen retorted.

111

"But she won't, you know. Not forever."

"How do you know?"

"That's something else I'll discuss with Marietta."

Coraleen, pouting, examined her hands. "You're a very stubborn man," she said, raising her head to meet his gaze.

"I am."

"It'll do you no good."

"Are you sure of that, Coraleen?"

She nodded.

He got up and drew her to her feet. "Now listen to me. We've bandied enough words here. Go and tell Marietta I'm waiting."

"All right," Coraleen agreed sharply. "I'll do it."

"Thank you. And I hope you'll speak for me, Coraleen."

This time, she noticed, he had dropped the courtesy title. It pleased her. She said, "Of course I'll speak for you. I promise you that I will."

Moments later she was saying to Marietta, "Lafe's down below. He wants to talk to you. You'll not see him, of course."

Marietta hesitated. She had begun to think that she had been wrong to avoid Lafe. Now that her anger had cooled, she realized that everything was exactly as before. Even worse, if that was possible. Oren still sought out Sara, continued his friendship with Gentry, treated her exactly as he treated Coraleen, like a well-loved sister and nothing more. She made up her mind quickly. She rose, went to the cheval glass. "Yes, please tell Lafe that I'll be down in a moment."

"You'll see him?" Coraleen said blankly.

"Of course. Why not?"

"But you've always refused. What's changed your mind?" the younger girl demanded.

"*I* have changed it." Marietta touched a bit of patchouli scent to her throat, smoothed her hair at the brow. "Will you tell him?"

"After the way he behaved toward you, Marietta?"

"I think now that he had cause. Though at the time I didn't see it."

"And after he allowed Oren and Gentry to go ahead with their duel?"

"I realize that he couldn't have stopped them."

"But, Marietta, Marietta, what if Oren had been killed?"

Marietta turned from the glass, said stiffly, "He wasn't, Coraleen."

As Coraleen approached her, eyes flashing, Marietta brushed past her. "Where is he? Since I'm ready to go down, there's no need for you to do so."

Coraleen seized a fold of her dress, held her. "No good will ever come of your seeing Lafe Flynn now or ever. I know it, Marietta. I feel it."

Marietta calmly detached herself. "I think I must be the judge of that. And I do wish you'd try to behave in a more grown-up fashion."

Color seeped into Coraleen's cheeks. A sheen of tears gleamed in her eyes. "I'm more grown up than you think."

"If you'd only show it more often," Marietta retorted, and left the younger girl alone.

Lafe rose when she joined him.

"You wanted to see me, Coraleen says." Her face was composed, her voice cool, though a sudden excitement passed over her in a quick and bewildering wave as her eyes met his.

"Coraleen was successful in her persuasions, then. I must be sure to tell her how grateful I am."

"Successful?" Marietta's brows rose. A glint of humor sparkled in her eyes. She thought of Coraleen's arguments, but forbore to mention them to Lafe. She seated herself in a small wicker rocking chair and waved Lafe to the love seat.

He sat down, concealing a sigh. When Coraleen had snuggled next to him, he'd felt crowded. If only Marietta had done the same. But no matter. One of these days she would.

He looked into her heart-shaped face. "Marietta, this has gone far enough. I want to tell you that though I'd do exactly the same again, I'm sorry to have offended you that

113

morning at Death Meadows. But there appeared no other way to get you to leave."

She felt the hammer of her pulses, and found herself suddenly blushing at the memory of how he had handled her. His hard hands clasping her fingers around the pistol, nearly crushing them. His arms enfolding her in the cloak. Though she had burned with anger against him then, she had felt the swift sweet juices of her body surge. Now she understood the effect he had on her. It was a quickening of the life force, separate from her feeling for Oren, who had always been part of her. On that thought, she was able to laugh, to say, "You'd do the same again, Lafe. How honest you are."

"I want to be, with you, Marietta." He stopped, finding it impossible to go on. His secrets must remain *his* secrets. He could be honest about his feelings for her, but about hardly more than that. Too much would be endangered were she to know the truth of his activities. He would not sacrifice his mission. But neither would he give up Marietta.

"I'm glad to hear you want to be honest," she said.

He grinned at her. "I wonder if you really are. And how you would take it if I were to tell you what I'm thinking right now."

"Now wait," she protested. "I don't ask to hear all your thoughts, you know."

"Ah, that's better. And now that we're friends again, may I suggest you come out for a drive with me?"

She hesitated, then answered, "Why, yes, thank you. I'd like to."

Elisha brought her a blue ruffled parasol that matched her gown, and a few moments later she and Lafe were driving down the road.

Coraleen, peering down from between barely parted curtains, saw Marietta tip her head back to look at Lafe, the sun shining on her face, and felt her own blood burn with rage.

"Is there a special destination you have in mind?" Marietta was asking.

"Why, no. I hadn't considered this far ahead."

"Ah, you didn't expect me to acquiesce, then."

"My dear, I didn't come out here once a week for the past four without believing I'd change your mind. I knew it would happen. The question was when."

She found herself laughing. "Your conceit gives you great confidence, doesn't it, Lafe?"

"Conceit? Confidence?" He grinned at her. "Well, I suppose I may be fairly accused of such qualities. But it wasn't either one that has continued to bring me to Galloway."

"What was it then?"

He gave her a direct look. "I simply couldn't stay away, Marietta, I've thought perhaps I should. I've tried to weigh it. Perhaps, I told myself, it was no good. We could never be anything to each other. But in the end, reason had nothing to do with it. I wanted to see you. I had to see you."

"I see," she said softly. There was no mistaking him. She gave him a long sideways look, considering the man and the effects his attentions might have on Oren. Had Oren seen her ride out with Lafe? And if he had, did he feel a stab of jealousy?

Since the duel, the whispers had spread through the entire county, she knew. Coraleen saw to it that every cruel word about Marietta was repeated, not once, not twice, but as many times as Marietta permitted it within her hearing. Mrs. Filene was quoted, and Sara Beckwith, and Mrs. Pinchot, too. But Coraleen was not the only bearer of tales. Letty Blandish had come to her as well, to say that the townfolk whispered behind their hands that more trouble was brewing at Galloway.

All agreed, it seemed, that Marietta was the cause of the duel between Oren and Gentry. That she, in her wickedness, never quite specified, was endangering her brother Oren and always would. And that he, as a chivalrous and honorable man, would continue to defend her name, no matter how worthless, until it cost him his life.

Suddenly Marietta shivered.

115

Lafe asked quickly, "Is it possible that you've a chill in this heat? Shall we turn back?"

"No," she answered. "I've no chill. I was simply thinking."

" And your thoughts make you cold?" he asked soberly. "Is it what I've been saying to you? If so, I'm sorry."

"No, no, it's not that, Lafe," she answered, forcing a smile.

They had been following a rutted track that led into Galloway's fields. Lafe drew up and stopped.

The tobacco plants stood high, their huge leaves a strong dark green.

"It's ready," he said.

"Yes. They've begun the first harvesting in the north acres. Now if only the weather holds fine," Marietta said, casting an anxious eye at the blue sky, "then they should have it all in."

"Yes, I've already spoken to Oren about buying."

"Oh? He didn't mention that to me."

"I'm surprised to hear it."

"I hardly concern myself with the running of the plantation," she said quickly. "Oren knows best about it."

"Is that so?" Lafe grinned. "I thought that you yourself knew a surprising amount."

"I learned from my father, as Oren did," she answered. But now she was thinking of the note she had signed. Once the harvest was sold, it should be paid off. She must be sure to speak to Oren. As long as it was outstanding, she would be uneasy about it.

"I'll deal with either of you, as you prefer it," Lafe said. "Be sure I'll be pleased to sample your wares, and offer you a price."

The color rose in her cheeks at his tone. Was he speaking of tobacco? Or something else?

Dryly, as if he had read her mind, he added, "I refer to tobacco, of course, Marietta."

She choked back a laugh, unwilling to admit she had understood the more suggestive meaning of his words. Instead, thinking of the note once more, she asked, "Will you be able to give us a good price, do you think?"

"The best," he answered. And then, leaning his elbows on his knees, the reins loose in his hands, he continued. "Do you know, Marietta, one day this harvest will be done by machine. And machines will roll the papers for cigarettes and cigars. And small fortunes will become tremendous ones."

"I suppose there are fortunes to be made, Lafe. But as for the machinery . . . we've found that our people can never learn to operate it. Even the most simple task, if it involves anything beyond hand labor, appears beyond them."

"And you believe it's because they're black, do you?"

"I suppose it is. I know of no other reason for it."

"I can think of several other reasons. But no matter. If it's true that they can't use machinery because they're black, then, surely, in a few generations that will no longer be a problem."

She gave him a puzzled look. "But how do you mean? Why say that? What's to change what's never been changed before?"

He laughed softly. "My dear Marietta, our black slaves have been receiving, and continue to receive, great infusions of white blood. What happens to the babies born of that lust? Almost always they grow up as slaves. So if it takes white blood to deal with mechanical devices, then the slaves should soon be able to manage them."

"Oh, that's not true, Lafe," she protested. "There's no such infusion."

"No? Truly? Is that what you think? Use your eyes, girl. Let them see without blinders. What of Elisha? His color, the shape of his nose? What of your cook, Essie? How about all the others on your place, those who have blue eyes and gray, golden skin and coffee? Surely you don't believe them to be the same pure breed of Africans that they were when they were dragged from their homes in chains?"

"But my father would never . . . I assure you . . . Perhaps some few depraved men . . . somewhere else . . ." Abruptly, she halted her protest. What was it Aunt Tatie had said? The murdered overseer had wanted the Beckwith wench. How many others had he wanted—and taken?

Lafe was laughing. "Don't you know that a man does what he wants with his property? If he owns a chair, he sits on it. If he has a gun, he shoots it. If he owns a woman, sooner or later he'll—"

"You mustn't speak of such things to me," she protested, color in her cheeks again. Yet even while she said it, she recognized her own joy in the conversation. It was stimulating to her mind, even though it challenged everything she had always believed. It set up a ferment in her. Always, she realized, speaking with Lafe did this to her.

"And why shouldn't I speak of such things to you?" he demanded.

She shook her head.

"You're a grown woman, Marietta. And you've a good head. That's another thing to be used, if one has it. Which isn't too often, I fear."

She was startled at the disappointment she felt when he turned the horse back and returned her to the house. And even as she left him, she began to look forward to seeing him again.

8

By early September, when the tobacco harvest was completed, and the bales were weighed, graded, and delivered to Lafe's warehouse for storage until they were transported to Durham's Station, Marietta and Lafe had become a familiar sight on the county roads, and in Darnal. Though Lafe was often away on his so-frequent business trips, they had managed to spend a good deal of time together.

Oren had plainly not liked it, though he didn't express his displeasure, when she insisted on joining him and Lafe when they rode in the fields to discuss the grading and pricing with Jed Blandish. He had liked it even less, but again had said nothing, when she told him, "What you receive from Lafe will surely cover the note with Marcus Swinton. You must be certain to see him at once." She supposed that he had, for she heard no more about it.

Meanwhile, she enjoyed her time with Lafe more and more. Twice he had taken her to dine at Jordan House, with Coraleen as a chattering chaperone, though none was necessary, thanks to Mr. Jordan, who appeared to have nothing to do but devote his entire attention to their care and service.

Both times, Marietta had seen Oren emerge from the gaming rooms, and though he hadn't come to speak with her, she waited hopefully for some sign that her attention to Lafe had sparked a response. But, except for his frequent absences from the house, and Mr. Blandish's complaints that Oren wasn't about when needed, Oren behaved much as always.

It wasn't until early December that she learned the note for the loan hadn't been paid off.

Elisha had driven her in to Darnal to pay a visit to the general store. She planned special Christmas gifts for the house servants this year. A warm red shawl for Aunt Tatie. A waistcoat for Elisha. A string of beads each for Dora and Essie. She still had to make up her mind about Beedle and Needle. Mr. Blandish would see to the barrels of rum, so that the field hands each had a tot both for Christmas and a New Year's celebration, as had always been the custom at Galloway. There was also the matter of sweets to be distributed then, and the new clothing, too.

She thought of these things as Elisha helped her down from the carriage. It was a gray day, and a cold wind blew dry leaves against her flowing skirts. She drew her cloak more closely around her and wondered if the chill presaged snow. It was something that happened rarely here, and when it did it brought such discomfort and suffering and so much illness in its wake that she dreaded it. She hoped Mr. Blandish had had an adequate store of cut wood put by.

She passed Jordan House and saw, across the street, the lamplit window of Hell's Tavern. There were several large broadsides hung beside the door. They rustled loudly in the wind.

When she reached the general store, other broadsides rustled at her. She paused to look at them. One was a huge poster that advertised the advantages of settling in the Minnesota Territory. It was torn, smudged. She wondered how many had read these glowing promises and set out to reach the Mississippi River for the long journey north. The other brought a frown to her brow. It promised a reward for the return of a runaway slave belonging to Alexander Beckwith. The thing was an old one, and it hung in wind-worried tatters. Soon it would tear through and be blown away along with the live oak leaves. After all this time Alexander Beckwith's man had not been returned. It was no longer probable that he would ever be. She remembered now the wild baying of the hounds they had loosed to hunt him in the trees near Galloway. She had been glad then that the runaway hadn't been cornered there. With a shudder she turned away and walked straight into Marcus Swinton's arms.

"My dear Marietta! How good to see you. I'm so pleased that you're in town. You were planning, of course, to stop by the bank."

She smiled up at him. "I'm doing my Christmas shopping."

His long thin body seemed to hunch over her. His hazel eyes were questioning. "Marietta, I must ask you—and please do forgive me for it, child—I must ask you. Did Oren give you my message?"

"Message?" she asked.

His young man's hazel eyes studied her from his old man's face. "I can see that you know nothing of it." He took her arm. "Come along. We mustn't stand here. What am I thinking of? We'll have tea together at Jordan House."

"Oh, but my shopping," she protested. "I truly must see to it." But it wasn't, in truth, the shopping that concerned her. She wanted to speak to Oren before she sat down with Marcus Swinton. The note should have been paid off long ago, immediately after the harvest. She had assumed it had been. She wanted no words with Marcus, however, until she had heard Oren confirm it.

But Marcus would have none of it. "There's time, dear child. There's plenty of time. I see by the pink of your nose that you're cold. A good strong cup of tea will warm you, and perhaps a gateau of chocolate with it, and we'll have a short talk in the meantime." He gave her no opportunity to argue, but propelled her along with him.

Within moments they were settled before the fire in Jordan House. The air was scented with the fragrance of burning pine wood. On the mantel, brass pots, polished and smooth, gleamed pleasantly amid clumps of red-berried holiday holly and firethorn.

The tea was set out before them on a small table.

Marcus rubbed his bony hands together. "You'll do me the honor, won't you?"

She served him with the thick black tea, poured a quantity of milk in it, and added sugar to his liking.

He held the cup, but didn't drink. He looked over it at her, his hazel eyes inquiring. "Marietta, you must tell me now what's happening at Galloway."

"Happening? Marcus, I'm afraid I don't understand."

"Dear girl, I know you had a good harvest. I learned that from Lafe Flynn, who bought it from you, and not only yours but all the others hereabouts. For a good price. I know that as well."

"Yes, yes, of course. I agree. But . . ."

Marcus went on: "If there's trouble, you have only to tell me so. Surely you know that. I was a friend of your father's. I count myself a friend of yours as well."

"You are," she said, bewildered. What was in Marcus' mind? Why was he hedging about?

"If Galloway's in trouble, dear child, you must only ask for my advice and, I might add, my help. You'll have both, and without stint."

"We've no trouble that I know of."

Marcus put down the cup. The small tinkle it made as it danced in its saucer seemed loud to Marietta. He said softly, "Marietta, when I renewed the note over your signature I specifically told Oren that I must speak to you. You are the owner of Galloway. You are, not he."

Marcus went on, but Marietta didn't hear his words. *Renewed the note over your signature,* he had said.

But she hadn't signed a second note. She hadn't known it had been renewed. She had thought that Oren had used the gain from the past harvest to pay Marcus what Galloway owed. Had Oren signed her name? Or had a new signature been necessary? She didn't dare to ask. To ask would reveal her doubts.

"Do you understand me, Marietta?"

She said, "Yes, yes, of course I do," although she had heard nothing of what he said. "I'll see to it at once."

He sat back, smiling. "As long as you understand. Now we'll say no more about it. Let's speak of other things. What do you think of Lafe Flynn, for instance?"

"A pleasant person," she said cautiously.

"More than pleasant, I should say. A very comely person indeed. And I don't think I'm exceeding the bounds of a banker's discretion when I tell you that he's very well fixed." He paused expectantly, but when Marietta made no comment, he continued. "And for all that, he works such hours as amazes me. The lamps burn late in that warehouse he's built—and already paid for, I might add. He rides here and there on his many affairs, though he could be a man of leisure if he liked." Again Marcus paused, but Marietta remained silent. He reached out, smiling, to pat her hand. "And I've often seen you out with him. That pleases me. You could do worse. And it's surely time you married and brought a master to Galloway."

She managed a smile for him, but said only, "How good it is to talk to you."

"It's more than good for me," he answered. "It's a positive delight. I wish I could say the same about certain others I know." He shook his head, and a thin lock of brown hair fell across his eyes. He peered through it at her. "Alexander Beckwith, for one. Good heavens, how that man annoys me. He's in and out of the bank, insisting that I increase the patrols. He reports to me every move of John Brown, the rabble rouser, as if the man's right here in Darnal. And when he's not harassing me, he's at the county building harassing some other hapless soul."

Marietta allowed Marcus to ramble, hardly giving him full attention, until she heard him say, "Did you know that John Farr has returned from Chapel Hill and has been paying Sara Beckwith court?"

To Marietta that was good enough news to provoke a bright smile. If Oren was infatuated with Sara, and Marietta thought he might be, then he would soon forget the silly young girl should she agree to marry John.

"And I would call it a suitable match," the older man was saying. "John should do well in the Beckwith family. He's as stiff-necked as Alexander himself. I've heard him maintain that North Carolina should secede from the union today. As if we had no responsibilities to it, or even to ourselves."

When Marietta heard him pause for breath, she politely made her apologies and escaped with a promise to visit him again soon.

She did her errands as quickly as she could, and with only half her mind. The shawl for Aunt Tatie was pink, not the red she had intended. The glass beads were pale green instead of the bright yellow she had visualized. She bought cards of red and green wool, and small pewter bells for decorating the tissue wrapping. Finally she grew so impatient that she left before her shopping was completed.

Elisha drove her home through the twilight cold. She was glad to see the lights of Galloway ahead. Soon Needle and Beedle were holding the horse's head, and she stepped down.

Jed Blandish was just going into the yard. She called to him, and noticed that before he turned to meet her he cast a glance at the house. Then he came toward her, saying as he removed his hat, "A cold evening, isn't it, Miss Garvey?"

She agreed that it was indeed cold. Then, "Mr. Blandish, you've remembered the barrels of rum for the holidays, haven't you?"

He hesitated, and again glanced toward the house.

She said impatiently, "Speak up, Mr. Blandish. I asked you a simple question."

He tugged his blond mustache. "I couldn't get it, not the rum, nor the sweets, nor much else I've been after for the plantation."

"You couldn't get it? What on earth do you mean? David Heller hasn't run out of rum, has he?"

"Miss Garvey, I've just been to see Mr. Henderson about it." Jed Blandish stopped. This was as far as he dared go.

"I see," Marietta said after a moment. "David Heller re-fused you." She didn't wait for confirmation, but went on: "Very well, Mr. Blandish. I'll see to it myself. Now, can you tell me, how is Letty doing on the stuffed toys for the children?"

"Well enough, I think. Aunt Tatie's been helping, and Essie and Dora, too, by evenings."

"All right, then. Thank you." She went slowly into the house, threw aside her cloak. It was warm, a fire blazed high in the morning room, where she found Oren seated in a big chair, his legs stretched before him, staring into the flames, and seeing what images she couldn't imagine. For a long moment he didn't turn to look at her, nor speak, although she was certain that he was aware of her presence.

At last he slid a look in her direction. "Coraleen told me you'd gone to town. Did you accomplish what you set out to do?"

"Some," she answered lightly. "And the rest I'll do another day." She perched on the love seat and tightened her fingers in the folds of her wool gown. "Oren," she said softly, "I'm very concerned about something I heard today."

He straightened up now and looked at her.

"Several things, in fact," she went on slowly.

"It's no wonder you didn't complete your errands if you spent all your time in gossip," he told her.

"What concerns me is hardly gossip. Though Marcus did impart to me a bit of that, too."

"What was it? Or did he give it a seal of confidentiality before he passed it on to you?"

"I gather it's no secret. Marcus says that John Farr has returned, and appears to be courting Sara."

"I knew he had come back, and I heard that he's spending some time at the Beckwiths', but that means nothing. Sara won't have him." He hoped he was right. He didn't know what he would do if he lost Sara to John Farr. It seemed to Oren that since Lawrence Garvey died, everything had gone wrong. The one joy in his life was his love for Sara Beck-with. He forced himself to consider a more immediate problem. Marietta had seen Marcus in town. What had the old banker told her? He waited, determined that she must bring the matter up.

She said finally, "Oren, we must speak of the note I signed last spring."

"Ah," Oren said. "I see now. Marcus has complained to you, has he?"

"He hasn't complained. He simply asked if there is trouble at Galloway. And I ask you the same thing."

Oren answered, "'And I told Marcus that you're not to be troubled. I'd never want you to worry. I told him very plainly that I ran Galloway."

"You do indeed. But you must have needed my signature to have the note renewed."

He had needed it but he hadn't been able to force himself to admit his failure to her. He was certain he only needed more time. Embarrassment forced him to stand, his eyes burning with anger. "Marietta, I'll not be questioned as if you suspect me of some crime."

"You misunderstand me," she said quickly. "It's just that I was puzzled by what Marcus said. I thought the loan was to be paid when we received the harvest money. Yet it wasn't."

"There wasn't enough. It didn't cover."

"But you still needed supplies, Oren."

"Of course," he agreed irritably. "And you insisted on such a list of them—unwisely, Marietta, I'm sorry to tell you —that I've not been able to meet our debts."

"So there's no rum for the holidays."

"Jed Blandish has been running to you again!"

"No, Oren. I saw him outside and asked."

"I'll see to the rum, to all the other foolishness, if you insist on it. For myself, I think we should do as the Beckwiths and others. Give the slaves a day off from their labors, and they'll be glad enough of it."

"We have always done differently at Galloway," she said.

"You must face the fact that your father is dead, Marietta."

Her eyes suddenly glittered with tears. "Oh, Oren," she whispered, "I don't know. I don't know what to do."

126

"You must leave it to me," he said. He went to her, touched her cheek lightly. "Leave everything to me, and I'll look after Galloway."

Later, as she climbed the stairs to her room, she suddenly realized that he had never answered her question about the note. She still didn't know if he had written her name, or received an extension from Marcus on the strength of her previous signature. She knew that she had handled the whole thing badly. She should have insisted that Oren explain why he hadn't paid up the loan, why there wasn't enough for all the necessary supplies. In her father's lifetime, there had been bad years as well as good. She expected them, and hoped to enjoy the one and survive the other. Why was this good year for the crop not as profitable as it should have been? That was what she ought to have learned from Oren. Yet she hadn't been able to bring herself to hurt him. If she reminded him too sharply that it was she, after all, who was ultimately responsible for Galloway and those who lived there, he might turn against her, and all her hopes would be lost.

On a Sunday just after the first of the year, Marietta returned from a drive with Lafe to find that Sara and Gentry had accompanied Oren and Coraleen from church services in town.

Her high spirits faded at once. The pleasure she had felt in Lafe's company vanished. To what purpose was she seeing him, leading him on—yes, even leading him on, she admitted to herself—when Oren hardly noticed, his gaze was so firmly fixed on Sara.

They exchanged greetings, and then, as Marietta and Lafe seated themselves, Gentry took up where he had apparently been interrupted.

"He came in right under their noses and stole eleven slaves, and murdered a good man in his bed to do it," Gentry said.

"What's this?" Lafe asked. "Is this something in this neighborhood?"

Gentry turned his angry blue gaze on Lafe. "You mean you don't know of it yet? I refer to the killer John Brown."

"Oh, I see. I thought you spoke of something more recent. The news of that came in on the telegraph at Jordan House a few days before Christmas. I'd nearly forgotten it in the press of other affairs." He turned his russet head to smile at Marietta. The press of affairs had consisted in these past few weeks largely of his courtship of her.

"Nearly forgot," Gentry snorted. "My dear Lafe, there's little of more importance than the killer we call John Brown. He and his abolitionist friends conspire to ruin us. They've taken up arms against us. Mark me, we'll hear more of him. He and his band of criminals and traitors will be a danger to us all until they're hanged and dead."

Lafe grinned. "Such bloodthirsty talk from a man so recently in church."

"But you agree?" Gentry demanded.

"Agree?" Lafe raised dark brows. "Why, man, how could I not agree?"

Coraleen, who had listened in fuming silence, said, "Lafe, you must come to hear the Reverend Filene with us one day. His sermons are rousing, and very good for the circulation of the blood."

"And the sermon today?" Lafe asked.

"Biblical proofs of the divine sanction of slavery, and the good of it for all mankind," she answered, imitating the Reverend Filene's deep booming voice.

"You could show more respect," Oren reproved her.

"For the Reverend Filene?" she scoffed.

"He's a man of God and preaches God's word," Sara murmured. "Perhaps, Coraleen, the respect should be for that."

Impatiently Marietta noted the approving look Oren bent on Sara. It annoyed her to see it. The girl was a ninny, suitable for John Farr, perhaps, but surely not for Oren. Why didn't he know that himself?

Lafe diverted her from her fulminations by leaning close to say, "Perhaps, Marietta, Coraleen's right. So if you invite me, I'll go to the Reverend Filene's church with you one day. But only to help you down from the carriage before, and up into it after."

"What?" she asked, smiling. "Do you mean you're not interested in the good reverend's sermons?"

"Oh, indeed I am. But you know that I must think for myself, and do what I think is right, and live as I think is right. In the end, remember, I alone must bear the consequences of my choices."

"Think for yourself, indeed," she retorted. "And without advice, I take it. You have a high opinion of your faculties."

He grinned. "I surely do, Marietta. And if it's the same in Darnal, and I daresay it is, as in my home, I can tell you now I have no interest at all in ladies' hats, nor their gowns and cloaks, nor the chitchat they exchange. So we'll arrive just in time for the service and depart immediately after."

"You were observant when you attended at home." She laughed. "It's much the same here. I confess I've not as much interest in the chitchat as I should have. Which is why I didn't go with Oren and Coraleen this morning."

Coraleen listened and was enraged. Marietta lied in her teeth. She had remained at home because she had been expecting Lafe to call, and for no other reason. And he! He was becoming impossible. He saw no one when Marietta was about. His dark blue eyes followed Marietta's every movement, every breath. It was ridiculous of him to be so besotted with her. Everyone knew what she was. Why, even at church that very morning there had been the usual talk about her.

Coraleen's eyes narrowed with malice. She leaned forward and said softly, "But today you'd have found the conversation among the ladies quite interesting, Marietta." She looked brightly at the others and paused dramatically before continuing. "They spoke of Mr. Edgar Allan Poe, the poet. You've surely heard of him, but did you know that his foster father dealt in tobacco? In Virginia, I think it was. Can you imagine? Just like us. But the man finally disowned Mr. Poe. Because he was much in love with his sister, or perhaps it was his cousin. No one at church seemed quite certain."

"Coraleen," Oren said sharply, "I'll ask you to go into the

kitchen and see if Essie will soon have dinner brought to the table. And tell Elisha to serve us some claret at once."

Coraleen rose, smiling sweetly, and left the room. When she had gone, Sara rose, too, saying that since there still appeared to be plenty of time, she would like a turn in the garden. Immediately Oren agreed.

Gentry ignored Lafe's expectant look and settled himself more firmly in his chair. "You've heard, I suppose," he said to Marietta, "that John Farr's back."

"Yes. I have."

"We see a good deal of him." A smile touched Gentry's lips, but not his pale blue eyes. "Sara's the cause of it, I believe. If you'd been at church today, you'd have seen his attentions to her."

"He's a very nice boy, I'm told," Marietta said.

"We believe so. And he has something behind him. The Farr plantation prospers."

"So I've heard. I hope all goes well for Sara."

Gentry's smile was as malicious as he knew how to make it. "I'm sure that you do."

In the garden, beyond sight of the house, Oren took Sara's hand and held it tightly. "I've been waiting all day for this. Why did you see to it that Gentry came home with us? I wanted to be alone with you, and you knew it."

She widened her eyes at him. "Oh, Oren, you know why I suggested Gentry come with us. How would it have looked otherwise?"

"I no longer care how it looks," he answered. "And neither would you if you cared for me truly. Now John Farr's come back, you're different. Why don't you admit it?"

"It's not true, Oren," Sara cried. "It isn't. But you know how my father feels. He likes you very much, and now that you and Gentry have stopped quarreling, he looks favorably on you for me. But—"

"But I have nothing," Oren said bitterly.

"Oh, if only Marietta would do what she ought to have done at the beginning. Why, never mind her father's foolish will. She should have signed Galloway over to you. You'd always have taken care of her. We'd always have taken care of her."

"She'll never do it, Sara."

She leaned her head against his chest and whispered, "Oren, you must understand, I can't wait forever."

His arms slipped around her, crushing her to his chest. "Sara, you love me."

She raised her head. Her fingertips settled lightly on his lean cheeks. She stared deep into his narrow dark eyes. "You know I do, Oren. I always have and always will. But you're not free to marry me. Because of Marietta. We must face that together. And I must think of myself in this."

"I won't let you go, Sara. You're all I've ever wanted, and I won't let myself lose you."

Downstairs in the morning room Gentry took a long swallow of the claret Elisha had served, and though the wine was good he made a bitter face. It seemed to him that Lafe Flynn was too much in evidence these days. He was forever running into him and the big black mute who followed him about, if not at home, then at the Farrs' or at the Swinton household, or in Jordan House. And if not in those places, then here at Galloway. There was no doubt that Lafe Flynn was more often at Galloway than Gentry had taste for. There was no doubt in his mind that, for all her feelings for Oren, Marietta was taken with this stranger. Gentry didn't like that. When she ignored Gentry in favor of her brother Oren, that was one thing. When she favored another man, that was something else again. He glared his dislike at Lafe, his disapproval at Marietta, and stalked outside.

Lafe gave vent to a long happy sigh of relief, then grinned. "At last! Do you know that man troubles me, Marietta? He's a bore."

"It appears we both trouble him," she said dryly. Then, rising: "Help yourself to more claret, Lafe. I'll just run upstairs for a moment."

"You need absolutely no refurbishing. Are you afraid to be alone with me here in the safety of your morning room?"

"I'm not afraid of you, Lafe, wherever we are," she answered.

He regarded her silently, then said without smiling, "Perhaps you should be. You might be the wiser, you know."

She gave him a pert smile from the doorway. "And perhaps you shouldn't have warned me. I might heed your admonition."

"I owe it to you," he told her, still unsmiling.

"And I thank you for it in that case." She turned then and went slowly up the steps. The pert expression faded from her face as if it had never been there.

She had left him only because she needed a few moments alone. Sara and Oren were in the garden together. A wave of heat swept Marietta's face as she paused before the mirror. She had thought to make Oren jealous of Lafe. Instead, she was made unbearably jealous of Sara.

She stood very still, her hands clenched at her sides. Why did Oren refuse to love her as she loved him?

There were voices down below. The others were gathering again. Gentry would be joining Lafe, and Oren and Sara, too. She knew she must compose herself and go down at once. She took a deep breath and told herself, I shall have Oren, and he will love me. I know it. I've always known it since he came to Galloway. It will be like that, as in the beginning, forever.

She noted as she passed that the door to the sewing room was ajar, the room beyond too dark for midday, as if the draperies had been drawn. Frowning, she wondered why. Letty worked there more often than anyone else and needed daylight to sew by. If Letty was inside, she would not have darkened the room; if it was empty, why was the door open?

Marietta regarded the darkness uneasily for another moment, then went to look. As she stepped over the threshold, the thin curtains and heavy draperies billowed out together on a chill breeze, sending shafts of sunlight into the room.

132

For an instant a long narrow shadow swayed and danced along the brightly polished floor. As her glance caught it, Marietta's eyes widened and burned. She gasped for breath and felt pain sear her lungs. Her heart seemed risen into her throat, tight as a clenched fist.

The chill breeze died. The shadow disappeared.

But Marietta remained still, frozen, caught in an old dream that had suddenly become real. She saw the four dangling figures in the dark of the live oak trees. She heard her mother's terrible scream.

Time spun around her. She was a child again, going down the hall to her mother's bedroom and opening the door, moving on tiptoe because her mother was ill, and she didn't want to waken her if she was dozing. Aunt Tatie had warned her against that many times.

Inside the door she eased open, the room was frighteningly dark. The air was still, heavy with the scent of dying roses. She tried not to breathe as she whispered, "Mama? Are you asleep, Mama?"

There was no answer, but the white bed curtains were drawn back. As she took a tentative step closer, the heavy blue drapes swung out on a sudden hot wind and the bright May sunlight filled Marietta's eyes, blinding her.

Slowly her vision cleared. In the brilliant rectangle of the exposed window she saw the single dangling figure that hung suspended, skirts awry around it, from the drapery rod.

She saw her mother's blue and distorted face framed in silken black waves.

She fell back screaming. Hands covering her eyes, she fled.

Somewhere in the hallway Aunt Tatie's warm arms enfolded her. . . .

9

Now the drapes billowed again.

An icy cold wind enveloped Marietta. She saw the single limp figure sway.

A piercing scream broke from her, and she sagged against the door, clinging to it for support.

The sound of her raw cry ripped through the idle conversation in the hallway below. For a moment no one spoke or moved. Within that same moment, Lafe lunged for the stairs.

"It's Marietta," Oren said.

"Whatever can be wrong?" Coraleen asked, while Sara gasped and Gentry swore.

Marietta stood frozen just inside the sewing room, staring into the shadows. Her slender shoulders were rigid, her slim throat taut with strain.

"Marietta!" Lafe said softly. "Marietta, what is it?"

She didn't move or reply. She seemed unaware of his presence, or that of the others who had followed him upstairs.

"Marietta, do you hear me?" he asked, his voice gentle. "It's Lafe, Marietta. I'm here with you, and nothing will harm you."

She remained silent, her wide amethyst eyes staring into the shadows across the room. Her heart-shaped face was a bloodless white.

Carefully he drew her into his arms and held her. He

warmed her body with his own and turned her away from the shadows. She obeyed lifelessly, allowing him to move her.

"What on earth's the matter?" Sara asked.

Coraleen sighed. "Oh, poor Marietta."

It was plain to Lafe that he held in his arms only the shell of the girl he loved. Her soul had retreated into some quiet place where he couldn't follow.

He said sharply, "Marietta, listen to me," and then shook her. Her head trembled on her shoulders. Her eyes went to his face, but they still held no recognition.

Even as he saw that, the draperies billowed out again, and in the bright, sudden light his eye caught the long narrow shadow, and he knew it for what it must be.

He moved Marietta aside, crossed the room, and jerked the draperies wide. Light spilled in, revealing a dressmaker's dummy wrapped in a length of fabric and suspended by a cord from the drapery rod.

He made an angry sound of disgust and pulled the thing down and hurled it to the floor.

Marietta drew a deep breath, but didn't speak.

Oren asked sharply, "What's that thing? Why was it hanging there?"

"Is it a game?" Coraleen demanded, her voice soft and insinuating. "Is it something we ought to know about, Marietta?"

She knew that they were all staring at her. Oren, Lafe, Sara, Gentry. They crowded around her, their eyes curious and condemning. But she couldn't speak. She couldn't answer. She couldn't explain what had happened to her.

She had walked into the darkened sewing room, the room that had once been her mother's retreat, and, seeing this stupid thing that Lafe had now thrown to the floor, she had become a child again, seeing, as she had the first time, her mother's body hanging in the window.

Now Lafe said, "It's just stuffing and a bit of cloth, Marietta. Come look at it and see."

Again she obeyed like a puppet. She stood beside him and

looked at the thing on the floor, but when he touched it with his boot, she shuddered and turned away, whispering hoarsely, more to herself than anyone else, "It's like with Snowball."

"Snowball?" Lafe demanded. "What do you mean?"

She shook her head slowly from side to side.

"Poor darling," Coraleen said worriedly. "She's all confused. Snowball's her big white cat that disappeared."

But Snowball hadn't disappeared, although Coraleen might think so. The memory of the broken animal lying under the stairs loomed in Marietta's mind. Someone had wrenched its legs to splinters and left it there to die in agony. Someone had hung the dressmaker's dummy in the window and left it there for Marietta to find.

Slowly Marietta's burning eyes moved from face to face. Oren and Lafe and Gentry. Sara and Coraleen. Each had been at Galloway when Snowball died. Each had been at Galloway today.

From below stairs there came the sound of the dinner bell. She raised her head. Lafe was watching her still, his dark blue eyes sharp and questioning. She said, "Go down, please, all of you. I'll join you in a little while."

She watched as they left her. Then, from the hallway below, she heard Coraleen say, "I don't know what we'll do with her. She's all atremble, Lafe. Did you notice it? And it's happened before, of course. We don't know why she does these things."

"*She* does these things?" Lafe demanded.

"Why . . . who else, Lafe? Who else?"

"Not Marietta," he retorted firmly.

"It was just a foolish prank." It was Oren's voice. "I shall have a long heart-to-heart talk with Needle and Beedle, and I'll soon get to the bottom of it."

Marietta smoothed her hair, drew a deep breath as she went down the steps. No, she thought, this hadn't been the work of the twins, no matter what Oren would prefer to believe. No more than Snowball's death had been. An adult intelligence had been behind these strange and awful works.

An adult intelligence turned against her, to frighten and destroy her. But who hated her with such cool and deliberate intent?

She joined the others at the table, at least outwardly composed.

Lafe smiled at her admiringly.

Coraleen, seeing that, allowed a bit of the burning anger she felt to escape. "But Marietta," she asked, "why on earth did you scream so? Did you think it was your mother hanging there? Did you think she'd somehow come back to haunt you?"

Later, when the others had gone, Marietta sat by the fire, her feet on a stool, needlework in her hands. The silken threads of blue and purple and green shimmered on her lap. The thin needle glinted in the firelight, although she didn't ply it.

Oren leaned against the mantel, his face in shadow. "You feel better now, Marietta?"

She nodded.

"I thought perhaps I should send for Dr. Pinchot."

"I don't need him," she answered. "There's nothing wrong with me."

"You were very upset."

"But I'm not upset any more."

He was silent for a moment. "Marietta," he said finally, "I've been doing a great deal of thinking lately, and now, after a lot of consideration. I have a proposal to make to you."

She raised her head, looked at him, her heart suddenly lifting.

He went on: "Your father left me a third share. If you would see your way clear to giving me one-third of the value of Galloway, as it stands today, then I would be able to do something with it. What do you say, Marietta? Will you think about it at least?"

Her heart sank. A wave of tiredness swept through her. She plucked listlessly at the colored silks that were to be stitched into the shape of a peacock's tail. She said slowly,

"Oren, I don't see how you can propose this. My father's will was very clear on the point. You are to receive a third of the income. Not a third of the value of Galloway."

He should have known she would recognize the difference. She was unwomanly in her attention to such detail. He frowned to cover his disappointment. "Yes, yes, of course. But that income gives me no independence."

"I don't understand what you mean. Or what you truly want," she answered. "Oren, this is your home. You belong here at Galloway. We all share in it. What else is there?"

"I told you, Marietta. I need my independence."

"And how should I manage without you?"

"You'd do nicely enough."

"It wouldn't be possible. No, no, without you, Oren, I would never know what to do."

"Then you won't even consider it."

"Oren," she said, "let's be sensible. Suppose I agreed to give you a one-third share of the value of Galloway. Suppose I should. What would it be when Marcus' loan is still outstanding and cannot be paid until the next harvest?"

"Ah, yes," he said bitterly. "You would bring that up."

She studied him, her amethyst eyes sad. "If we don't have the money to pay our bills, how could I pay you?"

He didn't answer.

"And if I should agree, then Coraleen would ask the same. It would leave no plantation. No Galloway."

"Coraleen's only a child, Marietta."

"True, but she'll come of age. And whatever I do for you I must do for her. You know that as well as I do."

He nodded, a dark flush spreading high on his cheekbones. "Perhaps you're right, Marietta. But I had hoped you'd understand." He hurried on now, the flush burning even darker. "And it could be done. Marcus would lend you what you'd need to give me my third share. Even with the note, he would do it."

"I wouldn't ask him to, Oren."

"Then I'm trapped here," he said desperately.

"Oren," she said softly, "you know what I feel for you."

"More's the pity that your feelings don't lead you to allowing me my freedom," he retorted.

"You can have whatever you want," she said stiffly. "You know that."

Shrugging, he answered, "Then we go on as we are, I suppose."

"Yes," she told him. "That's what we must do, Oren. Go on as we are."

But that wasn't enough. She wanted more. She wanted Oren's love. She knew that.

Oren knew it, too, but refused to admit it, even to himself. He also knew that no matter what was said they couldn't go on as they were.

Then, two weeks later, when he went to Beckwith plantation, he learned from Gentry that Sara had that day become engaged to John Farr.

He left Gentry standing, mouth still open, and rode wildly into Darnal. He strode into Jordan House and sat alone in the corner of the gaming room, trying to drown his anger and pain in drink, and succeeding only in increasing the heat of both.

Lafe, passing by, saw him and stopped to speak.

Oren glared up at him. "What do you want? Isn't it enough that I must see you constantly at Galloway? Why do you follow me here?"

"I intended to say good evening to you," Lafe answered. "Now I'm not so sure that I want to."

"You've said it," Oren muttered. "Now leave me alone."

Lafe pulled up a chair, eased himself into it, and crossed his long legs. "You're not very sociable this evening, Oren."

"I don't want to be," Oren snapped.

"Is something wrong? I wonder." Lafe wanted to ask about Marietta, but Oren's fierce mood stopped him.

"There's nothing more wrong than usual," Oren answered, surly as Lafe had never seen him before.

With his curiosity aroused, he leaned on his elbow, said lightly, "But you're not as usual, Oren."

"No. I suppose I'm not."

"We're friends. Perhaps there's some way I can help."

"You can. I told you," Oren retorted. "Just leave me alone."

Lafe grinned, didn't answer. He lifted a hand toward the bottle-lined bar, and Eamus Jordan trotted over.

"An ale, Mr. Flynn?"

"If you please. And for Mr. Henderson . . ."

"The same as before," Oren muttered.

Eamus cast a nervous look through his spectacles, eying the three empty glasses on the table. "Another bourbon?"

"You heard me."

Lafe nodded to the hotelkeeper, then said to Oren, "I was planning to ride out to Galloway. Shall we have this one for the road and go on together?"

"I'm not going home," Oren said stiffly.

"I see."

"You hardly see. I'm not going home ever," Oren muttered. "That's the thing. I don't want to. If only I had somewhere else."

Lafe didn't speak.

Oren went on, his words a murmur, only an echo of his thoughts. "It could have been different, should have been. That was the understanding when my mother married Lawrence Garvey. It was in Washington City. If it had all gone right, she'd never even have married him in the first place. There'd have been no need to."

"You lived in Washington City? Is that where you were born?" Lafe asked. "I didn't realize that."

"Yes, that's where I was born, and Coraleen, too. And that's where I wished we'd stayed. The four of us—my father, and mother, and Coraleen, and me. I wish we'd never come to Galloway. I wish I'd never laid eyes on the place, or Marietta, or even Sara."

"And what of your father?" Lafe wanted to know.

Oren's smile was narrow and bitter. "That was the beginning of it. He should have taken me with him. But he wouldn't. I had to stay at home, he said, with my mother

140

and sister, and be the man of the house." His voice rose in shrill mimicry. "The man of the house, he called it. When all I wanted in the world was to go with him."

"Where was it he went?"

"Oh. Didn't I tell you? It was the year of the gold find at Sutter's Mill in California. Eighteen forty-eight. Yes, that was the year. He heard of it, as everyone else did. And he was determined to dig his fortune from the ground."

Lafe nodded. It was a story he'd heard many times before.

"He packed up and left us with nothing but promises to send for us soon," Oren went on softly. "But soon never came. He drowned at Shepherd's Landing on the Mississippi. He died, and all our hopes went with him. If I'd been there, it wouldn't have happened. We'd be rich now. I'd be rich now, too. I'd have all I wanted." Oren rose suddenly. "But what's the use of talking about it? Everything's lost to me, and always has been, I suppose. I only face it now."

"Don't despair," Lafe said quietly, rising, too. "You're still a young man. There's time for you to recoup and more."

"There's no time." Oren turned from the table, staggered toward the door.

Lafe followed him into the stable yard.

There, Oren swung around, his face pale and sweaty. "Well, you've heard my life story. Now what do you want?"

"As I told you before, I'm going out to Galloway," Lafe told him.

"Then go and be damned," Oren answered. "I'm stopping in Hell's Tavern for a drink or two."

Lafe shrugged. "Do as you please." He watched until Oren had disappeared around the corner. Then he followed, walking slowly. He thought to allow Oren time to order his drink, to settle down into his morose mumblings, and then to join him, welcome or not.

But Duveen caught up with him as he approached the door of the tavern. The big man tugged his arm, tapped his right wrist. "You need me, Duveen?" Lafe asked, frowning.

Duveen nodded urgently.

141

"Then go back to the hotel and wait. I'll be there right away."

Duveen disappeared at a trot. Lafe frowned, wondering what the problem was, but he went into the tavern. Oren was hunched over a small wooden table, his back to another one where a large group of men sat drinking. Lafe knew none of them by name, but recognized their faces. Several were mechanics, another worked a small farm that barely kept him and his brood of barefoot children. Another lived by slave hunting. He decided that he didn't like the company Oren was keeping at the moment. They were a rough lot, and none had any liking for the plantation owners of the county.

He went back to the hotel, glanced into the gaming room in hopes of seeing Gentry. He was there, having come to look for Oren.

"That's why I stopped in here to look for you," Lafe said. "Oren's across the road in Hell's Tavern. And unless I'm mistaken he'll soon be drunk enough for trouble."

"It's what I feared," Gentry answered. "That's why I rode in after him. Oren finds himself disappointed in love. When a man's in that state, he's bound to get drunk, isn't he?"

"What are you talking about, man?"

"My sister's going to marry John Farr. For which, I don't mind telling you, I'm grateful. Even though Oren's my friend."

"Well, if he's your friend," Lafe told him, "then you'll see that he comes to no trouble this evening. I'd do it myself, but I've business to attend to that won't wait."

Gentry grinned, "You needn't worry for him. I'll see that he's all right."

"Very well," Lafe said, "I'll leave you to it."

Duveen was busily printing a note when Lafe reached his rooms. Lafe read the block-printed words as soon as he was finished. WE HAVE THEM. WITH A COMPLICATION. THERE'S A SON. OUR FRIENDS WON'T LEAVE HIM BEHIND.

"How old?" Lafe asked.

Duveen held up two fingers.

"It's much too young. If something happens and he's frightened and cries . . ."

Duveen nodded.

"So the warehouse hidey hole is out."

Duveen whistled softly between his teeth.

"But we can't ask a man to leave his family behind either. Who knows what'll happen? Who knows when we could manage to bring them together again, if ever?"

Duveen shook his head from side to side. His dark eyes were filled with an ancient sadness.

Lafe could read his thoughts. Here was almost the worst aspect of the peculiar institution, which some abhorred and some defended. Men and women who loved were torn apart. The father sold off, the mother and children separated. It was an unnatural act that deprived all concerned of what should be theirs.

Finally Lafe said, "Delay for two days, Duveen. I'll try to work out a way of minimizing the risk. And we won't use the warehouse."

Duveen grinned, nodded confidently.

When he was alone, Lafe took out a small cigar. He lit it with the note Duveen had written, then carefully crumbled the ash so that nothing was left of it. How could one transport a man, a woman, and a small boy beyond the county—hiding them by day, and by night avoiding the patrols—and leave no trace behind? He leaned back in his chair, his mind solely occupied with that problem.

Gentry was acutely aware of the words exchanged only a few feet away. He could hear them clearly, though they weren't spoken loudly. He could hear the tone of them, too. Snide, baiting comments, edged with low disgusted laughter.

"That's Henderson of Galloway."

"Is it? Well, I'll agree it's Henderson all right. But of

Galloway? How can that be? Galloway belongs to Miss Marietta Garvey, and everyone knows that."

"If he'd marry his sister, then he'd have Galloway, too, as well as her."

Gentry stared hard at Oren, but Oren's dark eyes were hooded. The hand holding the glass to his lips was steady.

"Are you ready to go home now?" Gentry asked finally.

"Home?" Oren asked.

"To Galloway," Gentry told him.

"It may be that he needn't marry her," a low voice said suggestively. "Or it may be that he already has, in a way."

Gentry rose, heat burning at the back of his neck and in his pale blue eyes. He'd made these same suggestions himself. But to hear them spoken now by others inflamed him.

There was an exchange of growling laughter. Then, "They were always crazy at Galloway. The old mistress hanged herself. The old master blew out his own brains. So what would you expect Miss Marietta to be?"

Gentry said urgently, "Oren, let's go."

Oren pushed back his chair, got to his feet. He stood leaning his two balled fists on the scarred tabletop, and turned his head stiffly. "Yes, let's go," he said loudly. "I don't like to drink where pigs do their swilling."

The noisy room suddenly hushed. The four men who had been speaking moved together, rising as if activated by a single breath.

David Heller came out from behind his bar shouting, "That'll do, that'll do, all of you," and brandishing his thick two-foot club.

In the skirmish that followed, he belabored every head he could reach, and by the time the deputy had arrived from the calaboose around the corner, he had quelled the disturbance and thrown its formenters bodily into the road beyond the door.

When Oren reached Galloway, he was sober again, but he had a black eye and a swollen lip. His coat hung in shreds from his shoulders. Both his boots were split.

Marietta cried out in terror as he came into the house, with Gentry, equally disarrayed, following after.

Oren turned away from her without a glance and went slowly up the stairs.

"It won't do," Gentry said quietly.

"What happened?" she demanded. "Why did you fight him this time?"

"This time I fought on Oren's side. If you don't believe me, then ask Oren."

"If you're not to blame, then who is?" she asked bitterly.

"We were in Hell's Tavern," Gentry explained. "The men there . . . We couldn't even call them out. They're not the kind to come. They'd sooner go for a shot in the back on some dark night . . . and so . . ."

She drew her breath in sharply. "Ah!" she exclaimed. "Then pray tell me, if you can, why you frequent such a low place. Isn't Jordan House quite nice enough for you, or is it too nice?"

Gentry looked sullenly at her. " I went to Hell's Tavern because Oren had gone there before me. Lafe asked me to. He'd spoken to Oren, and knew he was out to get drunk, and perhaps out for trouble as well. Lafe had a business appointment that couldn't wait, so he told me. And I went, which is what I'd have done regardless."

"Thank you for your trouble. Even though you couldn't keep Oren out of it."

"In all fairness to Oren, Marietta, you should know that he had to defend himself."

"Again," she said softly.

"Again," Gentry agreed.

As soon as he left her, Marietta went up to Oren's bedroom. She knocked at the door and went in before he could refuse her admittance.

He lay on the bed, still fully clothed, his arm folded across his face.

"Oren, Oren, what's to become of you?" she asked softly.

He didn't reply.

She leaned closer. A dark curl slid along her cheek. She asked, "Is there anything I can get for you? Are you all right?"

He lifted his arm from his face, looked up at her. "There's nothing I need."

For a moment there was silence between them. The lamplight flickered. The wick, burning low, guttered softly.

She noted the carpetbag that stood open on the table, but she didn't mention it. Finally she said, "Gentry's gone." When Oren didn't reply, she went on: "He told me there was trouble."

"So there was. As you can easily see by my face and clothes."

"Why couldn't you laugh at them, ignore them? What does it matter what that poor white trash says of you?"

"They're only repeating what they hear said by our friends, who are not poor white trash, Marietta."

"Ignore it all, Oren. It's meaningless."

He sat up slowly, swung his feet to the floor. "But it's not meaningless. And I would, no doubt, say the same were it Gentry who found himself in my situation, or John Farr. Or any other man. That's why I've determined to leave Galloway, Marietta. Whether you help me or not is your concern, your decision. But I shall go, regardless."

"Go where?" she gasped. "What are you talking about?"

"I don't know where, nor do I much care. Perhaps I'll return to Washington City. I wish we'd never left it. But anyplace will do, as long as it's away from here."

She saw his black eye, his split and swollen lip. She saw the bruises on his fists. As long as he was with her at Galloway, it would be the same. The talk would go on and on, and nothing would stop it. Yet there must be some way to protect him and still keep him here, keep everything the same as it had always been. She said quietly, "Oren, don't do anything rash, I beg you. I want to think about this a little. Surely there's something we can do."

"Did Gentry tell you about Sara?" he asked.

"Sara? Why, no. What about her, Oren?"

146

"She's going to marry John," Oren muttered. "It'll be soon, I think."

"I see," Marietta said. So this was why Oren had gone to Hell's Tavern to get drunk. Because of Sara Beckwith. She went to the carpetbag, snapped it shut, and put it away at the bottom of the wardrobe. "You won't need that for the moment anyway. Now rest, please, and I'll send Aunt Tatie up with some unguents to soothe your bruises."

He couldn't have Sara, she thought as she hurried downstairs. And he didn't want *her*. But he mustn't go away.

He mustn't go away, she repeated to herself as Coraleen called, "Marietta, Lafe is here, and refuses to be entertained even for five minutes by me. He wants to see you at once."

She smoothed her hair and her skirt and went toward him. As soon as she saw his russet head turned to her, saw his tall strong body, and felt the clasp of his fingers at her hands, she knew what she was going to do.

She turned to Coraleen. "Please go and tell Aunt Tatie that Oren needs unguents, will you?"

Coraleen grumbled, but withdrew in the direction of the kitchen.

"There was trouble?" Lafe said.

She nodded.

"I'm sorry to hear it. I'd hoped that Gentry could prevent it. I couldn't go myself, but when I heard from Eamus Jordan, I came directly here."

"Gentry told me. I know you did all you could do to stop Oren. And I know there was no way to do it tonight."

"Get a wrap," Lafe said. "It's a beautiful night for looking at the stars."

She hesitated, glanced up the stairs.

He caught a black velvet cloak from the hall tree and threw it around her shoulders. She remembered when he had done the same before, and thrust her away into the gig, his hands as strong then as now, and his face jus as determined. This time, instead of struggling against him, she smiled and allowed him to lead her out of doors.

147

It was cool on the gallery. The sky was dark. Over the ridges to the west a thin silver crescent moon shone brightly.

He said in a deep quiet voice, "Marietta, I want you to listen to me now."

She raised her eyes to his and nodded.

"I've waited, knowing it was only fair to you, to give you time, but I can wait no longer. I will wait no longer."

She was still. She felt him draw her closer, felt the strength of his hands spreading across her back. "You know how I feel, how I've felt since the first time I saw you. You've given me reason to hope. So now I tell you plainly. I want you to be my wife, Marietta. If you refuse me, I'll ask you again. I've made up my mind and nothing will stop me."

Briefly she thought of Oren. His lean dark face, his narrowed long eyes, the quick smile that had become so rare of late. He would never want her as she wanted him. And if she were married, he'd stay at Galloway. There'd no longer be reason for him to go. All would be as it had always been.

She looked into Lafe's face, saw that he was watching her intently.

"Well?" he asked. "What do you say? Is it to be a yes this time, or a no?"

Once again she thought of Oren. She could do anything for him, she told herself. She had made her decision before. All she need do now was follow through. She said quietly, "It's yes, Lafe. Oh, yes, I'll be your wife."

His sudden laugh was low, exultant. He swept her into his arms, crushing her to him. For a single moment she felt as if she'd been caught up in a high wind, swept away into some strange and unfamiliar place. There was a sweet rightness to the meeting of their flesh. Fear touched her at the strength of the emotions that burned through her. Then, smiling, she raised her lips for his kiss.

It was a long time before she remembered that in the instant Lafe's mouth claimed hers, his long hard body pressed to her, she had completely forgotten all thoughts of Oren.

10

Silence fell slowly on Jordan House.

Lafe pressed his ear to the closed door, listening while two politicians prolonged their good nights with a series of tasteless jokes. He waited, his lips curled with impatience, until their raucous laughter had faded away down the hall.

Now it was quiet enough to hear the stairs creak. To hear, from the gallery, the whisper of leafless wisteria. To hear the small fire sputter on the hearth.

In his hand he held the large brass key to the room next door to his suite. Once the warehouse had been completed, he had given up, much to Eamus Jordan's regret, the room he had used as his office. He'd bought the rosewood desk, which soothed the hotelkeeper's feelings somewhat, and moved it to the warehouse, where he placed it over the trap door that led to the hidey hole below. The key he had conveniently forgotten to return, believing it might someday be useful.

This night it would be.

In the room next door, now unoccupied, there were beds and quilts. Soon a family would sleep there.

Lafe turned the two lamps low, then listened once again at the door.

All was still. He took up a lamp and went to the gallery window. He pulled aside the drape and held the lamp high, then lowered it quickly.

Within a moment or two he heard a soft familiar whistle. He grinned, let the drapery fall into place.

Duveen had seen the signal and responded.

Waiting, he went back to the door to listen once more.

Soundlessly the drape at the window parted. Duveen stepped through, followed by a young man and a woman who carried a child on her hip.

Lafe greeted them with a smile, a finger to his lips, and eased the door open. The hallway was empty. The single light on the table was turned low. He stepped out, gestured the others to follow. Somewhere below a door slammed. A smothered gasp sounded behind him. He thrust the brass key into the lock and opened the door. It was only by the movement of the shadows that he knew his companions were still with him. Quickly he lit the candle stub he had brought with him. By its pale light he saw the young man nod, the woman sigh. The child she held opened his mouth in a broad grin, exposing a single white tooth against pink gums.

Lafe returned the grin, indicated the bed, and snuffed the candle out.

The family would spend what remained of the night in darkness, but soon the January chill would be warmed from their bones, and by dawn Duveen would have taken them on their way.

It went as planned. Duveen returned to the warehouse the next afternoon looking well pleased with himself. Within the hour Lafe was at Galloway, walking with Marietta in the gardens and making plans.

"Late March," Marietta said. "After the spring planting, Lafe."

"Need we wait so long?" he demanded. "Must you really have so long?"

She smiled teasingly. "Are you so impatient, then?"

"I am." His smile was teasing, too. "I'm tired of bachelor quarters, and bachelor living."

"And that's all that presses you?"

"That's all," he answered. But his look gave his words the lie.

A tremor of excitement shook her, even though she faced squarely the fact that she had consented to marry Lafe only

150

because of Oren. But she grew even more certain now that she could make a good life with Lafe. There would be happiness for them both at Galloway. They would all be one family, sharing their joys with each other.

She put a hand on Lafe's arm and said, smiling, "Bear with me, my dear. The preparations I am thinking of will surely take every day of these next two months."

"I'll bear with you this once, Marietta. But you mustn't think it sets a precedent. You'll learn I'm not always so patient."

"Then I'll make certain not to try you too far," she promised.

Coraleen stood concealed within the huge oleander bush only a few feet away from where Marietta and Lafe had stopped to talk. She heard all that was said. Now she watched as the two silhouettes blended together.

She tried to imagine that she was Marietta, her own body enclosed in Lafe's strong arms, her own mouth opening beneath his kiss. But she could no longer indulge in the fantasy as she had so many times before. What she had never believed could happen was about to happen. Fickle Marietta, who had always loved Oren to no purpose, would marry Lafe, take him from Coraleen and marry him.

Trembling, Coraleen shook her head slowly from side to side. No, no. It couldn't be. She wouldn't allow it to be. Marietta mustn't marry Lafe Flynn. He belonged to her, and always had and always would, and Marietta couldn't have him.

Her small face set with determination as she plucked absently at the shiny oleander leaves. She heard Lafe's soft laugh and watched as the two moved away and he followed Marietta up the steps, out of the cold sunlight into the house, speaking with a quiet urgency.

No, Coraleen thought again, it mustn't happen, and I won't allow it.

Here in the shade of the bush it was still. She nibbled at her fingers, thinking.

The Green Room, that was what her mother had called it

151

when she directed Elisha in the trimming out of the limbs of the old tree so that within it, sheltered and secret and scented, a hideaway was formed. The Green Room was where her mother had held small tea parties, trying with all her hopes to make Marietta and Coraleen friends and sisters. The tiny china cups painted with violets, which had been Beatrice Garvey's, brought from the South of France by her own family, had been fragile. So easily smashed beneath a rock when Coraleen could no longer bear the sweet smiling loving look her mother bestowed on Marietta.

She was still in the Green Room, absently nibbling at her fingertips, when Lafe rode away. Her lips burned from the juice of the leaves she had plucked. No, she thought, it mustn't be, and crammed into the pocket of her gown a handful of those bitter and oily leaves.

She went slowly into the house and crept up the stairs, hearing Oren and Marietta speak together as she passed the morning room.

She watched the sun rise higher in the sky and made her plans.

When, late in the afternoon, she saw Oren riding out, the hounds following after him, she ordered the twins to saddle her horse.

Just past the slave quarters she caught up with him. The air was sweet with the smell of wood fires. The smallest children raced about. She noticed nothing as she called, "Oren, wait up. I want to talk to you."

He stopped at her call, leaned frowning into the sunlight. His lip was still swollen, his eye dark with bruises. "What do you want?" he demanded.

"She's told you, hasn't she?" Coraleen asked hotly. "You know what's she's going to do."

"Yes, Marietta told me a few hours ago. But how do you know?"

Coraleen didn't answer. She stared at him. "You take it calmly."

"Why not?"

"Oren, you *are* a fool," she cried.

"And you're an impertinent child," he retorted. He kicked the horse in signal, but she leaned forward and caught the bridle.

"You mean you're going to do nothing?"

He sighed impatiently. "Coraleen, you're a nuisance. But to answer your question, no, I shall do nothing. Why should I? And even if there were some reason to, what could I do?"

"You could have had her yourself if you'd been clever enough to see it," she answered. "And that's what you should have done. I realize it only now. But I never dreamed she'd marry."

Oren slapped his knee angrily. "Coraleen, you're crazy! Marietta's as good as my sister. How could I ever think to marry her? And you already know the talk there's been. You've been anxious enough to repeat it. We'd never have lived it down."

"You don't see beyond the nose on your face."

"I don't?" he asked calmly. "Very well, then, tell me what I don't see."

"You'll never have Galloway," she said hotly. "Don't you know that? If Marietta marries Lafe, then our home, our very lives are gone for good."

"I think Marietta's marriage will be good for me nonetheless."

"Oh, do you?" Coraleen sneered. "Even if it means losing Galloway?"

"I'd not have it in any case. And what sort of man do you think me if you imagine I could marry Marietta only for control of the plantation?"

"I know you're a fool for not doing it. And I know it wasn't honor that held you back. It was Sara. You were besotted by her. In a few weeks she'll be Mrs. John Farr, and lost to you. So you could at least try to think of something else."

"There's nothing to do," he answered, thinking that it was true that he must forget Sara. But that changed nothing.

Though many a man took his marriage vows for profit, he couldn't do it. To be Marietta's dependent brother was bad enough. To become her dependent husband was unimaginable.

"She can't marry Lafe," Coraleen cried now.

"You'll not be able to stop her. No one stops Marietta when she sets her mind to something."

"We'll see," Coraleen shouted. "We'll just see about that." She whirled her horse and galloped wildly away.

In the second week of February Marietta took time away from her own wedding preparations to give a welcome-home party for Sara and John Farr, who had just returned from their honeymoon in Charleston.

The chandelier glittered, each drop a small sparkling star, pulsing with reflected candlelight. The table centerpiece, spread full and lush, scented the warmth of the room with a heady sweetness.

"Now Oregon," the Reverend Filene said. "Another free soil state. It'll do us no good."

"What of it?" Marcus Swinton asked. "Free or slave, it would change nothing now."

Marietta gave Oren a quick look.

He nodded, rose to his feet, and lifted his champagne glass. "Ladies and gentlemen, I'd like to toast the happy couple before us. To Sara. To John."

"To Sara. To John," the company murmured.

Oren seated himself, smiling still, his face revealing nothing of the heartsickness that was a constant pain to him. He had lost Sara, and though he had been present at her wedding, and seen her exchange her vows with John, only now did the finality of those vows touch him.

He let the conversation drift past him. The Reverend Filene's voice, Dr. Pinchot's, the simpering exchanges of their wives. He was relieved when everyone adjourned to the parlor for after-supper dancing.

Marietta had attended to it all. She'd had the rugs rolled up, the furniture moved out, the fiddlers brought in. She'd seen to the gay decorations of paper flowers and live green cuttings. It was, Oren supposed wearily, a rehearsal of sorts for her own marriage, which was to come at the end of March.

The newlyweds took the floor first. Sara's eyes were raised adoringly to John's face, Oren noticed bitterly, and remembered that she had once, and not so long ago, looked at him in just the same way. If he'd been master of this house, this plantation, now he would hold her in his arms. Galloway owed him for the loss of happiness.

At Oren's elbow, Coraleen said softly, "And here's a preview of things to come. Before we know it, Marietta will be married, too. This time it hurts you. Next time it will hurt me."

Oren left her without replying.

It was only a matter of time, Coraleen told herself, watching as Lafe took Marietta into his arms and led her into a waltz. It was only a matter of time. She would find the right moment. She would do what had to be done, as she had before.

"I'll be glad when this winter is over," Lafe said to Marietta. "I should never have agreed to delay for so long. I should have insisted that we go to Reverend Filene and have the knot tied and be done with it."

"How could we?" she protested. "I explained it to you, Lafe."

"You explained, and I listened. Still I'll be glad when the time comes. Though I still wish you'd agree to a New Orleans honeymoon."

"It's not a good month for me to be away," she answered. "You know it as well as I."

"There's Oren, Marietta," Lafe said.

"Yes, of course." She didn't go on to explain that she was less confident of Oren than she had been. She was determined to see more of the plantation's workings herself.

And she was somehow loath to meet Lafe's family. She had had a warm and charming letter from his mother, offering an invitation for a visit at the earliest possible moment.

She had had a letter from his sister Elizabet, too. And there had been a whole chestful of embroidered silks and hand-worked lace. Yet she had no desire to see Lafe in the place that had once been his home. She wanted to think of him as belonging only to Galloway.

"I suppose," he said now, sighing, "that two months doesn't matter, when I remind myself that I'll have you for the rest of my life."

"I must go and see to the wine bowl," she said hastily.

"You flee again," he reproved her.

She smiled and slipped away from him.

The wine bowl was full. Elisha stood close by, filling the cups as they were presented to him.

Marietta smoothed a small stain on a bit of silver, touched the fine linen cloth, and turned to greet Dr. Pinchot, and then to converse with Mrs. Filene.

She held a small cup in her hands, sipped at it occasionally. When the Reverend and Mrs. Filene made as if to take their departure, she put down her wine. She went with them to the door, bade them good night, returned, and took up her wine again.

Coraleen stood close beside her now. "It's a nice party, isn't it?" she asked, and watched while Marietta sipped her wine.

"I hope everyone is enjoying it."

"Oh, they are. I'm sure of it," Coraleen answered, adding, "I heard Sara say that she and John will give a party for you."

"That will be nice," Marietta said absently.

"I'll need a special new gown for that, of course," Coraleen went on. "Green, I think. Do you believe green will become me?"

"It would certainly." Marietta cleared her throat. There was a bitterness on her tongue, an odd burning at the back of her throat. She set the empty cup down as Gentry came to join her.

"A nice party, Marietta. We're all grateful to you for

going to the trouble, knowing how busy you must be with your own preparations."

"I'm glad we can be together," she said.

"It's good." His blue eyes were bloodshot and narrowed. A pink flush burned along his jowls. "We've been friends too long to allow trouble between us."

"Yes," she agreed.

"And Oren will get over his feeling for Sara. As I will get over my feeling for you."

"Surely there's room in every life for more than one love, Gentry," she answered.

But she wondered. Would she ever get over her feeling for Oren? She looked across the crowded room to where he spoke now with Lafe.

Lafe was the taller by several inches, the heavier, too, with a breadth of shoulder and chest that gave him an aura of physical power. Oren was more delicately made, his bones long and narrow, his features sensitive rather than rough-hewn and robust. Yet, as always when she studied him, she felt her heart contract.

Gentry said, "Your engagement to Lafe came as a surprise to all, although you did go about with him more than any of us expected you would."

She turned to him, put an impulsive hand on his arm. "You mustn't think that my acceptance of Lafe's suit is a reflection on you." She hurried on, seeing that Gentry's round face didn't soften, "Don't you see? It's just that we've known each other too long."

"You mean it's easier to marry a stranger than an old friend?" he asked quietly.

"Perhaps that's so, Gentry."

"A stranger, and a difficult man to know as well," Gentry said thoughtfully.

"I don't find him difficult to know."

Gentry smiled. "No, it would seem you don't. Yet what do you really know of him, Marietta?"

She stared into Gentry's eyes. "What are you implying?"

"Nothing, my dear. Just that we've never met his family, if he has one. We know nothing of his background, his past. He's been here—what is it now?—some nine months, I think, and has a thriving business in Darnal, which keeps him traveling about. But as for the rest . . ."

"I'll see you have all the details," she said dryly.

"When you have them yourself," he answered.

She shook her head and laughed. "I've had several letters from his mother, plainly a woman of breeding and charm. From his sister, too. He has an older brother who is an attorney at law. Lafe very much wished that we go on our honeymoon to New Orleans so that I could meet them, but I felt it would be a bad time to take such a long journey."

"You might have done well to take him up on the offer," Gentry told her.

She didn't reply. She found herself swallowing a bitter taste. The odd burning had become stronger in her throat.

She saw that other guests were gathering to leave. She excused herself to Gentry and went toward them, relieved, suddenly, that the evening was nearly at an end.

She was kissing the air close to Sara's cheek when she felt a terrible dizziness assail her. She caught her breath, clung desperately to Sara's hand for a moment. Then John smiled at her, thanked her, and drew Sara with him, followed by Gentry and the elder Beckwith. Within a short time the others departed, singly and in couples.

The last of the hoofbeats faded away under the live oak trees. The last of the carriage wheels jolted off into the shadows.

Marietta stood at the gallery railing. The night air was cold. A chill went through her. Yet her cheeks burned, and her forehead, too, and the fire at the back of her throat had spread and moved down now to encircle her heart. She drew a deep breath, and the fire exploded into quick sharp pain. She knew she must go in, lie down, rest. But she couldn't move.

She clung to the railing, fearful of releasing her hands, lest that single movement deplete the last of her strength.

She wanted to call out for aid, but her throat seemed bound in some throttling grip. She could scarcely draw air in, force it out. An icy film gathered on her brow, her cheeks. It spread along her shoulders and into the palms of her hands. Even her feet, encased in soft Morocco slippers, seemed to float in it.

There was a bright splash of light as the door opened. The chandelier glittered.

Oren and Coraleen were talking somewhere out of sight.

Marietta struggled to breathe. She stiffened her body, trying to ward off collapse.

As if from a distance she heard Lafe say, "Marietta, why are you standing here alone? It's too cold for you out of doors now."

She gasped, and with agonizing slowness she turned to look at him.

He made some small sound, and even as she swayed he caught her up in his arms.

He took her inside. There, holding her, he saw her face, pale and hollowed. Her eyes were wide, frightened. There were shadows around them, deep as bruises. Her lips seemed swollen and parched. He saw the too-rapid pump of the pulse in her throat, the heave of her full curved breasts beneath the tight blue velvet.

Coraleen cried, "Lafe, what are you doing?"

Oren stared.

Lafe raced up the stairs, holding Marietta's limp body tightly against him, the skirt of her gown trailing in whispers along the floor. Over his shoulder he shouted, "Send someone for Dr. Pinchot at once. You may catch him on the road if you try. Marietta's ill."

He didn't wait for an answer, but went on into the big room that he guessed to be hers. He swept the bed curtains aside, laid her down, and then covered her with a quilt. He lit a lamp and set it on the nearby table, and then stood back to look at her.

It seemed to him that she was worse, if that was possible. Now her face was gray. She made terrible choking sounds, and her hands were small fists pressing into her throat.

He bent over her. With one quick hand he loosened her gown, her stays. With the other he held her gently, moving her close to a big clay basin.

She was helplessly aware of his every movement, every touch. She wanted to protest at the pain, the indignity that he forced on her, but she was too weak. She could only obey his whispered orders.

There was a moment when Aunt Tatie was there, wiping her forehead with a cool cloth, another when Dora went racing from the room, only to return a moment later.

Aunt Tatie mixed a potion in a silver cup and handed it to Lafe, but he put it aside.

By the time Dr. Pinchot had come grumbling and laboring up the stairs and into the room, Lafe had brought Marietta to the brink of wretched sickness, and then past it. Whispering encouragement, he had made her spew forth the wine she had drunk, the food she had eaten.

By the time Dr. Pinchot leaned over her, Lafe had held the silver cup containing Aunt Tatie's potion to her lips, and Marietta's cold sweat was gone. She was warm, buried under a pile of quilts.

He examined her carefully, then said, "My dear girl, too much excitement, and too tight stays."

She asked hoarsely, "But how could those do that to me?"

"They did. Or perhaps a bit of spoiled food." He was soon on his way, with admonitions that she must rest.

She lay back, closed her eyes. She was certain it could not have been the food she'd eaten, the same food that all the others had eaten as well.

She remembered holding the cup of wine, remembered setting it down to see off Sara and John. Had someone touched it while it stood on the table? It seemed to her that everyone must have passed it and had the opportunity to add to it something which had made her so deathly ill.

Snowball, she thought. The dressmaker's dummy. And now this. Yet if she cried her suspicions aloud, everyone would think her mad. Were she to say that Coraleen had stood near the table, near the wine cup, she would be accusing her own sister, a girl hardly even grown. She dared say nothing, she told herself tiredly. There was nothing to say.

Lafe, still sitting beside her, got to his feet. "You must be more careful, Marietta."

"I will be," she answered in a sad whisper. But careful of what? Of whom? She might wonder about Coraleen, but how unjust that could be. Each time something terrible had happened, there had been others at Galloway.

Lafe bent down and kissed her, told her to sleep well. His tone was light, unconcerned. But as he left her, a frown deepened on his brow.

11

It was only a small chip, brownish and dry, but Aunt Tatie spied it. She bent, black skirts crumpling around her, grumbling aloud that Miss Coraleen could still make the same mess of her room that she had made as a fractious child.

Once she held the bit of leaf in her wrinkled fingers, she forgot what she had been thinking. She stared at it, sniffed at it. Her eyes seemed to sink in her skull. Her mouth folded in. She moaned softly to herself, pushing unpleasant thoughts and the sudden fear they brought away.

It wasn't possible. It couldn't have happened. Miss Marietta had come down sick from bad food. It had to be that. Aunt Tatie's head said one thing, but her heart said otherwise.

She stared at the small chip of dried oleander leaf and asked herself what to do. If only Mr. Lawrence hadn't died. He'd know what to make of it. It was like when Miss Marietta's pearls were gone. And then, turning up the mattress in Miss Coraleen's room, she'd stuck her finger into a torn seam, and when she set to mend it, she found the beads. She took them to Mr. Lawrence, and he looked sad, saying. "Don't say a word of this, Aunt Tatie. I'll deal with it." She nodded and kept her mouth shut, even when the beads turned up on Miss Marietta's dressing table, and nobody but she and Mr. Lawrence knew how they'd come there. The next day he was dead.

Now she was shivering, and her hands shook with fright,

and she felt that her tired eyes had seen more evil than she could stomach.

And Coraleen asked brightly, "What's that you're looking at, Aunt Tatie?"

"Nothing," she mumbled, balling her hand and thrusting it behind her.

"Nothing?" Coraleen laughed. "You're hiding something from me, Aunt Tatie." She widened her eyes. "Is it a surprise? Is it something nice for me?"

"Piece of nothing," Aunt Tatie insisted. "And I've got my work to do." She swung away so that she wouldn't have to look into Coraleen's eyes. She grabbed up the quilts and bustled out to the gallery to hang them for a sunlight airing.

She hummed to fight her terror, and tried to think what to do and whom to talk to, and how she would say it, and still she held tightly to the chip of dried leaf.

She was thinking so hard that she didn't sense the movement behind her. She was concentrating on framing her fears into unfamiliar words. A dried oleander leaf had dangerous effects, a fresh one even worse.

Suddenly she felt something slam hard into her back. The breath was knocked out of her, and she tipped off balance. She whimpered. She clawed at the railing.

The hands had the strength of the devil and shoved once more. She crumpled over the railing into a sunburst of brilliance. The quilts, trailing slowly after, enshrouded her where she fell.

Coraleen raced silently into the sewing room. Below, she heard Elisha's shout, the twins' screams, the yap of the excited hounds.

Her blood pounded in her ears. Her heart pounded, too. But she wasn't afraid. She had faced the threat and dealt with it as she had done before. It was easy if you weren't afraid, she told herself triumphantly.

When Elisha, entering the morning room, looked up and muttered, "Aunt Tatie's dead," Coraleen, trailing silver threads from her embroidery hoop, buried her face in Oren's shoulder and cried.

"Nobody knows how it happened," Marietta said tonelessly.

"Who found her?" Lafe asked, his brows drawn down and his eyes hard.

"Elisha heard the fall, and the twins, too, I think. He ran from where he was working and reached her first. But she was already gone."

Lafe saw the glitter of tears in her eyes, and he took her hand. "I'm sorry, Marietta. I know Aunt Tatie had been with you all your life. I know you'll miss her."

"Yes," Marietta said dryly, "I'll miss her."

Aunt Tatie had been there when the bad dreams wakened her, had held her warm and safe after her mother died. She had wept with Marietta when her father died. The old black woman had been a part of her life, and necessary to her. And now Aunt Tatie was gone. Like Marietta's mother, her father . . . "I'll miss her," Marietta repeated softly.

Something in her voice sharpened Lafe's attention. "What else is there?" he asked. "What are you holding back from me?"

She hesitated. Then, "Elisha . . . Oh, my God, Lafe, I've known him all my life, too. But I think he's lying to me. I think . . . I'm so frightened suddenly . . ."

Frightened. Yes. What she felt was fear mixed with grief. Ever since she'd been taken so ill at Sara and John's party, she'd been frightened. Only the greatest effort of will had allowed her to suffer her terror in silence. The suspicions she couldn't allay burned through her and singed her to the soul.

"Go on," Lafe said insistently. "Tell me, Marietta."

"Elisha first said Aunt Tatie spoke to him, and then he suddenly denied it. He said he was mistaken. She was gone, he kept telling me after, at the moment he bent over her."

"You think he lied to you?"

164

"Perhaps, perhaps, I just don't know."

"I expect it's a misunderstanding and nothing more, Marietta. You must put it out of your mind," he said. But he did not intend to take his own advice.

He found Elisha in the morning room, polishing the silver candelabra.

The old man heard him out, eyes sunken and dull. "I don't know nothing about it. I heard a fall, or some loud noise anyhow. And I ran around and found her."

"Dead?"

Elisha was ashen. He wet his lips. He looked down at his feet when he nodded.

"You're sure she was dead?"

Elisha nodded again, then muttered, "I was scared, Mr. Lafe. The dogs were barking and the twins were screaming . . ."

Lafe said softly, "Elisha, why are you scared now?"

"I ain't scared, Mr. Lafe. I just don't know nothing, that's all."

Lafe knew there was more. He looked at Elisha for a moment, then put a gentle hand on his shoulder. "You'd better say it, Elisha."

"It don't make sense," the old man cried. "Poor Aunt Tatie was out of her mind. She was near dead and groaning and whispering, and maybe I didn't hear her right. I ain't sure what she said. I ain't sure, so—"

"Then she did speak?" Lafe asked. "She's gone now, Elisha. Nothing can hurt her. What did she say?"

"It was Miss Marietta that Aunt Tatie always loved the best. She raised her up from an infant. No matter who she asked for, I know it was Miss Marietta that Aunt Tatie wanted."

"Who did she call for?" Lafe asked. "Whose name did she say, Elisha?"

"Miss Coraleen," Elisha muttered. "She asked for Miss Coraleen. And I could hardly believe it! Not for Miss Marietta, but Miss Coraleen. And you tell Miss Marietta that and it'll hurt her, because she was the one Aunt Tatie loved best."

Lafe forced a smile and said, "Well never mind about it. I won't say a word to Miss Marietta. I suppose poor Aunt Tatie just imagined that Coraleen was nearby and could help her."

It was easy enough to reassure Elisha, for the old man wanted to be reassured. He had only wanted to shield Marietta from knowing that Aunt Tatie had died asking for Coraleen.

But Lafe saw something else here. Perhaps Aunt Tatie had not been asking for Coraleen. Perhaps she had been accusing her instead.

He went outside, looked up at the gallery from which Aunt Tatie had fallen. Its door, he knew, opened into Coraleen's room.

There had been that business with the dressmaker's dummy. And then more recently Marietta had been so ill. No one else had been, so Lafe refused to blame bad food. And two days later Aunt Tatie had died saying Coraleen's name.

His suspicions disgusted him, but he couldn't put them aside. Not if there was danger to Marietta. He was impelled to act even though his doubts were stronger than his convictions.

Coraleen interrupted his ruminations. "Marietta wanted to know if you'd left without telling her," she said, smiling. "I swear, the way the two of you behave makes me wish I were getting married, too."

Her pink and white face shone with good will. The February wind tousled her brown curls. Her smile was sweet, but still Lafe felt its emptiness.

He looked into her bottomless brown eyes and thought, If I'm wrong and unjust, no harm will be done, but if I'm right she'll understand. She'll know that I'm watching, though she'll never know why. At last he said quietly, "Coraleen, I want to ask you to do me a very great favor."

"Of course," she answered in quick delight. "Whatever you like."

His dark blue eyes sought her gaze, held it. He towered over her, a man who found laughter easy, but could be dangerous when crossed. He allowed her to see that streak of granite in him. In a voice that was deep, edged with iron, he said slowly, "I want you to keep a good eye on Marietta for me. To make sure that she's well, and takes good care of herself. You must help her all you can, and make certain that no harm and no unhappiness befall her."

He knows, Coraleen thought wildly. He must know something. Fear swept her from head to toe in a chill wave. He would do anything, anything for Marietta.

Now he was saying, "Will you do that for me, Caroleen?"

"Of course. Why, nothing will please me more than to look after Marietta for you. And you needn't worry. All will be well." She managed to force the words through a fear-clogged throat. And even as she spoke her reassurance, she cursed Marietta, and Lafe, too. She looked down at the earth beneath her feet. This was the place to which Aunt Tatie had fallen. Lafe had been looking up at the gallery from this very spot. He had as good as told her his thoughts, though she couldn't imagine what had drawn them to her. Regardless, he couldn't *know*. He *couldn't* be certain. She concealed a desire to laugh. Why, for a moment, he'd actually managed to frighten her.

And then Lafe said, "I hope I needn't worry. For if something should happen to Marietta in these six weeks before we're married, I shall be very angry indeed."

12

"Miss Marietta, if you don't stop your fidgeting we'll never get it done right," Dora grumbled. "You wiggle here and you wiggle there, and pull and push until we don't know where we're at."

Marietta winced within. The words might have been Aunt Tatie's, but the old woman was gone now, and Dora, come to help with the fitting of the wedding dress, spoke them instead.

Letty Blandish nodded her head vigorously in agreement, but kept her pursed lips firmly closed around the pins they held.

"I wish it didn't take so long," Marietta said impatiently. "I've a million things to do besides standing here for hours on end."

"Rushing your own wedding dress," Dora said reproachfully. "You want it right, don't you? Then you ought to be willing to give some time to it."

"I know, I know," Marietta told her.

Letty's hands moved nimbly at the hem of the gown. "I'll get it basted in and then you can try it on again."

"Oh, do go on and sew it," Marietta told her. "I know it will be right."

"Miss Marietta," Letty protested, "why, you know we can't ever be that certain. And I'm not having everybody in Darnal whispering that Letty Blandish put a crooked hem into Miss Marietta's wedding dress."

"All right," Marietta groaned. "We'll try it on for the millionth time, if you insist. But let's stop for now."

"Never saw the like," Dora grumbled.

Letty cut in quickly. "There now. And if you'll bend . . ."

Marietta leaned forward, held her arms out straight, and allowed Letty and Dora to draw the gown over her head. Then there was the business of underskirts and crinoline, of laces and ties, and finally Dora helped her on with an everyday outfit of light green.

Only now did she permit herself a glance at the cheval glass. She had been resolute in not looking at her wedding gown, a fact which escaped both Letty and Dora.

Marietta felt that the less she saw of the white gown being readied for her and the less she thought of the wedding so speedily approaching, the better it would be. She didn't allow herself to examine that feeling too closely but put it down to the usual case of prenuptial nerves. Other women had married and survived, she told herself. And she would, too.

When she had told Oren that she had accepted Lafe's proposal, Oren had smiled and offered to give her away if she liked. Pained, she had agreed, saying in a light voice, "I've no one else to do it, Oren. And you are my closest male kin, I suppose."

She didn't know what she had hoped until that moment, but his equable acceptance had hurt her, though she made certain that no one knew it.

Lafe had sent to New Orleans for the enormous bolt of gleaming silk. He had sent to New York City for the tiny white seed pearls that would adorn it at neck and yoke. Time seemed to have rushed by while she made arrangements, sent out invitations to the county folk, discussed the refreshments to be served at the reception with Essie and Dora, the flowers with Elisha, their honeymoon plans with Lafe, which now involved his suite at Jordan House, to which he insisted they retreat for a few days, in lieu of the trip to New Orleans that she had refused.

Meanwhile, the life of the plantation had gone on much as usual. Oren hadn't liked it when she determined to ride with him and Jed Blandish to oversee the planting. Though he hadn't demurred, his grim face had spoken for him well enough. She had pretended not to notice. She remarked to Jed Blandish that the slave quarters would need a complete refurbishing this fall, since they hadn't had it the previous year, and Oren frowned at that, too. No matter. She would see to it when the time came, just as she would see to repaying Marcus Swinton immediately after the harvest. If the weather held, it should be a profitable one, and Oren would have no grounds for protest.

Time had passed so quickly. When in January she had spoken of late March after the planting, it had seemed far away. Now it was already upon her. The fields glistened white as fresh-fallen snow under the thin netting laid over them to protect the tender young tobacco plants. The corn was planted, the produce beds begun. She had found it good to be busy, to be so preoccupied that she remembered only in startled moments that within two weeks she would be Mrs. Lafayette Flynn.

Now, as she stepped into the hallway, she thought that the activity had eased her in another fashion as well. She had had no time to brood on the fear that had beset her when Aunt Tatie died. It had receded to the back of her mind, where she could remember it and reflect with cool wonder upon it.

As she started down the steps, Coraleen waylaid her. "Marietta, come and see my gown. Oh, I'm so excited. I think it's the most beautiful one I've ever had in my life."

"You'll be lovely in it," Marietta said. "The shade of pink is just right for you."

Coraleen hugged her arm. "Come and see," she insisted, drawing Marietta with her.

The pink silk lay across the big bed. Below it, toes peeping from beneath the spread, were shiny pink slippers.

"You'll be surrounded with beaux when you wear that," Marietta told her.

Coraleen made a small breathless sound. Her cheeks were suddenly fiery red, and her eyes gleamed with held-back tears. "Marietta, it's going to be so different from now on. I promise you it will be. I've been . . . I've been trying to show you these past months, but now I must say it. Before, I was jealous of you." She took a deep breath, hurried on. "Oh, I'm ashamed of myself, Marietta. But you're so beautiful, and everyone loves you. And then there was Lafe, taking you away from us, from Oren and me. It made me . . . I'm so bitterly ashamed, you'll never know . . . but it made me angry at you, Marietta. At you. I don't know what possessed me to say those things I said . . . about your mother, and . . . and . . . all that . . . All this time I've remembered, and wished I could tell you how sorry I am." She flung herself into Marietta's arms. "Please say you forgive me, please do."

Marietta held her, smoothed the damp brown curls from her pink and white face, the tears from her cheeks. "Never mind, Coraleen. I understand. It doesn't matter. I just want us all to be together, to be a family. You and Oren and me." And then, quickly, she added, "And Lafe, too. The four of us, our family."

She tried to stifle the still small question that arose within her. A whisper of uneasiness, some intuition that surfaced briefly to warn her. *I was jealous. Everyone loves you.* So many things had happened over the years. Coraleen was prone to quick tempers, quick tears, and quick regrets. She was partial to masks, and she donned and doffed them at will.

Marietta held the young girl closer and told herself, No, no. This is real. At last Coraleen's growing up and beginning to understand herself. She said softly, "We'll all be happy, Coraleen. You'll see. I'll make sure of it."

And Coraleen, her face hidden and buried in Marietta's warm shoulder, suddenly smiled. There was more than one way to skin a cat. Oh, yes, indeed. They'd all be happy together. She and Oren, and poor Marietta, too. The three of them. Though Marietta didn't know it yet. For Coraleen's love for Lafe had now become a deep and intense hatred. Lafe had spurned her. Lafe had become a threat to her. He would stand between Oren and Galloway. She had tried to turn Lafe against Marietta, and hadn't succeeded. She had tried to stop Marietta, and had failed in that. But it didn't matter. She would wait. Afterwards, some way or other, she'd drive Lafe Flynn away from Galloway for good.

"Now then," Marietta said after a moment. "I must go down and see to the week's menus with Essie. And I'll discuss with her at the same time the menus for when"—she drew a deep shaky breath before she went on—"for when I'm away. On my honeymoon with Lafe."

Coraleen freed herself. She smiled brilliantly. "I'm so glad I talked to you, Marietta. Oh, honey, I feel so good now. I feel like a different person now that I've told you the truth."

"Mr. Flynn, Mr. Flynn, a word with you, if you have a moment?"

Lafe allowed himself to be detained by Eamus Jordan's plump hand. "What can I do for you?"

"It's about the suite, sir. You'll want whatever fresh flowers I can find. And several bottles of champagne, of course?"

"Your best champagne, Mr. Jordan."

"And the new drapes are ready to be hung." Mr. Jordan wrung his hands. "Though what's to be done with them after, I'm sure I don't know."

"After?" Lafe inquired. "Why, after, as you put it, they'll continue to hang."

"Indeed? You'll just leave them?"

"Leave them?" Lafe laughed. "Ah, I see. Perhaps I should have told you, Mr. Jordan, I don't intend to give up my suite here at Jordan House after my marriage. I shall need it for those times when the weather's bad, when Miss Marietta and I wish to stay overnight in Darnal."

Mr. Jordan beamed. "I'm delighted to hear it, sir. A guest such as yourself isn't too often come by in these parts."

"My business in town goes on, Mr. Jordan," Lafe said

easily. "The warehouse will be full in a few months. We'll be just as before, I assure you."

"And what of your man Duveen?" the hotelkeeper inquired.

"I shall take him with me to Galloway, along with my clothes and certain other belongings. But he'll come in with me as needs be."

"You'll be a busy fellow, I should think," Mr. Jordan remarked. "And now let me offer my congratulations, belated as they may be, on your coming marriage. You'll have for wife a beautiful girl."

Lafe heard the faint question in the hotelkeeper's voice and chuckled. "A beautiful girl, albeit one from a family you believe to be strange?"

"Mr. Flynn," Eamus said hastily, "I had hoped you'd forgotten those foolish words of mine. What do I truly know of the Garveys? If you choose Miss Marietta—" He stopped, tilted his head. "What's that on the road outside, I wonder?"

Lafe listened, too. There were shouts, galloping horsemen, hounds baying.

"The patrol," Mr. Jordan said. "I wonder what's wrong now. They brought a runaway in a few hours ago."

"Oh, did they?"

"There was a lookout for him. It came in on the telegraph two days back. I took it to the deputy sheriff myself." Mr. Jordan turned, went to the door, and cast an anxious glance outside.

Lafe looked over his shoulder. The road was full of men on horseback and yapping hounds. Torches made circles of brightness in the dark.

Eamus shook his head and backed inside, his breath a white plume at his lips. "A sorry business, Mr. Flynn. A sorry business indeed."

Lafe said nothing. He strained to listen. He thought he had heard a familiar whistle over the sounds of search in the square. Suddenly he smoothed all expression from his face. Yes, there it was again. Duveen.

173

"I must get to it," he told the hotelkeeper. "I shall, as you said, be a busy man these next few weeks." It was true, and it was a thought that pleased rather than oppressed him. But now he must find Duveen.

He went, humming, to his suite, in hopes his intuition led him aright.

Duveen was waiting for him. The dour look on his face warned Lafe. "Do we have trouble?"

Duveen nodded, jerked his thumb over his shoulder, and turned to enter the bedroom behind him.

Lafe followed, frowning. It had all gone so smoothly so far. He wanted no complications now. In two weeks he would be married. He foresaw no problems arising from that change in his situation. Though he knew Duveen had certain doubts, Lafe was determined that all would go on as before. But he needed a free mind, and free time, for these next days.

Duveen lit a lamp, held it in one hand, and advanced upon the wardrobe. He eased the door open.

Lafe bit back a quick exclamation.

A small foot in a dusty boot, a clenched fist, lay partly exposed from behind his trousers and jackets and waistcoats.

He raised his brows at Duveen, who nodded soberly. At that signal Lafe said, "Would you come out please."

A small man of some fifty years emerged cautiously from his hiding place. He wore ripped trousers, stained with blood on the left leg. His shirt was more tattered than whole. His face was round and smooth and dark, and his nose was wide. He eyed Duveen accusingly, then burst out, "What did you bring me here for? If he's to find me?"

In the brief silence that fell after his words, Lafe clearly heard the commotion below. The horses, the dogs, the shouts of the men. Indeed, he thought, what *had* made Duveen bring this small man here?

Aloud he said, "Duveen knew what he was doing. It's all right."

"Duveen? Is that his name?"

Lafe nodded.

The small man advanced on Duveen in a slow dragging,

limping walk. He thrust out his hand and caught Duveen's. "Thank you, brother. I don't know how it came about, except that the good Lord sent you. But thank you." He turned, his shoulders sagging. "And now . . ."

"Sit down," Lafe said, leading the way into the front room. He touched the bolt on the door, assuring himself that it was secure. He turned back to the small Negro. "I see your leg is hurt. We'll attend to it. Are you hungry?"

"Hungry?" A glint of humor glowed in the man's eyes. "Hungry? Of course. When isn't a man who is chattel hungry?"

"Hungry for food," Lafe said.

"For that, and for freedom, too. Or do you first feed a man before you turn him over to the patrols or the sheriff?"

Lafe didn't reply. He glanced sideways at Duveen, who gave the small Negro a long thoughtful look and then went out. Lafe went and leaned his shoulders against the door.

"He doesn't say much," the small man said.

"He can't speak," Lafe answered. "His name's Duveen. He can write."

"He's strong, and brave. He must be a little crazy, too. Do you know what he did? He looked in the window of the calaboose. I was chained there. I couldn't stand up and I couldn't sit. It seemed like a lifetime. I saw him look in. I saw him disappear. Two hours later he came and got me. He broke in the back door the minute the deputy stepped out. He yanked the chain out and brought me here."

"How did you come to the calaboose?"

The small man cocked his head. "Listen, you hear them? They're looking for me again. They left me in the calaboose for safekeeping while they celebrated with whiskey. They picked me up first in the woods out of town."

"Where were you going?"

"Now I learn why Duveen brought me here to you."

"Where were you going?" Lafe repeated evenly.

"North to feed my greatest hunger. If the good Lord so pleases."

"You're a preacher, aren't you?"

The small Negro looked startled. "How do you know? It's rare that a white man should recognize me as such."

"You sound like every preacher I ever heard, black or white." Lafe grinned. "And what's your name? If you don't mind saying."

"Moses," the preacher answered, and chuckled. "Good, isn't it?"

"Moses what?"

"Moses Jasper."

"The Reverend Moses Jasper, are you?"

The preacher nodded. "And I can probably thank my name for my calling. My former master saw to it that I had schooling, and taught me the Bible himself."

"Your former master?"

"My former earthly master," Moses Jasper said. "He's dead now, and God rest his soul. His daughter didn't want me, so I was sold."

"Where do you hail from?"

Moses put his small balled fists on his knees. "I don't know that I should say."

"I'm not turning you over to the patrol, Reverend Jasper. Haven't you figured that out yet? Duveen wouldn't have brought you here if he thought I would do that."

"They're looking for me."

Lafe nodded.

"There's a price on my head," Moses went on, almost whispering. "A big one. More than I'm worth. I expect they know it outside."

"I expect they do."

"It's not for any evildoing," Moses went on. "You'd better know that, too.

"I've not asked you, have I?"

"This meeting with you is only one more proof that the Lord moves in mysterious ways. You don't ask, but I'll tell you. I came up from Georgia, where I was taken by my new master. I couldn't stay with him. He resented my teaching the word of the Lord, you see. My small sermons among

176

my people, he said, had the kernels of rebellion in them. As if His words could stir men to violence." Moses drew a deep breath. "Even when there's justice in it."

Lafe thought of John Brown, but said only, "And you want to go on."

Moses nodded.

The door at Lafe's back suddenly moved. He asked, "Duveen?" At a soft tap-tap, he moved aside, jerked the door open quickly.

As soon as Duveen was inside, Lafe closed the door and set its bolt.

Duveen put a tray on the table. He arranged knife, fork, and napkin neatly, then gestured at the fried chicken legs, the sliced ham and bread. When Moses had begun to eat, Duveen fetched a basin of water and some cloths and knelt to clean the cut on the preacher's thigh.

When he had done that, and been thanked, he took a piece of paper and printed.

Lafe read the note quickly. CAN WE HELP HIM OUT OF TOWN? "We can and will," he said. "But you'd better get him some other clothes. And it'll take some time. We want to be sure they've given up searching the town."

"Tomorrow?" Moses asked.

"We'll wait until tomorrow to see."

The next morning at dawn Lafe was on the road outside Jordan House. He looked up and down, then walked slowly across to the courthouse. He surveyed the road again, then retraced his steps, this time passing Hell's Tavern before turning the corner to go by the calaboose. The glass-paneled front door was locked. Inside a pale lamp burned at its wick.

All of Darnal seemed quiet.

He ran into Eamus on the front steps of Jordan House. "You're out early, Mr. Flynn," the hotelkeeper said.

"I wanted the freshness of the morning," Lafe told him.

"They didn't find him, you know."

"Find who?"

"The runaway. It seems someone broke in the back door

of the calaboose to get him out. The deputy had apparently gone around the corner to Hell's Tavern for a moment. Young Beckwith and Farr were fuming. There was a price of five hundred dollars, you know."

"Remarkable," Lafe said dryly.

"They've telegraphed his master, and a slave hunter's on the way. The men are in a rage. They've lost the nigger, and even if they find him, the slave hunter will get the reward, if he can manage it."

"What a pity," Lafe said. Then, "Oh, I meant to mention it last night, and then forgot. But Duveen and I will be going off for a few days to Raleigh. I'm in search of a special gift for Miss Marietta. You'll keep a weather eye on the suite for me, won't you?"

"Indeed I will. And all preparations will go forward."

"Thank you, and good morning. I doubt I'll see you before we go."

Inside the suite, he told Duveen, "The town's quiet enough now, but slave hunters are on the way, and our own patrol is angry for losing the reward. I think we'll have to take the reverend out of here today."

Duveen nodded.

"We must begin to move certain of my things to Galloway, I think. Will you get a stack of my clothes together and fold them well? Put some sheets and quilts on top, if you can."

Duveen suddenly grinned.

"You know what I plan?"

Duveen pointed at the big red wooden chest in the corner. It had a great mass of yellow daisies painted on it. The centers of the flowers were black, and in each one was a neatly drilled air hole.

Now Lafe threw up the lid. "I think it'll do. We'll fill it up, bypass to Durham's Station, and then return to Galloway to complete the unloading."

Duveen went to the wardrobe and began lifting out clothes.

Moses, watching, said, "I want to help. What can I do?"

Duveen shook his big bald head.

178

"There must be something," Moses insisted.

Duveen turned to give him a wide grin.

"You'd like me to keep quiet?"

Duveen nodded and concentrated on his chore.

Moses looked at Lafe. "Do you do this on a regular basis? Or is it just to help me?"

"I don't know that I'm obliged to answer questions, Reverend," Lafe said gently.

"You mean you think that the less I know the better?"

Duveen made a soft warning sound in his throat. Moses didn't look at him.

"I may mean that," Lafe answered.

"Perhaps I should explain why I want to know."

"You may, if you like."

"Mister, I don't know your name, and I don't know who you are. I wouldn't want to know, the circumstances being what they are, except for one thing."

"And that is?"

"I'm tired of running away. This is as far from Georgia as I think I have to be for now. The Lord brought me to you for a purpose. I want to stay and help you. And that's why I asked."

Lafe shook his head. "It'd be too dangerous for you. You'd be recognized."

"I don't think I would be. Nobody got a look at me in good daylight, and wouldn't remember me if they had. A new suit of clothes . . ."

"You'd be risking your life," Lafe said.

"And what of Duveen? Didn't he risk his life for me last night? And you? Aren't you endangered every minute I sit and talk with you? I need to help," Moses continued before Lafe could object. "And I can. If you keep me here with you, I can be Duveen's voice."

Duveen had stopped packing. His dark eyes were fixed on Lafe's face.

Lafe asked, "What do you think, Duveen? You have a vote. Use it now."

After a moment, Duveen gave a brief nod.

179

Lafe grinned. "All right, Reverend Jasper, you're on. But you're going to learn how to keep quiet, aren't you?"

Moses grinned. "Yes, sir. Yes, sir. Don't worry about that, sir. I know when to keep quiet and when to talk."

"I believe you do," Lafe answered. "I hope you do." In response to Duveen's questioning look, he went on: "Finish packing. We'll leave as soon as you're ready."

"Leave?" Moses demanded. "In the good Lord's name—"

"I can't have you suddenly appear here, can I? Duveen and I are going to Durham's Station to pick you up. I'll bring you back with me from there. You see, my brother in New Orleans knew I needed a trained man to help me in the warehouse, so he's sent you to me as a loan. His name is Flynn, too. I'll give you all the details you'll ever need. We'll leave in a little while, and go from Durham Station to Raleigh for some shopping I must do. And we'll be back, all three of us together, by the end of the week."

Within half an hour, by broad morning light, and in full view of half of Darnal, Lafe and Duveen carried down the big wooden chest, put it in the wagon, and set off at a leisurely pace for Durham's Station.

13

The room was dark and still. It was hours before dawn, and Marietta lay awake, staring at the white canopy overhead. A heavy weight seemed to press her deeper into the pillows. A lethargy seemed to wrap her slender body in leathery bonds. A cottony dullness afflicted her emotions.

Her eyes burned, and her lips were stinging as if she had pressed them deeply into a sheaf of nettles.

The first hours of her wedding day were upon her, and she could no longer pretend to herself that the reality she had never quite allowed herself to face would never come to pass.

A large wardrobe, deeply carved in the French manner, and polished until it shone, hulked in the corner. A similar style of chest, with two silver-backed brushes and an enamel box of cuff links and collar buttons, rested beside her dressing table.

The whole room, from canopy to carpet, had been refurnished to make way for Lafe. Soon, in hours only, she would be his wife.

Her dream of love with Oren must be put away forever.

Suddenly she could lie in bed no longer. She sat up, threw back the coverlet. She caught up a frilly pink wrapper and went to stand outside on the gallery. She looked down the road between the faint greening haze of the live oak trees to where the two white pillars marked the entrance to Galloway.

It was just there that she had first seen Lafe when he came in with Oren. She remembered her fear that night, and the knowledge that it was she who endangered Oren.

She clasped her hands tightly before her. She knew that what she was doing was right. Then why was she so assailed by doubts?

A small sound made her turn quickly.

A shadow moved at the corner of the gallery. A muted footfall seemed suddenly loud.

She whispered in a dry tone, "Who's there?"

"Marietta?" It was Oren's voice. He appeared out of the shadows, came toward her. "What is it? Can't you sleep?"

"I wanted a breath of air."

"At this hour?" He smiled at her, his long face alight. "Do you suffer bridal nerves?"

"No," she said.

"Then you should sleep. This day will be full of excitement for you."

"For us all, I suppose." But she was looking hard at him. All her hopes and heart must be in her eyes, she thought. All her dreams, for so long held back, must surely show now. Oren, she whispered silently, turn to me now. Tell me not to marry Lafe. Tell me that you want me, and always have, and always will. And I'll refuse Lafe. For you, I will, no matter what anyone says.

But Oren said, laughing, "You may deny it, Marietta, but you're having the usual second thoughts that all brides have, I think."

She made a sound of impatience.

He laughed again. "Do you deny it truly? Then I only think it all the more. Though I confess I never expected such a thing of you. You have always known your own mind so well. Still, let me try to reassure you, Marietta. You've nothing to fear from your choice. Lafe appears to me to be an eminently suitable husband for you."

"Indeed?" she asked. "I knew you approved, but I didn't realize you were so enthusiastic."

"I am. But I didn't want to influence your thinking. When you were in doubt I was constrained to hold my tongue. And even after you told me of the engagement, I believed it to be better to encourage you, but not to take too strong a position. I always wanted you to be free to change your mind, if you so desired it."

"I'm still free to do that," she told him, and looked into his face, hoping to see approval there.

"Change your mind? Why would you do that after waiting so long?"

"I would if I wanted to."

"Headstrong Marietta . . . and do you want to?"

"I . . . I don't know, Oren."

"You see?" His voice was gentle, almost indulgent. "As I told you, you suffer from bridal nerves." He moved closer, turned her chin up. "Listen to me, Marietta. It's the fear of taking a large and irrevocable step that troubles you. Yet this is what we all must do sooner or later. It's a part of life, and we must simply face it."

A cold wave swept slowly over her. She felt it begin at her toes, pass smoothly through her limbs and body, to touch her cheeks. She shivered uncontrollably.

"Now then," he said briskly. "I know just what you need. Wait here a moment and I'll bring it to you."

He disappeared for the space of a long breath, and when he returned he was carrying a decanter and two glasses. He grinned at her. "Some warmth will be good for you. Have this, and then go to sleep for what little remains of the night." He poured sherry until it reached the brim of the glass. "A full medicinal dose. Drink it down quickly for the best effect."

She took the glass from him, her fingers touching his. She felt their warmth, raised her eyes to his, and saw that he had noticed nothing. She drank the wine in quick swallows, choking a little at the sharp sweetness of it. It spread a delightful warmth in her chest. It tingled at her lips.

"I don't know," she said in a whisper. "I don't know, Oren."

"To bed with you." He gave her a brotherly pat on the shoulder. "Go on now."

183

But she swayed toward him, her face lifted, her eyes wide and glowing as they searched his for some sign that would guide her.

The smile he bestowed on her meant nothing. She couldn't read it. She reached out hungrily to touch his cheek. She slid tender fingers over his lips, caressing them, and she whispered, "Oren, Oren, tell me what I must do."

He jerked his head away, repugnance suddenly twisting his features. He stepped back. "Marietta, you must go to bed at once."

She had had her sign. He didn't want her, and he never would. The only way to keep him content at Galloway was to marry Lafe Flynn.

She said quietly, "Yes, I must go to bed, Oren. It'll be morning very soon, won't it? My wedding day is already begun." She took the decanter from his hands. "I'll have another in my room. Thank you. Good night."

"Good night, Marietta." There was relief in his voice. He bent his head, pressed a quick empty kiss on her cheek. He watched, she knew, as she went inside.

She drew the curtains on his unmoving shadow. She poured a second glass of sherry to the brim and placed it on the table beside her bed, and when she had settled herself beneath the coverlet, the bed curtains drawn, closing out the world, and the day, too, she drank the wine quickly.

Once again she felt its heat. She lay back against the stack of pillows.

By this time tomorrow her life would be joined to Lafe's, her body would be joined to his.

She tried to imagine his face and form, but she couldn't summon either to mind. It was Oren's image that she saw, Oren's laugh that she heard.

She sank drowsily into sleep, and dreamed of Oren.

The morning bell awakend her.

She was instantly aware of a bustle and stir within the house and without. There were voices, chattering and giggling. There were footsteps near and far. There were bangs and rattles and hammerings.

Her head ached. Her mouth was dry. She lay still against the pillows for a moment. Then, with a mutter of impatience, she flung back the bed curtains and swung her feet to the hooked rug. An open chink in the drapes allowed a single ray of pale sun to enter the room. It lay like a crumpled ribbon on the wall. She looked at it, then with a shrug she went to the window. She drew back the curtains and drapes. The room filled with light.

It was her wedding day.

She went to the table, took a quick sip of sherry from the decanter, and sighed as its warmth touched her.

It was her wedding day.

As she dressed quickly in a morning gown, she looked around the room. Soon it would no longer be hers alone. She would share it with Lafe from the moment they returned from their few days in Jordan House. She kept her eyes resolutely away from the huge wardrobe and chest that Lafe had had brought from his rooms in Darnal by Duveen and the newer servant, only lately arrived from New Orleans.

The two men had brought in the furniture and placed it at her direction. Then they carried in the huge red wooden chest, and unpacked it. The two men had worked quickly, not speaking. Duveen because he couldn't, Moses because he was shy, she supposed. Within moments their chore was done, and they had gone. It was with such ease that Lafe had become a permanent part of her life. And she had willed it so. There was to be no last-minute turning back. She wouldn't change her mind.

She took another quick swallow of sherry from the decanter before she went downstairs.

The last of the carriages had rolled off. The last hoofbeats had faded, and the final chirrups of laughter had drifted across the fields. A stillness lay on Galloway.

Within the big house the lights of the giant chandelier

had been snuffed out. The lamps had been lowered, so that long black shadows lay along the white walls and draped the paintings that hung there.

Now Marietta cast a slow lingering look around the big hall and, smiling, raised her eyes to Lafe. "I'm glad it's over, I think."

"You must be tired. You danced every dance, and a few between."

"How else does one celebrate one's wedding day?"

"There are ways," Lafe said. Then, "Are you ready to go now?"

"I'm ready." She paused, looked carefully around the hall. "There must be something else to do."

"Do you think it's possible?" he asked, laughing softly.

"Ah, well, I did want to see that all was properly disposed of, Lafe. I shouldn't like to think that we returned and were confounded by unbearable litter and confusion. It would be so wrong a way to begin."

"I agree." He took up a lamp, and she saw that there was a tired patience in him that was surely wonderful. "But you've arranged it all," he went on. "We'll not be confounded by any confusion when we return. Wait a minute, and I'll get you a wrap to wear. You look worn to me, Marietta."

"Not worn," she answered. "But I'm sure you're right. I'll need something, won't I?"

"You will indeed, and I'll get it." He left her as she sank to the steps. The white veiling of her headdress made a halo around her head. The silk and pearls of her gown were an armor.

The house was still, scented even now with flowers and wines and the heat of excitement. Lafe smiled at the quick hunger that rose in him as he went to the room that was soon to be his and passed Coraleen's door, not noticing that it was opened a single inch on darkness.

He didn't know that she stood just beyond listening to his footsteps. He didn't know that her face was contorted with

186

the fury that had forced her, hours earlier, to creep away to her quarters. She still wore her pink gown. Now she took it off, having torn the silk and listened to the sound of it, and told herself that it was Marietta's moan of pain. She ripped the flowers from her hair and destroyed them, petal by petal.

She hated them both. Oh, how she hated them! They would pay for what they had done to her. Marietta. Lafe. Somehow, someday, they would pay.

All unaware, Lafe caught up a cloak that Dora had laid out. It was of white silk, quilted and padded. He hurried downstairs.

"Ready?"

"I think so."

He threw the cloak around Marietta's shoulders and held her close, leading her outside. The carriage was lit by two small lanterns and decorated with wreaths of white flowers. The seat cushions were draped with white silk.

He placed her carefully beside him, and took up the reins. Overhead the sky was a dark blue, sprinkled with a brilliance of diamond stars. He felt Marietta shiver, and he drew her close against him. "We'll soon be in Darnal. You'll be warm in your bed."

"Will I be warm, do you think?" she asked dreamily.

"Wait and see." He laughed, but he wondered. Did she doubt that he could keep her warm?

"I'll wait," she whispered.

She sank boneless against his arm, her head tipped back. He thought she had fallen asleep, and then she suddenly cried, "Lafe, Lafe, where are we going?"

"We're going to Jordan House, to our own rooms to sleep," he answered.

"Ah, yes," she murmured, sinking back against his arm again.

When they reached Darnal, he helped her down from the carriage. She trembled, and he said, "You're frightened, Marietta. And there's no need. There's no need at all. Don't you know I'd never hurt you?"

"Frightened?" she asked. "Why, Lafe, how can you think that?" She forced a quick warm smile.

He led her to the door of the suite. "Go in. I'll have a cigar before I join you."

"You're a discerning husband, aren't you?" she asked.

"I love you," he answered, and he left her.

As soon as the door was closed behind him, she ran on tiptoe to the table where she saw the champagne that Mr. Jordan had set out. She breathed deeply of the scent of flowers as she took a long gurgling pull at the wine.

Some of it splashed on her white satin gown, and she brushed at it absently but took another long drink. When she finally set the big bottle down, it was half empty, and at last she was warm again.

All through this, her wedding day, she had kept her uneasiness under control by turning to the sherry decanter, and now to the champagne. She had maintained her pose, her mask of smiling joy, her will itself, by taking quick drinks of wine when no one was looking.

Now, through the shadows, she saw a haze of brightness. She walked slowly through it as she paced the suite. She was Mrs. Lafayette Flynn, and no one could say differently. She had married the most eligible man to come to the county in years. And through that marriage she had made certain that all would be as before.

Galloway would go on, with Oren, and Coraleen until she married, too. And Marietta herself would be mistress there. Lafe had made plain to her that he had no interest in the plantation regardless of the legalities. He would attend to his affairs in town, run the Golden Leaf, see to the warehouse, ride to distant plantations on buying trips. He would take his place at Galloway, of course, but he wouldn't interfere. He would have her, and that was what he wanted. So all would be well. She would no longer fear that Oren would be endangered defending her good name, nor fear that he would leave. For why should he? He would have all that he wanted. And he always would. She would see to that. She would see that he never wanted to leave.

Now she found herself in a gown of the most delicate white lace. She turned slowly, looking around the big room that had been newly decorated for her wedding night.

There were fresh flowers on the mantel. Tall white candles awaited the touch of a flame. The canopy of the bed was of glistening yellow silk, with curtains to match, and an oval rug of braided yellow had been spread beside it.

She smiled slowly. It was all as she'd imagined it. Only she herself was different. She hadn't thought to be giddy on her wedding night. She hadn't supposed that she would have to fight back the desire to burst into raucous laughter.

She lit the candles and reached up to draw the pins from her hair, and outside in the hall she heard Lafe's step.

She turned from the mirror as he opened the door and smiled at her, saying, "I'd thought you'd be in bed by now."

"Oh, no, I've been thinking." She drew out a final pin, and her curls fell free to her waist, shimmering with light. Every night since she had grown up, Aunt Tatie first, bless her heart, and then sweet Dora had helped her with her hair, with the strings and tapes and buttons of her gown. But now she was alone. She plucked at the buttons, but didn't undo them. Instead she went to the settle, patted the place beside her.

"Will you sit down for a little while and talk to me, Lafe?"

"Of course. For as long as you like." He sat next to her, then offered her a glass of brandy. "I thought you might like this."

"I think that perhaps I've had enough sherry, and enough champagne. See the bottle, Lafe? But if you offer me brandy . . ."

"I offer it to you, Marietta."

She accepted the glass he gave her, and watched as he raised his own to his lips, his dark blue eyes smiling at her over it. "To my bride."

189

"And to my husband," she said. The drink was fire, pure clean hot flame, going down her throat. She coughed on it and breathed deeply and heard him laugh aloud.

Blinking back sudden tears, she demanded, "Do you think to poison me, Lafe? That's loathsome stuff, you know."

"I agree," he said. "It's loathsome indeed. But it's the best I could do hereabouts. Someday you'll taste brandy from my father's cellar, and you'll be startled to find what a delight it is."

"You miss your home, don't you?" she asked softly. She leaned back in the settle, feeling the rough cloth through the silkiness of her gown. "Tell me why, Lafe?"

He was intrigued by this new being he saw before him. One who asked questions. One who demanded answers. "Miss my home?" He looked deep into her eyes. "My dear Marietta, how could I? My home is here now. In Darnal. At Galloway, With you. Don't you know that? Most of all it will always be with you."

"Yes," she breathed. A sudden wave of warmth passed over her, a sweet singing began in her veins. She put her hand out to him, and he took it, wrapped it tightly in his strong clasp. "Yes," she repeated. "That's what I want. For you to belong to us."

"For me to think of Galloway as home?" he asked softly. "And what of the rest?"

Now she leaned toward him confidentially. "Oh, yes. For that'll make it all right."

He understood suddenly that the last bit of brandy he had offered her had turned her head. He saw it in the bright softness of her eyes. He saw it in the quick rise and fall of her high curved breasts. He heard it then in the slurred words she uttered as she went on in a tremulous and dreaming whisper.

"Yes, yes," she said. "That'll make it all right. Make Galloway your home, Lafe. Then everything will be perfect. I'll have no fear for Oren any more. And it'll be the way I've always dreamed it would be. We shall live out our lives here. Not here in Jordan House, but in Galloway, together. And be happy, oh, yes, so happy. We will, Lafe, won't we? You'll make us happy, won't you?"

"I shall make *you* happy, Marietta," he said softly. "Believe me, and trust me. That much I can do."

He saw her eyes widen. She cried, "But Lafe, what are you denying me?"

"Listen, my darling. You and I will be happy. That's all I dare promise you."

She stiffened as he drew her closer to him, and he felt it, and a chill began to grow in him. "What do you mean when you say, 'You and I will be happy'?"

"Why, Marietta, surely you understand." He was watching her now, his eyes narrowed, a sharpness in him that he didn't want to acknowledge. "One day Coraleen will marry, I should think. And, of course, Oren will, too. And then it'll be the two of us, won't it? Then we shall be our own family."

She closed her eyes against his searching look. "No," she whispered. "No, Lafe. That's not how I planned it. Not at all. Oren won't marry. He won't go away. Why should he? He'll have all that he wants here, here, at Galloway with me. I shall see to that."

"He won't have everything that a man wants, Marietta." Lafe's eyes had narrowed. His voice was cool, but there was a tightness in his face.

"Yes, yes, he will," she insisted. "I promise you that I'll see he's content."

"Can you?" Lafe asked. His voice was very deep, rough. "Can you, Marietta? You forget that Oren's a man, and not a child. A man, Marietta. One day he'll want a woman, a wife. Soon he'll forget Sara and find someone else who pleases him. And when he does, you must let him go, you know."

She sat up straight, her spine rigid, her head flung back. The walls of the room seemed to shimmer, fading away into some hazy distance. She braced herself, but the floor beneath her feet seemed to sway. "Let Oren go?" she whispered.

"Why, no, Lafe! No!" She shook her head back and forth like a small stubborn child refusing to give up a well-loved doll. "Never, never, never, Lafe. Why, since the first I saw Oren I loved him. He came down out of the carriage after my father. I was watching from the front window. I ran out and flung myself down the gallery steps and into my father's arms, and he hugged me and kissed me, and over his shoulder I saw Oren standing there. And I knew then what the future must be. And at that same moment, Coraleen came flying and dragged at my father's coat tails, and he took her into his arms, too, while Oren smiled at me."

Listening, Lafe hardened himself against hurt. She didn't know what she was saying in her brandy-slurred voice. She certainly didn't know what she was telling him so openly. *In vino veritas*, he thought. Well, perhaps. But there were many truths, and many ways of looking at them. He wondered if she would remember her words by morning, and what she would make of them then.

"I knew," she went on, whispering hoarsely, "that I would love him forever and ever. And I knew that someday, if only I waited long enough, he would love me, too. It was that which sustained me all these years, Lafe. It hasn't been easy. There have been . . . there have been frightening moments. And then, when my father died . . ." She swallowed, breathed deeply, a shadow passing over her face. "It was so strange that he died as he did. Such a lot has happened since . . . Only the three of us left. Oren, and Coraleen, and me."

"And now there are four of us," he said lightly. A grim smile flickered on his mouth. Here was an irony to amuse him indeed. Some deep-grained honesty within her had required that they begin their lives with no secrets between them. He wished that she had held her tongue. For whether she remembered her words or not, he knew that he would. He got to his feet. "You must ready yourself for bed, Marietta. You're a great deal more tired than you realize."

"Oh, no," she cried, though her shoulders sagged now, and

her eyes were glazed. "No, I'm not tired. I like talking to you." And then, with a little-girl giggle, "The truth is, I can't move, Lafe. Something is gone wrong with my arms and legs. I can't move. And I shan't be able to undo my gown."

He picked her up easily, carried her to the bed.

Her slender body was light, warm. Her heat spread to him. He laid her against the pillows and turned her and undid the long row of pearl buttons. He eased the gown from beneath her and then over her head. She sighed deeply as he carefully drew off the many layers of shifts beneath her crinolines, the lace-trimmed camisole that covered her breasts. She sighed again and snuggled her cheek to his hand when he brushed the soft silken curls from her forehead.

When he left her side, she murmured wordlessly, but didn't stir.

He listened to her breathing as he stood at the window and looked into the dark, smoking a small cigar that was bitter to his taste. When he flung it away, it fell in an arc of bright embers that winked out one by one in the shadows below. He watched them die, as if each were a dream he relinquished unwillingly. At last he turned back to the room.

When he lay down beside her, she started and opened her eyes wide. "Lafe?"

He didn't speak. He couldn't. During the past moments the haze of brandy had left her. She had whispered his name, and no other's. Whatever had been hidden in her heart before would be hidden away again. There would be no one between them in this bed. It seemed to him that he had waited all his life to possess her. And now, even knowing how she had used him, he wanted her still, and knew he would want her forever.

He leaned over her, pressed his lips to hers, his arms tightly enfolding her, and made her his.

BOOK TWO

14

Lafe put a warm hand on her shoulder. "I'll say goodbye for a few hours, Marietta."

She raised her cheek for his kiss. Instead he brushed his lips lightly across hers and straightened up, a smile slanting his mouth.

She glanced quickly at Oren. He seemed not to have noticed, but Coraleen chuckled. "Three months wed, and still so passionate."

Lafe's smile became a teasing grin. He managed it with an effort. He used it to cover what had become, in these past months, an intense dislike of Coraleen. He believed now that the suspicions he had harbored against her after Marietta's strange attack of illness, and then Aunt Tatie's sudden death, were unjustified. Though he had watched her carefully, he'd seen nothing to suggest that he could have been right. But he had come to feel that she was spoiled and immature, undisciplined in her nature and disrespectful to her elders. Her affected and flirtatious ways with him were no longer amusing, but irritated him.

Marietta sensed his feeling and said in quick reproof, "Coraleen, you're too forward."

"But a man may kiss his wife." Coraleen pouted. "And if he does, why not remark on it?"

Oren said absently, "Coraleen, hush," and then, to Lafe, "You'll be in the warehouse today?"

"Yes. There, or at Jordan House."

"I'd like to stop in and see you. Would it be convenient in an hour or two?"

Lafe nodded, smiled again at Marietta, and left the room.

"My, I do like to see a man work hard," Coraleen said. "The hours Lafe keeps . . . and for a newly married man, too."

But Marietta ignored her. "Oren, you're going to town?"

"As you heard, Marietta."

"Letty mentioned that Jed Blandish was coming. Have you forgotten? Surely you don't want to miss him."

"Letty mentioned it to you?" Oren demanded. "Or did you ask her when he expected to see me?"

She was startled by the heat in his voice, but she said only, "Why should I do that, Oren?"

"I don't like this dealing behind my back, Marietta. Either I'm responsible for Galloway, or I'm not."

"You know you are," she said hastily. "I'll explain to Mr. Blandish when he comes."

"Thank you. You may tell him I'll see him tomorrow."

Marietta nodded, beginning to wonder what Oren wanted to discuss with Lafe. But she felt that she'd asked enough questions.

Coraleen, however, wasn't concerned with delicacy. "What's this special visit to Lafe about?" she demanded. "You see him at breakfast, sometimes at dinner, always at supper. Why can't you talk to him then?"

"I prefer to do business in a business place."

"And what business do you have with Lafe, I'd like to know?"

"I'd like to discuss an investment with him. Who better than my own brother-in-law could advise me?"

Coraleen hooted. "Investments with what? You don't have anything."

"I have my third," he said. "Just as you have yours."

"And you think Lafe'll help you double or triple it?" Now there was no mockery in her voice. "How would he?"

"I don't know, Coraleen. That's what I want to ask him."

"Then ask him for me as well. I could surely do with a windfall." She smiled sweetly at Marietta. "As generous as

198

you are to me, my dear sister, and no one would ever deny it, there's always a need for more."

"Cash money isn't easy to come by these days," Marietta answered. "I don't see how Lafe could help either of you." She drew a deep breath, trying to restrain herself. But then she burst out, "And besides, what do you lack? You have a beautiful home, all the clothes you could wear in a lifetime, food, and servants, and friends. What do you lack?"

"I," Coraleen said, "would like to have a small surrey of my own. So I could go about when I want to."

"Then you'll have it," Marietta promised. "Why not?" She looked expectantly at Oren.

But he said nothing. He refused to name any material thing that he desired. Of such goods there was plenty, as she said. It was something else that he yearned for. He wouldn't say it to her. She would never understand. To be a whole man, to be looked up to, to have independence, these were what he wanted. What he wanted now. Since he could no longer have Sara, Marietta could provide him with nothing important to him.

"You don't mind my talking to Lafe, do you?" he asked her at last.

"Why, no. Why should I?"

Oren got to his feet, dropped his napkin to the table. "Then I'll do it," he said.

Marietta absently picked up his napkin. She smoothed it carefully, rolled it into a neat cylinder, then slipped it into the silver ring marked with an ornately engraved "O." Unaware of the tenderness of the gesture, she laid it at Oren's place and looked away.

Coraleen was staring at her.

"We must remember to have a napkin ring made and inscribed for Lafe," she said.

"Indeed we must," Coraleen agreed dryly. "It surprises me that it's one thing you didn't remember to do before the wedding."

"It surprises me, too," Marietta answered.

"Did you mean it about the surrey?" Coraleen asked.

"You know I did. I'll speak to Mr. Blandish when he comes."

Coraleen jumped to her feet, hugged Marietta tightly, and whispered, "You're the dearest sister in the world." But the words were meaningless to her. Inside she fumed. Marietta thought to buy her affection and loyalty with a surrey. One day she'd dearly pay for thinking she could, Coraleen told herself as she left Marietta alone, still tenderly stroking Oren's napkin ring.

It was difficult to understand him, she thought. He could speak to Lafe at any time, yet he must do it now, today, just when he should have met with Mr. Blandish. And why had he believed she was interfering just because she mentioned the appointment with the overseer? Uneasily considering that, Marietta wondered if there was something he was hiding from her. Something like the renewed note about which she had learned only through Marcus. Well, by autumn it would be paid off. But why was Oren so touchy?

There was a hum of bees at the window. They swooped over the camellia hearts, sucking out sweet June nectar. It seemed a long time now since the day in late March when she and Lafe had been married. She had not, in that time, had an instant's regret for the decision she'd made. There were moments, though few and far between, when she confessed to herself that she wondered if it was the same for him. She sensed a certain reticence in him, a withholding. She could put no name to it, nor did she try. They were husband and wife, which was all that mattered to her, and she tried to be to him what he wanted. Of her wedding night she remembered only a little. The ride through the darkness, stars agleam overhead. His arm holding her tight to his side. The glow of lights in Jordan House. The champagne in the room that had been redone just for her. She could hear her own voice saying, "I've had enough sherry, and enough champagne," and her own laughter. She remembered accepting the brandy he offered her. After that . . . Warm hands at her breasts, fingers as delicate as butterflies caressing her nipples. A growing liquid heat that spread through her limbs and finally singed her when arms with muscles of iron clasped her tightly. She remembered a second of swift and penetrating pain, and then a long soaring sweetness of pulses drumming. A sudden lifting glory that brought a cry to her lips, and she knew, certainly, that she had shouted, "Oh, Lafe . . . Lafe . . ." before she fell into sleep.

When she awakened, he was leaning on an elbow looking down at her. She had a moment of alarm to see sadness in his face, and said, whispering, with a blush burning her cheeks, "Lafe, what's wrong? Do I disappoint you?" His dark blue eyes had gleamed at her as he answered, "No, no," and took her into his arms again.

There was by now no part of each other's bodies that they didn't know. He must be pleased with her. She must be the wife he wanted, as she had determined to be. Yet she felt the restraint in him, and knew it was there, and didn't understand it.

Now with a last look at his crumpled napkin, a second reminder that she must have a silver ring for him, she rose and went through the covered walkway to the kitchen, where Needle and Beedle were giggling with Dora, to discuss the menus for the next two nights with Essie.

Lafe sat with his boots on the desk, his chair tilted back on two legs, his head wreathed with cigar smoke.

Duveen was hardly inside when he tapped his right wrist urgently.

Immediately Lafe put down his cigar. "What's the matter?"

Duveen pointed with a thick finger at the gallery doors.

Lafe went to look out and saw Moses below. He stood with his head down, his hands hanging at his sides, while Eamus Jordan harangued him.

Lafe started outside, but Duveen caught his arm and offered him a note. WE NEED TO HURRY. THE COUNTY LINE. MOSES KNOWS.

Lafe nodded, went quickly into the yard. But even from

there he heard Eamus' raised voice. "You're not to do it. I've spoken to you before. Talking the word of God around as if you'd a right to it. I've had complaints from my guests. They don't want their people contaminated. Yes, that's what I said, contaminated by your ideas. So you stop it, or I'll have a word with Mr. Flynn." The small plump man was red-faced. His spectacles were steamy and askew on his nose.

Lafe, looming up behind him, asked softly, "What's this now, Mr. Jordan? Do you want a word with me about my Moses here?"

"Moses! That's another thing," Eamus Jordan grumbled. "Moses!" He raised his eyes to heaven. "I ask you, what kind of a name is that?"

"Moses? Why, Mr. Jordan, surely you read your Bible. Surely you know who Moses is."

"And that's why I ask . . ."

Lafe smiled thinly. "Moses is the name given this man by his previous master. If you've a quarrel with it, then I suggest you go down to New Orleans and take it up with him. This man was baptized Moses, has been called Moses all his life, and Moses he shall remain. As long as he wants to, and as long as I own him."

Eamus shifted his weight uncomfortably. "Now, Mr. Flynn, that's not my complaint." He swung irritably on the small black man. "Tell him. You say what this is all about."

"Yes, sir," Moses said, and stopped.

"Well?" Eamus demanded. "Well, what about it? Are you going to tell him or not?"

"I read a passage out, Mr. Lafe. To a girl back in the kitchen. She'd lost her babe a couple of weeks back, and I saw her crying for it."

Duveen had said there was an emergency at the county line, and Moses knew about it. Lafe decided to waste no more time. He dropped a hand on Moses' shoulder. "You come inside with me." And moving away, his hand still holding Moses, he said to Eamus, "You needn't worry. I doubt a passage from the Bible will spoil a kitchen girl for you."

Mr. Jordan trotted beside them, saying quickly, "Oh, I know it won't. But this man talks of salvation and freedom, and I don't know what else when I'm not there to overhear him. It's close to sedition."

Lafe grinned at him. "Mr. Jordan, are you telling me that our Bible, the one you and I were both raised by, is seditious?"

A wave of red suffused Eamus' face. "You realize that I'm not, sir. *We* understand. But for the slaves to hear such ideas—"

"I'll see to it," Lafe said firmly. "And now, if you'll do me the favor of seeing to something for me? I should like a box lunch for four at once. At once, mind you. I'm off in less than half an hour. Some cold chicken, if you please, and ham, and I'll have a carafe of wine with it, and whatever fruit you can manage for me."

"Chicken, Mr. Flynn, and ham. And we've plenty of fruit," Eamus murmured, completely diverted. "And what of a cobbler? They're just fresh from the oven. And by the time you're ready to eat—"

"Fruit cobbler it is," Lafe agreed. He hustled Moses up the steps and into the suite, the grin dropping off his face. "What is it? What's this Duveen wants me to find out from you?"

"I had word. There was trouble. I don't know what kind for sure. But it's just over the county line. We have three men coming through, and they can't make it the way the roads are watched. I think, and Duveen thinks, too, we'd better go."

"Duveen and I will. But not you."

"I want to go with you."

"No, Moses. You have to be at the warehouse."

"Let Duveen, then."

A low grumble came from Duveen's chest. His eyes flashed. He was saying that it was his job to ride with Lafe. He always had. No small Moses was going to take his place.

Lafe didn't look at the big man. He told Moses, "As you know, you're specially fitted to be at the warehouse. To keep an eye on whoever comes in, while you do the bookkeeping for me. And being nimble with your tongue, you'll know what to say if anyone asks after me."

"What will I say?"

"I was called away to Raleigh on sudden business. I'll be back as quickly as I can, or will send word if I'm delayed."

Moses nodded, sighed. "Should I go now?"

"Right now," Lafe answered, and bent over the table to take out his gun.

They drove the horses hard through the empty roads, circled the few small hamlets on byways that were hardly passable.

They had a quick meal as they went, and not long after midday they rode sedately into Digleytown. Its single road was somnolent and empty under a still high and hot sun, but when they tied up the wagon, a small boy appeared from around the corner of a tavern.

"I won't be long," Lafe said. "You wait."

Duveen nodded. He tipped his hat forward and appeared to close his eyes.

Lafe smiled to himself. It was Duveen's way of watching.

He gave both horses quick pats as he passed them, and winked at the small boy who stood staring at him.

"You from the patrol?" the boy asked.

"What patrol is that?"

"The one looking for those runaways," the boy said. "They been through here three times already."

"Haven't found them yet, is that it?"

"Nope. They haven't. But they will."

"And how do you know that?"

"There's so many of them. When there's that many, they're bound to get them. That's what my dad says."

"I expect your dad's right."

The small boy nodded solemnly. "My dad's always right. And he says we've got to fight. We've got to kill."

"That so?" Lafe asked.

"Else we'll lose everything," the boy went on. And now his eyes were wide and questioning. "Everything."

Lafe rumpled the blond head. "Well, before you fight, you've got to figure out who your enemy is, don't you?" With that, he went into the tavern.

It was empty but for a man behind the small bar, and a single customer. Both leaned on their elbows and drank ale.

Lafe greeted them, then said, "It seems quiet enough in Digleytown. I'd heard there was trouble here."

"That's why it's quiet. Everybody's home where they belong, making sure nobody's hanging around their places, nor stealing any more stuff from them. Everybody else is out beating the bushes," the bartender answered.

The other man took a long swig from his mug, then wiped his mouth with his left hand. The right sleeve of his coat was tucked into his pocket. "Everybody but me, that is," he said dryly. "And I'm sitting here minding my own business. Which is what, I might add," he went on with slow deliberation, "I believe that people should do."

Lafe grinned at him. "I expect, sir, that I seem to ask many questions."

"Not seem, if you don't mind."

"I'm here to help," Lafe answered. "So if you'll direct me—"

"I'll direct you to hell," the one-armed man replied. "Somebody stole a few chickens because he was hungry. I don't hold with hanging a man for that."

The bartender said quickly, "Mr. Ridgeway, you know you don't believe in letting slaves run from their masters."

"Don't I?" the one-armed man said menacingly.

"Now then," the tavernkeeper said, with an anxious look at Lafe. "Jonathan Ridgeway, you and I are old friends, and I understand you. But this gentleman here, he's from other parts—"

"Oh, go on," the one-armed man growled. "Go kill the niggers. What do I care? It's on your head what you do."

The tavernkeeper winced, drew Lafe outside. The small boy raised his head. "Hiyah, Dad."

"Run and play, Jimmy," his father answered. And when the boy looked downcast, "Go in and keep Mr. Ridgeway company. Pass him another mug of ale for me, and mind you, don't taste it first."

The boy dashed into the tavern.

His father said uneasily, "Don't pay him any mind, mister. The one inside, I mean. Since he lost that arm of his, he's so bitter he doesn't care what he says."

"How'd he lose it?" Lafe asked.

The man shrugged. "It's got nothing to do with you. You asked after the patrol. Follow the road out until you see a grove of three tall pines and, just past it, a logging mill. Across that same meadow is where they're looking. But, I tell you, when it gets dark, they'll come in." He nodded earnestly. "And I'll be ready for them, because they'll surely be ready for me."

Lafe thanked the man, made his farewell, and climbed on the wagon. He nudged Duveen, who jumped as if stung by a hornet, an action approvingly observed by the tavernkeeper.

Within moments, Digleytown, still quiet in the hot sun, was left behind. Within moments more, they had made the right turn and spotted the pines and the mill beyond.

"We'd better be careful," Lafe said. Duveen nodded at that. "We'll separate here. I'll drive on and join the patrol. Duveen, you go on on foot. Two hours after sunset, or as close to that as you can, draw the patrol off. I'll help you from my end however I can. When you meet your people, get them well hidden and find me at these pines." Duveen nodded. "You understand?" Duveen gave him a wide grin.

He slipped from the wagon, disappeared silently into the brush, which accepted his big body without a ripple of movement.

Lafe drove on, humming softly. He could plan no further than this for a time.

Long before he was able to see the fifteen men, he heard the sounds of them. There was the clump of horses' hooves, the snorts and whinnies of excited animals. There were the shouted exchanges, some questioning, some profane remarks. Familiar sounds he had expected. Yet something was missing. He listened, puzzled. And then he knew. As backdrop to all the other noise he should have heard the baying, snarling, yelping of hounds. It would be good if there were none, but it seemed an unlikely prospect.

He was still humming when he rode slowly up to the group, having hailed it first from a safe distance. He shoved back his hat, lounging on the seat, and said at large, "I guess you've not found what you're looking for. To judge by the oaths I've heard this last half hour."

"And who the hell are you?" a heavyset man demanded.

Lafe introduced himself, smiling, and added, "I heard of the trouble when I was driving through. I thought I'd come out to see."

"Not much to see," one of the mounted men grumbled. "Or else we'd not be riding in circles."

"Is there a lot on these niggers' heads?" Lafe asked.

"There won't be anything on their heads when we get through with them," the big man retorted. He jerked his thumb at the thick trees that surrounded the searchers. "There's a whole band of runaways inside there. They don't know how to live, and they steal and scavenge whatever they can get. We're going to drag them out, burn them out if we have to. Some way we'll get shut of them for good."

"I thought there were only three, or was it four?" Lafe observed.

"By now they've joined with the others."

"And do you have tracks or sign to follow?"

"Not yet. But we'll have them soon."

"I'll help if you'll allow me," Lafe offered. "I'm not in a hurry to be on my way."

"I don't know why you'd bother when it's not your own trouble."

Lafe grinned. His dark blue eyes were bright. "A bit of hunt is good for the liver, I find."

"As you please." The big man shrugged. "Another pair of eyes, and another gun, won't hurt, I guess. Though I doubt they'll help either."

Lafe fell in, asking, "You don't have dogs?"

"They'll be coming up soon."

Lafe concealed his disappointment. He nodded. "They'll make the difference."

"They'd better," the big man grumbled. He rode ahead of the wagon, the other horsemen bunching around it.

But soon they were strung out along the narrow trail, riding away from it, then circling back.

In the distance there was the baying of the hounds. Very quickly they came leaping and snarling through the brush, changing the tempo of the hunt. They pressed ahead, dodging, circling. They ran, muzzles close to the earth, ears flat, and eyes gleaming.

The men followed after, quickened with excitement now.

Soon the dogs set up a great howl and dodged off the narrow track and down a small embankment. There, on a thorny bush, a small scrap of cotton cloth hung like a blue pennant. The hounds charged it, snarling.

The heavyset man grinned his satisfaction. "Oh, yes, we're heading right. They're somewhere about. We've as good as got them."

The words were an echo of Lafe's thoughts. The scrap of fabric was of the cheap sort used for slaves' garments.

He imagined shadowy faceless men, listening to the yelps of the beasts, the voices of the hunters. He imagined them frozen in dread, and perhaps exchanging long silent desperate looks.

He whipped his horses to a faster pace and drove on briskly.

A mockingbird chattered an angry warning from the limb of a pine tree. The air was hot, bringing out a film of sweat on the flushed faces of the men. Mosquitoes swarmed in for fresh blood. Slowly the hounds circled and circled again, and the men's elation faded.

The sun set, and dark fell. Shadows thickened around the trees. The meadows turned dim and black as midnight seas. Neither stars nor moon pricked the skies, with light.

They rode more quietly now, with less conversation, fewer oaths. Against the hush of the forest, the rattle of the wagon wheels, the thud of the horses' hooves, and the panting of the dogs were loud and threatening.

Lafe imagined men crouching, watching as the hunters passed, breaths held, heartbeats suspended.

The dogs slowed but kept moving.

At one point Lafe thought he saw a second scrap of cloth. He said nothing. The dogs trotted by. A horseman trampled the scrap into the dust.

Gradually the searchers' ranks thinned. From fifteen their number dwindled to ten, and then to seven. Lafe made no comment, but enjoyed his delight that the odds were changing more and more in his favor.

At a tall point of rocks the men stopped to confer. Lafe passed them by, then drew up to wait.

"The hounds have lost it," the heavyset man growled. "They don't know where they're going."

"Give them a while longer," another rider answered.

There was a grumble of agreement.

Lafe drove on. Suddenly, the dogs streaked ahead. The men raced around him, following. A curtain of dust rose up behind the flailing pounding beat of hooves. A thunder of sound seemed to explode the hush of the forest.

Lafe, well behind now, saw the faint shadowy movement among the slim trunks of the trees. He squinted to look and caught the movement as it ended.

For a single instant he stared into a thin dark face. Dark eyes, burning with fear, met his own head on. It was as if the man were impaled on his glance. He waved once, quickly, and then rolled by. When he looked back, the man was gone.

He rose, whipped the horses, and when they broke into a

fast gait, the rumbling of the wagon wheels covered all sounds of movement in the brush.

It was soon after that he noticed the first faint drift of smoke, but again he made no comment.

A horse whinnied as the wind stirred the leaves of the trees. The heavyset man reared up in his stirrups, and then shouted angrily, "Look! Look over that way. The sky's red, isn't it?"

Lafe peered upward and agreed loudly that indeed the sky was red, and now he observed, loudly still, that he believed he smelled smoke, and would stake his life on it that there was a barn burning somewhere, though on whose property he couldn't say.

One of the men peeled off. "I'm taking the dogs with me," he cried. "They'll do me more good than they'll do you here." He disappeared into the darkness. Soon even the baying of the hounds was gone.

"We'd better see," the heavyset man said suddenly. "Maybe the ones we want are there."

Shouted agreement came from all sides. The six remaining men swung off with one accord, and Lafe turned his wagon to race after them, thinking that Duveen had done his work well, and now he, Lafe, must make certain that the risk had been worth while.

For a single instant he sensed watching eyes, a stillness that touched him as if it were a warning sound. He imagined an unmoving shadow just beyond the range of his vision. He cracked his whip loudly and shouted wordlessly, as if the elation of the hunt had overcome him.

He drove hard until he saw ahead of the racing men a narrow wooden bridge. He could hear the rush of the stream below, but couldn't see it. Then, whipping his horses, he yelled, "Hey, wait. Something in the creek. Something moving." He jerked off the track, circling hard as the brush closed around him.

The men swung behind him to follow, yelping signals at each other, and soon had circled and passed him, plunging deeper into the darkness.

He turned the wagon about, went back to the bridge at the best speed he could whip from the horses. He started across, and halfway, he hauled hard on the reins. The horses fought him, rearing and straining, but they obeyed finally. The wagon swung sideways, clamped wheels hooking between the two railings.

When the six men came galloping up in rampaging confusion, he was calmly releasing the team.

"What the hell happened?" the heavyset man demanded.

Lafe gave a disgusted shake of his head, gestured at the stuck wagon, and led the horses off the bridge.

"There was no sign back there," the man went on, breathing hard.

Lafe gave him a tight-lipped grin. "When I was fighting my stupid animals, I hadn't much mind for anything else. But I have a feeling something moved below, downstream."

"Why didn't you say so?" the leader cried. "Downstream, damn it! Let's go."

But another shouted, "Hell with it! I'm going to see about the fire," and plunged off into the dark.

The others exchanged silent looks and followed.

Alone, Lafe paused to wipe the sweat from his face. Then he took the bridge railings out, led the horses back, and hooked them up. Very soon after he was on the way to the three pines.

He sat over breakfast in the Digleytown tavern.

His boots were dusty, his fawn trousers streaked with stains of drying mud, but his russet hair lay neatly in place, and his eyes were bright. He had enjoyed himself, and it showed in his humor and his face.

Big Duveen leaned against the wall behind him, close by the window so he could watch the wagon, which was now stacked with cut logs.

Lafe sipped his steaming coffee and shook his head at the tavernkeeper. "No, they didn't have any luck. At least not while I was with them. Of course, I don't know what happened after. But of all of us, I think my own luck was worse.

My wagon's damaged, and I don't know what it'll cost to have it repaired. And I still can't figure out how it happened."

"There's snakes in that stream, bad ones," the small boy said, and yawned widely. "Maybe your horses knew it and got scared."

"Maybe," Lafe agreed thoughtfully. "I never saw them act that way before. But anyway, your men went off without me. So I don't know how they made out. I had to free the wagon, and that wasn't easy, believe me, and then I lost my way coming back. It took me so long that I'm surprised your men didn't return first."

"They had the barn to look after. Not that they could do much," the tavernkeeper said dryly, "since it was nearly burned to the ground when they got there."

"Oh? A pity! How do you know that?"

"Mr. Ridgeway rode out to see," the small boy said. "He wanted to know what was going on."

Lafe finished his meal, dropped a coin on the table to pay for it, and rose. "Tavernkeeper, I thank you, but now I must be on my way. I'd hoped to wait for your friends to hear the news, but it's growing late. So give them my good wishes, will you?"

The tavernkeeper nodded. His son trailed Lafe and Duveen outside, stood watching while they both got into the wagon, and then waved them off, yawning again.

Half a mile out of town Duveen heard the sound of approaching horses. He glanced sideways at Lafe.

"I believe we've seen enough of that bunch," Lafe told him.

Duveen pulled at the reins. The wagon rolled off the track and into the brush. Lafe hunched down, his hand on his gun, while Duveen held the horses to keep them still.

The group of slave hunters swept by, shouting among themselves. When silence had fallen, Lafe and Duveen resumed their ride. They had covered two miles when Lafe said, "You gave them the food? I heard they were hungry."

Duveen nodded.

"All three made it?"

Duveen turned his head to look at Lafe, and from his throat there came a deep rumbling chuckle.

15

Oren leaned back, crossed his long legs, and said reassuringly, "I'm sure you needn't fret, Marietta."

A small frown marked her brow. She braided her fingers together, and then separated them. She moved her slender feet in an impatient dance beneath the fringe of her gown. Finally she got up and went to the gallery doors. Looking out into the dark, she murmured, "But it's very odd, Oren. Lafe said nothing to me about such a trip, as you know. And he was gone all night last night, all day today. And he's still not returned."

"I agree that it's odd. But I'm sure there's a sensible explanation. Moses was vague. And for all that Lafe says he's so well trained with the books that he couldn't do without the man, I don't think Moses has much sense in his head."

Oren had arrived in town early the day before and stopped by Jordan House to learn from Eamus that Lafe had departed, taking box lunches. Puzzled, Oren had gone to the warehouse.

There he'd been greeted by Moses, who peered at him expressionlessly over a big ledger until, probably in response to Oren's grimace of irritation, the black man reluctantly remembered to rise to his feet and ask, "Can I help you, sir?"

"I'm looking for Mr. Lafe. He expects me."

"He had to go away," Moses answered. " A message came. He went to Raleigh, I think. He said if he's delayed he'll send word somehow."

Oren shrugged, turned away, stifling his resentment. "I suppose he forgot he had an appointment with me."

"He didn't say."

Now Marietta turned from the dark gallery doors. "Lafe knows Moses better than you do, Oren. It's for him to decide." Then, with a sound of annoyance, "If only I knew what it is. Nearly two nights! Where has he gone? Why?"

"He can take care of himself," Oren told her. "You've no need to be concerned."

She knew Oren was right, yet her uneasiness refused to subside. In the months since their marriage, Lafe had never been away overnight. He had taken any number of day trips, it was true, in the course of his affairs. Often he was gone from sunup until well after sundown. Yet she had always known him to be close by. At one of the plantations. In Darnal. Off to Durham's Station. But now he'd gone to Raleigh, it appeared.

She'd scarcely slept the night before, so conscious was she of the width of the bed, its great expanse of emptiness without his large warm bulk to fill it.

And then, along with her concern for Lafe, she had had the troubling interview with Jed Blandish on her mind. She hadn't yet mentioned it to Oren. Knowing how he'd resent her questions and dreading it, she wanted to think it all over first.

She had been waiting for Jed Blandish when she overheard Needle and Beedle, crouched in the bushes below the window, doing their weeding chores.

"You'd better do it right," Needle said threateningly. "You know what Mama said. If you're bad, Miss Marietta's going to send you down to the fields. And you'll be hungry like the hands are."

Beedle smugly answered, "Mama's teasing."

"They *are* hungry, 'cause the ration's cut. I know it."

"Miss Marietta won't make us field hands," Beedle answered. "She won't."

"But Mr. Oren would."

215

She wanted to lean out and cry, What nonsense, boys! Nobody's hungry at Galloway! But she heard Elisha admit the overseer. She went quickly into the hall. "Oh, Mr. Blandish, Mr. Henderson had to go into town. He'll see you in a day or so."

A look of relief passed over Jed Blandish's face. He turned away quickly.

"But please come in for a moment," Marietta went on. "I must speak to you."

Jed Blandish followed her silently into the morning room. He gave a single glance at the portrait of her father, wishing the man were still alive, and then cast his eyes down, waiting.

Marietta asked, "Is everything going as it should be, Mr. Blandish?"

"Mr. Henderson has told me I'm to talk to him about business affairs, Miss Garvey."

"Indeed? I believe I've heard that once too often."

He raised his head and looked at her. He hadn't expected that nor hoped for that. Ever since Mr. Garvey died, she'd been under Oren's thumb. Letty insisted that now she was married it would be different. He himself hadn't believed it. Now he began to think she was right. But it made his situation no easier.

She sat looking at him, not knowing how to begin. What she had heard beyond the window frightened her. Children such as Needle and Beedle repeated only what they had heard the adults around them say. Were conditions so bad that Oren was actually skimping on food? She could hear the echo of her father's dictum: Hungry men can't work. Her heart clenched within her. She knew that behind that practical conviction there was a more important one. It was wicked to starve those who were dependent on you for sustenance. At last she said, "I don't mean to interfere, of course, Mr. Blandish, but I'd like you to leave the books with me. I wish to go over them."

"Mr. Henderson . . ."

Her eyes glittered. Her voice sharpened. "Mr. Blandish, I'll deal with Mr. Henderson myself."

Jed hid his relief. The matter was out of his hands. He offered her the ledgers, saying, "These begin with the first of the year."

"Thank you," she answered, and went on so smoothly that at first he didn't understand her. "And now, Mr. Blandish, I'll ask you to do me a favor. Will you ride home and return at once with some older ledgers? Go back two or three years, will you?"

"I will, Miss Garvey." He hurried out. Returning half an hour later, he didn't go in, but left the ledgers with Elisha to be handed to Marietta. She wouldn't need him, he told himself. She was a clever woman, and she would understand the figures and what they said without any explanation from him. Besides, he was convinced now that Letty was right. Mr. Flynn must be the one asking the questions. It had always seemed unnatural to Jed that the man had ignored Galloway's affairs. Now Jed began to understand. He believed, with his wife, that the questions Miss Garvey raised were actually Mr. Flynn's questions. As far as Jed was concerned, Lafe Flynn's interest was all to the good.

But his assumption was wrong. Marietta had no help. She studied the figures and they told her only that there was trouble, but not where the trouble was. She went over them several times, then began a comparison with the ledgers that had been in use when her father was alive.

She saw first that in this past January prices on every item were much higher than they had been in the year 1858. She saw that footages of lumber for roofing had been delivered, and she recalled that new roofs hadn't been put on the slave quarters. Several hours of study sharpened her understanding of the pattern. She knew she must discuss it with Oren at once.

Now was as good a time as any would be. And though she tried to frame the words, she found that she couldn't. Her eyes strayed again to the window.

Where was Lafe? Why hadn't he returned last night? Why hadn't he sent word? She dreaded the long hours that lay ahead.

217

Oren yawned, rose to his feet. "I think you should go to bed, Marietta. You'll not bring him home more quickly by staring out the window."

"In a little while," she answered.

"Then, if you'll excuse me."

"Of course, Oren." And, "But what of Coraleen? Isn't she home yet?"

"You're like a mother hen. No, Marietta. Coraleen's staying over at the Beckwiths'. I forgot to mention it."

He went slowly upstairs, a grim smile on his narrow lips. Once Marietta had waited up for him. Oren was delighted with the change in the focus of her attention. It was a relief, and it made what he did all that much easier. Not that he wanted to do it, he thought sullenly. Her intransigence forced him to it, led him deeper and deeper into a situation he could never admit to her.

He was sound asleep when the quiet hoofbeats came slowly up the track, moved under the live oaks, and proceeded to the house.

While Duveen went back to the cabin he shared with Moses, Lafe spoke softly to the barking dogs to quiet them.

Then he went inside. He had had a long hard ride, and showed it. His usually elegant clothes were wrinkled and dust-covered. His russet beard was rough on his cheeks. He started up the steps, saw the glimmer of the lamp in the morning room, and peered into it.

Marietta was curled in a big chair, her chin resting on her hand, the line of her shoulders soft and rounded.

It was all he could do to keep from sweeping her into his arms. He said quietly, "Marietta?"

She jerked upright, her hand flying to her throat. "Oh, Lafe, how you've startled me!"

"Were you asleep with your eyes open?"

"Just musing, I think. But I didn't hear you come in."

"I'd hoped to awaken no one."

She rose slowly. "I was waiting for you. And very troubled. I couldn't imagine what had happened. When you didn't return last night . . ."

"Ah, it was nothing," he said lightly. "And you mustn't worry if I happen to keep strange hours sometimes. You already know that my interests keep me moving."

"But what kept you?"

"As I say, it was nothing. Although I thought it might be. I had a message from Raleigh concerning my latest shipment. The New Orleans people are so unfamiliar with our North Carolina ways. Anyhow, I set off in a hurry, taking a box lunch and Duveen with me. And when we got there I saw that a few words would attend to the problem. I spoke those soon enough, I assure you, and returned as quickly as I could. But still it took time."

The casual words told her nothing of how hard he had ridden to get back to her, flogging the horses so that the wagon fairly flew along the rough tracks, how he had hurried to put the wagon away in Darnal, and saddle his horse for the last gallop to Galloway.

It did take time, too much time, Marietta thought, angry now that the first wave of relief of seeing him safe had passed. But she said nothing of how she felt. Instead she asked coolly if he was hungry, and when he answered that he was, said softly, "Then sit and rest, and I'll bring you a tray."

But he was at her heels when she left the morning room. They went along the covered passageway together, and soon he was sitting at the big worktable while she put cold sliced ham, potato salad, and thick pieces of bread before him.

As she seated herself, he said, "It feels good to be home."

Home, she thought. Oddly, she had never actually considered that this was now his home. She said slowly, "Lafe, is all well with you? Are you comfortably established here? Is there perhaps something I've overlooked that you'd like to have?"

He leaned forward, took her hand. "I have everything I want, Marietta."

There was one thing, though, that he didn't have yet, but he fully intended to. He would have her heart for his own. One day soon now she would awaken to discover that she was in love with her husband, that she had forgotten her childish infatuation for Oren, and learned the love of wife for husband—that single-minded love that left room for no other. But he coudn't speak of it to her. She must learn it for herself, and with no urging, no prompting from him.

She drew her hand away with casual care. There was something in his face that challenged her, yet she couldn't put a name to it. "If you've done . . ."

He rose with her. As they went up the stairs together, he slid an arm around her small waist, drew her close to him, and when they were inside the room, the door closed, the drapes drawn against the night, he pulled the pins that held her hair, and buried his face in the soft silken perfumed mass, and kissed her mouth until it burned with the bruises of love.

He carried her to the bed, and there he held her with the weight of his body, and looked long into her eyes, and then he took her to him with a new intensity of desire.

The clang of the bell awakened her. She lay listening until it faded away. She stretched, smiling. When she turned toward him, she saw that his eyes were open and there was a faint smile on his mouth.

"I thought at first you were still asleep," she said.

He shook his head.

"But why so quiet then?"

"I was considering."

"Considering?" She smoothed the curls from her face, and hunched her shoulders. "You must tell me what you are considering at breakfast."

His arm moved along the pillow and settled around her. He drew her to his chest, holding her tightly against her resistance.

"I should rise now," she whispered.

"And why?"

"I must speak to Oren this morning."

"It'll wait," Lafe answered, his smile broadening.

"I think not."

"He'll still be there if you want to lie abed a little longer."

"I suppose, but I'd like to see him before he rides out."

"The longer you protest, the longer your brother will have to forgo the pleasure of your company."

She frowned, opened her mouth to argue, then suddenly she laughed. "Ah, Lafe, I don't put the plantation before my husband. If you want my company, you need only say so."

"Say so," Lafe repeated softly. Then, "Perhaps I should prefer that *you* want *my* company."

"But I do. Whatever do you mean?"

"Right now. At this moment. So that you can think of nothing else?"

"There's a time for everything. The wake-up bell has rung. The fires are all alight. It's broad day of a summer morning. We've things to do, both of us, many things."

"I know," he said soberly. "But I don't care. Then why do you?"

She put her head on his shoulder, whispered, moving her lips against the warm bare flesh, "I suppose I don't."

But at that moment, Oren spoke beyond the door. They could hear his words clearly as he said, "I'll kill those two half hands if the dogs are in the oleanders again. I'll wear the skins right off their backs."

"Mr. Oren," Elisha answered, "the dogs ain't in the bushes. They're in the side yard, and Needle and Beedle are in the kitchen where they belong."

"You're always protecting the little devils, Elisha. You spoil them as bad as Aunt Tatie did. You'd better stop it before you're sorry, and they even more so."

His voice faded on the last few words, and there was a clatter of bootheels as he went down the steps.

Marietta drew away from Lafe, saying, "I'd better get up now."

"No," Lafe said, and pulled her back to him.

She smiled. "Yes, my dear husband. Now it *is* time. You heard Oren. He's in a state. I don't want him to frighten the boys needlessly."

"No," Lafe said again, this time more insistently.

"Yes, my dear." She leaned over, pressed a kiss at the corner of his mouth. "We've time together, remember. We've all of our lives."

"Who knows how long that is?" he asked softly.

He pulled her down over him, feeling the softness of her breasts. He turned quickly, holding her still.

"Lafe," she whispered. "Lafe, not now, please . . . you know . . . you heard . . ."

"I know nothing. Except that I want you," he answered.

"Lafe, dear, now I must . . ."

He covered her mouth with his, her body with his, and buried himself in her with a hunger that he knew would never be wholly satisfied.

Her eyes were bright. There was a fullness to her lips. But as she went over the ledgers one last time, the glow faded from her face. Oren had been gone when she and Lafe came down. Lafe left immediately after the morning meal for Darnal, taking Duveen and Moses with him. She had repaired to the morning room with the books, hoping for Oren's return. Now there were voices outside, and she stepped out onto the gallery.

Gentry had just climbed down from the carriage. He had offered his hand to Coraleen, but when he saw Marietta, he seemed to have forgotten he was about to help the young girl down. He turned and grinned. "Good day, Marietta. How are you?"

She nodded. Then, "Did you have a fine time, Coraleen?"

"A very fine time," Coraleen murmured. She gave Gentry a sour look. "And with the proper assistance I might get down."

Gentry flushed, turned quickly, and helped her off the high step.

She ignored his muttered apology. "Marietta, I've news! You'll never guess what it is!"

"Then you'd better tell me, hadn't you?"

"It's Sara and John," Coraleen answered. "Gentry's going to become an uncle."

"How very nice." Marietta turned to Gentry. "You must take my good wishes home with you. Tell Sara we're all very happy for her. And will hope to see her soon."

"My father's the happy one," Gentry said. "Since I've delivered no heir he acknowledges, he thinks all the more highly of Sara these days." His plump pink face was suddenly sullen. "Not that I didn't try to please him."

Marietta ignored the sour look and the sour tone of his voice. "And you shall do so soon. Your life's not over yet, Gentry. You mustn't speak as if it is."

"You seem happy enough," he told her, plainly not pleased with the observation.

"And I am."

"I wouldn't have expected it," he said. "That's the truth, Marietta. I'd have wagered everything I owe that you'd not be pleased with your choice."

She looked him up and down, then replied, "Is that so? I wonder why, Gentry."

"Because you didn't take the man you wanted."

Anger flashed through her. She would have liked to slap his face smartly, or box his ears, and send him on his way. But there was no point in it. Let his rudeness be his burden to bear. She said, turning away, "Poor Gentry, I'm sorry you're still so dog in the manger. I never meant to hurt you."

Coraleen, having listened with amusement, swung on Gentry with pretended anger. "You hush, Gentry! What I want is to become an aunt, just as you're to be an uncle." Her smile curled at Marietta. "But if Lafe goes off by night, and stays away . . ." She cocked her head. "Has he returned yet, Marietta? Have you heard from him at least?"

"Of course," Marietta answered softly. "He came home last night." She blushed, remembering, but went on, still very softly: "And you verge on impertinence, Coraleen."

"Why, I didn't mean to, Marietta. But when husband and wife don't sleep together, then how can they produce a niece or nephew for me to love?" She turned to Gentry, "And you misjudge Lafe, Gentry. He's the most wonderful husband in the world. He never goes off without bringing a present on his return. He's thoughtful, and dear, and . . ." Coraleen looked to Marietta for more, and was rewarded beyond her expectation.

"He's all that I want in a husband," Marietta said simply, and turned away.

Later, she heard those words echo in her mind and was startled to discover that they were true. She could think of no way in which Lafe failed her. Then why, she asked herself, did her thoughts still return always to Oren? Why, even as she lay in Lafe's arms, had she planned how she would speak to Oren?

16

"Miss Garvey asked for them," Jed Blandish said.

"Miss Garvey?" Oren demanded.

"I mean Mrs. Flynn, of course," Jed hastily amended. He tugged hard at his long blond mustache to conceal the satisfaction he felt. "And when she asked, I couldn't say no, could I?"

Oren's face grew dark with rage, but his voice was soft. "Mr. Blandish, I'll have no disrespect from you. Not now. And not ever. Tell me at once what led her to become so interested in the ledgers."

Jed shrugged. "She didn't tell me, Mr. Henderson, so how would I know? I can't read her mind, and wouldn't dare it if I could. I certainly didn't think it my place to demand an explanation."

"Did she mention Mr. Flynn?"

"She mentioned nothing but the ledgers, which I handed over, as I was bound to."

Oren said nothing more. He kicked his horse, led it in a tight turn, and raced back to the house. Beedle caught the reins Oren flung at him, and Needle led the horse away. This time Oren didn't acknowledge with a smile the careful closing of the gate. He stood for a moment on the gallery, breathing deeply, before he went inside.

He found Marietta in the morning room.

She sat near the window, the curtain agleam with bright sun behind her. A silver napkin ring engraved with an ornamental "L" shone against the deep blue of her gown.

She made a picture that was lovely to behold, but Oren didn't notice.

His gaze took in the "L" on the napkin ring first. Lafe's initial. It was on Lafe that he blamed this trouble now. Then he saw the ledgers, prominently placed on the table at her side.

Though it was cool in the room, the heat of his anger burned high in him. He said, "Mr. Blandish says you have the books, Marietta. And I see them here. What's this all about?"

Her slender fingers tightened around the napkin ring until the knuckles whitened. She leaned back in the chair, but even so, her body remained tense. "I've been wanting to talk to you, Oren."

"I assumed that to be the case. Since you took the books from Blandish. I still don't understand." And then, unable to stop himself, he rushed on. "It's Lafe, of course. I knew it would happen. Sooner or later he had to interfere. I've been waiting for it. I expected it. No plantation can have two masters!"

She deliberately set aside the napkin ring and tilted her face up, answering, "You're quite wrong to blame Lafe, Oren. He has nothing to do with Galloway. Nor has he ever tried to."

"Nothing to do with Galloway." Oren sneered. "How can you pretend that? You know as well as I do that when a woman marries, her husband controls her property thereafter."

"But Lafe doesn't control Galloway. Nor is he interested in doing so."

"And how can you be sure of that? Has he said so to you? Has he signed a paper swearing to it?"

"He hasn't needed to do either. He's proven it by his actions." Now she smiled at Oren. "Tell me. How can I talk to you when you stand there stiff and angry, towering over me?"

He flung himself into a chair. "All right, Marietta."

"You've decreased the rations, haven't you, Oren?"

"Who's been complaining to you? If that Blandish—"

"Oren"—her voice was still soft—"there's been no complaint made to me. Blame no one in this."

"Then how do you know about it?"

"You *have* done as I thought, then."

"A mite only."

"And why is that?"

"Because we can't afford to go on the way we have been. This is one of those times when we must be more careful."

"Then we shall save elsewhere, Oren. I won't have my people go hungry."

"If I'm not allowed to make these decisions, Marietta, then I can do nothing at all for you, believe me."

"I hope that we'll decide together that we can save elsewhere," she said, smiling. "I'm certain that if we bend our minds to it, we can."

So, she'd discovered what he had done. Still, if this was the worst that she had gleaned from the ledgers, then he could deal with it. He said unwillingly, "I'll increase the distribution of staples as much as I can. But I believe you cosset the slaves too much. You make them expect more than they should. And then it becomes dangerous to disappoint them."

"I suppose you believe so. But I must insist on this, Oren. And I must insist the repairs to the quarters be done. It wasn't done last autumn, and I shan't let another year go by without it."

"You know we couldn't afford to do it. And as for this autumn, that depends on the harvest, doesn't it?"

She waited through a slow breath, then said quietly, "You had delivery of the roofing supplies at least, so you won't need to order them in again."

"I returned them," he said quickly. "When I realized the problem, I had all the supplies taken back."

"Oh? Did you? I didn't know. There's no credit shown on the books that I could find."

She was still smiling sweetly. Her gaze was direct and open and unaccusing.

But he could meet it only briefly. He rose, paced the floor, saying, "I'll check myself, Marietta. There's either an error, or else you've missed the entry."

"I've no doubt missed the entry," she told him.

But he knew she'd seen too much for his comfort. He was frightened now at what he'd done. To distract her, he said angrily, "Blandish is getting sloppy, Marietta. We must begin to think of replacing him. Or, better yet, we should send him away, and I'll take over his chores myself."

"Oren!" she gasped, stung out of her calm. "You don't mean it!"

He meant only a part of it. He would certainly prefer to replace Blandish with someone he could himself control. He had no intention of doing an overseer's job. It was beneath him, and beyond him as well. And he knew it. He answered only, "Marietta, for the good of Galloway—"

"I won't hear of it!" she said flatly.

He gave in immediately, knowing that he'd never move her. She wouldn't bend on this. And all he wanted now was to put an end to the conversation. He said, "I think you're right. Perhaps I am too hard on Blandish."

"You blame him for what isn't his responsibility," she said, and went on softly: "I can remember when he first came. I was a tiny child then. I've grown up in the security of his labors for us, for the Garveys, and for Galloway."

"I know," Oren said impatiently. "I know all that, Marietta. And I've just told you—"

"Yes, yes. But that you should even think for a moment that I would send him away—"

"I'm only considering means to make the plantation better paying, Marietta."

"I know. But we must remember how my father did it, Oren. His way was best. He knew best. We must always remember that."

"I try to, you know." Now that she was mollified, he allowed himself to mop the sweat from his brow. The hot angry color began to fade from his face. He continued: "I'll try even harder."

"And the note," Marietta said thoughtfully. "You haven't forgotten about that, have you? It'll be repaid after we sell this autumn?"

"If it's possible," he told her.

"We must make it possible, Oren. I won't have it otherwise."

"Have you ever thought, Marietta, that Lafe could help if he chose to?" Oren asked tentatively.

"Lafe?" Now her lips were suddenly compressed. There was no soft smile in her eyes. "Lafe, Oren? Only moments ago you accused him of interfering in Galloway's business affairs. Now you ask that he do so."

"I didn't mean that, and you know it."

"We couldn't ask Lafe for his help. And why should we? The plantation can and must sustain itself as it always has."

"I was thinking only of some emergency." Oren forced a quick teasing smile. "Or some wild extravagance on your part."

She didn't smile in return. She said evenly, "There'll be no wild extravagances. We shall be very, very careful."

"So you tell me now. But can you keep to it? You've promised Coraleen a surrey. Do you know what it'll cost you?"

"No, but I shall find out."

"Very well. Then I'll leave that to you. But I'd suggest, before you make any more promises, that you know what you are doing."

"I'll remember," she promised as he turned to leave.

The room seemed less bright with Oren gone. She considered their conversation with a vague but growing feeling of dissatisfaction. She had won her point, as she'd known she would. And he hadn't been nearly as angry as she'd expected. But having won it, she saw that the cut in the slaves' rations—an extreme act, no matter how Oren denied it—had

229

been only a symptom of something far worse. Something had gone very wrong at Galloway. But what?

Lafe brooded on that same question, though he didn't allow himself to ask it aloud. He leaned back in his chair and looked blandly into Oren's face. "I'm sorry," he said. "I've no need for any investment, Oren."

"It wouldn't be much," Oren said hastily. "I don't have much, as you must know. Not much that is my own, I mean. But still, if I could put something in with you . . ."

"You want to increase your income," he said at last. "Is that it, Oren?"

"Of course. Don't we all?"

"I suppose we do," Lafe answered.

"So even if you've never thought of it before, will you consider it now?" Oren asked eagerly.

But there was no use thinking about it. Were Oren to invest in the Golden Leaf, he would have the right to examine the books. Dreaming of larger and larger profits, he would begin to concern himself with the movement of produce through the warehouse, how many bales came in and how many went out. In the end, he would know more than he needed to know about Golden Leaf. It was better to stop it now, firmly, than to have to deal with it later. While Oren dreamed of profits, others had larger dreams, and more and more who had heard Duveen's whistle followed. The less Oren, or anyone else, knew of Lafe's business the better it would be for all concerned.

"Oren, I'm sorry to tell you that I can't accept your offer," he said at last. "The Golden Leaf Tobacco Company isn't mine entirely, though you may well have thought so. I have a small outstanding interest in it, but that's all. My father owns the rest, and the decision to sell is his. I can tell you now I doubt he'd sell any part of it. He believes strongly in holding full control. That's why I have so small a part in this myself."

Startled, Oren burst out, "But you led everyone to believe that the company was yours."

"Perhaps I did," Lafe agreed. "Though I don't recall," he went on smoothly, "that anyone ever asked me."

"Perhaps not," Oren answered coolly. "Since they'd assumed you to be owner." He rose to his feet. "I'm sorry to have troubled you, Lafe."

"It's no trouble." Lafe, too, rose. "In fact, I wish I could have accepted the offer. But as it stands . . ."

"I understand," Oren said quickly.

What he understood was that one more door had closed in his face. He wouldn't have Galloway, and now it appeared that he'd never be able to leave it.

He told Marietta nothing of his conversation with Lafe. By the time he returned to Galloway late that afternoon, he'd already talked out his irritation and disappointment over ale with Gentry in the Jordan House gaming room.

Gentry had been adequately sympathetic, saying, "I don't understand it, Oren. It's an odd way for a man to treat his kin by marriage, isn't it? I thought you two were on friendly terms."

"So did I." Oren's dark eyes narrowed thoughtfully. "It always seemed so." But he remembered Coraleen's angry warning now. If Marietta married Lafe, then Galloway would be lost to Oren for good. Coraleen had been right. And Lafe no longer was the laughing indulgent fellow he'd been at the beginning.

Gentry was saying. "I guess there's a lot we don't understand about Lafe Flynn, Oren."

"It appears so."

"Like why he come to Darnal in the first place," Gentry went on. "It would have made much better sense to locate himself in Durham's Station, and make buying trips into the countryside."

"I agree," Oren said. "No doubt you're right. However, he had his reasons. Or else his father had the reasons."

231

"His father?"

"The company is owned by his father," Oren informed him bitterly. "Lafe has only a small piece of it."

"That's interesting news indeed." Gentry regarded Oren thoughtfully. "He certainly speaks freely of his family in New Orleans. But, of course, you've met none of them, have you? Nor has Marietta, I believe."

"Marietta refused a honeymoon in New Orleans," Oren said. "A foolish decision. She'd have had the opportunity to see his people for herself. She didn't seem to care for the idea."

"I wonder if there really is a Flynn family. Or if our Lafe has run a clever bluff on us."

Oren looked startled. "Why do you say that?"

"I don't say there isn't one, Oren. I only say I wonder." Gentry grinned suddenly. "And it's not something too difficult to determine."

"It shouldn't be," Oren said softly. "But will you?"

Now he was suddenly hopeful. If Lafe were a fraud . . . if Marietta were to realize that the man she'd married was not what he appeared to be, then she would trust him again. She would lean on him as never before.

Gentry was saying, "I think I might try to determine it. I'll let you know what I decide."

Now, nearing the parlor, Oren heard Coraleen ask, "You've talked with Mr. Blandish about my surrey, Marietta? What did he say? When will he get it for me?"

Marietta answered, "I shall do it tomorrow morning. But, Coraleen, I must tell you now that I doubt we can order a new one."

There was a brief pause. Then Coraleen said in a sweet high voice, "You *did* promise, Marietta."

Oren crossed the threshold quickly, greeted Marietta and Coraleen, and said, "What's this about?"

"The surrey," Coraleen told him. "Marietta first promised me, and now . . ."

Oren shrugged. "And now you can't have it? Must you be

232

such a spoiled child? Well, blame me for your disappointment, Coraleen. I've explained to Marietta just this morning that if she's determined to feed the field hands like princes, then she must save on something. She's apparently decided to save on your whims, and I suppose that's right enough."

Marietta said quickly, "You've not allowed me to explain to Coraleen. I fear we must give up the idea of a new surrey. But surely Mr. Blandish will find something else. Perhaps one of the gigs could be repaired and polished and painted. And Coraleen would have her own conveyance, which is all that she really wants."

"Oh, oh, I'm sorry," Coraleen cried. "Marietta, I didn't understand you. Whatever you find for me will be perfect. I don't need a new surrey. I never meant to imply that I did."

Oren concealed his sudden suspicion. When Coraleen spoke thus, she was up to something, and though he saw nothing in her face to confirm his uneasy feeling, it remained with him. He knew his Coraleen too well for it to be otherwise.

Her smile was sweet, her brown eyes candid, as she looked happily at Marietta. "Anything with wheels will do for me," she said.

Two days later Jed Blandish brought the gig to the yard and presented it with a proud flourish to Coraleen. It had been scrubbed clean and polished. Wheels and braces and shafts and step shone brightly. Letty Blandish had re-covered its tattered brown cushions with a bright red rep. The black mare in harness was groomed to perfection.

Coraleen smiled with false pleasure, while her heart was heavy as a stone within her. This small old gig was not what she'd imagined. She'd dreamed of a surrey, its top fringed in red balls, its wheels trimmed in red, too. She'd imagined herself dashing about the countryside in that dashing conveyance, and riding sedately into town, the envy of all who looked at her and waved and smiled.

But the old gig had its own sturdy wheels, and the red

233

rep seat was bright, and within days she had become a familiar figure on the roads about the plantation.

She rode into the fields to watch the beginnings of the harvest. Now the first full-grown leaves were being primed, pulled from the still-expanding plant, and strung on stakes. The men worked quickly and smoothly, their black muscular backs shining with sweat. Soon they would load the wagons, and the packed stacks would be delivered for hanging in the curing barns, where already the small charcoal fires were alight, sending a haze of blue smoke over even the far reaches of Galloway.

Soon bored, Coraleen went farther afield. By harvest's end Coraleen and her gig had so often been seen in town that her presence was taken for granted and no longer remarked upon. She drove in alone, left the gig in the yard at Jordan House, and did her small shopping at the general store. From there, always, no matter how often she made the trip, she never failed to visit the warehouse to spend a little time with Lafe.

She would saunter in, swinging her parasol, and find him sitting at the rosewood desk. Moses would shoot her a glance over his books and wrap his thin legs more tightly around the high stool on which he sat. Duveen, if he was there at all, would immediately disappear.

He had seen Coraleen close up for the first time at Galloway. He and Moses had been hauling a chest up the staircase and had paused at the landing so that Moses could catch his breath when Coraleen came out to look. Duveen stared at her, and shrank from the sight—from the swift intuition of some dark evil behind the pretty face. He had never been able to communicate his feeling. Instead, he had avoided Coraleen whenever he could.

Lafe, seeing her come in, would sigh to himself, but ask, "How are you, Coraleen? Was it pleasant riding in?"

More often than not she would fling herself into a chair close by and smile at him. "Oh, pleasant indeed. Do you have time to come for a drive with me?" Another day she would pout. "Oh, it was boring. I asked Marietta to came along, but she had chores to do. Your Marietta is too busy to spend her time with me."

He'd move his papers impatiently on his desk and say with deliberation, "We're all busy these days, Coraleen."

"All except me."

"You must find it tiring to be idle."

"I'm not idle," she'd answer. "I'm having a good time."

This afternoon, having first spent a thoughtful hour on the bench in the town square, she didn't pretend at frivolity. She stared around the warehouse, sniffed the pungent air. She frowned and nibbled at her nails. "Lafe," she said, "I'm concerned about Marietta. I don't understand. She's terribly worried."

"Worried? Do you think so?" he asked.

Coraleen nodded, frowning more deeply. "I'm sure of it, Lafe. Though she says nothing about it. But . . . well, it's difficult to say, since she isn't candid—she never is, you know. I only wonder why she's so troubled. Is it Oren, do you suppose? Or is it the finances of the plantation? She wouldn't buy me a new surrey, and only gave me the old broken-down gig we've had for years. And there's other things as well that makes me think something must be wrong."

"She's said nothing to me," Lafe said. It was true. Marietta had confided no problems to him. On the other hand, he'd seen no real sign of worry in her either. Now, suddenly, he wondered. Had he been attending to her properly?

"Oh, Marietta wouldn't say anything," Coraleen replied. She pretended at amazement. "Surely you realize that Marietta considers Galloway totally her own, and would share it with no one, not even with her husband."

"It *is* her own," Lafe said. "And no one else's, and it's her right to feel so."

"When a woman marries, her property falls under control of her husband," Coraleen retorted pertly. "You know that as well as I do."

"Only if he wishes it. And I don't."

"How nice you are to feel so." Coraleen smiled. "Still, I think it odd of her. I know that Oren once suggested she ask you to lend her some money to pay bills with, and she was quite angry with him. She said she'd ask nothing of you."

Now Lafe's eyes held amusement. "I think you're making that up, my dear small sister."

"Then ask Oren. I'm sure he'll tell you the same. I believe that Marietta fears becoming obligated to you."

"And I," Lafe said, laughing aloud, "think you want only to make trouble wherever you can. But I want you to know that you'll make no trouble between Marietta and me."

She bounced to her feet indignantly. "I've always been on your side, and you know it. If you accuse me of trouble-making, then what can I do?"

He rose, his bulk towering over her. Suddenly there was no laughter in his voice, no smile of amusement in his eyes. "You can be quiet, and go home like a good child. I have work to do if you haven't. And I need time, and silence, in which to do it."

She thought suddenly of another time when he had stood thus and looked down at her. Then he had said, *I shall be very angry if anything happens to Marietta.* For the first time in her life, Coraleen had known fear. She knew it again now, and trembled with it.

But when she left the warehouse, she was well satisfied that she had sown a few small seeds that would one day bear bitter fruit for Marietta.

She ambled across the square smiling to herself. In Jordan House she made her way quickly up the steps, unobserved except by a girl who was polishing the grandfather clock. She found the door to Lafe's suite locked, so she went down again and around to the back. There, in full day, though no one was about to see, she hoisted her skirts, climbed up, and let herself into the rooms through the open gallery doors.

The last time she had climbed to the gallery, it had been dark. She'd hidden herself in the rocking chair to wait,

236

hoping for a pleasant hour of flirtation. Instead Lafe had treated her like a child and made sure she returned home by going with her.

She remembered that as she looked around the room. Here Lafe and Marietta had consummated their marriage. Here Lafe had held Marietta in his arms and smoothed her silken black hair on the satiny pillows, and kissed her smiling mouth, and ground his big body against hers in a passion that Coraleen could only imagine.

She cursed the bed and sheets, and set to work in search.

She left disappointed. She hadn't known what she was looking for, but she had been certain she would find something. Something. Anything. She was determined to find whatever was necessary to damn Lafe Flynn and drive him from Galloway for good.

17

Eamus Jordan pushed his glasses higher on his nose; he read and read again, and cried aloud, "Well, I'll be damned!"

Lafe, passing by, stopped and grinned. "I hope not, Mr. Jordan."

But the small plump man only flushed darker. "Look here at this, Mr. Flynn, before I take it over to the courthouse. It just came in over the telegraph machine." Eamus' eyes flashed, and his pudgy jowls quivered. "Nobody can do such a thing and expect to get away with it!"

Lafe scanned the brief message quickly. There had been trouble in Harpers Ferry, Virginia. John Brown had attacked the federal arsenal there, killed four men, and taken as hostage Colonel Lewis Washington, a descendant of George Washington.

"Trouble indeed," Lafe murmured, handing the message back to Eamus.

He went directly to the warehouse through the bright mid-October sunlight and put his feet up on the rosewood desk that covered the trap door to the hidey hole below. There now, in darkness, another traveler awaited nightfall.

Duveen had already heard of the attack on the arsenal. He, and Moses, too, were grim-faced.

Lafe knew that these two felt as he did. John Brown's call for general insurrection among the slaves could lead only to death—to death, to terror, to the slaughter of the innocent. The path of the fanatic was strewn with broken bodies and broken dreams. And there would be ripples from the explosion at Harpers Ferry that would reach even this North Carolina backwater, making his job all the more difficult.

Later, Lafe's expectation was confirmed. In the gaming room at Jordan House, the serving girls moved quietly, their dark faces impassive, their eyes lowered, while among the guests, excitement flushed cheeks and raised voices.

"They must go in and kill them all," Gentry said. "It's the only way."

Oren nodded his agreement, dark eyes afire. "And we must make plans in case there's trouble here as well."

"I'll speak to John Farr," Gentry promised. "The three of us will form a safety committee. If there's a general insurrection, then we'll be ready for it."

Lafe greeted Oren and Gentry, refused their suggestion that he join in their planning, and moved on after one quick ale. He considered that Oren spent too much time in Jordan House these days, and not enough at Galloway. But he knew he wouldn't speak of it. He had made sure always, since his marriage to Marietta, to refrain from any interference with her family or affairs.

He didn't know that Oren and Gentry had not granted him the same privacy. Gentry, watching him leave, said, sighing, "One thing we do know, Oren. He's all he says he is. Lafayette Flynn exists. He's the younger of two sons of the New Orleans shipping magnate. There's no doubting it, now that I've had news from my relatives."

Oren grunted. "A pity, isn't it? I'd hoped to learn otherwise."

"There was a duel," Gentry said thoughtfully. "He never went back."

"Because of Marietta," Oren retorted.

"Too long ago," Gentry answered. "But never mind, there'll be something, Oren. Just wait and see."

At the end of that week, when Marcus Swinton came to the warehouse asking to speak privately with him, Lafe found that he could no longer follow the policy he had chosen of separating himself from Galloway affairs.

Duveen quickly and conveniently found chores to perform elsewhere while Marcus seated himself and studied Lafe, hazel eyes bright and speculative. At last he said, "I've come to you because I don't know what else to do. And it's a concern that affects you."

Lafe nodded. "It's about Marietta, Marcus?"

"Indirectly." Marcus sighed. "Directly, too. I've been remiss in my obligations to my old friend Lawrence Garvey. But I feared to make trouble when it might prove unnecessary. Now I begin to believe that I've made a grievous error."

"Perhaps you'd better explain."

"It's about Galloway, Lafe. The plantation is all Marietta's ever had. The plantation and its buildings and its slaves, and the crops they can produce. It was left to her by her father, and there was a reason for the way he wrote his will. I know what the will stated, for I not only witnessed it but I helped him write it as well. I understood the problem as no one but he did." Marcus paused, waited for some comment, but Lafe didn't oblige him. With a sigh he went on: "This concerns you, too, Lafe. Now that you're married to Marietta, Galloway is part of your estate, too."

"I've never considered it so, and never will." Lafe was frowning now. "But go on. What problem is it that you understood?"

"Lawrence felt that Marietta must be protected against the Hendersons."

Lafe's impassive face gave nothing away, but he was suddenly alert. "Protected" was the word Marcus had used. Had Lawrence Garvey perceived some threat to Marietta?

"I don't know his reasons, though I know he had them. In any event, he believed that whoever held the purse strings would be all right. So he gave Coraleen and Oren only third shares in the profits of the plantation. After Lawrence's death, the profit dropped. It has continued to drop since."

"And to what do you attribute this falling off?" Lafe asked.

240

"Oren's management is a part of it, I believe." Marcus stopped, waited with obvious expectation.

Lafe said slowly, "My dear Marcus, I'm not quite certain that you've told me all you know, or all you think. Or else I haven't understood you. I know what price Marietta has received for the last three crops. I paid it myself, bale by bale, hogshead by hogshead. It was a good one each time. She made a profit each time as well. And so did I when the tobacco arrived at market. There's simply no reason for a problem."

"Yet there is a problem," Marcus said softly. "A year ago this past spring, Oren asked for a cash loan to cover the costs of planting and expenses until the harvest was in. Marietta signed for it, of course, as I'd not take Oren's signature. He has no collateral to offer, you understand. And he has no legal standing in connection with Galloway."

"And?"

"The loan has not been repaid. Oren asked that it be renewed twice, and twice I've done so. Though in at least one case, I know that Marietta wasn't aware of the renewal until she learned it from me."

"I see," Lafe said.

"There's more. While the note has been renewed each time, Oren's personal account has grown larger." Marcus fumbled for a cigar, drew it out, absently lit it. He puffed three times, examined the ash at the end of it. He crossed and recrossed his long thin legs. At last he said, "I don't like this, Lafe. It's a violation of a banker's ethic, but I tell you this for Marietta's sake. There is some trouble at Galloway. I don't know what it is, and though I've tried to speak with her about it, she either doesn't understand or doesn't want to."

Lafe nodded grimly. "I believe I follow you, Marcus. I'll see what I can do. But first I'll take care of the note immediately."

Marcus looked pained, held up his hand. "It's not my money I'm after, Lafe. I'd be offended if you should think that. I just don't want to see Marietta lose what her father left her. And I greatly fear that she doesn't quite see through Oren. He's using her, her affection for him, I might add, since she thinks of him as her brother, to feather his own nest. I know that's what's happening. And I don't like it. And I know it's not what Lawrence intended."

"Nonetheless," Lafe answered, "I shall come to the bank tomorrow morning. I shall pay what is owed in full and take the canceled note."

"And then?"

"And then I shall do whatever else must be done to see that Marietta fully comprehends what has happened, and what it can lead to."

He was as good as his word. The next morning he wrote out a draft that covered Marietta's indebtedness to the bank in full.

Soon after he rode back to Galloway. He spent three hours with a nervous Jed Blandish and the plantation ledgers. He spent another two hours with Jed in a slow drive from storeroom to storeroom, from shed to shed, taking a complete inventory of supplies and equipment. Then the two men did an hour-long inspection tour of the slave quarters.

All through the rest of the day and evening he covered the anger that boiled in him with an air of abstraction. Neither Coraleen nor Oren knew what was in his mind as he bade them a pleasant good night and withdrew to the bedroom he shared with Marietta.

There, as he sat watching her brush out her hair, he said quietly, "Marietta, I've a grave matter to discuss with you."

She put down the brush, turned quickly. Her amethyst eyes widened with concern. "A grave matter? What is it, Lafe?"

"You know that I've never attempted to involve myself with your affairs. And I wouldn't do so now unless it was absolutely necessary."

"My affairs?" she said softly. "What on earth are you talking about? I've no affairs separate from yours."

"But you do," he answered, smiling slightly. "Of course

242

you do. There's Galloway. Which belongs to you. And which I want to see in your hands for as long as you want it to be."

"Forever," she answered. "You know that, Lafe."

"Forever," he repeated, no longer smiling. "I doubt that there's such a thing as forever in this. But never mind that. I want you to know that Marcus spoke to me today. The loan has now been repaid."

A flush burned in her cheeks. "Lafe, I don't know why Marcus spoke to you. He shouldn't have done it. There was no need for you to become involved."

"Indeed? Marcus seemed to think otherwise. Perhaps because I am your husband."

"You still have no obligation to pay Galloway debts."

Now Coraleen's words came back to haunt Lafe. *She doesn't want to be obligated to you.* And what did that mean? Why not? Because of her feeling for Oren?

"I have the obligation to pay my wife's debt," Lafe said softly. "Whether you like it or not. And I'm surprised that you might think different."

"Ah, I see," she said. "Now you remind me that when I married you, all I owned became yours."

"Is that what I remind you of?" he asked dryly. "How interesting. I believe I spoke only of my own obligations. In fact, I was about to say that I'd be delighted to put all my resources into Galloway, but for the one thing that holds me back."

"You're not invited to put any resources into my plantation," she cried.

"I don't require an invitation. It's a right I have by law. Should I choose to exercise it. Which I would never do. Not as long as Oren supervises what's done here."

The room was suddenly still. The small fire on the hearth whispered. The candlewicks sputtered.

At last Marietta said quietly, "Now I do begin to see. It's Oren you're complaining about, isn't it?"

Lafe gave her a long speculative look before he answered. "I've not yet made a complaint, Marietta."

"But you will. I see where you're going." Her voice was

243

high and sharp. Spots of color burned in her cheeks. "And you've no right to do it. You knew I had Oren, Oren and Coraleen, with me when we married. You knew we would all be together. And now . . . now . . ."

"And now I tell you that Oren isn't doing as he should for your interests."

"He does as well as he can," she said defensively. "Every-one has a few bad years. Ask Alexander Beckwith. Ask Marcus Swinton himself."

"There've been no bad years. We both are aware of that. Not recently anyway."

"I've been paying more heed than I had before," she answered. "It'll be all right now. I should accept part of the blame, Lafe. Surely, you can see that. Had I paid more heed—"

"You're not to worry about it any more. As I told you, I've taken care of the loan." Lafe took a parchment from his pocket and passed it to her. She recognized it immediately. "I want you to study this."

She gave it a single glance, saw that she had signed once, and that Oren had imitated her signature twice more. A wave of sickness rolled over her. She breathed deeply, fighting for control. Lafe must know nothing of how she felt now. She tossed the document aside, shrugged her shoulders. "Well, what of it? I've seen it before, you know."

"You saw it only once," Lafe said softly. "The other two signatures aren't yours, as you realize without my telling you."

"Marcus renewed the note. It was no problem. I can't think why you're making such a fuss. I do thank you for your help, but it wasn't necessary. And I prefer that Oren attend to these matters."

"Even if he cheats you?" Lafe asked.

"You're not fair to him," she cried. "I don't want to discuss it any further. Everything will be all right."

"Not as long as Oren Henderson is in charge," Lafe said softly. "I've looked at the ledgers with Blandish, and I've ex-

244

amined the plantation itself. There's wealth here, Marietta. A wealth of disrepair and neglect. The storerooms are empty or nearly so. There's scarcely an inventory of tools. Yet the bills indicate the delivery of vast orders of supplies." Lafe sighed. "Marietta, shall I draw a picture for you? You understand as well as I do what Oren has been doing."

"No," she said hotly. "No, Lafe, you accuse him wrongly. I'll not listen to you any longer. And I won't permit you to speak to him about this."

"You won't permit me," Lafe echoed softly. "What an interesting turn of phrase. And how do you propose to keep me from doing what I know I must do to protect your own interests?"

"I forbid it, Lafe," she said coldly.

He leaned back, crossed his long legs, and braced his chin on his fist. He regarded her through dark blue eyes. At last he said, "You order me to allow Oren to steal from you, from the plantation, for his own benefit and to your detriment?"

"I do."

"Would you like to tell me why, Marietta?"

"Because I shall take the matter up with Oren myself. In my own way."

"Will you?"

"I will, Lafe."

"When?"

"Immediately." Her voice was firm. "The first thing tomorrow."

"I wonder if you'll be able to force yourself to it" was his only answer.

"Of course I shall," she retorted, still firm in her resolve.

But that night she hardly slept.

She was aware of the warm bulk of Lafe beside her, and conscious of the care with which he avoided the slightest touch of his flesh against hers. She knew that he was tense with anger, but that didn't trouble her. He'd had no right to interfere. She had not asked for his help, nor had she wanted it. Galloway was her responsibility, and she would deal with it.

But what was she to say to Oren now? She could no longer pretend that she didn't understand what he had been doing. Lafe had seen the ledgers just as she had. He'd checked the figures, rechecked the stores. Lafe, even more than she herself, was totally aware of the depths of Oren's perfidy. She hadn't wanted to know it. As soon as she'd realized what was happening, she'd tried to close her eyes to it.

How could she call Oren dishonest?

How could she accuse him?

Surely there must be some explanation for what he had done. If the two of them could speak quietly together, he would tell her, and she would understand. There was no reason for Lafe to treat her as if she were an idiot. She would show him she was competent to deal with this.

There were dark circles under her eyes when morning came. She was no nearer then than she had been the night before to knowing what she would say to Oren.

She avoided Lafe's eyes at the breakfast table and spoke lightly to Coraleen and Oren. She was relieved when Lafe departed for Darnal with Moses and Duveen.

Coraleen raced off soon after, but even when Marietta and Oren were alone, finishing coffee together, she couldn't gather herself to tell him what she had learned.

He left her in a little while and rode away, and she still hadn't warned him that Lafe knew what he had done. It was that which frightened her the most. Lafe knew. He would do something about it.

That evening she realized that by delaying the confrontation she had made a dreadful mistake.

At supper Coraleen was full of news. She had been at the Beckwiths' when word came that John Brown had been captured at the Harpers Ferry arsenal. "Colonel Lee led the Marines in," she announced, "and two of Brown's sons are dead, and eleven others as well. They'll hang the old man, and the rest of them, and then we'll be quit of them for good."

"They may hang them," Lafe agreed, "but we'll not be quit of them so easily, I fear."

"But we will," Oren said. "There's nothing else to do with them, and they'll make a fine example to anyone who thinks he can do the same."

"And make martyrs for the abolitionist cause," Lafe went on, as if Oren hadn't spoken. He rose to his feet then. "But we'll not settle it here. So instead, will you take a turn around the garden with me, Oren? I've something to discuss with you."

Marietta jumped to her feet and caught Lafe's arm. She smiled gaily into his face, crying, "Now, my darling, you do remember what I told you, don't you? Why, everything will be just as we agreed. So"—she tugged at his arm—"so sit down with me."

But he was immovable. He gently took her hand from his arm, then let go of it. "This is no time for you to use your wiles on me. I know they're false. I'd rather you scream aloud like a banshee than to see you simper and smile and burn inside."

Surprise froze her for a moment only. Then her anger rose up. "Very well,' she gasped. "Then it's banshee I shall be. No, Lafe. I won't allow this!"

Coraleen's bewildered brown eyes moved from her brother to Marietta, then to Lafe. What was this? There were tears in Marietta's eyes.

Lafe ignored Marietta, looked inquiringly, at Oren, who immediately got to his feet. "I'll be glad to walk with you."

"No," Marietta cried. "Oren, no, you mustn't listen to him."

His brows drew together. A dark flush spread over his face, but he said nothing. He followed Lafe to the door. They both took coats from the hall tree and then went outside.

Slowly, carefully, Lafe presented to Oren the information he had received from Marcus, what he knew of the books, what he had seen of the plantation. It was an unpleasant bill of particulars. He made his voice neutral, and chose his words with precision.

247

When he was done, he said, "Oren, there may be some explanation of which I am unaware. If so, I apologize. If not, then I think you must answer to me."

Oren said hoarsely, "You've no right to accuse me. This is no business of yours, Lafe Flynn."

"And that's all you wish to say?" Lafe drawled.

"I've the right to do as I wish," Oren went on. "Even up to, and including, the making of certain mistakes. The plantation should have been mine."

"But it isn't," Lafe retorted.

"I'll not discuss this with you," Oren said at last.

"If that's all you have to say to me, then you'd better listen instead," Lafe answered. "You'll go inside, and Marietta will tell you to forget this conversation. She'll say that she's mistress here, and she doesn't care what you've done, or how, or why. And when she says that, you will tell her that you're sorry that you've cheated her, and stolen from her, and forged her signature. You'll tell her you're sorry you betrayed the trust she so unwisely placed in you."

Oren hitched his coat more closely around his shoulders. He turned his face up, so that the moonlight made a silver death's-head of his features. He said harshly, "I'll do no such thing."

"But I think you'd better. And you will." Lafe took Oren's arm, and though his voice was mild, his fingers bit deep into the younger man's flesh. "For if you don't do as I say, I shall go to the law in Marietta's name, and in my own. I assure you that Marcus Swinton will be witness for me. You'll embarrass Marietta needlessly, and endanger yourself. I'll see that she's protected, no matter what. I'll not protect you, Oren."

"I can't do it," Oren answered. "I tell you, I cannot."

"But you will." Lafe's fingers tightened on Oren's arm. "And you'll do it right now. You'll also tell Marietta that you don't feel you want to handle her affairs for her any more. You'll tell her that you feel, regretfully, that you must leave Galloway."

"Are you out of your mind?" Oren demanded.

"You'll leave," Lafe answered, "or I shall throw you out bodily, and with the greatest of pleasure and the least tenderness I can manage."

Oren stopped in his tracks, stared hard at Lafe. The words said were the words meant. Lafe would do as he said.

Inside, Marietta was waiting.

Oren felt the granite bulk of Lafe behind him and found that all he could do was murmur, "Marietta, I'm . . . I'm—"

"Oren," she said, cutting in gently. "Oren, I asked you not to speak to Lafe, and now I ask you that you forget whatever it is he told you."

"I can't do that," Oren answered. "I'm leaving Galloway, Marietta. In just a few moments I'll be gone out of your life for good."

The color faded from her face. She whispered, "But what is it? What have I done to you? Why should you leave your home, Oren?"

"I've been ordered out by your husband," Oren said coldly. "What else can I do but go?"

"Ordered out!" She turned furiously on Lafe, who had stood by silently, watching and listening. "You've no right, Lafe. I told you . . . I told you—"

"And I made it quite clear that I would act if you didn't," he answered. "You didn't, and so I did."

She clutched at Oren's sleeve. "Listen, my dear, listen to me. I don't care what you did. It doesn't matter to me. Everything will be all right. I promise you, everything will be all right. The note's paid off. We'll manage somehow until next spring. I don't care what you did, believe me. It's of no consequence."

Oren shook his head slowly from side to side. "You don't understand, Marietta. Lafe's accused me of being a thief. I couldn't stay here. With your forgiveness or without it, I could no longer live in this house." He turned away, went slowly up the steps.

She sagged against the wall, tears streaming down her face.

"It's your fault, Lafe," she whispered hoarsely. "It's your doing, and I'll never forgive you for it. Never, never, never."

Elisha came then to darken the globes of the chandelier. Marietta covered her face, turned, and ran upstairs.

Watching her, Lafe thought that it would have been easier to have departed this place himself. If only he could have left the three of them—Coraleen, Oren, and Marietta—together, as he had found them, then it would have been easier on him. But it was impossible. He couldn't abandon Marietta to Coraleen and Oren. Now once again, and more than ever before, he sensed danger around Marietta. Now, more than ever, whether or not she wanted him, she needed him.

Moments later, she confronted him in their bedroom doorway, her nightdress and brush in her hands. He closed the door firmly behind him and leaned against it. In a mild voice he asked, "What are you doing, Marietta?"

"You can see well enough," she said, her eyes flashing defiance. "You need no explanation from me."

"Oren is leaving you, and therefore you are leaving me. Is that it?"

"You had no right to force him to go away from Galloway," she retorted.

"I had no right to protect you against theft?" Lafe asked, his voice still mild.

"Oren's not a thief! He's a man of honor. How dare you speak so of him?"

"I dare speak the truth, Marietta."

"It's not the truth."

"Do you say I've made it up?"

"I say you're wrong. And I say you interfere where you've no cause to," she cried.

He stared at her silently for a long time. At last he sighed. "My poor Marietta, how difficult all this is for you. Seven so hard months they've been, haven't they?"

" 'Seven so hard months'? I don't know what you're talking about!"

"But, my dear, of course you do. I mention the months of our marriage. Surely you remember that March day when we took our vows together."

Her color faded. Her breath stuck in her throat. She choked out, "What are you talking about?"

"You mustn't pretend. You understand well enough, Marietta. You should force yourself to some honesty. You've always wanted Oren, haven't you? And have looked, for a long while now, to have an excuse to keep your distance from me. Now you have your excuse and you seize upon it."

"How dare you, Lafe. You're my husband. I've never given you cause to speak so."

"I dare, I dare," he said softly. "Because it's the truth, whether or not you care to admit it. Be alone then to dream of your Oren. Pretend to yourself that his arms enfold you, and his lips kiss you. Dream all you like. but it'll never happen."

She slapped him as hard as she could across the face. The slender red marks of her fingers bloomed along his cheek.

He caught her wrist, held it tightly, pulling her close to his chest, and holding her there in a grip of steel. He looked down into her face, laughing softly. "My dear, I hope that makes you feel better, but it doesn't change what I've said from truth to lie."

She struggled in his grasp, cried, "Damn you, Lafe, I'll never forgive you for this."

"Be careful," he answered. "If you strike again, I may strike back. And I deal out hard blows when I'm driven to them."

She pulled away from him. "Let me out," she said coolly. "Let me pass."

He stepped aside, gave her a mocking bow. "You're free to go, Marietta."

She threw up her head, her eyes flashing. "And when will you go, Lafe?"

"Never fear, and never think it," he answered. "You won't be alone, Marietta. I'll not leave you."

18

"It's all your fault," Coraleen said in a bitter voice. "This was his home, always, always, until you so stupidly brought Lafe Flynn here."

Marietta bowed her head, said nothing. What could she answer? How could she defend herself?

Coraleen pressed the advantage. "Tell me, what will you do, Marietta? How long will you allow this to go on?"

"I don't know," Marietta whispered.

"Then when will you know?" Coraleen demanded. "In God's name, when will you do what you have to do?"

But Marietta only shook her dark head, swallowing hard to keep herself from sobbing.

"Come with me to the Beckwiths'," the younger girl pleaded. "At least do that. At least talk to Oren for a little while."

"Not yet," Marietta choked out. "Must you harry me? I need time to think."

"Then when?" Coraleen demanded. "When will you do it?"

Lafe said from the open doorway, "She'll do it, my dear Coraleen, when she's figured out a way to get rid of me."

"Lafe, will you please stop it?" Marietta said. "There's no need for you to involve Coraleen in this."

"It would seem to me she's brought herself into it, hasn't she?"

"And why not?" Coraleen demanded hotly. "It's Oren I'm talking about, and I'm Oren's sister. Someone must look out for his interests if Marietta won't."

Lafe smiled faintly. "What spirit, Coraleen! Still, I must tell you, Oren will not be back. That's the end of it. The two of you, Marietta and you, may do as you like, of course. But I tell you now that Oren won't return to Galloway."

Coraleen stared hard into his set face. She saw the small muscles tensed in his square jaw, the thin hard line of his lips, his hard dark blue eyes that met hers with a granite gaze. Oh, but this man was sure of himself, she thought.

And he was right in a way to be so sure. No doubt Oren would never return to Galloway while Lafe was here. But Lafe might not be here forever. No one knew of his comings and goings better than she did. No one saw a pattern beginning to emerge from them as clearly as she did.

That foolish gig that Marietta had given Coraleen stood her in good stead these days. No matter that it wasn't the pretty fringed surrey she had hoped for. It took her here and there in Darnal, and in the countryside. She observed Lafe and big Duveen, riding away with the wagon toward Durham's Station, coming back.

She had begun to be certain that there was more to Lafe Flynn than met the casual eye. She didn't know yet what it was, but she was sure it was something that couldn't bear the light of day. She watched him now, a bland innocence in her face, and finally said, "Perhaps you're right, Lafe." And then, "And perhaps you did what you had to."

Marietta gasped. "Coraleen, will you be quiet? You know nothing of what's happened. You don't realize what you say."

Coraleen grinned at her. "You only imagine so, dear sister. I spoke with Oren before he left. I know everything. He explained it fully. I think we must be good to him, because he's all there is of our family, Marietta. Yet I still think perhaps Lafe was just, as he had to be."

He made a small mocking bow. "I thank you for your kind words. Perhaps your sister will take them to heart and to mind."

Marietta set her lips, turned her face away.

Late that afternoon, she and Coraleen rode to the Beckwiths' in the gig. It was cold and gray, the air scented with the pungent smoke of wood fires. Her breath floated before her lips in a plume of white, and her eyes teared, straining for their first look at Oren.

But when Sara greeted them, complacently folding her hands over her swollen belly, she said, "What a pity you've missed the boys. Gentry and Oren talked late into the night, and now the two of them have gone to Darnal. I don't know why."

"To drink in Jordan House," Coraleen answered.

"Perhaps," Sara agreed. "If so, they won't stay overlong. My John went with them."

Heartsick, Marietta made conversation for a little while, then rose to go, and Sara asked, "Coraleen, will you stay over and see Oren since you've come? I know he'd like that, and I know you would, too."

"I will indeed," Coraleen answered. "You don't mind, do you, Marietta? I've so much to talk about with Sara, and it's been so long since we've had a real visit. And then, too, I *do* want to feast my eyes on Oren for a little."

"I don't mind," Marietta said, hearing the mockery in Coraleen's tone. *She* wanted to feast her eyes on Oren for a little. No doubt she also wanted to confide all she knew to Sara. Within days, the whole county would have been apprised of affairs at Galloway.

As she drove home in Coraleen's gig, she told herself that she didn't care. Galloway was always talked about. This would be only one more subject for discussion.

But the house was so still that evening. It was empty of feeling. The scent of loneliness hovered about it. Oren was gone, and Coraleen, too, and Lafe hadn't returned for supper.

When Elisha came to light the lamps, he had given her a sympathetic look. She had forced herself to eat the food Essie prepared, but it was all tasteless to her and didn't stir her dulled appetite, and Dora, noticing, asked if she knew of what would tempt her more.

Later, as she sat warming her cold hands before the fire and wondering what to do, she heard the horse come up the driveway and stop, snorting and stamping. She didn't move, but only leaned closer to the flames. It would be Lafe, and no one else. And she didn't care, she told herself. She didn't care if he came or went. She'd never care again.

He appeared in the doorway, his face ruddy with the October chill and his eyes bright. "I'm sorry to be so late, Marietta. I was delayed in town."

"I see." Her voice was cool. "Shall I have Essie prepare something for you?" she asked, and instantly remembered the night she had taken him into the kitchen with her, set out food for him, and leaned close by, enjoying his enjoyment as he ate.

But now he said, "No, thank you," and grinned. "I didn't want to be any trouble to the routine of the house, so I had a meal, if you want to call it that, in Jordan House."

"You needn't bother with that in the future," she answered. "This is your home. We shall always provide you with what you wish."

"Oh, will you?" He laughed softly. "Now, there's a pleasant invitation if I ever heard one."

"An invitation? What are you talking about?"

"Come, come, don't pretend with me, my dear."

"I've invited you to nothing, except to take your meals at home," she snapped.

"Ah, you've already changed your mind, have you? First you offer to provide what I wish, then you pretend you don't understand my acceptance. Still angry, are you?"

"Angry?" she demanded. "What do you know of how I feel?"

"I think you've made it plain enough, my dear. I thought that perhaps, once your temper had cooled, you'd allow yourself some sensible second thoughts."

"I have thought about it, believe me. I have not changed my mind. You had no right to send Oren away."

"Are you certain of that?"

"I am. I am. And what do you care?"

"I assure you, I care deeply."

Tears stung her eyes. She whispered, "No, no, you insist on mocking me, and I can't bear it."

"I'm sorry for that, Marietta."

"You could mend what you've done," she said urgently. "If you wanted to."

His eyes narrowed. He said harshly, "Are you asking *me* to apologize? Is it to you or to Oren that I must go on my knees?"

"I want it the way it was before," she said, her voice and hands trembling.

He drew a deep breath, controlling the urge, the hunger, to take her into his arms, to promise her anything she wanted. He waited until he was certain of his voice, and then said harshly, "You can't have it the way it was before, not ever again. The clock cannot be turned back. I'm going to protect you from Oren Henderson, no matter how much you despise me for it."

"But I've told you I don't need protection."

"I believe you do," he said more gently and, with a bow of his head to her, left her standing there without another word.

She sank down into the chair before the fire and was still there when Coraleen returned, saying only that she had changed her mind and decided not to stay over with Sara after all.

Gentry had ridden with her and returned to the Beckwiths' without coming in, she explained to Marietta's question.

She did not explain that Oren had ordered her to return to Galloway at once. "You're not to leave Marietta alone with that man," Oren had told her, his dark eyes gleaming. "I forbid it. You must stay there with the two of them. He'll no doubt try to send you away, too. Be sure you give him no excuse for that, Coraleen. And I mean you to listen to what I tell you."

She had laughed. "Why, you can wager I won't give him an excuse for turning me out, Oren. Why should I? He thinks me a child, and hardly notices what I do."

256

"Perhaps," Oren said. "Though I wouldn't be too certain of that, Coraleen. In any event, don't let anything happen."

"I won't, I promise you."

"And stay there."

"I will."

She had returned to Galloway immediately. She saw now —far better than Oren did, she was sure—that she must be clever, and vigilant, if she was to rid Galloway of Lafe and bring Oren home again.

That night when she went up to bed, she left the curtains open and pulled a deep soft chair close to the window. From midnight until dawn, she was aware of every dry leaf that dropped from the trees outside. She knew when a mockingbird awakened. She knew every creak of the floors in the house.

But she didn't know that soon after she had settled to watch, Lafe took a candle and went down the hall to the room to which Marietta had retreated. He eased the door open and went in, closing it softly behind him.

She sat up in alarm as he drew the bed curtains back.

"It's all right," he told her, and he noticed that her alarm didn't fade. "I hope you weren't already sleeping."

"What do you want?" She carefully pulled the bedclothes up around her, clutching the quilt to her throat. Strangely, she felt as shy of him as she had once thought she would be on her wedding night. She didn't recall having felt that way then, though now she did.

He set the candle on the table, sat down beside her. "A few words, Marietta. Are you awake enough to listen?"

She waited, shivering. It wasn't cold in the room, she knew. The chill was within her, within her very flesh and bone.

"I think we must talk a little, Marietta," he said slowly.

"What's there to talk about?" she asked. "What's done is done, isn't it?"

"Not quite." He gave her a faint smile. "Do you propose to remain here forever?"

"Yes, I do," she said coldly. "And it should please you,"

she went on, her voice sharp and bitter. "If you recall what you said to me . . ."

"I may have been somewhat angry," he answered dryly.

"But you spoke what you felt!"

"I don't deny it."

"Then there's no more to be said," She leaned back into the pillows, turning her face away.

"Are you sure you know what you're doing? Don't you realize that the more nights that pass the more difficult it will be for you to change these new arrangements?"

"I contemplate to change nothing," she retorted.

"Then Oren will have permanently separated us. Is that what you want?"

"Not Oren," she spat at him, turning to glare her anger from hot eyes. "Not Oren, Lafe. You. You did it. And you must take the responsibility!"

"I thought you'd have calmed yourself by now. I thought you might have considered further."

"I'm perfectly calm," she told him. She waited a moment, allowing her breath and her pulse to slow. "I *have* thought. And nothing's changed. You've destroyed my family, and I can't pretend that nothing's happened."

"Then I won't pretend either," Lafe told her.

He rose to his feet, stood looking down at her for a long silent moment. Then he leaned down. His warm hands closed around her shoulders. He said softly, "You're my wife, and I want you."

"No," she cried. "No, Lafe, I'll have nothing of you."

He murmured against her mouth, "I think you will, Marietta. Wherever your heart has gone, your body's here." He bent her head back and stared long and hard into her eyes. And then he took her face into his hands and held it and kissed her until her lips felt bruised.

When, finally, he allowed her to turn her head away, she said, "And now are you satisfied?"

He laughed, but there was no amusement in the sound. "How could I be? There's such a fire in your anger, Marietta. It stirs me more than you can imagine."

She lay back against the pillows, limp now and still. If her anger stirred him, she told herself, then she wouldn't be angry. She would offer the meek compliance of the sacrificial lamb.

She burned at his touch, but she didn't move or protest. She closed her eyes when his hand curled over her breast, stroking until her heart seemed to halt its beat. She set her lips when he pulled her into his arms. She was a dulled and useless thing when his weight settled on her.

She lay staring at the bed canopy above, looking past the wide curve of his bared shoulders, while he made urgent and harsh love to her.

She lay silent when he drew away and bent to cover her gently, and then left her alone. When he was gone, the last whisper of his footsteps faded, she found herself suddenly choked by sobs. Bitter tears spilled from her eyes and soaked the pillow, still warm from his body. She wept painfully, and didn't know why. Nor did she dare think on it.

At the breakfast table she was pale, silent when she served him coffee.

He thanked her with his usual courtesy, and she nodded acknowledgment but didn't speak.

Dividing a look between them, Coraleen sighed. "Oh, how grim we all are. I wish something would happen. I wish there'd be some excitement."

Marietta said nothing, merely shook her head.

Lafe grinned, "Well, perhaps there will be."

"Oh, do you think so?" the younger girl asked eagerly. "Tell me what, so that I can enjoy it ahead of time."

"I don't know what," he answered. "How could I? But you'll have your excitement, I'm sure."

Coraleen refused to be teased. "You're impossible," she said. "I don't know why I talk to you at all. Except there's no one else to talk to."

"Coraleen," Marietta cut in, "would you please stop chattering so?"

"Do you have a headache, Marietta?"

"Yes, I do."

"I'm sorry. Shall I find you something for it?"

Marietta raised her eyes to heaven. "Silence. Can you find me that?"

It crossed Coraleen's mind that there was adequate silence in the grave. She'd wish Marietta there but for Galloway. Aloud she said, "I'm sorry, Marietta. I truly am. I'll be quiet, I promise you."

Lafe said softly, "I'm sorry, too, Marietta, that you had such a bad night."

She turned her head stiffly. She looked at him, and then suddenly, with heat rising in her face, she lowered her eyes. When she could, she got to her feet, saying, "Excuse me, please. I've much to do today."

"Let me help you," Coraleen cried.

"Plantation business," Marietta answered crisply. "I shall just have a talk with Mr. Blandish first, and then we'll see."

She didn't look forward to telling Jed Blandish that Oren would not be working with him any longer. It would be embarrassing, if not worse, to say those words. She would have to make certain that the repairs on the slave quarters had begun. She would have to determine what else needed to be done, and what supplies the overseer required for the coming winter. Beyond that, one day very soon, she would have to see Marcus Swinton, to learn how Galloway's account stood. These tasks suddenly loomed ahead of her, joyless and heavy. When Oren had taken care of her affairs, she had been interested in them. Now suddenly, they were horrid duties that brought her no satisfaction, only weariness and fear.

She didn't know that Lafe had placed in Marcus' bank enough cash funds to carry the plantation for two full years even if no profit were made. She didn't know that he had sworn Marcus to secrecy and that Marcus had promised to keep Lafe informed, never breathing a word to Marietta.

Thus she was deeply troubled when she saw Jed Blandish. But she soon found that she needn't have been. He greeted the news of Oren's departure with open relief. Tugging his long blond mustaches, he assured her that he could manage the plantation, and that she needn't trouble her head about it. He said he'd get to the repairs immediately, and go about ordering the same winter supplies that had been ordered when her father was alive.

By the time she returned to the house, she was greatly relieved. She could see that she could manage her affairs without Oren's help. But that didn't cool her anger at Lafe, her heartache at having Oren gone.

Oren had been misguided, dreadfully misguided. Still, she could understand. His man's pride had driven him. He had not wanted to admit that he was beholden to her for everything he owned. He'd wanted a small nest egg for himself, and he hadn't seen that he was taking from her what was rightly hers. If Lafe had allowed it, she would have stopped Oren without driving him away. She would have made him see what he was doing without accusing him. She managed thus to convince herself that she was in the right, and Lafe completely in the wrong, about Oren.

Lafe Flynn, she told herself, was completely in the wrong about everything he did. He'd had no reason to come to her room the night before when she'd made clear enough that she didn't want him, and never would again. He'd had no right to force himself on her. No, no, no. No right at all.

Thinking of those moments, of her tears after, a flush rose in her cheeks. She dreaded the night ahead.

But she had no cause to fear.

Lafe didn't come to her that night. Nor did he come on the nights that followed, though she waited more and more anxiously for him, and listened to his slow footsteps pace off the floor of the adjacent room.

Lafe, listening as the silence deepened and the walls closed in on him, swore to himself that he'd never go to her again. He felt the fool for having forced himself on her, and he wouldn't allow himself to feel the fool a second time. What kind of a man wanted a woman who didn't want him? What kind of a husband took his wife when she didn't want him?

He determined that he wasn't that kind, whatever it was.

And as the days and nights passed, he was relieved that he had. For it became clear to him that he needed the privacy of a separate bedchamber.

Quite suddenly things fell into place just as they should.

Now he could slip out at night when he had to, and slip back again in good time for the morning bell, with no one to witness his coming and going.

No matter that he paid a bitter price for this convenience, that he walked the room more than he slept in it, that he leaned against the wall and listened to Marietta sigh.

He had the convenience. He would use it.

19

The moment he crossed the threshold of the suite in Jordan House, Lafe sensed that something was wrong. There was at first no one thing he could put his hand on, but he felt a change there, an alteration of the atmosphere itself.

Then he saw on the table where he had left some pages of correspondence a framed mark in the dust that showed those papers had been moved, then replaced. He saw that the candle on the mantel had burned an inch lower than he had left it.

Duveen and Moses, both with him then, watched with questioning eyes as he studied the rest of the room, then examined the gallery doors. Finally, satisfied that his intuition was correct, he turned to them and asked, "Has anyone been questioning either of you about me?"

Duveen slowly shook his head.

Moses said, "Nobody has, and nobody would." Then, "But what's the matter?"

"Someone's been in here, and I'm wondering who's so interested in me suddenly."

"You don't keep papers, do you?" Moses asked.

Lafe shook his head.

"Then the good Lord alone knows what anyone would find."

Lafe agreed, but the incident continued to trouble him. He made a careful search of the suite. Together, he and Duveen and Moses lifted the carpets, carefully probed the packing of the chairs and settle. They moved and examined the looking glass, and then the two paintings on the walls. If there had been an intruder, he had left no trace behind.

He sent Moses and Duveen to the warehouse, and sat at the table, fingers tugging a lock of russet hair, his thoughts straying to Marietta and how she had looked the first time he'd seen her, waiting in silver moonlight for Oren to come home.

Soon, with a muted curse, he rose and left the room, carefully locking the door behind him as always.

Gentry accosted him in the lower hallway. Red of face, shining of eye, Gentry stood very straight, saying, "I have a message from Oren for you, Lafe."

Lafe nodded.

"He asks that you meet him. You've defamed him, and he wants satisfaction."

Lafe laughed softly, "Oh, he says now that he's been defamed, does he?"

"Will you meet him? That's what he wants to know."

Lafe looked into hot blue eyes. "Let him come to me, Gentry. Let him ask me himself. I prefer my dealings direct."

"I act as his second. It's completely regular for me to do so. I'm empowered to say that if you refuse to meet him with pistols, you'll prove yourself the coward that Oren suspects you are."

Now Lafe threw back his head and laughed heartily. "My dear Gentry, take back word of what I've just told you to Oren. And you might add that I consider him a fool."

"You refuse to answer me?"

"I've just told you. I won't deal through seconds. I'll talk to him, and only to him."

"Very well. If these are your last words, I'll tell him," Gentry said. "No doubt you'll soon hear from him."

"No doubt," Lafe agreed dryly. "But tell him I suggest he take another week or so to allow his head to clear. I'm a very good shot, you know. And though Oren bested you once by luck, I'm not certain he'd be so lucky twice." When Gentry had turned away, Lafe called him back. "And, Gentry, do me the kindness of giving my regards to your father and to Sara, will you?"

Gentry's only response was a brief bow and a cold look.

When he reached the warehouse, Lafe found Coraleen waiting. She had flung back the fur-trimmed hood of her cloak and it lay curled around her shoulders, framing her pink and white face and giving it a vixenish look.

"Oh, how I'd love to know New Orleans," she was saying dreamily as Lafe entered the office. "You don't imagine, Moses, that it'll stay the same forever, do you? And if I don't see it soon, surely then it'll be too late."

Moses' round face was stony. His eyes lit with relief when he saw Lafe.

It was enough to tell Lafe that Coraleen's comments had been part of an inquisition. Only an hour before Lafe had asked if anyone had been questioning Moses. Now Coraleen was doing so, with New Orleans the excuse. And poor Moses had never seen that teeming city. Lafe could only hope that the man had acquitted himself well. He sent Moses off to help Duveen, who had ducked into the unloading sheds the moment Coraleen approached.

When Moses had gone, Lafe seated himself at the rose-wood desk, propped his chin on his fist, and grinned. "And now, Coraleen, what can I do for you this morning?"

"You can say good morning," she said, smiling.

"I'd have gladly done so at breakfast, if you'd been up to put in an appearance."

She gave a mock shudder. "Oh, I can't bear it. It's too grim. You stare at Marietta. She stares at you. Dora scuttles about, and Essie scolds in the kitchen."

"So you cower under the quilts and then visit me here instead."

"You don't object, surely."

"No. I suppose I don't. But is there a purpose in your coming, or is it just for the pleasure of my company?"

"The pleasure of your company, of course." She herself

heard the dry edge in her voice, and chuckled softly to cover it.

Lafe rose, went to the window, and opened it slightly. A cold wind slipped through, rustled the papers on the desk, and lifted a curl of Coraleen's hair. When he turned, he said, "Thank you for that. I'm glad someone has joy in seeing me." And the identical dry edge was in his tone.

Her brows lifted. She said, "But what could you expect, Lafe?"

He didn't answer her. What had he expected? He'd known from his wedding night where Marietta's heart was. He would have known before that if he'd only allowed himself to recognize the truth.

Coraleen went on: "And what will you do, Lafe? Will you remain at Galloway, the husband to an unwilling, unloving wife? Or will you go back to New Orleans?" She smiled broadly. "By all accounts, it's a beautiful place, and there are plenty to welcome you there, while there's none to welcome you here. But me, of course," she added hastily.

He gave her a long speculative look. "Do you indeed?"

"Of course I do. For I don't blame you for what's happened. I blame Marietta. She's deceived you, Lafe. She ought never to have married you. I tried to tell her so. And I tried to tell you."

"You meddle too much in affairs that don't concern you, Coraleen. Run along now like a good girl, and allow me to get to my work."

She pulled the hood up over her hair and rose in a flutter of gown and cloak. "You'll never be able to keep Oren and Marietta apart, Lafe. Don't you realize that? Don't you see it? You'll hurt us all and yourself, too, in the attempt, but you'll never keep them apart."

"We'll see," Lafe answered softly. "We'll see."

At dinnertime, when the gaming room was crowded with the midday rush, Oren and Gentry, full of bourbon, sat together waiting.

"Are you sure you want to do this?" Gentry asked. He had

spent the better part of the morning reporting Lafe's remarks, and agreeing that each was insulting beyond bearing and belief. But as he contemplated the plan he and Oren had devised, he became less and less sure of himself. He wished suddenly that he were at home and had no part in this. He looked into Oren's narrow face, hoping to see the same uncertainty, but Oren seemed at ease.

"I'm sure," he answered, barely glancing at Gentry. His dark eyes were hooded, studying the smoky crowded room and tallying his friends and foes.

The Reverend Filene would be an ally, as would Dr. Pinchot, a gentleman of the old, stern school, who believed that honor came before all.

Marcus Swinton, though, was no friend. It was he who had first gone to Lafe with that tale about the renewed note and Oren's growing bank account. One day he'd rue his action, Oren reflected bitterly, when he learned that the growing bank account had not been for Oren's use but for the county's well-being and for Marcus' own safety. But enemy or no, he would bear witness. And so would all these others, men who had been reared in the code and believed in it, and applauded those who lived by it. Lafe Flynn would soon learn that he could insult no Henderson with impunity in Darnal.

Oren's smile was narrow, but satisfied, when he saw Lafe make his way through the room to lean at the bar.

When he had a drink before him and had sipped at it, and not until then, Oren approached him, said quietly, "I'll have a word with you, sir."

Gentry, close by, nodded with importance, his uneasy eyes slipping about to observe the audience.

Lafe took another swallow of his drink, then set it down and turned to face Oren. "Yes. What can I do for you?" he asked politely.

"I sent you a challenge," Oren said coldly. "You've said to my second, Gentry Beckwith, that you'd deal only with me. I'm here now."

"So I see. In the flesh. And well primed, too, I suspect."

Oren ignored that. He demanded, "Well, what do you want to say to me, sir?"

"I?" Lafe's brows rose. "I? I have nothing to say to you. Whatever made you think I did?"

Oren raised his voice. "Sir, you told Gentry—"

"I said," Lafe interrupted mildly, "that if you had anything to tell me, I would listen. But only if you delivered your comments in person. You are here, in your person, what there is of it. Deliver your comments. Or leave me alone."

The group standing at the bar wreathed in cigar smoke had begun now to listen. Some half turned, the better to observe the corner of the bar where Lafe leaned, confronted by Oren and Gentry. Faint smiles touched some mouths. The beginnings of frowns grew on others.

"I demand that you meet me at Death Meadows," Oren said loudly. "You've blackened my name. I must have my satisfaction."

"At all costs?"

"I must have satisfaction," Oren repeated loudly.

"Your death is to be your satisfaction, is that it?" Lafe asked, his voice silky now.

"If it is, then it is," Oren cried. "But you must give me the opportunity to see how it goes."

"I must, must I?" Lafe grinned suddenly. "Oren, let me tell you, such words as *must* mean little or nothing to me."

"Then you refuse me!" Oren said triumphantly.

"Hah!" Gentry cried. "Lafe Flynn has refused the challenge." Turning to face his audience, he asked, "You hear?"

There was a murmur. The small pretense of polite inattention was gone now. All the men in the room had turned, were staring at Oren, staring at Lafe. All other talk had ceased.

Eamus Jordan, summoned by one of the serving girls, danced nervously in the doorway, weighing whether to interfere. Mr. Flynn was a valued customer, had been since his arrival in town. Oren Henderson was a young blood of the county, adopted son of the landed class. It was a hard choice. Eamus groaned and did nothing.

Lafe said in a soft voice, "Nothing would please me more than to meet you, Oren."

"But you dare not. You're a coward. You play at a courage you refuse to demonstrate."

"Is that so?"

"You've just proven that very thing." Oren turned his dark head and looked at Dr. Pinchot, who stood frowning, at the Reverend Filene, who was open-mouthed, at Marcus Swinton, who had turned pale. "These men are all witness to your cowardice, Lafe Flynn."

"They are witness only to my refusal. You may call it cowardice if you like."

"And what else is it?"

"I call it patience," Lafe answered with an audible sigh. "Patience, Oren. I don't know how much more of it I have. You might try to recall, please, if you possibly can, that you're related to me by marriage. Do you imagine that I'd meet my wife's brother in a fight to the death?—for that's what it would have to be."

He saw it in his mind as he spoke. Marietta's bloodless face, pale with anguish, wet with tears—and that look of never-ending hatred that would burn at him from her amethyst eyes. With Oren dead he would lose her forever, if he hadn't lost her already.

"What a fine-sounding excuse." Oren sneered. "Is that supposed to appease me, to wipe away the insults you've given me?"

There was a whispered grumble among the listening men.

Lafe ignored it. "I'm hardly trying to appease you. And since nothing could, I'll consider this conversation closed and bid you good afternoon, and good dinner, or whatever else you think fitting."

"Damn it, Flynn, do you think you can just walk out of this?" Oren demanded shrilly. He looked at Gentry, at the others again. "You all see? You all bear witness? Lafe Flynn is a coward, hiding behind Marietta Garvey's skirts. He's just plain scared despite his fancy excuses. He'd rather be dishonored than dead."

Now Lafe's dark blue eyes gleamed. He gave vent to a long sigh. "Oh, how you press me, Oren." He emptied his glass, made a wry face, and set it on the bar. He straightened, smoothed his cuffs, adjusted the cravat at his throat, and began to turn away.

"Not yet," Oren cried. "I'm not finished with you yet."

"But I am finished with you," Lafe told him. "Quite finished indeed."

Oren seized Lafe by the shoulder, pulled him around, and struck in a wild, free-swinging backhand at Lafe's face.

The sound of the blow was like an explosion in the room, followed by shocked silence.

Lafe stood very still. Then, in a hushed voice, he said, "Now you've gone too far, Oren."

He caught Oren by the waist, lifted him as easily as he would a small boy, and flung him halfway across the room to land sprawling against a table. The table tipped over and sent glasses and platters and bottles flying as Oren fell heavily to the floor.

Lafe stood over Oren, hands balled on his hips, his russet head bent. "Listen to me. Listen well. I'll say it only once more, and never again. You may insult me as you please. You know and I know why you do it. I'll not soil my hands with the blood of my wife's brother. I'll not bring her sorrow. So we shall not meet at Death Meadows. For if we did, I'd surely walk away, and you'd surely be carried. Now leave it, Oren. Go on as you can, and as you please. But stay away from Galloway. And be glad for your own sake that Marietta's my wife."

He turned on his heel, brushed his way past the watching men, murmured to Eamus, "I'll pay the damages," and left Jordan House.

By the time he returned to Galloway that evening, Marietta had already been treated to a full description of what had happened. Coraleen had had it from Sara, who had had it from Gentry, in the absence of Oren, who had returned to the Beckwiths' too drunk to stand on his feet, or to talk, and had retired to his room.

"Refused him!" Coraleen chortled. "Can you imagine it? I should have thought Lafe feared nothing in this life. At least that's how he's always acted, isn't it? But there you are! One can never tell! He refused Oren! Can you imagine it?"

Marietta listened, paling at first, then with spots of red burning in her cheeks. A brightness filled her eyes, and her lips trembled. Finally she said, "You might be glad that Lafe is as he is, Coraleen."

"Glad! Why, he should be ashamed to show his face. Just think what everyone is saying." The younger girl rushed on: "And do you know? He killed a man in New Orleans! That's why he left there. In a place called the Dueling Oaks! So imagine how fearful he must be of our Oren."

"He killed a man in New Orleans?" Marietta asked. "And why was that?"

Coraleen shrugged. "I can't tell you. Gentry didn't seem to know. But what does it matter what happened there? He's refused Oren here, and will never be able to hold his head up again. That's your husband, Marietta."

"How little you know of it," Marietta said.

"I know more than you think," Coraleen retorted.

Marietta didn't answer.

"I know that you'll rue the day that you married Lafe Flynn. You'll be sorry for it forever," Coraleen cried.

You'll be sorry. Those words again, Marietta thought, and she shuddered, though the fire was high on the hearth and warmth filled the candlelit room. *You'll be sorry.*

She turned her head from Coraleen to hide the tears that suddenly burned her eyes. She was sorry already, wasn't she? Sorry for what had happened to Oren. Sorry that she had hurt Lafe by accepting the love he had offered her in good faith, and given him nothing but heartache in return.

Coraleen wandered off, but Marietta remained in the morning room and waited for Lafe.

He made no mention of what had happened. He spoke just as usual in these days of their estrangement, politely, about the coldness of the weather, and whom he had seen

271

in town, and what news he had received from his family in New Orleans.

He did not speak of the coded telegram delivered to him at the warehouse only moments after he'd left Oren and Gentry in the gaming room, in which his brother Claude urged him to give up at once the activities in which he was engaged. Within the year, his work, now merely illegal and punishable by fines and imprisonment, would become treason, punishable by death. In the North the abolitionist fever was reaching a new pitch, and in the South the long shadows of war had already been cast. Lafe knew, though, that he would not be persuaded. What would come would come. He'd go on as before.

Marietta listened dutifully to his casual remarks, her hands folded tightly in her lap, her heart-shaped face framed in the blond lace that trimmed her green velvet gown. But at last she could no longer bear it. She burst out, "Lafe, I've heard what happened in Jordan House today."

He raised his dark brows. "Oh? And am I supposed to guess just what you heard? Was it that some new drummer has come to sell his wares? Or a traveling journalist has stopped to study the ways of our county? Or that one of the politicians disgraced himself with a serving girl?"

"Stop it," she cried. "You know what I'm talking about."

"I see." A small smile lifted a corner of his mouth. "And how do you know about that so quickly?"

"Coraleen told me."

"And she had it from Sara, of course. Who had had it from Gentry. Who was present at the great moment."

"She told me all."

"No doubt," he said dryly. "Our Coraleen is a messenger of speed at least. I'll not vouch for her accuracy, but never mind. You know what happened, Marietta. I'm sorry. I'd hoped not to trouble you."

"Trouble? Lafe, I understand what you did. You could have killed Oren, and I realize it."

"Oren." Again a smile lifted the corner of Lafe's mouth.

272

"Do you know, my dear Marietta, I believe I've heard all of Oren Henderson that I care to. Shall we agree between us that we won't mention his name again?"

She braided her fingers together. She kept her eyes on them, on the wedding ring Lafe had placed on her hand. She whispered, "Lafe, I want to thank you."

"You owe me no gratitude, Marietta." He spoke quietly, but the aperitif glass he had been holding snapped in his hand with the sound of a pistol shot, and blood seeped from between his curled fingers.

She jumped to her feet with a gasp, but he smiled at her, waved her back. "It's nothing, nothing. Don't disturb yourself." Saying that, he took out a silk handkerchief and bound his hand in it. He knew she was only waiting for his attention so she could go on. But he had no desire to hear what she had to say. He got to his feet with a casual glance at the window.

"You're not going out before supper?" she asked.

"No. I thought I heard the dogs."

"The boys will look after them." Then she burst out, "I know it can't have been easy for you, Lafe. I realize how trying Oren can be. And to challenge you before all the others in Jordan House. Just there, where everyone would know it . . ."

"Don't think about it."

"I can't help but think about it!"

He said, his smile wider, "The risk to your Oren's life?"

"No! No! Not that! I know you'd never kill him! No matter how sorely you were tried."

"I've forgotten it. I wish you'd do the same."

"It took great courage, Lafe."

"Why, thank you for saying so, Marietta."

"I've never said otherwise," she flared, rebuffed and angry at it.

"No, I don't believe you ever did."

"Oren shouldn't have done it. I tell you, when he's in the wrong, I admit it. I shall tell him so myself. He's behaved

273

badly all around." Her voice became softer. "But if you would only see your way to make amends with him somehow, I'm sure we'd be happy again."

Lafe looked into her eyes for a long moment. To make amends with Oren. Did she know what she was asking? A bitter smile curled his lips. His voice was silky when he said, "Why, Marietta, my dear, I'm glad to hear that you know when Oren's in the wrong. And now, if you'll forgive me, I prefer, as I mentioned before, not to concern myself any longer with your brother. Shall we go into the dining room? Or do you wish to sit here alone and dream your dreams?"

The next morning when Lafe arrived at the warehouse with Duveen and Moses, a broken side window gleamed in the cold sunlight; and when the three men went in, they found the office in total disarray. The rosewood desk had been emptied, the contents of every drawer strewn upon the floor. The cabinets had likewise been opened, and sheets of paper, bills of lading, purchase orders, and receipts had been scattered to the corners of the room.

Duveen grunted in dismay, the scars around his mouth suddenly pale against the black of his skin.

Moses murmured, "Lord help us."

Only Lafe was still, surveying the damage with speculative eyes.

Oren, he thought. Oren in a drunken rage and out for his revenge.

Or was there more to it than that? Had his comings and goings engendered suspicion? Had someone learned, or guessed, about the hidey hole beneath the rosewood desk that Eamus Jordan had had polished so lovingly? And there was the search of his suite at the hotel to think about. Could Oren have been responsible for that, too?

At last Lafe said softly, "We'll have to move our base. We can't continue here any longer." And again he realized that often things fell into place just as they had to. Oren was gone

274

from Galloway, and through his own doing. And Lafe shared his room with no one.

Duveen knew what he was thinking. His big shoulders hunched up. He shook his big dark head from side to side.

But Lafe said, smiling, "What better place than Galloway to do what we've got to do?"

20

There had been time, plenty of opportunity as well, Marietta thought. Oren could have sent her a message through Coraleen, who often came and went between the Beckwiths' and Galloway. Oren could have come himself when Lafe was off on one of his trips. Instead there had been nothing, not a single word. She tapped her foot impatiently as she thought, If he won't come to me, then I shall go to him. It was easy enough to plan an accidental meeting. All she had to do was have Elisha drive her in to town. All she had to do was linger near Jordan House.

She considered it for several days, hoping always that Oren would feel the need to see her, to return to Galloway, even for a brief and surreptitious visit.

He didn't come.

On a cold Thursday morning she dressed carefully, listening to the tick of the clock as she did up her black curls. She set a small flowered hat on them, though the velvet petals were unseasonable. The gay colors lifted her spirits only slightly. Her cloak was warm and weighed on her shoulders, as her spirits weighed on her heart. She changed her slippers twice, undecided about the color.

After all her preparations she was suddenly impatient, and she swept out leaving her mittens and shawl behind, so that by the time Elisha brought her to Darnal, her fingers were as numb with cold as her heart was.

"Where to now, Miss Marietta?" Elisha asked, his voice disapproving and his eyes avoiding hers. "You want the warehouse? Is that it? You going to see Mr. Lafe?"

"Just here," she answered tartly. "Before Jordan House.
"And then? What do I do then?"

"Stop and wait," she answered.

"Yes, Miss Marietta." His tone was submissive, but the
look he gave her was sharp enough to cut the ice she'd seen
on a puddle alongside the road. She thought briefly of Aunt
Tatie, who'd have done more than look. But Aunt Tatie was
dead now, and there was no one left to scold Marietta with
the sharp words of worry and love.

The carriage pulled up at the square, jerked to a halt
that further expressed Elisha's disapproval. The horses'
breaths steamed in the chill air.

Marietta leaned forward to look from the window. The
square was empty. No one lingered on the stone benches.
The broken railing of the hitching post moved slowly with
the wind and then sagged down again. There were pale lights
flickering beyond the steamy windows of the courthouse.

When she looked back at the hotel, she saw that from
there, too, pale light gleamed, spilling out through the open
door.

Her heart gave a great leap, and she gasped and said,
"Elisha, I'll get down now, and quickly, if you please."

She was halfway out before his hand settled at her elbow,
easing her from the high step to the frozen mud. "Miss
Marietta?"

"Hush, and stay here," she said in a furious whisper. With
that she was off and away, running in quick small steps,
crying, "Oren, I want to talk to you. Oren, wait. Don't go in
yet."

The so carefully planned accidental meeting was forgotten.
She didn't care that he would realize she had deliberately
lingered near the hotel waiting to see him.

He doffed his hat, bowed. "Good morning, Marietta." His
voice was cool, his face stiff, concealing the embarrassment
he felt. That she knew what he had done and still forgave
him only made his humiliation the more difficult to bear.
His very spirit cringed within him at the effusive warmth
she poured out at him.

277

"Good morning!" she mimicked him, laughing now, but reproachful as well. "Good morning. Is that all you have to say to me?"

"Is there anything else?" he asked.

She said, "Oren, please, are we suddenly become enemies? Is that possible? What have *I* done to you? Why am *I* now your enemy?"

He hesitated, then said, "Marietta, please don't make a scene. You'll embarrass us both."

"I don't care," she said hotly. "It's nothing to do with anyone else. I don't care what they hear or see or listen to or think. I must talk to you, and I won't wait a day longer. Too much has happened to be ignored. We must talk of it calmly together. We must decide what to do."

"To do?" He gave her a quizzical look. But then he took her elbow. "Very well. Let's sit down on a bench in the square. And tell me what you propose to do."

She pressed close to him. "Oren, if only you knew what it's been like since you left Galloway."

"I didn't leave Galloway, Marietta. Your husband ordered me out. I had no recourse."

"And you blame *me* for it?"

He waited to answer until they were seated together. Then he said, "I can't blame you for his acts, I suppose."

"Well, thank you for that. Then why didn't you send me a word, a message? Why didn't you do something, anything, so that I would know you were all right?"

"You knew I must be. Coraleen surely told you that. And besides, I didn't think it would matter to you, Marietta." What he meant was that he didn't think it *should* matter to her. The unbearable urgency with which she stared at him made him want to get up, walk away. But her small hand was fastened onto his sleeve with an iron grip. There was, he decided, nothing he could do but hear her out, and then go back to Jordan House and get himself drunk.

"Not matter to me?" she echoed. "Oren, are you gone mad? How can you imagine I no longer care about you?"

278

He squirmed anew at that, but decided to ignore it. He answered, "I sometimes think I *have* gone mad, after all that's happened. But why do you ask me that? Have I developed a twitch?"

She dismissed his small attempt at levity. She said, "Look, you must know I opposed Lafe, and begged him to do nothing. What do I care what happened with the note, the ledgers, or with anything else, in fact? These are only material things. And besides, I know full well you'd have made restitution when you could, had Lafe given you the time to do so."

"And *I* thank *you* for that, Marietta." He went on defensively: "But I see you think I did wrong. And I didn't. I only took what was owing to me, not a cent more. I swear it to you."

She knew better, for there'd been nothing owing to him. Yet she realized he must believe his excuses. She said, "Ah, you're bitter against me, and when there's no reason." She drew a deep breath. "Oren, I want you to come home. And I shall find a way. Believe me, trust me, I shall find a way."

"Do you really think to talk your husband into welcoming me into my own home, into the home from which he unjustly ordered me?"

"I'll try. I . . . he's an obdurate man in some ways. But I'll try. And perhaps, with time, I shall succeed. For though he's stubborn, he's reasonable, too. And if I knew you'd accept my invitation, and could say so, then—"

"I'd accept an invitation from you, Marietta. But only when Lafe Flynn is gone forever from Galloway. I'll not set foot on the place as long as he's there."

"You want me to send him away?" Her voice and her eyes showed her surprise. She hadn't expected or even thought of that. She had merely imagined the four of them together once more, peace restored. The taste of the suggestion was bitter. She said slowly, "Oren, I *am* married to Lafe. He has some rights. I have some obligations to him."

Oren shrugged and said nothing. He was comfortable with

the Beckwiths. He had no desire to return to the hearth of Galloway. He needed only money to be content. He wondered if he could persuade Marietta to see his need. It was, he told himself, only a portion of what was truly his.

She had heard her own words, *some obligations to him,* and she tried to conceal instant embarrassment. Certainly her wifely obligations were no longer fulfilled. A memory of his body against hers . . . His lips pressed to her mouth . . . A breath shared between them as they clung together . . She closed her mind swiftly. Whatever her obligation had once been, it existed no more. Indeed, she had no reason to believe that Lafe wanted it otherwise. He never came to the room she used now, and hadn't for a long while, not since she had wept in his arms. As for the rest, she saw to it that his clothes were kept in good repair. He had his meals. His boots were shined. His quarters were always aired and warm. She was his wife.

She said, "All I want is a reconciliation between the two of you. If that were possible, I would do anything."

Oren smiled grimly. "Your dream does you credit, I suppose. But I don't share it. I have no desire to be reconciled with your husband." Oren leaned a bit closer, adding softly, "And I hate him for more than his interference between us, in our lives, Marietta. Do you know he refused my challenge? He's a coward. You live with a yellow-livered coward, and I don't see how you can bear it."

"I doubt he refused to fight you out of fear, Oren," she said dryly. "It was for my sake, and mine alone."

"Gentry was right," Oren said bitterly. "He said you'd take Flynn's part and defend him no matter how the affair ended. And Sara and John—"

"They know nothing of it!" she snapped. "Nor of my feelings. They know nothing of Lafe either, except through you, and that's hardly an unbiased view, is it, Oren?"

"It seems, since they were right, they know more than I did. I never believed you'd accept his explanation."

Her teeth chattered with the cold that had slowly seeped

into her. She drew a deep painful breath and coughed a little, shaking her head from side to side. "His explanation! You really don't know him very well, do you? Lafe explains nothing. I learned the facts from Coraleen, who left nothing to my imagination. But I know Lafe. And I know why he wouldn't fight you."

"Have it your own way." Oren shrugged. "It's nothing to me. Except that I despise him."

"You despise him for thinking of me?"

"Of you? You've nothing to do with it. For thinking rather of his own skin."

"He thought," she said softly, "of me. Of me, Oren. I know it."

Oren shrugged again.

A shadow fell over them. Lafe's towering form stood above them. He looked at them for a moment, but said nothing. Slowly, while Oren stared at the ground and Marietta stared at him, he stripped the gloves from his hands and dropped them in her lap. Then, still not speaking, he walked on.

She smoothed them onto her own hands absently, feeling the warmth of his flesh that still remained in them.

Now Oren got to his feet. "I must leave you now, Marietta. I'm sorry that Lafe had to see us together."

She jumped up, too, her body stiff and cramped with the cold that seemed to have settled so quickly into her bones. "I'm not sorry. It doesn't matter. But won't you meet with me again?"

"I see no purpose in it."

Tears stung her eyes, ran down her cheeks. "No purpose," she said softly. "Of course there's none. Just that we might be together, as we were before."

"Then come to the Beckwiths' to see me, if you must. You'll generally find me there. And we can talk then. Oh, and I suppose you've not heard of it, but Sara had a child early this morning. She and the infant are well."

"And you didn't tell me the moment we met?"

"It slipped my mind, Marietta."

281

"What is it? A boy or a girl?"

"It's a boy."

"They've named it?"

He shook his head, grinning suddenly. "Oh, so like a woman! I don't know what they named it, Marietta. Coraleen will tell you, if you truly want to know."

"Does it still hurt you," she asked softly, "that you lost Sara to John?"

"No," he said grimly. "It no longer hurts. I've lost more than Sara, haven't I, Marietta? I have more to think about, haven't I?" With that, he turned and walked away and left her alone.

Lafe was waiting for her in the carriage with Elisha, and he came out to open the door for her and help her in.

"You've completed your errands in Darnal, Marietta?" he asked, settling into the seat beside her.

"I had no errands. I wanted to see Oren. And since he doesn't come, and can't come, to Galloway, I came to find him here."

"And you sat for an hour in the cold. Do you know that your lips are blue?"

"There was no place else to sit and talk privately," she retorted. With that she took his gloves from her hands and dropped them on his knee. "Thank you for these. But I'm not cold any more." Even as she spoke the words, a shiver assailed her. It shook her whole body and set her teeth chattering.

He took off his cloak, and though she protested, he bundled her in it. "Not cold," he said. "The fire within you doesn't seem to warm your flesh." After that he was silent until they had left the town well behind. Finally he said, "If you want Oren to visit you occasionally at Galloway, you need only ask him. I'll not object to that."

"You've changed your mind?"

"Only on the matter of an occasional visit. I don't like the idea that you must meet him clandestinely away from your own home."

She looked at the stern set of his mouth and answered,

"I might as well tell you that I've already asked him, provisional to your agreement, of course, and he refuses to come. He won't set foot on Galloway again."

Lafe's stern mouth softened into a faint, knowing smile. "As long as I'm there?"

She didn't answer. She bent her head, regarded her fingertips fixedly, and tried to still the cold shivers that beset her.

"We're at loggerheads," Lafe said at last.

"I suppose we are." And then, with a sob in her voice, she demanded, "Is it so wrong of me to want us all to be together? Why do you make me feel at fault? I've done nothing."

"You've no reason to feel at fault. I've not complained to you," he answered quietly.

"You've not complained in words," she conceded. "But in your looks, in your manner, I see that you blame me. And for what?"

"If you don't know, then I can't tell you." He grinned suddenly. "But never mind, Marietta. I'm sure that Oren'll soon decide to visit you, at least when I'm not about."

"I'm sure he won't. How can he?"

"You must make the best of it, then."

"There was no need to be so cruel to him, Lafe. I could have arranged it. I'd have seen to his silliness some way or other."

"And gone bankrupt in the process," Lafe retorted grimly. Then, "But we needn't cover that ground again, Marietta."

"But what shall I do?"

"Don't you see it yet? There's nothing for you to do."

"You'll not relent?"

"No, Marietta."

She made a sound that was part cough, part sigh. "I don't understand you, Lafe. Truly, I just don't understand."

He said, not looking at her, "You find it strange that I should be determined to protect you from your own misguided instincts?"

"Protect me from nothing, you mean." She stared at him, unsmiling. Her voice was level. "I think you're jealous of

Oren. I think you found the excuse you needed to send him away from us only for that reason."

"You may think as you please," Lafe answered coldly. "I won't try to dissuade you."

"I never dreamed this could happen. All I wanted was to keep things as they were."

Lafe said, "And was the past so good? Was it so perfect that you can't let it go?"

Was the past so good to remember? she asked herself. It surely seemed so now. The three of them, Oren and Cora-leen and Marietta herself, bound close by shared experience. Suddenly in her mind she saw the green light of the oleander house. Small shattered cups of china gleaming palely against the moist black earth. She brushed the memory aside.

She said firmly, "It was all good." And then, "Almost all good."

"Until I came," he finished for her.

She said nothing to that.

"I'm sorry, Marietta. When I asked you to marry me, I meant to make you happy, and I thought I could."

He had believed that until his wedding night. And even after, he had still believed it, realizing that she had given her heart to Oren, but thinking that she loved her husband more than she yet knew. He had thought he could teach her to see what was in her heart now, and forget her girlhood infatuation for Oren. He was less sure today than he had been. But he wasn't a man to give up hope.

"It would have been all right," she said. "If only you'd not interfered with Oren."

"If only I'd not determined to protect you," Lafe retorted.

"Then you won't ask him to return to Galloway to live?"

Lafe laughed softly. "You know I won't."

She leaned back, closed her eyes. "There's no more to be said, is there?"

"There's one more thing," he told her. "In fact, it surprises me that you've not already mentioned it."

"And that is?"

"Marietta, look at me." His voice was hard now, and with no laughter in it. A hard hot light burned in his eyes. "You can tell me to leave Galloway," he said in slow, deliberate words. "You can say that you no longer want me with you there."

When Oren had suggested it, she had demurred. But now it was on the tip of her tongue to agree. The phrases were on her lips. All she need do was utter them, and Oren would be home again. She felt the quick hard drumming of her heart, the hammer of a pulse in her throat. It should have been so easy, she thought in angry astonishment. Yet it wasn't. It was impossible. She couldn't say the words that would release her from Lafe, return Oren to her. She found herself bound to the man she'd married in a way she couldn't name. She remembered now that when Lafe kissed her for the first time, she'd gone to his arms with no thoughts of Oren between them. She remembered saying to Coraleen that Lafe was all she wanted in a husband, and being surprised to find that she meant the words with all her heart. She couldn't bring herself to tell him she didn't want him.

At last she said only, "I married you, Lafe."

"How nicely you put your affection and need of me," he answered. "And it's wise of you. I might as well tell you now that no matter what you say to me I won't abandon you at Galloway. I would not, Marietta, even if you pleaded with me to go. I'd see you through, even against your own will, and without your help. You may not thank me for it, but I'll at least have the satisfaction of knowing I did right."

"You're impossible!" she flared.

"I must seem so to you." He looked ahead. "How nice Galloway looks from here. The lights in the windows, the smoke over the chimneys . . ."

But she looked up into the bare limbs of the live oak trees, and the shivers beset her again as she saw four long narrow shadows hanging there.

21

Lafe stood at the center of the midnight dark room. The embers on the hearth made a faint red glow, but he had snuffed the lamps out, so that shadows enveloped the big canopied bed and lay like heavy black quilts along the floor. Outside the dogs barked fitfully, settling down after he'd disturbed them when he returned.

Within the house all was silent. Yet a feeling of discomfort grew in him. He was tired, but he couldn't lie down to sleep. He moved restlessly now, first to the window to look out at the moon-silvered yard, then to the bare dressing table that Marietta had once used. He imagined he could still smell the sweet odor of the patchouli scent that she sometimes wore.

Unable to bear the torment in her face, he'd given way more than he intended to. He was certain that Oren would soon make his appearance at Galloway. He was just as certain that when Oren did he would have a reason for it.

Lafe shook his head. Was there to be no end of Oren Henderson? he asked himself.

He went back to the window. The stars hung so low that they seemed almost as bright as single candles held against the wall of a darkened room. But starshine had been no danger that night. He and Duveen had slipped past the patrol one more time. He wondered how often they could manage it again.

A quick harsh barking caught his attention. He raised his head, listening. When the sound came once more, he frowned.

He crossed the room quickly, eased open his door, and went to stand before the door to Marietta's room, uneasily remembering the last time he had gone there hoping to make her understand his feeling and his need.

He forgot that when he heard a moan, another harsh bark, a choking strangling sound from within. He tried the door, and found it locked. He took no time to consider the pained grief that assailed him, realizing that she must have kept the bedroom door locked against him since that night, though he'd never tried it, hence never known it, before.

He called softly, "Marietta, can you hear me? Are you ill, Marietta?"

There was no response, but he thought he heard a sigh.

He backed off from the door as far as he could move, and then came forward swiftly, with his right boot raised, and smashed the latch open with a single kick.

A lamp burned low inside. The bed curtains were drawn back.

Marietta lay still, the quilts trailing on the floor beside her. Her black hair was spread like a shining cloud on the pillows. Her face seemed small, hollowed out at cheek and temple. Her nightdress, soaked with perspiration, clung to the smooth round curves of her breasts, clung to her slender hips. It seemed to him that he could very nearly see the steam of fever rising from her limp body.

He caught up the quilts and covered her quickly. He bent and pressed his lips to her forehead, and its heat seemed to sear his mouth and blister it.

As he straightened up, she opened her fever-glazed eyes and stared at him, moving her parched lips wordlessly.

He didn't know if she recognized him. He didn't wait to ask.

He roused Coraleen with a shout that brought her running, told her to get Essie up, to have a steam kettle made, to send Elisha immediately for Dr. Pinchot.

When he returned to her side, she had thrown off the quilts again. She moaned, breathing in hard rasping sighs.

As the others came and went—Dr. Pinchot shaking his

head at lung congestion, Essie with the steam kettle, Coraleen with some of old Aunt Tatie's recipes—Lafe sat beside Marietta watching her struggle for breath, and remembering how she had sat shivering and blue-lipped with cold on a bench in Darnal's square with Oren.

It was three days before she was conscious, five days before she could speak, and thirteen before she could rise from her bed and walk slowly about the room, leaning on Dora.

She barely remembered the time of her illness. She had faint recollections of Lafe bending over her, but didn't know that he hadn't left her side until she spoke her first words. She didn't know that he had prayed over her for hours, days.

She was still very tired, her face pale, with more flesh gone from her bones than she could spare. She leaned back in a chair in the morning room, regarding the fire on the hearth, and the lamps lit against the dark of a gray afternoon, the day that Oren came at last to see her.

He said, handing his coat to Elisha, "Marietta, I'm sorry for your illness. Coraleen's kept me informed."

"Thank you for coming, Oren," she answered. "Oh, I'm so glad to see you. So glad. It'll do me more good than all Dr. Pinchot's bitter tonics."

He sat beside her, took her hand. "You've had a bad time, but now it's over."

"Yes, thank goodness." For a moment her gaze turned inward. The bad times . . . they had seemed to go on forever. But there had been one good thing about them. In all her dreams she had known she was protected. Some unseen hand had hovered close beside her, gripped her, and never let her go. She remembered arms raising her higher on the pillows so that she could breathe. She remembered a big rough hand gently smoothing the hair from her face. She looked at Oren. "Lafe was good to me, Oren. You must be sure to thank him for it."

"I shall. If I see him."

"He's in Darnal. But if you'll wait . . ."

"I won't wait. Not this time." Oren got up, paced the floor restlessly. It was painful to have to return to the scene of his failure and shame. But it hadn't been just for himself that he came. He said, "There's so much going on, Marietta, yet I don't know what to talk about."

"We're not strangers who need to make idle conversation." When he didn't reply, she went on: "You're troubled. Tell me what it is, Oren."

"May I? Dare I speak frankly to you?"

"Why not? We always have spoken frankly together before."

He sat down once more, again took her hand. "Marietta, I'm in desperate need for money. For myself, but also for something else."

"Yes," she agreed slowly. "I thought you must be. And what's this *something else* you mention?"

"Marietta, very few see it yet, but trouble is coming. Dr. Pinchot mentioned to me that he has heard that hundreds of Southern medical students are withdrawing from Northern colleges and returning home. Abolitionist public opinion in the North is growing stronger and stronger. Why, even the plays, many, many of them, idealize the slaves, make a hero of John Brown. We shall soon need arms to protect ourselves. And they're expensive. You must help me."

It crossed her mind that it was strange behavior to come on a convalescent call to ask for money, but she brushed the thought aside. She was well enough now, and Oren had no way of knowing the weakness that still lingered in her. She considered what he had told her, and said finally, "Oren, I don't like the idea of your raising a private army."

"You don't understand. But never mind. Will you do it?" He went on: "I only want you to advance me my share of the profits for the coming year."

Drawing the lacy softness of her blue shawl more closely around her shoulders, she answered, "I'll think about it, Oren, and see if it's possible."

289

"Do you have any idea how much it might be?"

"Not yet. I'll have to find out."

"You mustn't ask your husband," Oren said quickly. "He mustn't know about this, Marietta. You do understand that?"

"Yes, I understand. I don't like going around him, Oren, but I'll think about it, and I'll speak to Blandish."

Soon after that Oren left her with a promise to return in four days. He didn't say that he hoped to have the full draft for the money then, but he didn't need to. She knew what was in his mind.

When she was alone, she rested for a moment. Then she rang for Dora and said when the girl appeared, "Send down to Mr. Blandish for me, Dora. One of the twins can go. I want to see him at once."

"Now? Oh, you don't want to talk to him now," Dora protested. "You need a hot cup of milk, and a nap, so you can stay down for supper the way you planned."

"Don't argue," Marietta retorted with an imperious wave of her hand. "Just get Blandish for me at once."

"First Oren and then him," Dora grumbled, but at a glance from Marietta she did as she was told.

In less than half an hour Jed Blandish stood in the morning room, his face ruddy, his eyes uneasy when he heard the question Marietta asked.

He tugged his long blond mustaches, repeating, "How much do I calculate we'll profit by next year, Miss Marietta? How do I know? How can I tell? We've not got the seed in. I don't know what the weather will be. I don't know what the market will be. So how can I tell?"

"You can make a guess from experience," she said tartly.

He shrugged, then asked, "But why is it so important? Why do you need to know now?"

She lay back in the chair, shaking her head tiredly. "Oh, never mind, Blandish. I'll decide for myself."

"You'll decide for yourself what next year's profits will

be?" He gave her a small grin. "That'll be a neat trick. When you've no idea what the prices will be."

"Never mind," she repeated. "Just forget I asked."

"Was there anything more?"

"No," she answered.

"We'll need to be thinking of Christmas soon."

"Yes, yes, we will. But not at this moment. You may leave me, Mr. Blandish."

He started for the door, then turned back to say, "I'm glad you're better, though you still look peaked to me, and Letty says the same."

"I'm fine," Marietta murmured. "Goodbye, Mr. Blandish."

"What do you expect?" Dora asked. "First Mr. Oren was here, and then Mr. Blandish came. I told her she was doing too much, but she wouldn't listen to me. When Aunt Tatie talked, she listened, but now there's nobody to run her, so she's going to get herself sick again."

Out of this spate of words, having waited patiently for them to come to a stop, Lafe picked out only two facts. One was that Oren had made his call. The other was that Marietta had sent for Jed Blandish.

Lafe considered that briefly as he went up the steps. He stopped before Marietta's door. All was silent within.

He touched the door, and it swung open. By day it remained unlocked, he thought, a grim smile at his lips.

He found her sound asleep, a frown still on her brow, a faint sheen of sweat on her upper lip. He leaned close to listen to her breathing. It was slow and easy, and he allowed himself to breathe again. She was worn by having too much company, and no more than that.

More than anything he wanted to hold her close in his arms, but he turned away.

Downstairs again, he sent Beedle for Jed Blandish.

He stood before the fire, waiting impatiently until the overseer appeared. When he did, Lafe moved directly to the point. "Miss Marietta sent for you today. What did she want?"

Jed shrugged. "Mr. Flynn, I don't know myself. She had a silly question to ask, and it surprised me, for she's not a silly woman and never has been."

"The question?"

"What will next year's profits be. That's what she wanted to know."

"And you told her?"

"That I'd no way of calculating it, and therefore couldn't say."

"Her answer?"

Jed had a glimpse of Lafe's blazing eyes, then quickly looked at the corner of the room. "She said something about figuring it out for herself."

"Thank you," Lafe told the man. "Good evening to you."

Jed backed hastily from the room. He felt as if he'd had a narrow escape, but he didn't know from what. He knew only that Lafe Flynn was in a temper, and showing it, and that he himself had no desire to be around when it finally exploded.

Four days later Oren returned to Galloway. He made certain that Lafe wasn't there by cutting across the fields to the slave quarters and sending one of the children to question the twins at the stable.

Reassured—but wrongly so, for Lafe had actually only ridden a mile toward Darnal and then turned back—Oren went up to the house.

Marietta was downstairs in the parlor, waiting for him before the fire. She had dressed carefully in an afternoon gown of lavender, becomingly trimmed with white ruffles at the throat and cuffs. Her hair was piled high, and her cheeks were powdered, hiding the shadows of sleeplessness that lay beneath her eyes. It had taken many long night hours of pondering before she came to her decision.

Oren greeted her with the highest of spirits and gave her

the bonbons he had brought her, and then paused expectantly.

She raised brilliant eyes to look at him and said, "Oren, I'm sorry. I've decided I can't give you the money you ask for."

He stared at her without understanding.

She went on: "It's nothing to do with the use you intend to put it to, though I don't approve of that. But I simply can't calculate what the future profits will be. Nor can Blandish, for I asked him. And even more, Oren"—she drew a deep breath—"it would in the end be a disservice to you."

"But you promised me!" Oren said bitterly. "What shall I do? You promised me, Marietta."

"I told you only that I would think about it. You must find another source of income."

"I can't," he yelled. "Don't you understand me? I need the money now." He hadn't the courage to tell her that he would appear a fool and a braggart before his friends, before so many important men in the county, if she didn't cooperate with him.

Her face paled as he came to stand over her, white-lipped and fiery of eye. "Oren, believe me, I've decided what's best for you."

"You've chosen to ruin me!"

"No, I haven't, and I won't." She patted the red settle. "Now sit beside me and tell me what else you can do."

"How do I know? Why should I care?" Oren shouted. "You promised to give me a portion of what was mine. And you've gone back on your word."

"But I didn't . . ." Now her resolution faltered. Perhaps she was wrong to deny him. She whispered, "Oren, if you'd come back in a few days' time, perhaps when I'm stronger, perhaps then—"

"I don't think so." The words were soft, but spoken with brute finality from the doorway where Lafe stood watching. "I don't think so," he said again.

He stepped forward and stood aside. He jerked his

head once at Oren, and the younger man understood.

Without a glance at Marietta, without a word, he took up his coat and hat and went into the hallway. He heard Marietta's faint cry, but didn't turn back. He knew that Lafe was one step behind him.

Elisha, white-eyed and hunched, held open the door. Oren passed through into gray afternoon sunlight. He let his breath out slowly. It was all gone wrong. Now he must think what to do. He'd counted too strongly on Marietta's love for him. And this was where it had brought him.

He had reached the gallery steps when Lafe said softly, "Just a moment, Oren."

He swung back impatiently. "What now? You've wrecked my life. What more can you want of me?"

"You may well have wrecked it for yourself, you fool," Lafe said.

He caught Oren by the velvet lapels of his cloak, shook him hard, and then pressed him against the railing.

The door behind the two men swung open. Marietta stood there. "Lafe, don't!" she cried. "Don't!"

Lafe ignored her. He shook Oren again, lifting him from his feet. "Now you listen to me, man, and pay heed. The next time I see you here, I'll kill you with my bare hands! Is that clear enough for a bonehead like you? Do you understand me?" With each question he gave Oren another shake, then set him on his feet again. "You come to my house to demand money of my wife. When she finds that she can't oblige you, you abuse her. What a pleasant sound that has as it's put into words."

"You lie!" Oren grated. "I asked only for what was mine."

"Nothing's yours, nor ever was," Lafe retorted.

He raised Oren from his feet again, and flung him bodily over the vine-draped railing.

Suddenly, as Oren lay sprawled in the frozen dirt, Lafe was upon him, straddling the thinner form that struggled to rise, flinging wild blows at his face.

Coraleen came screaming and threw herself at Lafe's

shoulders, clawing at him. Without even being aware of it, he shouldered her away. He struck short sharp blows at Oren's face while his knuckles split and bled and swelled, and Oren's features became a bloody and smeared mask of bruises, his eyelids swollen grotesquely and nearly closed.

Lafe was unaware of Marietta, leaning now against a pillar and weeping. He was unaware, too, of wide-eyed Needle and Beedle, of Duveen and Moses, watching in frozen stillness, of Essie, come from the kitchen, and Dora, clutching a frilled apron.

Rhythmically Lafe struck, and rhythmically Oren rolled with each blow until, finally, he was still.

Lafe straightened, stood swaying above the limp body. He wiped blood from his mouth with the back of his hand and gestured at Needle. "Get the gig, boy. Bring it around right away."

The whole group waited in captivated silence, only Marietta's sobs a distant music, until Needle brought up the gig.

Then Lafe raised Oren into his arms and threw him into the gig, where Oren lay like a broken doll, not conscious, with a bubble of blood swelling at his torn lips. "Take him to the Beckwiths'," Lafe growled at Coraleen. "Take him there, and be sure to tell them to keep him. For if he comes back here, I'll kill him, and nothing will stop me."

White-faced, she climbed into the seat and drove away.

Lafe turned, looked at the others. Slowly he let his eyes pass over Essie and Dora, over the two small boys, over Elisha, and Duveen and Moses. But he didn't see them. He saw no one but Marietta, where she leaned against the white of the pillar and wept soundlessly.

He stared at her for a moment, then went up the steps and passed her, not speaking. He allowed the door to slam behind him. Inside, he detoured into the morning room to grab up a decanter, then went up to the room he once had shared with Marietta.

He sat in the big chair near the window, with the curtains and drapes drawn and the lamps unlit, and allowed the early night to cover him as he took great gulps straight from the decanter.

Much later he heard his door open. He turned to look, and saw the silhouette of Marietta. He rose to his feet. "What do you want?"

"Lafe? Are you all right?"

He laughed softly. "No, no. I'm not. But I'll recover." He wiped his mouth with the back of his hand, and winced at the pain from his torn knuckles. He held the decanter aloft. "Will you join me?"

"No," she said coldly. "That's not what I came for."

"Then why did you?" he demanded. "To tell me that I've been wrong again? Well, I won't listen. Your Oren's a rogue and a bully, and I despise him."

"Oh, do you?" She advanced slowly into the room. The light behind her outlined her willowy slimness, the curves of her breasts and hips. "You despise him? When you won't listen to me? When you don't want to know what happened? When you behave like a brute yourself?"

"We'll not talk now, Marietta," Lafe said. "Go away."

"Go away. Is that all you can say in your own defense?"

"In your protection," he muttered.

But she didn't quite hear him, and demanded, "What? What? Say what you really mean."

"All right," he told her. "I'll say it. Take yourself out of here now, this instant. Get away from me, Marietta. I mean it."

She gasped and stood still, and he took a step toward her.

"Get away from me, I tell you, or you'll regret it!"

"Regret it? What's there more for me to regret? Can you tell me that?"

He was close to her now, swaying. His eyes gleamed at her. A strange smile curled his mouth. She could smell the whiskey on his breath, the sweat of his body. His hair was tousled as she had never seen it, and his face twisted into that of a stranger.

He said, "I've warned you, Marietta."

296

Some instinct made her turn and run as he reached for her. Some deep and ancient fear sent her fleeing from the room.

As she locked the door of her own room behind her, she heard him laugh.

22

It was a cold day in early December.

The sky was so dark that it seemed twilight at noon.

Lafe rode along the track a few miles beyond Galloway. In his pocket he had a second coded telegram. This time it was from his father.

It had been sent one day after John Brown was hanged at Charlestown by the Virginia authorities. In brief and urgent words the older Flynn had suggested that Lafe immediately cease his activities, either to remain with his wife at Galloway, or to bring her to New Orleans. Trouble was coming. How soon, no one could guess. But the time for argument and discussion was very nearly past. Next, and imminent, was the resort to arms.

Lafe believed it. He knew that any man caught transporting slaves out of their owners' control would be dealt with harshly. Imprisonment and fines would no longer satisfy high-running passions. There was hungering for blood.

But he couldn't stop now. In a month perhaps, or two, he would consider it. And when he did, what of Marietta? They had never spoken of the beating he had given Oren; and Oren, of course, though well recovered by now, had never returned to Galloway. Nor would he, Lafe was certain, as long as Lafe himself was there. Though the days went by quietly, his separation from Marietta was proving more painful than Lafe could ever have imagined. But he knew of no way to bind the wounds that had caused it. He knew of no way to try.

Still, what of Marietta when his activities in Darnal must cease? Could he just abandon her? Or would he stay at Galloway with her, the respectable proprietor of the Golden Leaf Tobacco Company, until, with the advent the bloodshed he was certain now would come, he could no longer continue there? He saw where his love had brought him, and he knew Duveen's unspoken questions had been justified. A man with a mission had no right to love, nor any right to dream of it either. He'd not thought far enough ahead. He'd not wanted to.

Marietta . . .

To stay with her, seeing her, hiding the depths of his hurt, his hungers, beneath polite smiles, was more difficult with each day that passed. How long now since he had held her in his arms? How long since she had freely laughed with him? How long since he had kissed her?

He forgot his brooding at the sudden crackle of sound in the brush ahead of him—a crackle of sound, a crash, the loud curse of a single and somewhat familiar voice.

Lafe kicked his horse into a gallop and pounded around the curve ahead, to the small wooden bridge he and Duveen had favored as a convenient meeting place some time before. They used it no longer. For it had become favorite of the patrols, too.

Now a cart sat squarely in the narrow approach. Its one horse was down, struggling. Dust rose up in a cloud around it as it flailed its three good legs and helplessly heaved and rocked its thick body. A man stood nearby, pistol at the ready, but the animal thrashed in and out of aim until, just as Lafe pulled up and dismounted, the horse subsided to stillness for a moment, and the one-armed man with the pistol thrust it out, fired it, and in the same motion swung away.

The horse died in that instant, and the one-armed man, muttering to himself, leaned his heavily bearded face against his cart loaded with logs.

Lafe raised his hand in greeting. "Mr. Ridgeway, isn't it?" he asked. "Mr. Ridgeway of Digleytown?"

The one-armed man jerked his head in a nod. His eyes were hard. "Yes it is. I recall you, sir. But not your name. You were part of a group of slave hunters, weren't you?"

"You might say so," Lafe agreed. "I contributed my share, I suppose. But I found no one. Nor did the others, I would imagine."

"You would imagine rightly," Mr. Ridgeway answered. A light gleamed deep within his eyes. "A barn burned down that evening."

"So I was given to understand. Though I never saw it for myself."

There was a brief silence. Then the bearded man quickly shuffled his feet. He was, Lafe knew, attempting too slowly to cover the sound of an anguished groan coming from the logs, which Lafe pretended not to have heard.

At last Mr. Ridgeway asked, "You live in the area?"

"Yes. At a plantation called Galloway. I run the Golden Leaf Tobacco Company in Darnal."

"You do?" Mr. Ridgeway asked.

Lafe nodded. "This information takes you by surprise?"

"Indeed it does." The one-armed man looked at the tipped cart, its load of logs askew. "I was on my way to the Golden Leaf Tobacco Company itself when this misfortune overtook me on the road."

Alerted, and certain now, Lafe said, "Then I take it you've heard of me and heard of my business, too?"

"Perhaps."

"Perhaps," Lafe repeated. "An interesting word that. So exact. So careful. So full of information."

"It's full of what I want it to be," Mr. Ridgeway answered with a grin.

"I believe you need some help here," Lafe said. "Shall I find a horse for you, Mr. Ridgeway? I see very plainly that you'll need something to move your cart."

"Do you think you can do that for me?"

"I know that I can."

"Then we're well met indeed, aren't we?"

"I think we are." Lafe waited a moment, listening. When he heard the faint groan again, he said quietly, "Mr. Ridgeway, may I offer some advice?"

The bearded man nodded, shooting an anxious look at the cart.

"If you're thinking to unload any of your cargo here, I must tell you that it wouldn't be safe."

"Cargo?" Mr. Ridgeway asked, his bearded face blank.

Lafe said, "Should there be something, anything, under the logs you carry—what it is, I couldn't guess, of course—it's safer where it is now than it would be anyplace around here you could possibly find. I happen to know that this place has been used once too often for certain trips, and is very well watched by armed patrols."

"I see," Mr. Ridgeway said. Then, "You'll return soon with a horse I can buy from you?"

"I'll return soon with a horse you can borrow from me."

"Tell me," Mr. Ridgeway asked, "do you own slaves?"

"In a manner of speaking."

"You might say *perhaps*," Mr. Ridgeway said dryly.

"I've two men who work for me," Lafe replied.

"Yes?" Mr. Ridgeway asked.

"One is called Moses, is small and round-faced. The other is a great whistler. In fact"—Lafe grinned now—"I believe he has an extraordinary reputation for the music he makes between his teeth and lips. He has no tongue and therefore can't speak a word."

The one-armed man laughed softly. "I quite agree with you. Your man Duveen does have a reputation, as does Moses. But then, it seems, so do you."

"Not too far and wide, I hope," Lafe answered.

"My knowledge doesn't extend to that."

"Then let me get a horse for your cart," Lafe said. "And when we have reloaded you, and can go on, I'll invite you to my wife's plantation, Galloway, for the night."

"The Golden Leaf—"

"Mr. Ridgeway, I'd like nothing better than to show you

301

the place, and all my works in it; and believe me, when I think it safe, I shall. But at the moment it's best we not go there. You must stop at least this evening with me at Galloway."

"I'm in your hands, sir, and will do whatever you think best."

Lafe wheeled, rode away. It wasn't very long before he returned with Duveen, who led a strong workhorse on a bridle.

Lafe introduced him to the one-armed man, who nodded and looked relieved, saying, "We're well met this afternoon, I can tell you."

But Duveen, staring at the one-armed man, shook his head. He showed nothing on his dark face, but a black sadness grew in his eyes.

Lafe saw it and wondered.

There was, in spite of his doubts, nothing to do then but go ahead as already planned.

Duveen and Lafe managed to right the tilted cart, its load disarranged but still intact. They put the fresh horse into the traces.

In a little while Lafe set out, Duveen at his side, for Galloway, Mr. Ridgeway and his cart following.

The hounds barked when they turned between the two white stone pillars, and barked again when the wagon rolled into the side yard.

"Mr. Ridgeway, you must be my guest this evening," Lafe said. "Duveen will see to your cart and things. You needn't fear for them. He knows just what to do. In the morning we'll go into Darnal, and I shall show you the warehouse so that you'll be familiar with it. And then, since I have an errand in Durham's Station, I shall ride along with you, if you like."

"You're very kind," Mr. Ridgeway said. "Am I suitably dressed for your home, though?"

"You'll do, never fear," Lafe answered, leading the way inside.

"I could hardly ignore the man," he said later to Marietta. "After all, I've known him some time, and have accepted his hospitality."

"Of course," Marietta responded. "You're certainly welcome to have a friend here. I'll tell Elisha to prepare a room for him."

"Thank you, my dear. You're very accommodating."

When the two of them entered the parlor together, Mr. Ridgeway leaped to his feet. "Mrs. Flynn," he said, bowing. "This is a real pleasure."

"How do you do?" Marietta murmured.

"I've long heard of the Garveys of Galloway, but I never expected to have the honor."

"I'm glad you've come," she said. "But do sit down, please, and tell me how you come to be acquainted with my husband."

Mr. Ridgeway gave Lafe a helpless look.

"We met through business of course," Lafe said easily. "In my travels I've passed through Digleytown many times. And it was there that we first ran into each other."

"And your business is?" Marietta asked.

"Lumber, ma'am. Lumber it is. And the best for charcoal that you can get. I don't doubt that you've sometimes used it for your own curing. And if not, then you should have, and should still. If I say so myself, it's top grade."

Moments later Lafe heard a familiar whistle. He got to his feet, went to the window.

Duveen stood outside.

Lafe turned back to the room and said, "If you'll excuse me for a moment."

"You'll not be long?" Marietta asked. "We'll sit down for supper in a little while."

"Not long at all."

He met Coraleen in the hallway.

"Is there company?" she demanded. "I heard a strange voice. I saw you drive in with someone, a cart, or something."

"A friend of mine, Coraleen," Lafe explained.

303

"Will he stay?"

"Overnight, I believe."

"Oh, how nice," she cried. "It'll be a change, won't it?"

"I hope you find my friend entertaining," Lafe said as he went outdoors.

Duveen stood waiting patiently, shifting from boot to boot in the cold. When he saw Lafe, he tapped his right wrist, then turned and walked quickly away.

Lafe followed him past the cart, where the load of logs seemed hardly disturbed, and then back into the slave quarters to the cabin he shared with Moses.

The small man sat on his haunches, leaning over a shadowed pallet. His round face was puckered with worry.

"What is it?" Lafe asked. "What's wrong?"

"This man's hurt," Moses said. "And I think it's bad."

"Hurt?"

"The logs rolled when the cart tipped. It's his leg."

Lafe looked down at the young man who lay shivering under the thickness of two heavy quilts. His glittery eyes widened when he saw Lafe. His head turned restlessly.

"We'll take care of you," Lafe told him. "You'll be all right. I'm a friend of Mr. Ridgeway's, and I'll see you get through somehow."

Moses whispered, "If he can."

Duveen brought a lamp and thrust it at Moses, then bent down and drew the quilts away.

Not a muscle moved in Lafe's face, but he turned sick inside.

The young man's leg was crushed at the ankle, still oozing blood, though the wound had been cleaned, and splinters of shattered white bone showed through the mangled flesh.

Lafe knew there was no way to heal or mend or put together that smashed part, but he said only, "What's your name, my friend?"

"Justin Cooley" was the answer.

"You sleep, if you can, and rest," Lafe told him, and he saw the pain-filled eyes close obediently.

Lafe looked at him a moment longer, then jerked his head at Duveen and went outside. "Bring in one of the older women to tend him, Duveen, and tell her not to say a word."

Duveen nodded.

Moses materialized out of the shadows. "I don't like having him here."

"I can't blame you, Moses. But there was nothing else to do."

"And that leg's going to have to go."

"How far can a one-legged man run?" Lafe asked. And then, "We'll wait a few days and see."

"Mr. Ridgeway," Coraleen was saying as she rose from a deep curtsey, "how nice to meet you. We've so little company these days at Galloway. And to see and speak to a friend of Lafe's, something we also have little opportunity to do, is so very exciting."

Mr. Ridgeway smiled. "I expect he likes to keep his beautiful family to himself. And I don't blame him there. Were I in his boots, believe me, I'd not bring too many of my acquaintances home with me."

"And where is your home?" she asked.

"In Digleytown. I'm in lumber, as I was just telling your sister."

"Digleytown? And what brings you here to Darnal?"

"Oh, a matter of business."

"Business," Coraleen repeated. "I see. And you'll stay awhile?"

"Much to my regret, I assure you, I must go on tomorrow."

"What a pity. Here was I, planning on having the pleasure of entertaining you."

"I shall be the disappointed one at missing that," Mr. Ridgeway answered.

"How gallant." Coraleen laughed, tossing her curls. "Much more so than my brother-in-law could ever be."

Marietta frowned slightly. "Coraleen, Mr. Ridgeway will not understand your humor."

"No matter," Coraleen said, shrugging. "Gallant is as gallant does. Isn't that right?"

"We all have our rough spots," Mr. Ridgeway said hastily. He cast a hopeful look at the door, and was relieved to see Lafe standing there. "You have no trouble, I hope?"

"Nothing of any consequence," Lafe answered. Then, "You'll have a drink with me before the evening meal?"

"I'd be pleased to. I'm well ready for it after all that happened on the road."

"There was an incident?" Marietta asked.

The one-armed man described how the horse had stepped into a pothole, broken his foreleg, and fallen, tipping the cart. "Well, I just stood there, swearing," he said. "I was so damned, oh, I beg your pardon, ladies, so disgusted, I didn't know what to do with myself. And then Mr. Flynn appeared, out of nowhere, it seemed to me."

"You'd not visited him for some time?" Coraleen asked.

"Oh, not for a very long time."

Lafe, listening as he poured drinks, frowned. He hurried the chore, and served the one-armed man. The fewer questions Coraleen asked, the better it would be. Ridgeway was on dangerous ground, and knew it, though he was sensible enough to appear quite unconcerned.

To relieve him of the burden of inquisition to which Coraleen was subjecting him, Lafe said, raising his glass, "Your good health, Marietta, and Coraleen." And to Mr. Ridgeway, "And yours, with our welcome to you."

It was pleasant to have guests, Marietta thought as she led the way into the dining room. She looked across the candlelight at Lafe, who, acting the genial host now, was telling Mr. Ridgeway about his life in New Orleans.

His eye caught hers. He paused for a moment, and a brief smile flickered at the corners of his mouth.

She looked hastily away, unable to imagine what his thought had been. The separation between them had grown wide as an ocean.

She didn't know how to bridge it. She told herself that she didn't want to. How could she want to? Yet doubts tormented her. Was the man whose gentle touch at her cheek she remembered from the nights of her illness the same man who had so ruthlessly whipped Oren to the ground? Though she willed it away, a small voice always whispered in answer that Lafe had acted in defense of her. Still, she could not bring herself to forgive him, and the sense of loss cut deeply. Once they had held long conversations, which left her excited and stirred and often amused. Once they had shared laughter, and that, too, had wrapped her in a cocoon of joy. Once she would have been able to tell him of the small incidents of her day. He would have laughed to hear that Needle and Beedle had both solemnly sworn to her that Galloway was haunted, that a ghostly man and a ghostly woman walked its halls by the shadows of night. But now he was remote, his ironic courtesies only pained her. She could say nothing to him.

She found herself wondering, not for the first time, how he had become celibate so easily. She had learned him well enough to know he was a man of intense and demanding passions. Yet he hadn't approached her, not even so that she could refuse him, since the night he had sent Oren away. Could he have lost his need for her, when she knew only too well how empty the bed was without him, how she had missed his warmth, the sense of his body beside her? She spent countless night hours struggling with desires he had taught her, knowing now that when she had met him in joy it had nothing to do with wifely obligation. If he had similar feelings, he concealed them well.

It was only after she withdrew from the table with Coraleen, leaving the two men to speak alone over their wine and walnuts and to smoke their cigars, that Marietta began to suspect Lafe might be concealing something.

Coraleen curled like a kitten in the easy chair before the fire and said dreamily, "I'd like to be a fly on the wall. I'd like to be there, invisible, yet able to hear."

"And to what purpose?" Marietta laughed. "Men's talk isn't all that interesting."

"It might be," Coraleen retorted. She chewed a brown

curl, then spat it out. "It could be of politics, of course. But how much politics can they talk? No, I suspect they speak of women."

"Come now," Marietta answered. "You've no reason to think so."

"Gentry and Oren often speak of women. I've heard them."

"You shouldn't have been listening."

"Why not? I'm seventeen. I'm curious. I want to know more than anyone will tell me." Coraleen's smile broadened. "More than you'll tell me certainly."

"When you must know, you will," Marietta said. She turned away, took up her embroidery. "You dwell too much on unsuitable subjects."

"I believe marriage relations a very suitable subject," Coraleen said softly. "And especially these days. For I have so many questions, Marietta."

Marietta glanced at her, but said nothing. She bent her head over the hoop, frowning at the purple silk.

"You and Lafe, for example. You've taken the guest room and stayed there a very long time. And Dora has moved all your belongings to it, so plainly you intend to go on staying there."

"It's no affair of yours," Marietta said shortly.

"I suppose not, but I can't help but wonder. Tell me, Marietta, how do you propose to keep your husband, when you don't sleep with him?"

"I'll not discuss it with you," Marietta retorted, feeling a warmth in her face, a sinking in her heart.

"And how is it that you're so sure of him? I judge him a man who'd not go long without a woman. And since I do judge him so, I ask myself with whom he sleeps."

"I shan't listen to you, Coraleen."

"But you *are* listening, Marietta. You can't help yourself. You wonder as much as I do."

It was true, but Marietta said, "It's no concern of mine what Lafe Flynn does."

308

"It must be. As long as he's your husband."

That, too, was true, Marietta admitted to herself. She supposed it was her hurt pride that made her question his behavior. What else could it be? She was loyal to him, to the vows she had made him. She had the right to expect the same of him. But the voice within her whispered, You've always sided with Oren, haven't you?

Coraleen's tone had hardened now. She said, "You'll be sorry for marrying him. Just wait and see."

Marietta heard the long, long echo of those words over the years. Once again she shuddered at them. Yes, she had been sorry for so much.

"And do you know?" Coraleen asked in a new bright voice. "Do you know that he creeps out at night? Don't you wonder where he goes, and what he does, and who he sees on his midnight errands?"

"I don't know what you're talking about," Marietta said shortly.

"He reminds me," Coraleen went on with soft significance, "of Papa. Wandering about through the dark alone, thinking what terrible thoughts no one will ever know." She laughed quietly. "Yes, Lafe reminds me much of Papa. A man without a woman to warm him turns so, I suppose."

A tremor shook Marietta's body. She felt her heart pound once, violently, against her ribs. She set her embroidery aside and leaned her head back against the crocheted antimacassar, saying, "There's no likeness between my father and Lafe."

And at the same time she tried to dismiss her last memory of her father—the sprawl of his body . . . the dark pool at his head . . .

"No likeness except the one I mention, I grant you." Coraleen eyed Marietta, then went on: "But of course, Lafe's younger. So perhaps his midnight walks lead him to where there's a comfort you refuse to give him."

"That'll do," Marietta answered. She rose. "I'll go up now, so if you stay, make my apologies to Mr. Ridgeway."

Coraleen's insinuations echoed through her mind as she retreated to her room, and would not be banished. She remembered her talk with Needle and Beedle. Ghostly man, they'd insisted, walking, walking through Galloway. Ghostly woman, too, they'd assured her.

Was the man Lafe? And who was the woman?

She brushed out her hair, telling herself that Coraleen's word was not often to be trusted. She imagined things. She made things up. She had no reason to say that Lafe left the house at night. As for the twins, they were mere children, and if there was such a thing as ghosts, Marietta had never seen them for herself.

She lay for some time curled under the warm quilts, and then, at last, sighing, she rose. She bound up her hair in a ribbon, donned a dark brown riding dress, and hung a dark brown cloak on the chair.

Long after she heard the men pass on the way to their separate rooms, long after she heard Lafe close the door to the room they had once shared, she sat close by the window in the dark while the last of the embers burned out on the hearth.

The hounds bayed as the wind stirred in the leafless limbs of the trees. When finally they went still again, all was silence.

At last, sighing once more, she removed her clothing and crept back to bed, angry with her own behavior. She shouldn't have given credence to a word spoken by Coraleen. The girl was unreliable beyond belief. How could Marietta have permitted herself to listen? Lafe didn't wander abroad at night. Why on earth would he?

The question rankled. She told herself that she didn't care what he did. He could wander as far as New Orleans, and she would only be grateful for it. She owed him nothing, and he owed her nothing. The marriage had been a mistake from the beginning—her mistake, and she was willing to concede it. She didn't care what he did. She'd never care what he did.

Yet all through the night she lay still, staring with hot eyes at the silken canopy overhead.

Coraleen had been wrong about Lafe and Mr. Ridgeway. It wasn't women that they discussed.

Their voices lowered, they discussed Justin Cooley's injuries.

Mr. Ridgeway's bearded face paled. He touched his empty sleeve. "Is there no chance for him?"

"I don't know."

"Could you try? Could you give him as much time as you dare?"

Lafe nodded. "But you understand, I can call no one in. If there's to be an amputation, we must do it secretly."

"I'd not presume to ask you to do otherwise," Mr. Ridgeway answered. "How long do you think you can reasonably wait?"

"I don't know that either. Perhaps a few days, perhaps a week."

"You don't think the man can be moved?"

"Not in that condition. And not for a good while after."

"I don't like the risk you take, Mr. Flynn. If he's found here on your property—"

"I see no way out of it, Mr. Ridgeway."

The bearded man nodded slowly. "Then I'll be on my way tomorrow. Though I hate to leave Justin here."

"I'll get him through it," Lafe promised. "I'll get him out of here, too."

The following morning Ridgeway made his farewells and departed, taking his log-laden cart with him.

By the end of that same week Justin Cooley still writhed in silent agony on his pallet. Beneath the poultices placed on his leg, maggots had burrowed, thick and white with the poisons they fed on. The flesh turned to mush, darkening, and split in crevices. Long streaks of angry red rimmed with green reached as high as his knee.

Lafe stood over him one midnight, flanked by Duveen and

Moses. "You understand me, Justin? You know what I must do?"

The young man nodded, biting back an anguished groan. "Then I'll do the best I can."

When the fire was high, the water boiling, the knives honed, he fed Justin a full tumbler of whiskey, motioned to Duveen to tie a silence-ensuring gag at his mouth, and then to hold him firmly while Moses readied him for the sharpened knives.

The heat of the high fire, the stench in the room brought a sweat to Lafe's face as he squatted down, probing with delicate fingers before, with a deep rasping breath, he began the surgery.

Justin's agonized body shook beneath Duveen's weight, but Lafe worked quickly. He cut maggoty flesh away, and tendon and vein. He bound the remaining stump at the knee with a heavy twine, and wrapped it in poultices that Moses had brought.

When it was over, he fed Justin another glass of whiskey, and leaving Duveen to watch with Moses, he went out into the night.

There, in the dark, shielded by shadows, the sickness overwhelmed him. His stomach rose up and spewed its contents. A cold sweat poured from him, and he shook with it.

Finally he was able to return to the house. He moved as silently as he had left it an hour before.

Coraleen was watching. She saw him come slowly down the track and into the yard. She smiled to herself. He'd been to the slave quarters, of course. She asked herself who the woman was. Since he'd left the house, it wasn't that two-faced Dora, and it couldn't have been Essie, who was too old and fat. Some girl in the fields, then, Coraleen decided. She'd learn the girl's name soon enough. Surely Marietta would like to know.

23

It was a quiet Christmas.

Essie roasted a goose, which was hardly eaten, and made a plum pudding, which was only just touched.

They exchange gifts and thanks with empty smiles.

Elisha had hung wreaths of holly at every door and clumps of mistletoe on every chandelier.

Marietta, sitting alone in the morning room, her embroidery on her lap, heard Lafe's step in the hall and approached him to ask some trivial question.

He listened and answered, and as she turned away, he caught her by the shoulders and swung her back, holding her so that she couldn't move. He grinned, looking upward to the green leaves and white berries, and said, "I claim my rights, Marietta."

His arms closed tightly around her, holding her with such force that she felt all the hard tension of his body. He pressed her head back into the curve of his shoulder, and his lips came down on hers, forcing her mouth open so that she tasted the sweetness of his tongue and breath and was giddy with it. Hardly knowing what she did, she lifted her hands to caress his russet hair, and her arms tightened around his neck; and as he pressed to her, she pressed to him.

Then, quite suddenly, he broke free of her and set her aside. He gave her a small crooked grin, a lift of dark brows. "Merry Christmas," he said and turned away to leave her trembling there.

He rode, swearing all the way, to Duveen's cabin, spoke

briefly with Moses, and decided then that Justin still couldn't be moved for yet a little while.

By the advent of the new year, the young man was much improved; but there was a small bleeding still, and he hadn't learned to handle his crutch.

Lafe knew that the longer Justin remained at Galloway, the greater the risk grew. But he saw no way out, and contented himself with waiting.

Meanwhile Coraleen continued her spying, and she waited, too.

24

Marcus Swinton was too polite to get up and leave when Oren and Gentry joined him at the bar in Jordan House. He was, however, not hypocritical enough to pretend to be glad to see Oren. He jerked his head in a stiff nod, then half turned away.

Gentry said, "Mr. Swinton, I'd like a word with you, if you please."

Marcus swung back. "And that is . . . ?"

"Oren and I and John Farr have formed a committee in which you, as banker to Darnal, should have some interest."

"And what committee is that?" Marcus asked, displaying no enthusiasm. He'd already heard of it, and he'd made no effort to join, because he didn't approve.

"A committee for action in case of a general uprising," Gentry told him. "We must be ready, and organized, and armed."

"What makes you think such a thing will occur?"

Gentry's pale blue eyes flashed. "This is 1860, sir! Time has passed. It's more than possible that there'll be an uprising. It begins to appear to me, to the rest of us, indeed, that it's even probable."

"And what makes you think that, I wonder?"

"The situation."

"I see."

"I ask if you do see, Mr. Swinton."

Marcus carefully lit a cigar, blew out smoke. "We all have our opinions."

"Certainly," Gentry agreed. "But you'll join us, of course."

Marcus glanced sideways at Oren. "I must think about it."

"Think? What's there to think about? We know what needs to be done. We're arming ourselves. It's been forced on us. When the time comes, every red-blooded Southern man—"

"When the time comes is soon enough for committees," Marcus returned. "Sometimes merely the formation of a group to combat a fear brings that fear to reality."

"I'd expect the Reverend Filene to quote parts of the Bible to me, sir. But he doesn't. And you do, in your own way."

"It wasn't the Bible I thought of then," Marcus replied.

"The barrier is my presence, I think," Oren said quietly.

Marcus didn't turn his head to look at him.

"You've completely misunderstood what happened, Marcus," Oren went on. "I did what I thought was best for Marietta and Galloway. If I was wrong, I regret it, believe me. And I've lost by it, too."

Gentry cut in. "There's no room in politics for personal feelings. And, Mr. Swinton, my father's with us, too. We're all agreed. It's not just to combat an uprising either, to keep our women from being raped, to keep ourselves from being murdered in our beds. It's for true and permanent action."

Marcus said, "I wonder what you have in mind then."

"Simply this. The time is coming when we must make a stand against the abolitionists. They're out to destroy us, it's plain enough to see. When they begin to undermine us in our own lands, then we can be certain what they intend. They're shipping copies of that traitor Hinton Helper's *Compendium* all over North Carolina. Soon we'll be forced to make hard decisions. And we must be ready for them."

"Ready? You use the word with frequency. But I don't know what you want to be ready for."

Gentry sighed with restrained impatience. "Mr. Swinton, there'll be a vote one of these days. To secede or not. We know where *we* stand."

"I know where you stand, too," Marcus answered. "But it won't be easy. North Carolina won't come to such a move without a struggle. And you know that as well as I do. We've too many who aren't slaveholders. The mountain people would want no part of it. They've made that clear for generations now."

"We're well aware of that problem. And that's why we must get together. When the time comes, we'll see that the vote goes the way we want it, and no other way."

"And meanwhile?" Marcus asked.

"Meanwhile we'll prepare ourselves."

"I'll think about it," Marcus promised. With a nod at the two men, he walked slowly away.

Watching him, Oren said, "I believe you'd have had easier going, Gentry, if it hadn't been for me."

"Perhaps." Gentry shrugged his bulky shoulders. "But it doesn't matter. He'll join us when we need him, I think."

As they were leaving, they passed Lafe. Stiff nods were exchanged, but no words.

Outside Oren said, "He travels less than he used to. I wonder why."

Gentry shrugged. "It's the season, I suppose."

"Perhaps."

"But what does it matter?"

"It does to me. And I'll find out what it means."

"And how'll you do that, Oren?"

"Coraleen," Oren retorted.

"What makes you think she'll know?"

"She will," Oren answered, a sudden smile on his lips. He was soon to be proven right.

Coraleen sat in the Beckwiths' parlor with Sara's baby on her lap, and Sara herself watching nearby.

It was, Oren thought, looking at Sara, remarkable that whatever he'd once felt for her was gone. He'd believed at first that he'd never survive the loss. Now he hardly remembered how he'd once desperately wanted her, and how it had felt to him then. All that was left was a faint memory of it, but none of the feeling. The recognition was good. It gave him a sense of freedom.

He greeted Coraleen and said, "I just saw Lafe in town a while ago. He's not traveling as he used to, is he?"

"No." She tossed her head. "And I for one am sorry for it. He makes me want to grind my teeth and spit."

"Coraleen!" Sara's cry of reproof was pained. "How can you talk so? Your own brother-in-law, and the head of the house you live in."

"He's nothing to me," Coraleen retorted.

Oren grinned. "My dear and loyal sister."

"Someone must be loyal," she said, pulling a virtuous face.

"And what do you mean by that?" Oren asked.

"If you knew Lafe Flynn as well as I do, you'd know my answer."

Oren stood over her now, no smile on his face. "Tell me, Coraleen."

"He has a woman in the slave quarters," Coraleen said triumphantly.

A light grew in Oren's dark eyes. Gentry made a small sound.

"How do you know?" Oren demanded.

"Because I do. I've seen him coming and going at night."

"Who is the woman?" Oren asked. "Can you tell me that?"

"Not yet. But I'll be able to soon. If you want to find out."

"I do." Oren exchanged a glance with Gentry. It was the chance he'd been waiting for. It was illegal to cohabit with a slave woman. Though it wasn't a law often enforced, it could be made to work for Oren now.

"Does Marietta know?" Gentry asked.

"What a nasty conversation!" Sara cried. She rose, took her son from Coraleen's arms. "I must tell you that I think this preoccupation with Galloway ridiculous. And I think it's time you, Oren, began to live your own life and forgot the past and Galloway with it. I'm sorry for you, but there's no purpose in this."

"How simple you make it sound," Oren murmured, seeing in his mind's eye the white walls of Galloway and its vine-hung galleries.

Later, riding with Coraleen to the pillared gates of the plantation, he looked up at the house and his heart ached. It should have been his. It would still be all his.

He uttered the thought aloud.

"But you left me alone here. You deserted me, Oren Henderson," Coraleen said. "I've no one who cares for me now."

"It's time you stopped feeling sorry for yourself," he answered dryly. "As Marietta would say, what do you lack?"

"Everything that I want."

"I had no choice, and you know it as well as I," Oren told Coraleen. "One day, and soon, it'll be different. If you help me."

She nodded, her face suddenly softened and dreamy. "Yes, I do think it's possible, Oren. I can imagine a Galloway without Lafe Flynn. And with you home, returned to the place you belong."

He listened with mounting interest, but concealed it. He knew how Coraleen could tease when it amused her and pained others.

He said slowly, "It may be different after what's happened."

"The more fool you, Oren Henderson, if you don't know better than that. All you need do is rid us of Lafe."

"You really think so?"

Coraleen whispered, "And it won't be so difficult, particularly when she knows that Lafe goes to someone else . . . someone who gives him what she won't."

They were at the pillars of Galloway by that time, and Oren looked up the track toward the big house. It seemed suddenly forbidding to him. Grim in the light of the January afternoon, its windows dark with shadows, the vines that sheathed its galleries bare of lacy leaves.

He drew a deep breath and said softly, "Coraleen, you

319

must find out who this woman is at once. And when you do, let me know immediately. Do you understand me?" She nodded. "Can you?" She nodded again. "Then do it."

She watched him swing his horse about, and then she went on, lifting her head as the dogs bayed their usual warning against the approach of strangers, and smiling when she observed that Needle and Beedle raced frantically after them along the garden paths.

Soon Oren would be back, she told herself, and the twins would be sorry indeed if they allowed this to happen then. He'd have their hides for letting the dogs play in the oleanders. She looked speculatively at the big tree that had always been Marietta's favorite retreat. It was the perfect place, she decided, for what she wanted to do.

That night, well wrapped against the chill air, she secreted herself there, her black hood and black cloak making her one with the shadows, invisible to Lafe when he passed.

Three times during the next day she drove her gig through the slave quarters. No one paid any attention to her, though many eyes followed her. Each time she passed, Duveen sat before his cabin, whittling at a thin stick.

That evening she asked Marietta if Duveen could be ill, mentioning that he seemed no longer to ride to Darnal each day with Lafe.

Lafe heard the comment from Marietta, and the next morning Duveen went to the warehouse with him, and Moses remained alone at the cabin.

Coraleen, riding past on her own daily patrol, raised her crop at him, smiled, and called, "Good morning to you," pleased to see him, for he could be more easily handled than Duveen.

She proceeded to do just that. A little while later Needle came to tell Moses that Miss Marietta required him urgently at the house. He cast a worried look at the door behind him, shuffled and hesitated, and prayed a little, but at last he set out to answer the summons.

He was gone hardly a moment before Coraleen slipped from the cover of trees and danced up to the cabin. She peered in its two small windows and saw nothing but shadows.

She eased the door open, followed by a bar of bright sunlight.

It was dim within. She crossed the threshold into the tiny room.

There was the faint slow rasp of breathing, and as her eyes adjusted to the faint light she saw the empty pallet on the floor, and in the corner, close by the small fire, the ashen-faced man who lay asleep, one leg extended, the stump of the other one resting on a box.

A man with one leg, a black man whose thin wrists still bore the marks of manacles.

Coraleen drew her breath in sharply and set out immediately for the Beckwiths' plantation.

Behind her, Justin Cooley opened his eyes and moaned softly.

Oren slammed his fist into his left palm. "We have him!"

"What will you do?" Coraleen asked excitedly.

"You'll find out when it happens."

"I want to know now. I must know now." Coraleen gave him a sly look, then turned to Gentry. "Gentry, isn't it true that if I hadn't come to you with this news, you'd know nothing about it?"

"Of course it is," he said soothingly. "You're a clever girl. But you must leave men's business to us, Coraleen."

"You don't trust me." She pouted.

"I trust you more than you know," Oren assured her, smiling, his dark eyes alight. "Now go back to Galloway and, mind you, say nothing of what you've told us."

"Say nothing! Of course I won't. Do you imagine I want to spoil it for you?" Coraleen paused. Then, "But what will you do?"

"We'll take him, and with him the proof that he's been

harboring runaway slaves," Oren answered. "And that will settle Lafe Flynn's hash."

"And then?"

"We'll hang him," Gentry said coldly.

"And he won't come back to Galloway any more," Coraleen said, laughing.

When she had gone, Gentry said, frowning, "Do you think you can rely on her, Oren?"

"Why not? She hates Lafe as much as I do. And with as good a cause." Now Oren frowned. "But as for the hanging, Gentry, that was more than you needed to say. We'll turn him over to the law, of course."

"We will?"

"Certainly. What else can we do?"

"Shall we see when we have him, Oren?"

With that the two men sat down to lay their plans.

When the whistle came that night, Lafe rose. He dropped his napkin near the silver ring marked with his initial, excused himself, and left the dining room.

"I wonder where he's going now?" Coraleen observed with soft significance.

"It's no affair of yours," Marietta snapped.

"The whistle is Duveen's," Coraleen said. "And it's a summons to his quarters, where Lafe keeps the woman he really wants.

"You disgust me, Coraleen."

"I know." Coraleen's smile broadened. "But I can't help what your husband does."

"He had some errand for Duveen or Moses to perform for him. Don't make up such lies."

"I wonder who he keeps there? Some beautiful maiden perhaps that he brought from New Orleans in his red chest perhaps. Or is it one of our own women? A young girl that's grown since we last looked at her? Who do you imagine he couples with?"

Marietta rose so quickly that the chair fell away behind her with a clatter that brought Dora running.

"Go away," Coraleen told her. "We don't need you."

The girl righted the chair, gave a quick frightened glance at Marietta's face, and left the room at a trot.

Laughing aloud now at her own naughty cleverness, Coraleen said, "I shouldn't worry too much, Marietta. Men will be men, you know."

Marietta didn't answer. She gave the girl a long hard look and left her alone.

When she heard Marietta reach the top of the stairs, Coraleen rose, humming happily. She sang as she changed into her black riding outfit; then she sat down to wait impatiently for the hours to pass.

She knew what must happen.

She didn't intend to miss it.

"It wasn't a dream," Justin said tiredly. "She opened the door and stood there with the sun behind her so I couldn't see her face. I was still and didn't move, hoping she'd go away. But she came in and looked at me. She's small and plump and got brownish hair."

"And she said nothing?" Lafe asked.

Moses muttered, "Miss Coraleen," in a chagrined voice. "Riding by and riding by. And then that call from Miss Marietta that Miss Marietta didn't know anything about."

"Coraleen," Lafe agreed harshly. He got to his feet. "We'll have to move you, Justin. I'm sorry. I know you're not ready. But there's nothing else I can do."

"To the hidey hole?" Moses asked hopefully, for the trip to Darnal didn't seem so far to him now.

But the warehouse had been searched, the suite in the hotel as well.

Lafe said, "I'm afraid that won't do." He looked sideways at Duveen, who nodded quickly and took out his pad and wrote a few words: NOW. BEFORE SHE TELLS.

"If it isn't already too late," Lafe said.

Justin braced himself. Moses stuck the crutch under the young man's arm.

After that they all moved quickly. Moses kept watch outside the cabin as the wagon pulled away, jolting under the live oak trees, and then out between the two white pillars. It rolled from the deepest of shadow into the high moon's light as it swung in a wide turn, heading away from town.

Duveen handled the reins, and Lafe sat beside him, his gun propped against his thigh. Justin crouched in the back, squeezing his crutch tightly.

"We'll take him cross country and toward the hills," Lafe said softly. "If we can make it."

Duveen grunted, swinging his big head from side to side, eying the brightness around them.

"We'll find somebody to keep him until he can move on." Lafe pushed his hat back, eased the gun against his thigh, searching the area around the small bridge ahead, and then with a quick nod said, "Go on, Duveen. Give them your whip and ride it through."

The wagon pounded across the wood planks and plunged into the stand of trees beyond.

It was there that the first hint of trouble came.

Even Coraleen, following silently on horseback a discreet distance behind, was surprised. She spurred forward as a crashing ahead warned her. She wanted to see, to see, but the wagon had disappeared from view into momentary darkness.

It reappeared, lurching wildly, then stopped, the horses rearing up with fright. Duveen fought to control them as Lafe stared without surprise at the seven horsemen who surrounded them.

Gentry said, "You're out traveling at a strange hour, Lafe."

"I am?" Lafe looked at him. "Then so are you."

"We're patrolling," Gentry returned.

"Indeed?" Now Lafe's eyes found Oren among the other men. And David Heller, and John Farr. "And have you had good luck this night?"

"We think so," Oren answered. "Get down from the wagon."

"Get down?" Lafe echoed. "Why?"

"I prefer to see you on the ground while we search it, Lafe."

"Search it for what?"

"For contraband." Now it was Gentry speaking. "We're legally empowered to do so, and you know that as well as I do."

"And by whom are you empowered? And on what grounds?"

Oren gave a short bark of laughter. "As if you didn't know. We're empowered by the town, and the sheriff, and the landowners. And you're suspected of transporting a runaway slave."

"I am?" Lafe, still seated, didn't turn his head to look at the back of the wagon where Justin crouched in the corner under a thick pile of hay.

He hesitated as the knot of horsemen moved closer. Now he saw that Alexander Beckwith was with them, and two men unknown to Lafe by name, though he knew them to be habitués of Hell's Tavern.

Resistance was useless. Yet somehow he must play for time. He must make time work for him. Legally empowered or not, he knew they had no intention of acting legally. They'd not trouble themselves to take him to jail in Darnal. Instead, they'd be the jury and render a verdict which couldn't be overturned once sentence had been carried out. Yet the man in the wagon must be considered, and Duveen, too.

He said slowly, "I reject your claim. I refuse search. You're not the law, and can't pretend to be."

"The county gives power to the patron," Alexander Beckwith said heavily. "It's always been so."

Gentry moved forward, impatience written on his face. "There's no need for discussion. Oren, see to the contents of the wagon." He looked coldly along the barrel of the pistol he aimed at Lafe. "If you wish to protest further, you may do so."

Lafe smiled, shrugged, and at the same time, fired his gun

from the shadow of his thigh. The sound of the shot blended with the simultaneous blast from Gentry's pistol.

A great bloom of pain exploded in Lafe's shoulder. He was flung back, with the silver sky spinning around him.

Duveen threw himself from the seat with a deep menacing growl. Gentry fired again at the same instant that the great body crashed into him and then, with blood spouting from its chest, sprawled on the cold hard ground. Gentry went sprawling, too. But while Duveen remained still, he bounced to his feet, ready to shoot again.

Lafe, aware that he was encircled, dragged himself up. He let his legs dangle from the wagon, then dropped to the ground. He knelt beside Duveen for a long still moment, not looking up at the sounds of movement around him.

He hardly heard the exclamations of satisfaction as Justin was dragged shivering from beneath the hay. He didn't stir, though he felt a pistol press firmly into his side, the sharp prod of a boot.

Oren said softly, "Get to your feet. You're finished now. We've found you out, and with witnesses."

"We'll take you to town," David Heller said, "and turn you over to the deputy. The law will take care of you, Lafe Flynn."

"Ah, the sheriff's away, David, as you well know," Gentry remarked. "There's no deputy at the calaboose. We'll just hold him at the plantation until the sheriff returns tomorrow."

"Of course," Oren agreed. "That's by far the most sensible course."

"And the man in the wagon?" Lafe asked, rising clumsily to his feet. "What about him?"

"We'll see to him, never fear."

"He's one-legged, and only recently made so. He needs care."

Gentry laughed. "We'll cure him. And if his owner can't be traced—and I doubt we'll try very hard—then I shall claim him for myself. Since I lost one to you, I have the right to one back."

"You've no right, but you'll take it," Lafe replied quietly. Then, "And what of Duveen?"

"We'll see to him, too."

"He must have a Christian burial," Lafe insisted.

"Then he will," Oren replied.

And Gentry, stepping up behind Lafe and raising his pistol, softly added, "When *you* do."

Coraleen, watching, gasped as she saw Gentry strike Lafe down, saw the big man crumple soundlessly to the earth.

When they had thrown his limp body into the wagon, and Duveen's next to him, and Justin with them, they rode toward Beckwith's plantation.

Quietly, intent on seeing it all, she followed.

25

The lace of Marietta's gown whispered with every step. For hours she had paced the halls of the house, aware with all her senses of its emptiness.

Suddenly, where there should be the warmth and odor of wood fires burning, there was only cold and the rancid, mildewed scent of abandonment. This, though logs glowed here in the hearth of the morning room to which she had finally withdrawn. Beyond the pale circles of light cast by the lamps, the flickering arcs of the candles she had set aflame, huge black shadows lay massed and waiting.

Her father's eyes seemed to follow her from within the golden frame of his portrait as she took two steps this way, swung around, took two steps in another direction. With chilled fingers, she briefly held the old Bible, then replaced it on the desk.

Now she knew who the ghosts of Galloway were. Needle and Beedle spoke of the man and the woman who slipped silently about the house and walked forth from it on terrifying errands. But she could put a name to them, and they were living flesh and blood.

For an hour, then another, she had heard him pacing in the room she had once imagined would be theirs together forever. Unbidden, unwanted, she had imagined herself going to him there. She had seen her arms go around his neck, his head bend to hers, his lips find her mouth as he gathered her close to his warmth and strength. She had fought the yearning with angry admonitions: Let him come to her. Let him realize what he had done. He had driven Oren away, hadn't he? Then let him mend what he had broken. But all her arguments were meaningless. And at the last, though still unwilling, she had taken a candle and walked silently across the few steps—each a long long mile— to his door.

The room was empty. Their marriage bed was empty.

She ran across the room to look from the window, and saw him cross the yard. Moments later he'd ridden away, his tall figure bathed in the silver of the moon. She raced onto the gallery, stood staring, so cloaked in anger that she scarcely felt the January chill as she waited to see him go down the track that lead beneath the live oaks to the Darnal Road.

Then, faintly, she'd heard the sound of hoof on stone, and she knew he had taken the path to the slave quarters beyond the hill.

Coraleen's contemptuous, mocking words echoed in her mind. *He keeps a woman there. I wonder who.*

Marietta had turned quickly, gone indoors. As quiet as a wraith herself, she drifted down the hall. She opened a second door and gave the empty bedroom a single glance. Coraleen was gone.

These two were the ghosts about whom the slaves whispered.

Lafe, going first, on the way to the arms of a woman who was to him what Marietta herself should have been, and Coraleen, trailing after like a hound tracking a fox as it ran free in the fields.

Marietta had retreated to the morning room. There, under the watching eyes of her father's portrait, she paced the hours away, waiting to confront the two, one for his faithlessness and the other for revealing it.

But suddenly she could wait no longer.

She needed air, activity. She needed to see for herself the woman to whom Lafe went. Better that by far than to listen to Coraleen's words.

Within the moment, her cloak was wrapped snugly around her. She went into the darkness. The moon was lowering. The black of the sky was streaked with long layers of pale clouds.

She saddled her horse, noting that Lafe's black stallion was gone, and Coraleen's bay. As she mounted, the twins rose from their pallets, murmuring in fright. She told them to sleep again, and rode out quickly.

The black stallion was tethered to a post before the cabin. It nickered at her as she cantered from the trees and pulled up beside it.

At the same time, the cabin door burst open. Moses came hurtling out. When he saw her, he stopped short. Then he turned, plunged inside, and slammed the door.

She dismounted, tethered her horse, and went to the door. "Moses," she said softly. "Moses, come out."

For a long moment nothing happened. In the stillness she heard the whisper of wind in the bare limbs of the trees. She heard the faint sound of voices joined in a sad strain of melody. She felt the brush of eyes upon her, and knew that somewhere in the darkness someone stood and watched her. Was it Coraleen? she wondered briefly.

"Moses," she said again, her voice raised and sharp. "Moses, I demand that you come out."

The door opened only inches. Moses' round face appeared in the narrow opening, his body concealing the room behind him.

"Is Mr. Lafe here?" she demanded.

Moses shook his head.

"Moses!"

"No, Miss Marietta," the man said, fright etched on his face.

She gave him a contemptuous smile. "But his stallion is."

"He's gone, I tell you. He went in the wagon."

She turned, surveyed the clearing. Where was Coraleen? Where was the bay?

"He went, Miss Marietta. I've been looking for him to come back ever since."

330

But Marietta couldn't believe him. The man was so plainly frightened.

"Step aside," she told him. "I'm coming in."

"The Lord's my witness . . ." he began. A single glance from her anger-bright eyes silenced him. He moved away from the door and opened it wide.

She crossed the threshold into the dimness of a single burning candle. The room was cold; the small fire had been allowed to die. The walls were water-stained where rains had leaked through. The bare wooden floor was splintering, and on it she saw the three pallets. Three. Not two.

Her lip curled. What a fine place Lafe had chosen for his assignations. A slave's cabin, shared by Moses and Duveen.

She swung on Moses then. "Who is the woman who stayed with you?"

"Woman?" He stared at Marietta, eyes blank and wide. "Woman?"

"Yes, yes, the woman. Mr. Lafe's concubine. I want to know her name. I want to know how she came here."

"Woman," Moses repeated softly, understanding now. "There's not been any woman here, Miss Marietta."

That time she believed him. The truth of his words was evident in his face. Her eyes went back to the pallet. She wondered if Lafe had come here to sleep with Duveen and Moses. Had he escaped from his bachelor room to find better rest with his men? But no, it couldn't be. He was gone, and in the wagon.

"Where is Mr. Lafe now?" she asked Moses.

"I don't know. He went and didn't say where to."

"And Duveen?"

"He took Duveen with him." There was sweat on Moses' brow. He mopped it away, and his hand trembled.

"Why are you frightened?" she asked.

"He hasn't come back."

"And he should have?"

Ah, yes. He should have come back well before now. He should have slipped into the big house and crept ghostlike into his room, so none would have known that he'd been abroad that night. But he hadn't.

Her eyes went to the third pallet again. She asked quietly, "And who slept there?"

"A friend," Moses answered after a brief hesitation.

"What friend?" she demanded, suspicion leaping high in her once more.

"A man."

She moved to lean against the table, her hands gripping its edge, her eyes never leaving Moses' face. "Who was the man?" she asked.

"He was riding with Mr. Ridgeway, Mr. Lafe's friend," Moses said carefully.

"And?"

"He was hurt. We kept him here."

"How is it that I knew nothing of him?"

"Mr. Lafe can tell you," Moses faltered.

"But Mr. Lafe's not here, is he?" Her eyes traveled about the room now. "And neither is Duveen. So I think you must tell me yourself, Moses."

"I can't," he answered.

"And this mysterious man who was hurt, he went away in the wagon with the other two. Is that it?"

Moses jerked his head in a nod.

Her impatient gesture sent flying a worn piece of paper that had lain on the table. It fluttered to the floor at Moses' feet. He pretended not to see it, wishing it invisible with all his heart.

She said softly, "Oh, I'm sorry."

Moses didn't even hear the apology. With trembling lips he framed careful words. "If you'll go back to the house, Miss Marietta, as soon as Mr. Lafe comes I'll tell him you were here."

"Thank you," she answered, her tone dry. "Now you must pick that paper up. Whatever it is, you don't want it lost, do you?"

He knelt and took the document, crumbling it into a tightly closed fist.

332

"Is there a message on it? Does it say where Mr. Lafe has gone?"

He looked up at her, shook his head slowly.

"You're not speechless like Duveen. Come tell me what you have there."

He rose, but he didn't answer.

She held out her hand. "Let me see it, Moses."

The man's round face seemed to age as she looked at him. All light went out of his eyes.

"Let me see it at once," she repeated.

He brought the document to her, then retreated quickly.

It took her only moments to scan the blurring phrases. *From this day forth . . . in recognition of services rendered . . . swears to forgo and manumit all claim of ownership . . . Frank Duveen . . .*

She raised startled eyes to Moses' wizened face. "Why, Duveen's been a freed man for many years. Why does he pretend to be a slave still?"

Moses said nothing.

"Why does Mr. Lafe pretend he is?"

Still Moses didn't answer.

"And you? What of you, Moses? Are you a freed man, too? Do you have your papers from Mr. Lafe's brother in New Orleans?"

The room was so quiet that she could hear his shallow, fearful breath. At last he whispered, "No, Miss Marietta. I don't have papers."

"Then you do belong to Mr. Lafe's brother?"

"I belong to no one," Moses answered, "except to myself, and the Lord."

"If you've no papers, you're owned by someone."

He didn't reply, and she went on softly: "Unless you're a runaway."

Runaway.

The sound of the word hung in the room. Moses winced beneath it as if it were a lash that tore the flesh from his bones.

She saw and understood. Her eyes went to the third pallet

for the last time. She said softly, "And he, he who slept there, he was a runaway as well."

Now she saw it all: Duveen a freed man, the injured slave hidden away, Lafe's business comings and goings, his so lightly expressed opinions . . . He was one of the hated and hunted, a clandestine transporter of slaves out of their bondage.

For a single instant a warm wave of happiness very nearly brought her to tears. Lafe had had no woman hidden away for his pleasure. He had been true to her, even and in spite of her leaning toward Oren.

But the joy receded as swiftly as it had bloomed. Anger took its place and burned like a fire in her veins.

She saw it all clearly now. He'd only married her to use her. He'd never truly loved her. He'd needed a means of becoming respectable to the county, a place of operations. He'd needed a Galloway, and her, for his traitor's schemes.

Coraleen had been wrong, wrong! But this was even worse than the girl had imagined. Lafe had used them, endangered them all, by making Galloway a part of his wicked plots.

She turned on Moses. "Now where is he gone with Duveen and the other man?"

"I don't know, Miss Marietta." The dignity of truth was in his face.

She saw it, and said more gently, "Why did Duveen leave his papers with you, Moses?"

The small man gave her a haunted look. Then his eyes slid past her toward the door. He lifted his head to listen.

"No one's coming," she told him. Then, impatiently, "Well?"

"He wanted me to have them, I guess."

In her rage, she didn't understand. Her mouth curled in what was part a rictus of anger, part a smile of contempt. "And now this wicked arrangement is finished. What will Mr. Lafe do? What will you and Duveen do?"

"Wicked, Miss Marietta?"

"It's against the law."

334

"Even so, is helping a man to freedom so sinful?"

"You could be taken to the calaboose and put in the stocks and whipped for that," she told him.

"Yes," he agreed. "By man's law. But the Lord never said it in His commandments."

"But you'll be sent back to your rightful owner," she cried. "Don't you understand that? You'll be sent back!"

"Yes," he answered. "I guess I will be. But it won't matter. Not if Mr. Lafe and Duveen don't get here pretty soon."

"They'll not remain long if they do," she retorted. "And be sure and tell Mr. Lafe I was here. Be sure and tell him I'll be at the house, waiting."

Moses bowed his head.

With a last furious glance, she left him.

The clearing was still empty, dark, when she went outside. She caught her slipper in the hem of her gown as she mounted her horse, heard it tear, and felt the cold on her leg as she rode away.

She felt the same cold as she raced into the house. But by now it had spread through her whole body. Her teeth chattered and her hands shook. Her skin was puckered with it, and her mouth dry. But even so, the heat of fury burned in her blood.

She took a lamp with her when she flung open the door of the room she had once decorated for sharing with Lafe. All that she had done nearly two years before mocked her. The white of the bed canopy and the embroidered quilt, the dark sheen of the chest and wardrobe . . . More than anything else, the emptiness of the room mocked her.

You'll be sorry, Coraleen had said. And said it many times. The girl was wiser than her years. For she was right. More than ever before, Marietta carried the bitter weight of regret. To bind Oren to her, she had married Lafe. And Lafe had driven Oren away, not for Oren's silly errors and small deceits but only to ensure safety for his own schemes. Coraleen's awful prophecy had come true.

A fury possessed Marietta once more. She ran along the

335

hallway. She burst into Lafe's room and flung open the doors of the wardrobe. She dragged out his silken shirts and threw them on the floor. She ripped the jackets from the hangers, the trousers from the press, the boots from their racks. She scattered links and collar buttons and cravats on the pile.

At last, exhausted and spent, she crept down to the morning room. She sat at the desk that had been her father's, beneath the painting of him that seemed to watch her with living eyes.

What Moses had said flickered through her mind: *Is helping a man to freedom so sinful?*

Was it? She didn't know. She didn't care. She knew only that Lafe had married her to use her. But she would repay him. No matter what it took, she'd see him gone from Galloway for good. Suddenly, without knowing why, she put her face in her hands and wept.

Coraleen crossed the threshold silently, but the wind, following her through the briefly opened door, set up a tinkle of music in the hall chandelier.

She looked up at the dancing crystal drops, and a grin spread her lips wide and lit her dark eyes. No matter if Marietta awakened. She could come down if she liked, trailing her beruffled lavender gown, with the waves of her black hair framing her sleep-flushed face. She might stand and stare and rail and threaten. But it would all be to no purpose. For, though it would still be a little while before she knew it, she was no longer mistress of Galloway.

Oren and the others had Lafe Flynn now, and he could no longer protect her. Soon Oren would return, and Galloway would be his; and instead of Marietta, Coraleen herself would be its mistress.

She would have the slaves flogged if she liked, and even for the slightest impertinence. She would sell pretty Dora off for a whore. She would send Needle and Beedle into the fields where they belonged, and teach them their places as Marietta had never done.

She would have a surrey with red balled fringes at its top, and her bay would wear a bridle with silver trim, and she would drive it morning, noon, and night, wearing Marietta's jewels. By then, those jewels would be her own.

Smiling, Coraleen flung her cloak over the banister. Elisha could hang it on the hall tree in the morning. All would be different by the time the sun had risen.

It was just then, turning to go upstairs, that she saw the pale light in the morning room. She stared at it for a moment, her eyes widening, then went toward the source of the light.

Marietta sat in the big chair behind the desk, a dark shawl covering her shoulders. Her shining black hair was disheveled, a bit of pine twig caught in it, a shred of dried leaf. There was a long smudge on her lavender sleeve. In the pale light of the lamp, her face was white and set, her amethyst eyes darkened and expressionless.

"Why, Marietta, what's the matter?" Coraleen asked, holding in her laughter. Whatever troubled Marietta now would soon be forgotten. When she knew what had happened, this small pique would be meaningless. "What ever's wrong? Can't you sleep? Are you plagued by evil dreams?"

"You've been out, haven't you?" Marietta asked in a quiet voice.

"Have I?"

"Don't deny it, Coraleen. I see by the flush of cold on your cheeks, and by your dress. And even more, I looked in your room hours ago. You've been away from the house all this time."

"Well, then, yes, so I have. And what of it?" Coraleen flung herself into the big chair beside the desk and tossed back her head.

"Where did you go?" Marietta asked, her voice still soft.

"Where? If you must know, I went riding. It's been a beautiful night, Marietta. The moon was so high and bright."

"It's nearly gone now, and clouds are forming."

"Perhaps. But now I'm home."

"You followed Lafe, didn't you?"

"Did I?"

"I know it," Marietta answered.

"Then why ask me?" Coraleen chortled. "If you know so much, or think you do, then you've no need for information."

"No," Marietta agreed. "I've no need of information."

"But I'll tell you"—Coraleen smiled—"that soon you'll have your heart's desire. Oren will come home, Marietta. He'll be here, at Galloway, with us, where he belongs."

"Oh, will he? And how do you know that?"

But Coraleen only laughed.

Marietta stared at her for a moment, then said again, "How do you know it, Coraleen?" this time louder.

"Because I do." It was on the tip of her tongue, she could hardly bear to hold it back. But she must wait a little. She must savor it. And the longer the wait the better the surprise when Marietta knew.

Oren would soon be back, Marietta thought. Strangely, she felt no joy in it. The memory of forged signatures rankled. The recollection of his anger when she would not provide him with the money he requested, then demanded, was as fresh in her mind as in the hour it happened. She had thought she understood and forgave. But there was no joy in imagining Oren here with her again. She said softly, "Where did Lafe go, Coraleen?"

But the girl shook her head from side to side.

"I'm anxious to know. I must see him at once. There are things to be said."

Marietta's urgency soothed and pleased Coraleen. "You've no need to think he's gone to another woman," she said at last. "Your vanity remains intact."

"Ah, does it?" Marietta murmured. "Then where is he?"

"I won't tell you," Coraleen replied. "You'll learn that when you must, and not before."

Marietta leaned back in her chair. She smoothed the

338

lavender silk of her gown over her knees, watching Coraleen from beneath lowered lids. "It pains me to tell you, Coraleen, but whether Oren returns or not means nothing to you."

"Oh, doesn't it?" Coraleen cried. "You may think as you like, but when Oren comes home, everything will be different."

"Perhaps," Marietta told her. "But you won't be here to see it. For now I know I must do what I've been avoiding for a long while, Coraleen. I must send you away from Galloway for good."

Coraleen's face paled. She straightened her curled legs from under her and leaned forward, her bottomless eyes narrowed in a disbelieving stare.

"I shall send you away," Marietta repeated softly. "You'll not see Oren. Not ever again."

"He won't let you," Coraleen said tonelessly. "He won't let you. You'll see."

But even as she spoke, she saw that Marietta's face was changed. It wasn't Marietta who sat behind the desk. It was Lawrence Garvey, with his care-lined face, and that sad look in his eyes, and his jaw set in that awful determination which she had learned to know over the years when always he put Marietta first and she herself, young Coraleen, was always last.

And now Marietta was saying, "It's you who'll see. I should have done it long ago. Without you Galloway will be a better place. It'll be the way it was before you came."

A last thread of caution shredded and broke in Coraleen. She didn't care. Hate was a good tide. It supported her as always. It swept her with it now.

"Try," she said softly, rising to her feet slowly. "Try, my dear sister Marietta. You'll get what Papa got. Oh, yes, indeed you will. When Galloway is Oren's, then I'll make you mine. As I made Papa mine forever."

Marietta's fingers trembled on her knee. She said, "My father's gun went off and killed him."

339

"Oh, do you still believe so?" Coraleen laughed, still edging closer. "Then let me tell you that you're right. Papa's gun went off and killed him. But I was holding it."

"Coraleen!" The word was a horrified whisper. Marietta's trembling hand moved steadily toward the Bible on the corner of the desk. "If I'm to believe you, you must tell me why."

"The jewels. Your pearls. I had them and Aunt Tatie found them. Poor soul, she paid for that betrayal, too. And within the year she would have betrayed me once again. If I hadn't stopped her."

"You're mad," Marietta said. "You make up stories to frighten me." Her fingers closed around the Bible. She drew it slowly toward her.

"How nice it would be if you could convince yourself of that." Now Coraleen stood at Marietta's desk, her plump figure looming close over her. "Poor Marietta, I don't blame you for refusing to know the truth. It only proves that I shall always have my own way. Always, always." A smile lit her empty eyes and curled her lips. She went on dreamily: "Yes, I had the pearls for just a little while. But then Papa took them back. And afterwards he died. Because he was going to send me from Galloway. Because of you. But we were so happy, just the three of us, until Lafe Flynn came to court you. You had everything, and everyone. Lafe should have been mine, but you took him from me. So I took Snowball from you, my dear Marietta. Oh, yes, I took Snowball from you. And very nearly your mind as well. Remember the dressmaker's dummy? Remember your own mother hanging in the window and swinging on the breeze? Oh well, Lafe's kisses saved you. But after Aunt Tatie found the dried oleander leaf, and guessed I'd tried to poison you, I took her from you, too."

Pink and white of face and smiling, a picture of young innocence, Marietta thought, yet here was the evil that had plagued her for so long. Here the hate that had dogged her.

340

Pain shook her now, tiny arrows catching her at the heart. But she fought it down and mastered it. Later there'd be time for grief. She must be clever, strong. Her fingers tightened on the Bible.

"And this night," Coraleen said in joyful triumph, "I've taken Lafe from you."

"You haven't," Marietta answered. "He'll be back soon."

"No he won't. He'll never return. You've no one to protect you, my Marietta. No one. Oren and the Beckwiths have Lafe Flynn now, and Duveen is dead."

A new grief touched Marietta. Duveen dead. He'd left his freedom papers with Moses and gone out with Lafe, and now he'd never come back.

She allowed nothing to show on her face. She made her voice level, saying, "And how did Duveen die, Coraleen?" At the same time she rose slowly to her feet.

"There was no woman," Coraleen answered. "Lafe steals slaves from their rightful owners and sends them away. Don't you understand? Duveen helped him, and there was the one-legged man in the wagon. They were taking him away."

"You saw it happen," Marietta whispered.

"Oh, yes, I saw it all. Oren and Gentry and John Farr were there, ready at the small bridge, when they rode by."

"And how did they come to know of it, I wonder?"

Coraleen put her head back, and a terrible cackle of pleasure came from her throat. "I told them!" she crowed. "It was I, Marietta, I, who told them. Then Gentry shot Lafe—"

"Lafe?" Marietta said dryly. "It was Duveen, you said, Duveen. Not Lafe!"

Coraleen cackled again. "Lafe, too, my dear Marietta. And by now, perhaps, he's dead where they have him. And if he's not, he will be soon. For Oren will never allow him to return to Galloway."

Arrows of pain drew her breath from her. The shadows in the corners of the room moved closer and closer. The lamp sputtered once in the silence and jumped high, revealing clearly Coraleen's twisted face as she suddenly threw herself at Marietta.

Marietta stepped back, and swung the Bible as hard as she could at Coraleen's head.

The girl cried out, collapsed in a crumpled heap at Marietta's feet, and at the same moment the lamp went out.

26

Marietta raced blindly through the shadows and into the hall. She caught up the cloak Coraleen had thrown over the banister, and darted to the door. There she paused, wavered uncertainly. Then she turned back. She lit a candle with steady hand, though tears still streamed down her face. Her shadow flew before her as she ran up the steps. She emptied the cash box hidden in her room of its contents. She tied her jewels into a scarf and tucked it at her waist. In the scattered debris of Lafe's belongings she found a heavy great-coat, a broad brimmed hat, a thick muffler. She didn't think of how she had felt when she had torn his things from chest and wardrobe. She didn't think of how she felt now.

She knew only that Oren and the Beckwiths held Lafe, and he was injured. She only knew that she must find him. Even as she ran breathlessly down the stairs, she planned ahead. But at the door she stopped once more.

She must bring him a gun. They would have taken his.

She listened. There wasn't a sound from the morning room. She tiptoed into the darkness, holding her breath, carefully skirting the place where Coraleen lay, limp, still, and breathing heavily.

The desk drawer made a small sound as she pulled it open. She couldn't see, but her fingers closed at once on her father's gun. It had been used to kill him. Now it must be used to save Lafe.

Clutching the handful of bullets she'd grabbed and stuffing them into the pocket of her cloak as she ran, she raced into

343

the yard. Her horse was still saddled. She pulled herself up, kicked hard. The animal stretched out, bucked hard, and came down pawing at the frozen earth. She clung to the pommel with one hand and slashed with the reins at his hindquarters. He snorted and took off at a gallop. It took only moments for her to reach the slave quarters beyond the hill.

Not pausing to dismount, she called out, "Moses! Moses, come quickly! I need you."

The cabin door opened, and he came at the run.

"Mount the stallion and come!" she cried, aware even as she did so that other doors had opened, other ears listened.

He obeyed without questions. In only moments more they had passed from under the live oaks and the reaching limbs of the pines into the rolling meadows.

He saw the direction they were taking, and his face tightened with fear, but he said nothing until they had reached the Beckwiths' property and saw in the hollow the spread of the plantation house. Then he asked, "Are they here, Miss Marietta?"

"Yes, they must be." She drew a deep breath. "I'm sorry to tell you. Duveen is dead, I believe. And Mr. Lafe is wounded. We must find some way . . ." Her voice trailed off. She pointed. "Moses, do you see it? Do you see the wagon pulled up there in the shadow of the barn?"

"Yes," he breathed.

"Then that's where they're holding Mr. Lafe." She turned in the saddle. "Now listen to me. This is what you must do. Ride up to the door of the house. Make noise, and cry out, and pound loudly. When they come, tell them there's trouble at Galloway. Say help's needed. Then mount and ride out well ahead of them. Don't let them keep up with you, Moses. For I want you to circle back and meet me here, at the wagon. If I'm not there, then you must wait. Do you understand?"

He nodded once.

"Then go on."

"Miss Marietta . . ."

"Now," she said crisply. "Now, Moses." She spurred ahead and left him, then eased the horse to a slower pace, picking her way carefully and quietly into the hollow, always angling in the direction of the barn.

A good distance from it, shadowed by a bush, she stopped, her gaze searching the shadowed building. There was no light at its small windows. There was no guard outside.

A tiny smile touched the corners of her lips. Oren and Gentry would be in the house, perhaps drunk with the glory of their night's work. But the night was not yet done.

She rode on. As she went past the slave quarters, there was a stirring. A shadow wavered at the corner of a cabin, and then ducked back. No outcry came. No warning split the silence.

And then in the distance she heard shouts, and a drumming of hooves that faded quickly away.

She moved faster now, but in silence, alert to danger. She dismounted at the barn and peered into the wagon. The hay was disarrayed in some places, closely packed down in others. There were dark stains on it, and dark stains on the seat as well.

She didn't allow herself to give a name to them. With a heart that beat slowly, fearfully, she approached the barn itself. She stopped to listen, but could hear nothing.

She tried to see into a small window, but it was too far above her head. She moved silently to the big door. The thick bar lay solidly in its slot. With a quick prayer, she swung it up, fighting its weight with all her strength. It groaned, and at the same time a chicken cackled.

She pulled the door open and stepped inside.

The first thing she saw was the big mound of a faceless body, covered against a cold it could never feel.

Then, after a heart-stopping moment, she saw Lafe. He rose up on an elbow and stared at her, but didn't speak a word.

He thought in that still moment that he was dreaming.

345

How could Marietta be here? And if this was a dream, and not real, then why did she look so? Why was her face so pale and tear-streaked? Why was the silk of her hair so wild? Why was her gown torn? Surely, if he dreamed, he would see her heart-shaped face alight with a smile so beautiful that it had the power to hurt him. He would see the glow in her amethyst eyes.

He got to his feet slowly, using the wall for support, and leaned there, still staring at her, and at last he said, "Marietta?" thinking that he was in fever from the wound that Justin had bound, and seeing not flesh and blood but fantasy.

At last she said urgently, "Lafe, I know what you've done, and what's happened. I know that they'll kill you. Coraleen has told me. I've come to send you on your way. I've brought you the money you'll need to travel on, and the wagon's just outside. Moses will meet you, and you and he, and . . ." Her voice faltered. She looked at the one-legged man who lay sleeping in the corner. "And he, too, if you want him. You must go away at once. You must get beyond the county and the state as quickly as you can. If you do, you can get to safety. If you don't . . ."

She stopped, for he was smiling at her. She felt the familiar quick sting in the air between them.

"You're wonderful," he said softly.

"No, no," she whispered in a hoarse voice. "You mustn't stand like that. You must go. Now, now."

"And you?"

"I'll go back to Galloway and remain there," she said coldly. "What I do isn't involved in this."

"Then I'll go back with you."

"You can't. I've sent Oren and the Beckwiths there on a fool's errand."

"I'll wait until they return. I'll remain with you at Galloway until the sheriff comes for me."

"He'll never come, and if he does he'll find you dead. Gentry and Oren will see that you never arrive at the calaboose alive."

346

He believed that himself, but was willing to risk it. Then he glanced at Justin, thought briefly of Moses. He owed them a chance for freedom, for life. Without him, they'd have no chance for either.

But he said again, "And you, Marietta?"

"You married me only to use me."

"Is that what you really think?"

"Of course. But no more talk."

"I want to talk." A twist of pain etched his mouth as he came toward her. "I want it all straight between us."

"Not now, Lafe. Another time." Her voice broke. She saw the blood on his sleeve, the black crusting that had spread as far as his wrist.

"There may never be another time." he said softly. Now he stood over her. "Marietta, why did you marry me?"

"We'll not discuss it."

"For Oren, wasn't it?"

"Lafe . . ."

He grinned at her, "My dear, I only want you to know the truth. I want you to face it before it's too late. Whatever you once felt for Oren is gone. It's been gone a long while now. Why don't you see it? Why don't you admit that what we were to each other couldn't have come about if you hadn't given Oren up?"

She turned from him, went to the door. "If you won't leave now, then you won't. I've done what I could."

He nodded. He bent over Justin, whispering, and helped the man to his feet. He stopped beside Duveen's body and looked at him, and then bent and gathered the man in his arms.

Marietta made a small sound of protest, and Lafe said, "I can't leave him here. He was a good man, and must have a decent burial."

She said nothing more, but stepped outside. There was no one about. The sky had begun to pale. The gray clouds hung close on the horizon.

When she reached the wagon, she found Moses hiding in the hay. He asked the question with his eyes.

"Mr. Lafe's coming just now."

They both turned to look toward Galloway. At any moment Oren and Gentry and the others might come from that direction. They might burst from the trees, brandishing their guns.

Oren, with Gentry and John Farr at his heels, had found Galloway ablaze with light.

Dora and Essie clung to each other in a corner near the hall tree.

Elisha struggled to his feet from where he had been sitting on the stairs, and ashen-faced, he cried, "Mr. Oren, thank God you're here!" and pointed up the steps.

Oren ran upstairs, the others following. The big crystal chandelier burned brightly in the upper hallway. The door of Lafe's room had been flung open. Inside candles lit a scene of savage destruction, the furniture overturned, the bed in disarray, Lafe's clothing strewn wildly about the floor, much of it torn, knife-slashed.

In the next room Marietta's dresses, cut to gleaming ribbons, hung from the bedposts and canopy, trailed from the wardrobe.

It seemed as if a whirlwind had swept through Coraleen's room. There, not a single piece of furniture was undamaged. Rug and bed and chair and chest were ripped and gouged. Over all a drift of feathers stirred with the draft from the open window.

Coraleen herself was gone.

Gentry swore beneath his breath.

But Oren was still. He imagined Coraleen racing from room to room, her pink and white face twisted with madness while she ripped and tore and slashed.

He turned slowly and said, "We must find Marietta. We must find Coraleen."

Marietta wasn't in the house. He was soon certain of that.

When he went into the sewing room, the room that had once belonged to Beatrice Garvey, he found Coraleen waiting.

She hung from the drapery rod above the window, and when he crossed the threshold, crying out at the sight of her, her limp and dangling body, moved by the night wind, seemed to turn to greet him for the last time. . . .

There was little time left. Marietta's whisper was urgent as she said to Lafe, "You must hurry. They'll soon return."

He gently lowered Duveen's body into the wagon, tucking the greatcoat around it, then covering it with hay. He gave Moses a faint smile, then helped Justin in. He climbed awkwardly to the seat and took the reins.

Avoiding his eyes, she handed up the greatcoat and muffler she had brought him. She give him the pistol and put the extra bullets into his big hand. A tremor shook her when their fingers touched. She stiffened and hastily gave him the scarf-wrapped money and jewels.

He started to thank her, but she shook her head angrily. "No, no, don't misunderstand. Whatever you did, I don't want your blood on my hands."

"And that's all?" he said.

"That's all," she cried.

"We'll talk of it again," he said, smiling. "I must take these men away from here. But I'll return."

"No," she answered. "Don't do it, Lafe. It will be dangerous. And for nothing."

"Then come with me," he whispered. "Come now. We'll go to New Orleans. From there we'll go West. We'll start anew, Marictta."

"I can't. I won't, Lafe."

"Because of Oren?" he asked.

Oren, she thought. She had loved him as she had loved the days of her childhood, and clung to him, trapped in the memory of those days. Her woman's heart she had given to Lafe, not knowing it soon enough. Not knowing *him* soon enough.

"It's Oren," Lafe said again.

"Not Oren," she answered. "Galloway. I can't turn my back on my home."

"You must remain to see it all destroyed, then. Your fields scorched, your home in ashes, your slaves fled. You must see it with your own eyes, and weep for it, and for a past that's dead."

She didn't answer.

"So be it." He settled the greatcoat around his shoulders and tucked the pistol into his belt. His big hands tightened around the reins. "I won't say goodbye, Marietta."

He turned his grim face from hers and looked toward Galloway. Then he snapped the reins once. The horses moved out. The wagon rolled.

She climbed into the saddle, but sat there, not moving.

He was going away for good. She knew she would never see him again. The ache of loss began in that instant.

She imagined herself riding alone between the white pillars of Galloway. Coraleen and Oren would be waiting. They would be outraged when she sent them both away. They would argue and threaten; they would beg. But she would stand firm. She couldn't bear to look upon either of them again.

Now Lafe and the wagon had disappeared into the distant shadows. She peered at the place where she'd last seen him. Only an emptiness was there. An emptiness as vast as the one in her heart.

Her throat closed convulsively on a sob. Tears burned her cheeks.

She loved him. What else mattered?

She cried, "No, no," and the startled horse broke into a run.

She gave him his head, and he galloped across the field and into the trees.

The wagon creaked somewhere close by.

She narrowed the distance between them and caught up, and riding alongside, she smiled tremulously into Lafe's up-turned face.

"Wait," she said. "Wait for me, Lafe. I'm coming, too."

He stared at her for a moment. Then a light gleamed in his eyes. "For good? And no matter what happens?"

"Yes," she whispered.

The wagon jerked to a stop. She climbed from the horse to the seat and sank down beside him.

He drew her close, wrapped his greatcoat around her.

The wagon rolled on, into the first light of dawn.